The Great Dempseys

Book 1

BRIANNA MACMAHON

MACMAHON BOOKS LLC

Content Warning

Dear readers,

This book contains material that some may find potentially triggering or traumatizing, including:

- suicidal ideation,

- attempted suicide, and

- abuse.

I more than understand if you need to take breaks while reading this book. If the need arises, please check the resources at the back of the book.

Thank you so much, and please take care of yourself.

Contents

Part I

CHAPTER 1

Audrey

GREAT GRAY

C OMPLICATED. THAT WAS THE word Audrey would use to explain her relationship with mornings. For instance, she loved her and her father's tradition of waking up early on the weekends and, weather permitting, going for long walks along the Hudson. There was something magical about New York in the morning, something unknowable. In the early hours, while most still slept, Audrey could pretend the city was a secret only she and her father had discovered. He adored New York, more than Audrey ever had—or could. When she was with him, seeing the city through his eyes, she found herself appreciating New York a little more: its culture, its history, its people. And she loved that; she loved feeling more connected to a place that had never quite felt like home to her.

She didn't, however, love being unceremoniously awoken or going to sleep knowing she had to be up at a certain time. The city wasn't so magical then. No, instead, it was loud and obnoxious, with sirens, construction, and cars—not to mention people all screaming at each other over the most mundane things.

The morning of August 28, 1978 was the latter, as it was a morning when Audrey *had* to wake up early. It was her first day of school. Not just her first day of school but the first day of her sophomore year. And through some process

Audrey still didn't quite understand, she would now be attending Great Gray, one of the most prestigious private schools in New York.

It all started when Principal What's-His-Face from her middle school had put her name forward as someone who was "worthy" (whatever that meant) of attending Great Gray. No way, Audrey had thought. Impossible! Great Gray was an expensive school, for rich families—which the Nielsens were not.

Apparently, though, Audrey didn't need to worry about this, as she hadn't secured one of the scholarship positions for that year. Instead, for her freshman year, she attended a public high school, and all returned to normal. Unbeknownst to her, however, her parents had applied for her to be transferred to Great Gray for her sophomore year. Her grades were solid, as were her extracurriculars, and against all odds, she'd managed to procure her spot as a transfer student—on a full scholarship.

Though her family was not destitute, by any means—they lived in a two-bedroom apartment in Greenwich Village—Audrey knew they could not afford the tuition of a place like Great Gray. Alexander, her father, worked as a shoe repairman—or, as he called himself, a cobbler. And while he earned enough money to support his two daughters and his wife, Sophia, he didn't have a lot to spare. Claire, the oldest of the girls, was attending New York University, which was enough of a financial strain. Adding Great Gray into the mix would be, in Audrey's estimation, too much. Besides, the economy was tanking, and everything was a mess.

At every turn, though—and despite all of her thoughtfully reasoned objections—Alexander and Sophia assured her they weren't letting her give up on such an "amazing, once in a lifetime opportunity!" Yes, Audrey agreed, attending Great Gray would be an incredible honor, but she didn't even know if it was something she wanted. She'd been going to school with the same kids since preschool, and she'd already finished one year of high school. At Great Gray, she'd have to make new friends, whose lives were as far removed from hers as Antarctica was from a tropical climate. What if she didn't make friends there? What if she didn't belong?

But her own feelings on the matter were inconsequential, apparently, as her parents made the decision without even asking for her input. As soon as they'd heard that Audrey had, in fact, been offered one of the scholarship positions, they'd enthusiastically accepted on her behalf. She was now a member of Great Gray's Class of 1981.

"Isn't this amazing, sweets?" Sophia had asked her, her eyes twinkling with so much excitement that all Audrey could muster was a resigned nod.

And so, on the morning of August 28, Audrey wasn't in the best mood. Though months had passed since she'd learned about Great Gray, she still resented her parents for having made the decision without consulting her. Didn't her opinion matter? Didn't they know they were ripping her away from her comfort zone, her life?

"You'll make new friends," Alexander insisted at the breakfast table as he read *The Wall Street Journal*.

In many ways, Alexander was a mystery to Audrey; he was fascinated by the stock market and learned all he could about it, but he never dabbled. He was far too financially cautious to risk his money like that. It was the same reason he never went to casinos or bought a lottery ticket. Great Gray, however, was a different story; to him, it was not a financial risk but an investment in his youngest daughter's future.

"Maybe," Audrey said, shrugging. "Probably not, though."

"Don't say that. Of course, you will!" Alexander gave her a thumbs-up for extra encouragement, reminding Audrey of those horrid days when she had to run the mile, and the Gym teacher would cheer them on from the sidelines.

"Oh, thanks. That's real helpful. Just like that, all my nerves are gone. Poof. Like magic."

Alexander laughed. "Come on, Audie," he said, reassuringly touching her hand. "You're going to be just fine. Great Gray is an amazing school."

"Sure. But at the end of the day, it's just a school."

"A school that Supreme Court justices and senators have attended," he reminded her, as if either of those was a career path that interested Audrey.

Hearing all the noise, Sophia sauntered out of her bedroom, wrapped in her favorite robe. She beamed when she saw Audrey, and she placed her hand to her chest.

"You look beautiful in your uniform, Audie," Sophia said.

"Thanks," said Audrey. "It's not very me, but—"

"You look beautiful," Sophia reiterated, nodding for emphasis. She walked over to Audrey, a wistful smile on her lips. "Oh, I remember when I used to have hair like yours," she mused, running her fingers through Audrey's carefully styled, Farrah Fawcett-inspired hair.

"Mom! Careful!"

"Sorry, sweets! Here, let me ... there. Good as new!"

Sophia always loved to mention how much Audrey favored her, with her honey-blonde hair and green eyes. Every one of Audrey's yearbook photos, it seemed, reminded Sophia of the youth she'd once possessed. And while Audrey was deeply flattered by the comparison, she couldn't help but note a trace of sadness in Sophia's eyes when she looked at her, as if in disbelief that she was old enough to have one daughter in college and another in high school. Children, it seemed, served as a constant reminder of the passage of time, the growing distance between the adolescents parents had once been and the adults they now were.

Alexander averted his attention to the clock on the wall. "But you better get moving, love. Don't want to be late."

Audrey gave him a look. "If I miss the subway, another will come along."

"I know. It's just ... you're not all that familiar with Uptown, and it's a bit of a walk from the station to Great Gray, so—"

"She'll be fine," Sophia said, exchanging a knowing look with Audrey.

"I'm pretty smart, you know," Audrey piped up.

"Yes, I know." Alexander sighed. "Just ... keep your wits about you, yeah?"

"Don't worry. I'll be careful. I always am."

Alexander smiled. "I'm just so proud of you, Audie."

"Thanks, Dad." Audrey kissed his cheek. "Love you." She pulled Sophia into an embrace. "Both of you."

"Bye, Audie!" said Sophia, waving as though Audrey were departing on a transatlantic voyage.

Despite her father's fears, Audrey had little trouble navigating her way to Great Gray. She and her parents had visited the school over the summer, to scout out the area. ("Can't risk you getting lost, now, can we?" Alexander had teased, all too familiar with Audrey's embarrassingly poor sense of direction.) Audrey remembered joking whether they called it Great Gray because the building was big and constructed from—wouldn't you know it?—gray stone. No, her father had informed her with a chuckle; it was because the mascot was a great gray owl. And while Audrey had found that explanation to be lacking, Alexander had then pointed out the gray, black, and white crest above the front door that boasted what must have been a great gray owl in the center. (Audrey simply took her father's word for it, as her knowledge of birds was severely limited.) Thus, grudgingly, Audrey had to concede the point—but not without noting that the gray building wasn't coincidental.

Now, as Audrey gazed at Great Gray's exterior, she had to admit it was undeniably striking, with its polished stone and fenced-in courtyard. A few students were milling about, reacquainting before the start of a new year. Though Audrey had always been a social butterfly, she dreaded the prospect of having to make friends. Maybe she wouldn't be the only new kid; maybe some other sophomores were also transfer students.

"... out of this rat hole," a boy was saying to his four friends—or, more accurately, minions, as they struck Audrey as boys who had no existence outside of their appointed leader.

But their leader was certainly nothing to write home about, reminding her of every soon-to-be disgraced politician apologizing for his misdeeds. He would've been labeled a nobody at her old high school, but since his family was obviously wealthy—the boy proudly wore an expensive-looking, ill-fitting watch—he was probably one of the popular kids. Effortlessly, Audrey could envision him as that fifty-year-old man still telling stories about his high school glory days, living vicariously through his suffering son.

"But we're seniors now," the boy went on. "And you know what that means."

He removed a cigarette from his pocket, lighting it up with a clear aura of discomfort, as if it were something he'd never done before. "We can skip out whenever we want."

They all laughed at that, revealing just how pitiful their senses of humor were. One of the other boys called their leader Alistair, which cemented to Audrey that she'd truly entered another world. Only people with serious money were named Alistair. Perhaps naively, Audrey hoped these boys weren't indicative of the sorts of people she'd meet at Great Gray, but she wasn't all that optimistic. A part of Audrey had assumed that private school kids would be more well mannered than their public school counterparts, but clearly, regardless of their upbringing, teenagers were teenagers: entitled, boastful, and annoying.

Upon entering the school, Audrey saw that most of the students were already being escorted into the auditorium for what she assumed was the obligatory first day of school assembly. No doubt, they'd be subjected to the same speech they'd been given every year since kindergarten: bullying is bad, your teachers are here to help you, and detentions go on your permanent record. Audrey wasn't sure what a permanent record was, or if it even existed, but it'd been mentioned so many times she assumed it had to be real. At this point, Audrey could deliver the speech herself—and much more humorously, if she did say so herself.

"Name?" a student asked her, though it sounded more like a demand.

"Audrey Nielsen. I'm a sophomore, but—"

"Over there to the left."

Audrey scooted to the left. To her relief, most of the students around her looked just as nervous as she was. Hopefully, she would be able to find a good group of friends. She didn't want to feel like a pariah for too long.

Only one student stood in front of Audrey, and three were standing behind her. One girl with flaming red hair sat at the reception table, thumbing through the list of students and corresponding schedules.

"Next!" said the redhead, pointing at Audrey. As Audrey neared her, the redhead simply said, "Name?"

Were some of these "student helpers" planning future careers as drill sergeants? They acted as though they resented Audrey for simply existing and going through the same rigmarole as everyone else. The redhead was clicking her gum, her eyes on the *Cosmopolitan* magazine she had unsubtly placed underneath her list of student names.

"Audrey Nielsen."

The redhead nodded distractedly, then handed Audrey her schedule. "This will tell you where your classes are. Do you have any questions?"

Audrey stared at the schedule, struggling to take it all in. Yes, as a matter of fact, she *did* have questions—lots of them. For one, how was she supposed to know where these rooms were? Some of the rooms had numbers, and others had letters. And why did she have two different classes listed at the same time?

"Here at Great Gray, we alternate between Gray and Black days," the redhead explained. "Today's a Gray day. So, for fifth period, you'll go to Gym. On Black days, you'll have study hall."

"Oh, okay. That makes sense. Thanks!"

"Sure." The redhead cracked her version of a smile. "The auditorium's over there to your left. Principal Waverly will tell you more about what to expect here at Great Gray."

Audrey was spellbound by the auditorium's grandiosity. Four pillars lined the aisle, two on each side; windows flanked the left and right walls, reminding Audrey that the real world did, in fact, exist outside this place. The school crest hung above the stage, complete with some pretentious Latin words: *UIRTUS, VIRTUS, VICTORIA.* Audrey could hardly believe she was now attending a school with a motto—and a Latin one, at that.

She claimed a seat at the back of the auditorium, with no one immediately around her. Then, she surveyed the room. Everyone was wearing variations of the same outfit—black pants or a black skirt, with a white dress shirt and a gray-and-white checkered tie. Audrey found the ensemble to be dreadfully dull, with minimal room for self-expression. Some of the female students, though, embellished their outfits with the kind of jewelry Audrey had seen only in Fifth Avenue storefronts.

"Good morning, students. Good morning," said Principal Waverly, with pseudo enthusiasm and a matching smile. He looked like he should have been a librarian and lived every day perplexed as to how he'd become a principal. "I'm sure you are all ready and excited to start a new school year. As the principal of Great Gray, it is my honor to welcome you—some of you again, and some of you for the first time. Yes, I see many familiar faces out there, and for those I don't recognize, I look forward to getting to know each and every one of you—but hopefully not for the, uh ... unfortunate reasons," he added with an awkward chuckle.

From her vantage point, Audrey could see the rest of the auditorium. Most students were engaged in their own side conversations, acting as though Principal Waverly wasn't even there. Some students were even plucky enough to outright leave, and Audrey couldn't blame them—and secretly wished she had joined them. Principal Waverly wasn't a gifted public speaker, and he was delusional to think that teenagers—especially this early in the morning—would give him any of their attention.

"Here at Great Gray, we live by three words: *uirtus, virtus, victoria*," Principal Waverly continued, seemingly unaware that very few students were actually listening. "For those of you who do not, uh, speak fluent Latin, those words mean excellence, virtue, and success. It is our, uh, most sincere hope that what you learn here at Great Gray will carry you through the rest of your lives ..."

As Principal Waverly droned on about school policies and expectations, Audrey reminisced about warm summer days biking in Central Park. She fondly remembered staying in East Hampton for the Fourth of July and her birthday, grilling and relaxing on the beach. This was the last place she wanted to be, in a stuffy auditorium listening to a middle-aged man trying to relate to her and her peers.

Audrey knew she was zoning out, but she was too lazy to zone back in. A few seconds later, she felt a swift breeze, then heard someone sit down on the open seat to her left. Instinctively, Audrey turned, curious as to who this latecomer was.

It took everything inside Audrey to not stare. He was outrageously handsome, boasting what could only be dubbed movie-star good looks. While most adolescent boys opted for longer, feathered hairstyles, he did not; on the contrary, he sported an Ivy League haircut, with his dark-brown hair parted to the left. As he settled into his seat, his head turned slightly toward Audrey, and she caught a glimpse of his baby-blue eyes. He was zealously scrawling in his notebook, his hand racing across the paper. Audrey stared for a beat too long, as he finally felt her eyes on him and looked up.

"Hi," he said, offering a smile, revealing yet another attractive feature—dimples.

Audrey had never struggled to make conversation before, but in his company, she balked, scrambling to invent a suitably witty response to his simplest of greetings. She understood the importance of first impressions, and she didn't want him to think she was shy—or, even worse, boring.

"Hi," she said at last, instantly regretting her uninspired choice. She sank into her chair, cheeks burning.

Before she could say anything more to him, Principal Waverly informed the room that next Friday, there would be a fair for all of Great Gray's clubs and activities. Though many of the sports teams had already begun practicing, some were still open to new members. Audrey actually felt her eyes gloss over when she heard the word "sports." And, to her shock, he mentioned there was a polo team. People under the age of forty played polo? Was Great Gray trying to prepare their students for lives of leisure as members of some ridiculously expensive social club?

"Please be sure to attend the fair so you can get involved in all that Great Gray has to offer," Principal Waverly said. "Now, thank you all for your undivided attention," he went on, without a trace of irony. "Let's make this the best year yet! Please, at this time, make your way to your homerooms."

Principal Waverly walked up the aisle, waving at students as though they were fans of his. Only a few desperate brown nosers waved back. Audrey wondered what Principal Waverly had dreamed of becoming—and what had happened in his life to lead him to this point, where he required the adoration of teenagers to be happy.

Audrey pulled out her schedule to see where her homeroom was. Of course, she had no idea which rooms were where, so she'd probably end up roaming the halls for twenty minutes. By then, she would already be late for her first class. Hardly a good way to demonstrate how grateful she was to be here.

"Are you a freshman?" the boy asked her.

"No, I'm a sophomore, but I just transferred here."

"Oh." He smiled warmly. "Well, welcome to Great Gray."

"Thanks." She smiled in return, proud of herself for maintaining her composure.

The boy leaned forward. "I know they don't give you much help on where things are. If you want, I could walk you to your homeroom."

To Audrey's delight, his accent was decidedly New York. It wasn't as strong as a Brooklyn accent, for instance, but she clearly heard it when he pronounced "walk" more like "wawk."

"That'd be great! Thanks!" said Audrey, delighted she had an excuse to spend more time with him.

He grinned. "I'm Bobby, by the way. I'm a sophomore too."

"Audrey."

"So, Audrey ... where are we headed?"

"Let's see ..." Audrey consulted her schedule with furrowed brows. "Room four eighteen."

They stood up, and Audrey was surprised by how tall Bobby was; he had to be almost six feet tall. As they walked, Bobby asked her if she was nervous about her first day. Audrey admitted she was, as she'd never been good with change.

"It's different from my old school," she said.

"I'm sure you'll be just fine," Bobby said, suddenly stopping. "Here we are. Four eighteen."

"Oh." Audrey was strangely disappointed they were already parting. "Well, thanks again."

"Of course." He shifted on his feet. "I'll, uh ... see you around."

"Yeah, uh ... see you too!" Audrey said, waving awkwardly.

Luckily, Bobby couldn't hear her pathetic response over the swell of students who had just arrived in the hallway. With her head hanging low, Audrey entered her homeroom, trying to refocus her attention.

The first day of school was always absurdly monotonous, with every teacher giving the same speech on expectations and time management. Some tried to strike fear into the hearts of their students, claiming that tardiness and late assignments would result in automatic Fs. Others assumed the opposite approach, trying to be all buddy-buddy with the students—with equally ineffective results. Going from teacher archetype to teacher archetype was a form of whiplash for which Audrey had not been prepared.

Thankfully, though, she had lunch sixth period, so she made her way to the cafeteria. All the tables were rectangular, with three seats on each side. She glanced around the room, knowing very well that her social future depended on where—and with whom—she sat. Unintentionally, Audrey could ruin her whole high school experience by sitting with the wrong people—or, even worse, sitting alone.

To her surprise—and endless relief—Cassandra Irvine, a girl from her Geometry class, stood up from her table and waved her over.

"Audrey! Over here!"

Audrey didn't exactly know why Cassandra wanted her to sit with her and her friends, but she wasn't about to refuse such a kind offer. Instead, Audrey walked over to the table. As she did so, Cassandra signaled for one of the girls to move over so Audrey could sit in the middle chair directly across from Cassandra.

"Hi," Audrey said to the other girls at the table, none of whom she recognized from her earlier classes.

"This is Lisa," Cassandra started, motioning to the girl on Audrey's left, "and this is Shelly and Barb." She pointed at each girl in turn. "Girls, Audrey is new here."

Disconcertingly, Lisa, Shelly, and Barb were almost spitting images of Cassandra, with their shoulder-length half-dos and accessorized uniforms. The girls leaned forward, as a unit, their curiosity piqued.

Lisa placed her elbows on the table. "New from where?"

"I went to a school in the Village," Audrey replied.

"Is that a different country?" asked Barb.

Audrey laughed. "Maybe to some people."

None of the girls laughed with her. Barb, for her part, seemed genuinely perplexed, and Audrey began to fear that Barb actually thought the Village was, in fact, a different country. Perhaps money didn't equate to a better education after all ...

"I thought the Village was for poor people," Shelly interjected.

Before Audrey could respond to that, Cassandra shot Shelly a piercing look. "Oh, is that where you live?" Cassandra asked, redirecting her attention to Audrey. "Greenwich Village?" After Audrey nodded in response, Cassandra asked, "So, what are you doing here?"

It sounded like an innocent question, but Audrey sensed an underlying, accusatory edge. The girls were staring at her, waiting for her answer. Audrey shifted in her seat. She felt as though she were being interviewed for a job: one she was, evidently, woefully unqualified for.

"I earned my place here," Audrey said, perhaps a bit too defensively.

Cassandra broke into a conciliatory smile. "Of course, you did. We *all* did."

Audrey didn't know what to make of that. *Had* they all earned their place here? Barb didn't even know where—or what—the Village was, and Shelly certainly hadn't learned anything about manners, as far as Audrey could tell. Not willing to rock the boat, however—or ostracize herself from this potential friend group—Audrey simply grimaced.

"I guess we did," she said flatly.

"Well, we're happy you're here now," Cassandra went on, "and the girls and I will be more than happy to help you ... fit in with the rest of us," she added, her eyes on Audrey's unadorned uniform.

"Oh. That's ... nice of you." As Audrey said these words, dread pooled in the pit of her stomach.

"Cassandra is *always* so nice and thoughtful," piped up Shelly, which didn't do much to assuage Audrey's mounting doubts.

"I bought this dress one time," Lisa began, visibly eager to illustrate Shelly's point, "and Cassandra told me it wasn't my color. She was right, of course!"

Cassandra nodded sagely. "You look positively *garish* in yellow."

Audrey's eyes widened. Would this be her future—being told what to wear by some five-foot-two dictator? Maybe she would have been better off sitting by herself, if this was the alternative.

"Don't worry," Cassandra told Audrey. "I bet you look good in *every* color. Especially ..." She trailed off, absently stroking her many glittering bracelets. "... *green*."

"Jeepers!" gasped Shelly, eyeing Cassandra's bracelets. "Are those new?"

Cassandra shrugged. "Oh, these? Just a back-to-school gift from Daddy."

As the girls squealed with delight, Audrey took a large bite of her sandwich and, perhaps melodramatically, hoped she would choke.

THE LAST THREE CLASSES were much more enjoyable than the previous five. Audrey got to meet her English teacher, Mrs. Parker, who, though undoubtedly intimidating, possessed a dry wit that Audrey appreciated. And, dissimilarly to some of the other teachers Audrey had already met, Mrs. Parker did not allow her students to walk all over her. Within the first five minutes of class, Mrs. Parker sent some boy down to detention for flinging rubber bands at the back of a girl's head. He claimed he was just joking around, but Mrs. Parker wasn't in the mood for such juvenile antics. Audrey wished she had shown that same grit during lunch, that she'd called out Cassandra and her friends for their judgmental comments.

A little under an hour later, Audrey was back home. Her mother was in the living room, and as soon as Audrey walked through the door, Sophia sprung to her feet, peppering her with all sorts of questions about Great Gray.

"How was your first day? Did you make any friends? What are your teachers like? Do you already have homework?"

Audrey answered her questions as vaguely as possible, knowing very well she wouldn't mention Cassandra or the other girls. She knew how important it was to her parents for her to fit in, and she didn't want them to be worried about her. Audrey started giving Sophia her assessment of Mrs. Parker, the school's most daunting English teacher, and Alexander walked in.

"They say she fails students just to make them cry," Audrey told them. "I don't think I believe it, but … she *does* have that look about her. I kind of like her, though. She's funny. Has that Aunt Trina sarcasm."

"Oh, no. There's two of them?" joked Alexander.

"Well, we're so proud of you, Audie," Sophia said, unable to suppress her palpable glee. That was one of the things Audrey loved most about her mother—her unwavering positivity. "Really, Dad and me … we were saying this morning just how impressed we are by you. It's a big change, we know, but … you'll do great."

"And don't forget, love," Alexander piped up, "high school is the best years of your life. So, soak it all up!"

Sophia added, "Oh, and next Saturday, we're all going out to dinner, to celebrate this new school year."

"*All* of us?" asked Audrey. "Including Claire?"

"Well, of course!" said Sophia, oblivious to Audrey's tone.

Though Audrey loved Claire, the two had never been particularly close. And Audrey would have been lying if she said that having Claire out of the apartment and in one of the NYU dorms hadn't been a dream. In fact, when their parents had decided a dorm would be worth the extra money to ensure that Claire had the whole college experience, Audrey hadn't protested. Now, it was just Audrey at home, and she'd already gotten used to having the bedroom all to herself.

"Right. I won't forget," Audrey said.

"Well, dinner's almost ready, sweets!"

After dinner, Audrey handed over all the paperwork to Alexander to sign. Predictably, he made the same joke he always did, remarking how he felt like Elvis

Presley signing autographs. Audrey laughed, as she always did, not wanting her father to ever think he'd lost his touch.

Eventually, the evening morphed into night. Because the apartment contained only one bathroom, they had devised a schedule for who could use it when. It was a routine they had down to the minute. The wonderful parents they were, Sophia and Alexander always let their daughters go first. With Claire out of the lineup, Audrey was the first one on the list.

The night before, Audrey had been racked with anxiety, stewing over every possibility, living through every worst-case scenario. Tonight, however, her anxiety was more centered, grounded in the reality of how her first day at Great Gray had gone. As she closed her eyes, she saw Cassandra Irvine and her posse laughing and pointing at her.

"You don't belong here," they said in chorus. "You never will."

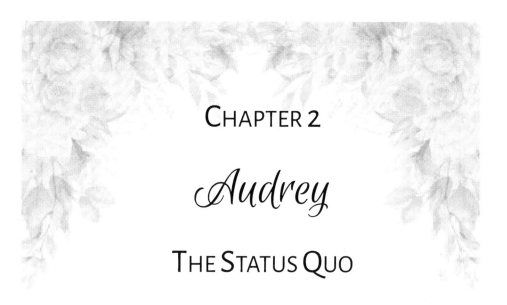

CHAPTER 2

Audrey

THE STATUS QUO

I N MANY WAYS, AUDREY thought, the second day of school was more difficult than the first. It was the definitive realization that summer was truly over. The next nine months of her life would be spent attending classes, lugging around a backpack heavier than she was, and navigating the complicated politics of a private high school.

She'd arrived at school a little early, to enjoy the emptiness of the hallways and actually read the various flyers already posted around. She was impressed by how many extracurricular activities and clubs Great Gray boasted. There were, of course, the staples, such as yearbook, pep club, key club, and drama. Some of the clubs, however, seemed so niche she wasn't sure how many students could possibly be enrolled. For example, there was a group dedicated to dissecting and analyzing each *Columbo* episode, and, according to the flyer, they were encouraged—maybe even required—to wear trench coats.

Slowly, more students filed in, dispersing in all directions, with varying levels of energy. Audrey could have used a cup of joe to power her through the school day, but her parents thought she was too young—even though Claire had been drinking coffee since she was twelve.

As Audrey approached her locker, she tried—but failed—to stifle a yawn. Bobby, the boy she'd met at the assembly, entered the school. Instead of a backpack, he carried a black messenger bag. It was slung across his shoulder, making him look charmingly adult. He struck Audrey as the sort of person who had never acted his age; he had probably been one of those kids who was more interested in what the adults were doing. While most of his peers preferred to have their ties slung across their shoulders or their blazer unbuttoned, Bobby was the epitome of prim and proper. Audrey couldn't help but wonder how early he'd woken up, as his shirt and pants were wrinkle-free, and his hair was perfectly coiffed. A bit self-consciously, Audrey glanced down at her own attire, noting the creases in her skirt and blouse. Bobby neared her, and Audrey attempted to smooth her skirt with the palms of her hands. Her heart lodged itself in her throat as she was once again made aware of just how handsome he was.

To her delight, Bobby's locker was not too far away from hers. When he opened his locker, Audrey caught a glimpse inside and was impressed by how organized it was. Everything was color coordinated, most likely lined up in the order of his classes. Bobby grabbed a couple of notebooks, placing them gingerly in his bag. Not wanting to pry or come across as stalkerish, Audrey pretended to be fascinated by her locker's drab interior. She made a mental note to decorate it with some posters.

"Hi again."

Bobby's voice came from behind her, and in shock, Audrey slammed her locker, nearly crushing her index finger in the process. Audrey collected herself and turned to face Bobby, who was standing near enough that she could smell his lemony, woodsy cologne but not so near that she felt uncomfortable. He didn't seem aware of his attractiveness—or accustomed to talking to girls. Rather, his left hand tightly gripped his bag, his posture was stiff, and he offered Audrey a sweet—but adorably timid—smile.

"Hi," Audrey said, absently playing with her collar.

"How was your day yesterday?"

"It was good, yeah," she lied. "I think I'm getting the lay of the land." She looked up and met his beautiful eyes. "Thanks again for walking me to my homeroom."

"You're very welcome." He cleared his throat. "I was actually ... I'm glad I saw you. Some friends and I, we're going to grab burgers after school, and I was wondering if you'd like to join us."

Audrey knew it would have been the better move to play it cool—maybe even reject his invitation—but she was far too excited by this turn of events to feign aloofness. A cute boy was asking her if she wanted to hang out with him and his friends. No way was she going to turn him down.

"I'd like that," Audrey said giddily.

"Great! Do you know Jack's?"

"No."

"Oh, okay. Here, I'll meet you by your locker after school, and we'll go together."

"Sounds good!"

For the rest of the morning, Audrey had a noticeable pep in her step. Nothing, it seemed, could sully her mood. She'd been hoping she'd see Bobby again, and she was flattered he'd sought her out on his own—and that he wanted her to meet his friends. Maybe this could be the start of something. Maybe—

"Audrey." Cassandra's voice knocked Audrey out of her daydream, bringing her back to the cafeteria. "Are you even listening to me? You were pretty zoned out there."

"Oh." Audrey looked up and saw all the girls glaring at her. "Sorry about that. I guess I just ... do any of you girls know a Bobby?"

Cassandra's face blanched. "Bobby ... Dempsey?"

Upon hearing that name, the other girls' eyes widened. Audrey wasn't sure where to direct her attention—or what to say. All the girls were staring at her as though she'd been speaking in a foreign language.

Audrey shrugged. "Maybe?"

"Well, what does he look like?" Cassandra demanded.

"He's tall with brown hair, blue eyes, and—"

"That's him." Cassandra furrowed her eyebrows. "How did you ... how do you know him?"

"He sat next to me at the assembly. Actually, he was really nice and offered to walk me to my homeroom."

"*He* offered?"

"Well, yeah." A pit opened in Audrey's stomach. "Why? Does he do that a lot?"

Shelly snorted, and Cassandra quelled her with a quick look. Audrey nervously glanced between the two, trying to decipher this exchange. Was Shelly trying to warn her about Bobby, or had Cassandra possibly dated him before? It was difficult to tell why they were reacting this way.

"He's never offered to walk *me* anywhere," Barb lamented.

"Please. He doesn't even know you exist," Lisa retorted, and Barb hung her head in shame.

Audrey smiled sympathetically at Barb before continuing, "Well, he invited me to grab burgers with him and his friends after school."

"He must like you!" Shelly chirped, and in response, Cassandra smacked her shoulder—too forcefully to be in jest.

The pit in Audrey's stomach became occupied by butterflies, lots of them, fluttering about, all crashing into each other. Shelly's comment—whether genuine or derisive—had alleviated some of Audrey's concerns. However, Cassandra's eyes were daggers, threatening—but failing—to deflate Audrey's buoyed mood.

There was a manic look in Cassandra's eyes. "You can't go out with him," she told Audrey.

"Why not?"

"Because!" Cassandra slammed the table, startling Barb, who squealed and squeezed her juice box, some of which splashed onto the table.

With her napkin, Audrey wiped up the spilled juice. "Do you ... *like* Bobby?" she asked Cassandra.

Cassandra scoffed. "He's *Bobby Dempsey*. Of course, I like him."

"Well, if it makes you feel any better, I'm not going out with just him. I'm—"

"It doesn't matter, Audrey! You can't just come in here and ..." Cassandra trailed off, shaking her head. She tapped her finger against the table. "Do you even know anything about him?"

"Well—"

"He's the son of Robert Dempsey—*the* Robert Dempsey. Surely, you know who *that* is?"

Audrey would have had to be living under a rock to not know *the* Robert Dempsey. He was the CEO of R.D. Dempsey Corporation, colloquially known as Dempsey Corp. Dempsey Corp was one of the largest, most influential conglomerates in the United States, if not the world. Audrey's father was nothing short of obsessed with the Dempsey family and their exuberant, lavish lifestyle, comparing them to past dynasties such as the Morgans, Rockefellers, and Vanderbilts. Alexander had always fancied himself a history buff, and he was particularly interested in "great men who defined their age"—which, evidently, included Robert Dempsey. Originally, the Dempseys had made their fortune in transportation—something to do with railroads, if Audrey remembered correctly. Usually, she tuned out her father's history lessons, finding talk of rich White men owning things to be incredibly boring. Still, despite her naivety about all things business and stocks, even she knew the Dempseys were a big deal. In fact, they were not only one of the richest families in New York but also in the nation, with an estimated net worth of well over one billion dollars.

"Of course, I know who he is," Audrey responded.

"So, obviously, you can see why it won't work out," Cassandra pressed on, "seeing as you're from the Village and all."

Lisa and Shelly snorted, looking at Audrey with an infuriating mixture of superiority and pity. Barb, on the other hand, offered Audrey a wry, knowing smile. Audrey's face was hot. She hadn't expected Cassandra to try and embarrass her by using her socioeconomic status against her.

"Why should that matter?" Audrey countered, her voice steady despite her simmering anger.

Cassandra scoffed. "Because it does. It just does. End of discussion." She then directed her attention to Lisa. "Did Alistair ever get back to you about where you're going Saturday?"

Lisa beamed. "He's taking me to P.J. Clarke's."

"Oooo!" Shelly clapped excitedly.

Audrey sat in silence. As far as Cassandra was concerned, the subject had been dropped, and Audrey wouldn't be permitted to speak about Bobby anymore. But that didn't stop her from thinking about him and their after-school meetup. In fact, throughout the day, Audrey found herself doodling his initials—BD—in the margins of her notebooks.

After classes finished, Audrey swung by her locker and gathered up her books. As he'd promised, Bobby escorted her to Jack's Burger Bar. It was just a couple of blocks from Great Gray, but Bobby and Audrey made friendly, lighthearted conversation on the walk over. Jack's was straight out of the 1950s, with black-and-white tile floors, a jukebox, and blue booths. The staff all wore those typical diner uniforms, complete with the little hats.

Bobby led Audrey over to the booth where four people—three girls and a boy—were already sitting. Audrey trailed behind his towering frame, not quite enthused at the prospect of meeting more Cassandras. She sincerely hoped his friends were nice.

"Hey, everyone," Bobby said. "This is Audrey. She's new here, so let's make her feel welcome. Audrey, this is Sebastian," he continued, gesturing at the only boy, who nodded politely at Audrey, "and this is—"

"I know you!" one of the girls piped up. "We're in Geometry and Gym together, but we haven't been properly introduced." She stuck out her hand. "I'm Florie. Florie Washington. To remember, just think: like the president but better."

Audrey smiled. "I'll remember that."

The girl with raven hair and bright red lips laughed. "Glad to know you're actually taking an interest in American history, Florie."

"Oh, come on, Sarah! You know how much I love history! Don't forget we saw *1776* together," Florie retorted.

"And that didn't help you much on the final, did it?"

"I almost passed! That should say something."

Sarah rolled her eyes. "You can't watch a musical and think that's real history."

"Oh, you mean our Founding Fathers *didn't* sing at each other?" Florie asked, hand to her chest in mock indignation. "You learn something new every day."

"History class *would* be better if they turned it into a musical," Audrey agreed. "Mr. Schmidt isn't exactly interesting to listen to."

"Ooof, you have Mr. Spit? Lordy." Florie shuddered. "I had him last year. Maybe sit in the back from now on. He tends to spray more than he says, if you catch my meaning."

"Ew!" exclaimed Sarah. "That's disgusting! We're about to eat!"

"Well, that man ruined many a lunch for me, let me tell you. Having that class right before lunch? Criminal." Florie scooted in, patting the seat next to her. "Sit next to me, Audrey, and I'll impart more of my wisdom onto you."

They all ordered burgers, fries, and shakes. As they chatted away, Audrey was surprised by how comfortable she felt in their company; it was a stark contrast to the two lunches she'd spent with Cassandra and her posse. The last girl, Helena, reminded Audrey of the activities and clubs fair next Friday, telling her it was a great way to meet new people and get involved in all that Great Gray had to offer. Audrey couldn't help but think that Helena would be a fantastic spokeswoman for the school; she certainly seemed passionate about singing its praises.

"Let me guess, that's where I can join the polo team?" Audrey joked.

"Well, we do have that," answered Helena, oblivious to Audrey's tone, "but, um, it's just for boys."

"Figures," said Audrey, shaking her head. "The one thing I was interested in!"

"Did you play at your old school?" asked Bobby, playing along.

"You know, I did. I was the star player. I got all the ... goals. Or whatever they're called."

Bobby laughed. "Well, don't worry. We have, you know, normal clubs, like the school paper, yearbook, soccer, all that."

"And Chordially Yours!" piped up Florie. "If you join, you could hang out with me and Miss Sarah Songbird here all the time!" she added, slinging her arm around Sarah's shoulder.

Sarah blushed, shaking her head. "You're the one who always gets the solos," she said cheerfully.

"Oh, is Chordially Yours a singing group?" asked Audrey.

"We are, indeed!" Florie boasted. "Best singing group Great Gray's ever seen! And heard! Do you sing?"

"Not very good," laughed Audrey.

"Music to my ears! Less competition for me, then," Florie teased, playfully nudging Audrey.

"What *do* you like?" Bobby asked Audrey. "You know, besides polo," he added, his eyes glinting spiritedly.

"I'm not sure yet," Audrey said, shamelessly fantasizing about what it'd feel like to run her fingers through his thick, gorgeous hair. "I guess I'll keep my options open."

Audrey didn't want to be too hasty, but she and Bobby seemed to be getting along especially well. Bobby asked all sorts of questions, including how she'd spent her summer. Later, Sebastian and Helena, the two seniors, complained about their SAT scores, fearing they wouldn't be able to attend their dream schools.

"I might have to take the damn thing again," Sebastian lamented. He then turned to Bobby and asked hopefully, "Maybe you could help me study this time, considering you're the expert and all?"

Bobby smiled. "I'll have to check my schedule, see if I can fit you in."

Sebastian patted him on the back. "Good man."

"You've already taken the SATs?" Audrey asked Bobby. "We're only sopho-mores."

Bobby shrugged. "I wanted to make sure I liked my score."

"And did you?"

"I was happy with it."

"Of course, you were," laughed Sebastian. "You got a fifteen ninety. Best score to come out of Great Gray since ... ever."

There wasn't any trace of envy or resentment in Sebastian's tone; rather, he sounded quite proud. Even now, he beamed at Bobby, who was clearly uncomfortable with the conversation being fixated on him; he simply claimed he'd "lucked out" with the questions.

"Jesus, Bobby," said Helena, her jaw dropping. "And here I was, happy with my twelve seventy."

"And that's a great score, Helena!" Bobby said earnestly.

"It's no fifteen ninety."

"It'll get you into Brown, and that's all that matters, right?" Bobby looked at Audrey, the intensity of his gaze nearly causing her to gag on her straw. "But, uh, whenever you're thinking of taking the SATs, I'd be more than happy to help you study too—you know, if you want."

Audrey stirred her milkshake with the straw. "Quite presumptuous of you to think I'd need any help," she teased.

In her peripheral vision, Audrey saw Florie and Sarah make eye contact and smile. Sebastian, who had been casually reclining in his seat, suddenly sat up with rapt attention; he propped his chin on his hand as he turned to Bobby in anticipation of his rebuttal.

Bobby, for his part, laughed, raising his hands in mock surrender. "All right, all right," he said affably. "If you change your mind, though, the offer still stands."

"I'll consider it," Audrey said, taking a delicate sip of her milkshake.

"*I'm* definitely considering it," Helena jumped in. "If you could help me with my cover letter to Brown, that'd be great."

"Sure," Bobby said. "As soon as I'm, you know, done writing the next great American novel."

At first, Audrey thought he was joking, but then she was brought back to the assembly. Bobby had been carrying a notebook, and as Principal Waverly droned on about school rules and policies and the polo team, Bobby had been writing away, his hand flying across the paper so fast Audrey hadn't been able to decipher a word. The notebook, clearly, was well loved; he was only a handful of pages away from its end.

"Thanks, Bobby," Helena laughed. "I just want to make sure I don't shoot myself in the foot by ... oh, I don't know ... putting a comma in the wrong place or something."

"I can help with that."

"Oh, here we go," Sarah muttered, shaking her head.

"What?"

"You're gonna give us that whole speech about how commas save lives."

"They can!" Bobby argued, unable to suppress his preemptive laughter. "It's the difference between eating your grandmother and telling your grandmother it's time to eat!" While the others groaned, Audrey laughed. "Okay," Bobby conceded. "You don't like grammar jokes! That's fine! I guess Audrey and I are the only ones with taste here."

"You know, I might take you up on your offer after all, if you'll be telling jokes like that," Audrey said, and Bobby grinned.

Slowly, the group started to disperse, with Helena being the first to leave, followed by Sarah.

"Well," Florie said grandly, standing up, "back to hell for me—Hell's Kitchen, that is. Where you headed, Audrey?"

Audrey gulped as Bobby and Sebastian turned to look at her. "Um ... I'm down in the Village."

She waited for the inevitable gasp, but it didn't come. Instead, Bobby and Sebastian offered to walk Florie and Audrey to the nearest station. Florie, however, assured them she'd get herself and Audrey there "just fine, thank you very much."

"I like you, Audrey," Florie said the second they rounded the corner. "Not the way *Bobby* likes you, but still." She smiled slyly. "And *you* clearly like *him*. Don't even try to deny it! I saw how you laughed at all his jokes. Even that comma one, which was just plain dumb. No offense."

"It was cute." Audrey bit her thumbnail. "*He* is really cute."

Florie threw up jazz hands. "Bobby and Audrey. I can see it now!"

"Whoa! Slow down, there! It's not like we're dating or anything."

"Yet. But just you wait." Florie clicked her tongue. "I'd put money on him asking you out. Mind you, I'm not sitting on a Dempsey fortune—far from it—but someday, I'll have so much bread they'll think I'm a baker." Audrey laughed, and Florie added, "See, unlike your future boyfriend, my jokes land. They're funny. Gotta have a sense of humor to survive at Great Gray."

"Don't I know it."

"Yeah, I saw you sitting with Cassandra and her clones at lunch. They wouldn't know 'funny' if it came up and bit 'em on the ass." Florie pulled a face. "Sorry. Don't mean to talk bad 'bout your friends."

"Oh, don't worry. They're not my friends. Cassandra made that *very* clear."

Florie stopped in her tracks. "What'd she say to you?"

"Nothing much. She just, you know, let it be known she won't ever be friends with a girl like me. And she kind of ..." Audrey trailed off, deciding Florie was someone in whom she could confide. "See, I'm on scholarship, which I guess makes me lesser in her eyes."

"As I live and breathe! A fellow scholarship student! I wasn't sure we actually existed!"

Relief poured over Audrey. "You're one too?"

"Of course!" Florie grinned. "But, see, people like us ... we're a rare breed at Great Gray. Most everyone there eats with forks made of gold and sleeps on linens English kings died on. And the rules ... they just don't apply to them. Like Cassandra. See, last year, her daddy paid for the new library 'cause she got caught smoking in the bathroom. No detention. Nothin' on her record. Just the Irvine name on a plaque outside the library. Gotta love how money talks in this town."

This news didn't come as a surprise to Audrey, though it did turn her stomach just the same. She'd warned her parents these were the sorts of kids she'd be going to school with—privileged heirs who would never have to face any consequences for their actions—but they'd insisted she was exaggerating.

"Anyway." Florie sighed. "At least we have each other."

"Do Bobby and the others treat you differently because you're a scholarship student?" Audrey asked, hoping Florie's answer wouldn't disappoint her.

"No. Now, I don't know Bobby that well—he's more Sarah's friend—but he's always been kind to me. He'll be kind to you too," she added, as if reading Audrey's mind. "I mean, he'd have to be, right? Seeing as he'll be your boyfriend and all." She winked at Audrey. "I bet by lunch tomorrow—'cause yes, you'll be sitting with me and Sarah from now on—you'll be telling us he asked you out."

CHAPTER 3

Audrey

THE PRINCE OF THE UPPER EAST SIDE

I T TOOK ONLY ONE day for Florie's prophecy to be proven correct. Audrey dawdled at her locker, waiting for Bobby. She wanted to speak with him some more—and hopefully show she was interested in more than just a friendship with him. Luckily, she didn't have to wait too long, and as soon as he saw her, Bobby smiled.

"Hey, Audrey." He walked over. "I was hoping I'd see you. We didn't really get a chance to talk yesterday, just the two of us."

"Yeah, sorry, I had to get home. I didn't want my parents to be worried, wondering where I was."

"They sound like good parents."

"They are. The best. But I would've liked to talk to you more. And not just, you know, about commas and the SATs."

Bobby laughed. Audrey noticed the specks of white in his irises, like icebergs set against the Arctic Ocean. If his father had been someone other than Robert Dempsey, Bobby would have undoubtedly been scouted by Hollywood film producers, eager to find the next John Travolta.

"So, I hope this isn't too forward," Bobby went on, "but ... I think you're really cute, and I was wondering if you'd be interested in maybe going on a date with me sometime."

Audrey ran her fingers through her hair, hoping her cheeks weren't as red as they felt. Bobby Dempsey thought she was cute. No, not just cute—*really* cute.

"I'd really like that," she said.

Bobby grinned. "Are you free next Friday, after the clubs and activities fair?"

They arranged the details. A first date should be casual, they agreed; accordingly, Audrey recommended they go to Sal's, one of her go-to pizza places.

"It's in the Village, just a short walk from my place," Audrey told him.

"That sounds great! I've never been to the Village."

It was odd to Audrey, hearing Bobby say he'd never once stepped foot in the neighborhood that had been her home for her entire life. Though New York was technically one city, it was almost like each neighborhood existed independently of one another. Audrey, for her part, didn't even know where Lenox Hill was; for all she knew, it might not even exist.

"The pizza is amazing," Audrey said. "Some of the best in the city."

"That's a high bar."

"You'll see for yourself. And if I'm wrong, dinner's on me."

Bobby smiled. "Well, I'd love to stay and chat, but Mrs. Parker actually wants to see me to talk about the piece I'm writing for this week's paper."

"Don't let me stop you!"

Audrey watched as he headed toward the staircase and disappeared from her view. She then opened her locker and started loading up her backpack, making sure everything was in its rightful place.

"You didn't listen to me." Cassandra's voice came from behind her.

Audrey turned to face her, her eyebrows furrowed. "I don't—"

"I told you not to talk to Bobby Dempsey."

"I really—"

"No, you know what? I don't want to hear it." Cassandra glared at her. "Don't even think about sitting with us at lunch today—or ever."

Audrey laughed, despite herself. "Okay."

"Is that funny to you?"

"It kind of is, yeah." Audrey closed her locker. "Anyway, I should go. But, uh … have a good rest of your day, Cassandra."

"It won't last, you know!" Cassandra called out as Audrey walked away. "He won't … it won't work out!"

Though a part of Audrey wanted to say something sarcastic in response, she decided against it. Cassandra wasn't worth her time—or her energy. Besides, it was obvious she was just jealous that Bobby wasn't waiting for her by *her* locker, asking *her* out on dates.

Audrey had seen the messages in the girls' bathrooms; she knew how many of her peers would have gladly given their eye teeth to go out with Bobby. For the rest of the day, she was bolstered by the knowledge that she was going on a date with Bobby next week. It was tantalizing, keeping the secret, but Audrey didn't want to share the news with just anyone.

Finally, lunchtime arrived, and Audrey did her best to avoid all eye contact with Cassandra and her friends. She could still hear them whispering amongst themselves as she passed, though. Cassandra had plainly done what she could to poison them against Audrey. With her head held high, Audrey joined Florie and Sarah at their table, and she informed them that she and Bobby would be going on a date next Friday.

"I knew it!" Florie exclaimed. "I just knew you two liked each other! I told you, didn't I? I told you you'd end up dating him."

"It's just the first date," Audrey insisted. "It's not like we're boyfriend-girl-friend."

"Please. Oh, and just so you know, I expect a full report. I need to know what kind of boy Bobby Dempsey is. Does he hold open doors? Is he nice to waiters? Does he tip well? All of it." Florie turned to Sarah. "What can you tell us? Give us the skinny."

"Well, I've known Bobby since we were kids," Sarah explained. "My *baba* works at Dempsey Corp, and our families have always been close. Bobby's a good guy—very sweet. I can tell he likes you, Audrey. He was talking about you in

Spanish today."

Audrey wanted to investigate this further, discover what Bobby had been saying about her, but before she could open her mouth, Florie cut in, saying, "You know what the girls call Bobby, right?"

"No, what?" asked Audrey.

"The Prince of the Upper East Side. So, you're dating royalty, honey. Royalty." Florie hit the table for dramatic emphasis. "You're Grace Kelly."

"Hardly!"

"No, you are. And ... hey, you know what?" Florie looked at Audrey intently, as though seeing her for the first time. "I was joking around, but ... you really look like her!"

Audrey raised an eyebrow. "What, because I'm blonde, and all blondes look alike?"

"No. Because you look like her. Your hair's a bit ... wilder than hers. But still! You've got The Look. Bobby *clearly* thinks so."

WHEN AUDREY RETURNED HOME, the aroma of Sophia's family-favorite turkey hung in the air. She greeted her mother before she got started on her homework. Thankfully, she didn't have too much yet—just some light reading assignments. She breezed through them in under an hour, then changed into more comfortable clothes, just in time for dinner.

"How was your day, Audie?" asked Alexander, turning to her.

"Well." Audrey rested her fork and knife on the edge of her plate. "I actually ... I have a date next Friday."

"A date?" Sophia's eyes widened. "It's only the third day of school!"

"I know."

"That's so fast! You don't even know anyone yet—not really! Definitely not enough to go on a date with them!"

"But I think you'd like him."

"I'm sure we would," said Alexander, reaching over to pat Audrey's hand. "But Mom's right, love. It's too soon."

"But I already said yes."

"Well, tomorrow, you can tell him no."

Audrey silently picked up her knife and fork and resumed cutting her turkey. She knew her parents meant well, but they were acting as though they'd sat her down over the summer and relayed their expectations for her. They'd never once brought up the word "dating"—and they'd certainly never told her she was too young to even consider it.

"There's nothing wrong with just being friends with this boy," said Sophia after a few minutes of awkward silence, no doubt sensing her daughter's frustration.

"But Bobby's really cute. I don't want to just be friends with him," Audrey explained.

"Bobby. That's the boy's name?" asked Alexander absently, cutting his turkey.

"Yes." Then, with purpose, Audrey added, "Bobby *Dempsey*."

Audrey had never known her parents to be so dramatic. Alexander dropped his fork, and Sophia nearly spit out her water.

"Dempsey?" asked Alexander, the color drained from his face. "As in ... the son of *Robert* Dempsey?"

"That's the one."

Alexander propped his elbows on the table, his interest suddenly piqued. "Where was he planning on taking you?"

"We were going to grab a couple slices at Sal's. But since you and Mom think I'm too young to be dating—"

"Now, hang on." Alexander shook his index finger at her, in that typical Dad Way. "When you told us a boy had asked you out, we were picturing just a normal high school boy. But the son of Robert Dempsey ... that's special."

Audrey resisted the urge to roll her eyes. She was all too familiar with her parents' social agenda. Though they'd never explicitly admitted it, she knew they'd been so gung-ho for Great Gray so Audrey could live out their fantasy of life amongst the upper echelons of New York society. Still, never could they have imagined that their youngest daughter would attract the attention of someone like Bobby Dempsey. The quick, one-hundred-and-eighty-degree shift in their opinion, merely because of Bobby's parentage, was enough to make Audrey lose her appetite—which was upsetting, as she loved her mother's turkey.

"He, you can go out with," Sophia agreed, nodding earnestly. "We don't mind you dating young Robert."

"Bobby," corrected Audrey.

"What?"

"Bobby. He goes by Bobby."

"Why on Earth would he do that? Robert is such a handsome, regal name."

"Do you know how much Robert Dempsey's worth?" Alexander blurted, leaning forward so much Audrey thought he'd get gravy on his shirt. At last, all those hours he'd spent reading *Forbes* had paid off. "One billion dollars. Billion! And he only has the one son. Imagine, inheriting all that money?" Alexander whistled through his teeth, his mind probably dancing with images of yachts, mansions, and sports cars. "Not too shabby. Not too shabby at all."

Audrey took a deep breath. "I'm not interested in Bobby because of his dad's money. He's really nice."

"And cute," Sophia added, winking at her. "You said he's cute."

"Well, yes. Obviously. Or else I wouldn't have said yes."

"Now, now, Audie," piped up Alexander, ignoring Sophia's and Audrey's laughs. "Let's not be shallow."

"Shallow?" Audrey crossed her arms. "You're the one talking about his dad's bank account!"

"Well, I ..." Alexander tried to talk himself out of the hole he'd dug. "It's just a lot of money, that's all. But like you said, I'm sure Bobby ... I'm sure he's a lovely boy."

"Yes, bring him over next Friday, will you? Before you head out?" asked Sophia, a bit too intently.

"It's the first date," Audrey reminded her. "I'm not bringing him home to meet you on the first date. That'd guarantee there won't be a second date."

"Of course, there will be a second date! It's you!" Sophia beamed. "Now, who wants dessert?"

CHAPTER 4

Audrey

FIRST DATE

THANKFULLY, THE NEXT WEEK flew by. As soon as classes ended on Friday, the students were funneled into the gymnasium, where they could decide if they wanted to try out for a sports team or join any clubs. As Audrey wandered the gym, she was amazed by how crowded it was. There must have been about one hundred students, all grabbing flyers and inquiring about the ins and outs of each club. Across the gym, Florie was manning Chordially Yours' booth, chatting up the people in line.

After a few minutes, Audrey found the table for The Great Debaters, the school's debate club. The student heading the table was already deep in conversation with other potential members, so Audrey stood in line, scanning the gym. The sports tables were particularly busy, with keen freshmen trying to prove themselves to the upperclassmen. Audrey was relieved she'd never been interested in sports; it seemed like a nightmare, having to endure various rounds of tryouts and hazing, only to be told you weren't good enough. Eventually, Audrey made her way to the front of the line, enduring tedious small talk with the girl running the table before she was finally set free.

A couple of football players were horsing around, tossing a football back and forth, to the chagrin of one of the teacher supervisors, who kept catching the ball, tsk-tsking them, then returning it. Clearly, he wasn't paid enough to care, as he kept glancing up at the clock, dismayed by how much time remained. He must have pulled the short straw, having to spend his Friday afternoon watching over kids who had spent all week terrorizing him. The boys, meanwhile, waited until his back was turned before they tossed the ball again. Few were less daunted by the prospect of trouble than privileged teenage boys.

Gradually, the fair wound down, and the crowd thinned out. From what Audrey could tell, the fair had been a success; a lot of the clubs had managed to recruit new members. For her part, she had joined The Great Debaters and Helping Hands, the latter of which was the school's volunteer club. Audrey admired Helping Hands' mission, and she was eager to make a positive difference in people's lives. Briefly, Audrey saw Florie, who filled her in on all the people who had come up to Chordially Yours' booth.

"A couple of them sang at me, Audrey. Yeah, not *to* me—*at* me. It was mortifying."

Audrey laughed. "Were they any good at least?"

"No. But, you know, it's not my job to tell them that. They'll find out for themselves when they get axed after the first round." Florie jerked her head toward the cross-country team's table. "Oh, and you probably already knew this, but your boyfriend is right over there."

"Huh." Audrey put her hands on her hips. "I wouldn't have pegged him as a runner."

"He's also on the baseball team."

"Baseball?" Audrey scrunched her nose.

Florie's jaw dropped. "You don't like baseball?"

"My dad's into it. But I've never gotten the appeal. It's so boring—and long. Why are there so many rounds?"

"You mean innings?"

"Sure." Audrey shrugged. "It's just not for me."

"Oh, Audrey! You've got to get into baseball! Bobby's the shortstop."

"What's that?"

Florie heaved a deep breath, collecting herself. "Just ask your dad, okay? I've got to go."

"Okay," laughed Audrey, waving as Florie left. She then made her way over to Bobby. "Need some help?" she asked, watching as he rolled up the tablecloth.

Bobby looked up. "Hey!" He flashed her a smile. "No, I'm just about finished up here. Thanks, though. Just give me a second to put all this stuff in the team's storage locker."

Within five minutes, Bobby had cleaned up his table—which was more than most of the other clubs could say—and he and Audrey left. A few straggler students saw them together—including Shelly—and Audrey knew she would have to brace herself for next week's rumor mill. She hoped the date went well; otherwise, it would be very awkward, having to tell Florie she had dubbed her the next Grace Kelly far too early.

"Did you join any clubs?" Bobby asked as they descended Great Gray's front staircase.

"I did. I guess you could say I'm now a Helping Hand and a Great Debater." She made a face, realizing how stupid that sounded. "I joined Helping Hands and The Great Debaters," she clarified.

Bobby laughed, waving down a taxi. "You know, Seb's in The Great Debaters. So, you'll be seeing a lot of him."

"Well, I heard you're on the cross-country team and the baseball team."

"That's true." Bobby nodded distractedly. "I also write for *The Bulletin*."

"Which do you like best?"

"I love them all. But ... writing is my first love. Ah. Here we are."

A taxi pulled over. Bobby opened the door, and Audrey noted that Bobby was, indeed, the type to open doors. Florie would be pleased. Already, things were looking good.

"After you," Bobby said.

"Thank you," said Audrey.

Audrey relayed the directions to the driver. As they rode off, Bobby positioned himself so he could face her. Vaguely, Audrey wondered how many girls had been where she was before, going out with Bobby Dempsey. For all she knew, this could be a part of Bobby's charm; maybe he simply feigned interest in women before abruptly cutting things off. She'd seen Claire get hurt in the past by boys who'd promised her the world. Still, Audrey's instincts told her that Bobby was different—that he wasn't one to play those sorts of games.

"I've been looking forward to this all week," Bobby admitted, knocking Audrey out of her thoughts.

"Me too."

"I actually ... I have something to confess." He chuckled, despite himself. "This is kind of ... well, it's my first date."

"Really?"

"I know, it's weird. I'm a sophomore in high school, and I've never been on a date before."

"No, it's not weird. That's not what I meant." Audrey rested her hands on her lap. "It's my first date too. I was just surprised is all."

"Why?"

"Well, I thought it was obvious. Lots of the girls think you're the cutest guy in school." She met his eyes, warmth flooding her cheeks. "And I definitely don't disagree with that."

In response, Bobby grinned. Audrey couldn't decide what she loved more—his eyes or his dimples. Sitting so close to him in the cab, she could see the beginnings of scruff on his cheeks. If he was already this handsome as a sophomore, she couldn't imagine how handsome he'd be in a couple of years.

"Well, just so you know, the feeling is mutual," Bobby assured her. "I really ... I'm very taken in with you."

Audrey laughed, shaking her head. "That's the kind of thing my grandparents would say."

"What, 'taken in with you'?"

"Yes! It's very old school. But on you, it works. And I guess it goes with your whole Prince of the Upper East Side persona."

"My what?"

"That's what some of the girls call you. And the bathroom stalls seem to back that up."

"I don't quite know how I feel about that, but ... I suppose it could be worse."

"Oh, it could. And it is for some guys. Like Alistair Amherst. No one has a good thing to say about him—except for his girlfriend, who's head over heels for him, apparently."

Bobby smirked. "Maybe that's how Lisa feels this week. But knowing them ... let's just say, they've never exactly been a ... stable couple."

Bobby leaned closer to her, his finger unintentionally brushing her thigh. When he did so, bolts of electricity jolted through Audrey's veins. She impulsively sat up. Her heartbeat quickened, and she struggled to regain some sort of composure. What was wrong with her? She was sitting in a cab, not running a marathon.

"What do you think of Great Gray so far?" Bobby asked, apparently incognizant of the effect his touch had on her.

Audrey cleared her throat. "I'm liking my classes so far—well, most of them. French is sort of kicking my butt. We're going much faster than we did in middle school."

"If you ever want some tutoring, I'd be more than happy to help."

Audrey cocked her head to the side. "But I thought you took Spanish, like Sarah."

"I do, but ... I had some language tutors when I was younger, so I'm rather good at French too."

"Well, if you're really offering, I'll take you up on that." Playfully, she asked, "What's your fee?"

"Entirely free of charge. I promise."

Curious whether the sensation she'd felt just moments before was a fluke or something that could be recreated, Audrey slowly lowered her hand to meet Bobby's. The sheer act of their fingers touching sent even more powerful currents through Audrey's body. Something that had, for fifteen years, been dormant awakened within her, and its novelty exhilarated her. Bobby, for his part, appeared equally affected. He looked down at their hands, then back up at her, wide-eyed. He shifted his hand so he could interlock his fingers with hers. There it was again—that electric jolt. They both sat in stunned silence, unable to explain the flood of emotions pulsating through them.

"Here you are," the taxi driver announced, and Bobby reached for his wallet and paid him.

"Thank you so much," Bobby said.

"Yes, thank you," added Audrey.

The taxi driver sifted through the wad of cash Bobby had handed him, letting out a low whistle. "Thank *you*. You have a good weekend, now."

Audrey made another mental note. Bobby was also a good tipper. So far, he was two for two on Florie's criteria.

Sal's was crowded, which came as a shock to Bobby but not to Audrey, who knew how adored the place was. Vince, the owner, instantly recognized Audrey and demanded that a booth be found for her, pronto. As soon as Bobby and Audrey were seated, Tony, Audrey's favorite waiter, dropped two Cokes off at their table and informed them their garlic knots and pepperoni pie would be out in a few minutes.

"It smells amazing in here," Bobby remarked as he sat down across from Audrey, eyeing all the film posters, memorabilia, and autographed photos from the past few decades. "Lots of big names up there. Elvis Presley, John Wayne, Audrey Hepburn, Yogi Berra." Bobby continued surveying the restaurant, like a kid entering a toy store for the first time. "This place is really cool."

"My dad and Vince go way back, so ... we get treated like royalty."

"What's your father like?" asked Bobby as he delicately placed his napkin on his lap. Audrey had never known a teenage boy to be so well mannered.

"Oh, he's the best," gushed Audrey. "He owns his own shop just a few blocks away. He's a cobbler."

"Wow. That's hard work."

"Yes, it is. He works so hard—really long hours—and he does everything for me, my sister, and my mom."

"You have a sister?"

"Claire. She's older. She's actually a freshman at NYU."

"Are you close?"

"Um ... not so much. I mean, I love her, but she and I are very different." Audrey met Bobby's eyes. "But enough about me. I want to know more about you. But, to preface, I should tell you ... I already know a bit. See, my dad is kind of ... obsessed with your dad. That's the kindest way I can put it."

"He reads *Forbes* and the like?"

"Religiously. So, I know you're an only child, who your dad is, what he does, all that. But who are *you*? Who is Bobby Dempsey?"

Bobby laughed, running his index finger along the table's grooves. "That's quite the loaded question."

"Is it?" Audrey leaned forward, her elbows on the table. "Do tell."

Bobby drummed his fingers on the table. "I just don't think my life's as interesting as you'd expect. People have these grand ideas, I think, of what it's like being the son of Robert Dempsey, but ... it's not like that."

"Then what's it like?"

Bobby sipped his Coke. "You should write for *The Bulletin*."

"Are you saying that because you do, and you want to see more of me?" she teased.

"I certainly wouldn't mind that." He smirked coyly. "But you're a natural, asking questions, getting to the root of things. We could really use someone like you."

"What do you write for the paper? Are you the ... sports person or whatever it's called?"

"No, I'm the features editor. I write columns highlighting a particular student, for instance, or an event going on at the school. I really love it."

Finally, Audrey was getting Bobby to open up. Since they'd arrived, he'd been instilled with a new, highly attractive confidence; his sleeves were rolled up, his tie was undone, and his right arm was slung over the back of the booth. Talking about writing imbued his eyes with a bright twinkle. Audrey could easily imagine him hunched over his desk, typing away on his typewriter into the early hours of the morning. He struck her as the poetic type, as someone who gazed up at the moon in wonderment, dreaming up worlds far different from their own.

"Do you want to be a writer?" she asked. "Is that your dream career?"

"It is." As quickly as it'd appeared, though, the twinkle in his eyes dulled, and he heaved a sigh. "But I don't really ... when the time comes, I'll take over Dempsey Corp."

"Is that something you want? Taking over Dempsey Corp?"

"I'm it—the last of the Dempsey line. It's expected."

"And your dad wouldn't be okay with you doing your own thing?"

Bobby traced the condensation on his glass. "He's been grooming me to be his successor ever since I took my first breath—even before that, probably. And my whole life has just ... revolved around that reality."

The abrupt change in Bobby's mood saddened Audrey. She missed the upbeat, excitable Bobby who'd commented on the décor, the Bobby who'd lit up when talking about writing. But now, he sat before her, his shoulders slumped and his eyes downcast.

"What does your mom have to say about all this?" asked Audrey.

"She died, a couple years ago."

"Oh my God." Audrey could have kicked herself for her ignorance. "I'm so sorry. I didn't know."

"It's okay."

"No, I ... I shouldn't be assuming ... or prying. I—"

"You're not. You're being nice. And I don't want you to feel badly about it. My mother ... well, she was sick for a while, and ... she and I ... we weren't all that close. But, um, I'm extremely fortunate. I have a lot of security. It's not like I don't know what I'll be doing twenty years from now. And I guess there's a, uh ... a comfort in that."

"Not if it doesn't make you happy."

Bobby wiped his lips with his napkin. "I want to make my father proud. I need to. He's done so much for me. I ... I can't let him down."

Audrey wondered what kind of father Robert Dempsey was. Obviously, he harbored high expectations for Bobby, as most fathers did of their only sons, but what was their day-to-day relationship like? Did Bobby's father love him like her parents loved her? Did they watch films together, visit museums, take in Broadway shows, go to dinner, discuss everything from sports to politics to dating?

"I'm sorry," Audrey repeated, reaching across the table and taking his hand in hers. "I wish you had more ... freedom."

"Thank you," he said softly, tightening his grip on her hand. "That means a lot."

As they ate their garlic knots and pizza, they continued chatting away—about much lighter topics. They realized, for one, that they had vastly different music tastes. Bobby, similarly to most boys his age, was into Aerosmith, Paul McCartney, and—most passionately—Billy Joel.

"I see," said Audrey, taking a long sip of her Coke.

"You don't like them?"

"Not really. I'm more into disco. I love the Bee Gees!"

"I take it you saw *Saturday Night Fever* last year?"

"Of course! Three times! Why, what was the last movie you saw?"

"The last movie in general or the last good one?"

"Last good one, let's say."

"Oh, easy. *Star Wars*."

Audrey made a face. "That movie with the weird robots?"

"Weird robots?" laughed Bobby.

"I remember seeing a picture in the *Daily News* last year. It was this tall robot next to a short one."

"C-3PO and R2-D2. They're droids."

"Sure. And wasn't there an ... ape?"

"He's a Wookiee." Bobby folded up his napkin. "Not important. What *is* important is that it was a great movie."

"I'll take your word for it. My dad loved it. But space stuff isn't really for me."

"Well, let's see. There's got to be some sort of movie we'd both like to see. How do you feel about ... mysteries?"

"Love them!"

"Excellent! So, I guess we know what we can see next time."

Audrey met his eyes. "So, there'll be a next time?"

"If you want there to be."

"I think I'm warming up to the idea."

Afterward, they strolled around the Village for a couple of hours. It was remarkably easy, being with Bobby. Audrey pointed out some of the places her family frequented. They passed the bodega, the bookshop, the secondhand store where her family bought most of their clothes, and the coffee shop with coffee that tasted like liquidized metal.

"Then why do you still go there?" asked Bobby.

"Mom's friends with the owner. I think it's kind of a pity thing."

Audrey had saved Washington Square Park for the end, as she knew Bobby would love its vibrancy—and he did. He giddily fumbled for a penny when they stood at the fountain, then made a wish and tossed it in.

"What'd you wish for?" asked Audrey.

"I can't say, now, can I?" said Bobby, a mischievous spark in his eyes. "That would spoil it."

They sat for a while on the fountain's edge, watching as the world passed them by. The smell of freshly cut grass permeated the air, tantalizing Audrey with memories of summer days—all of which would, within the month, be replaced with cool, autumnal ones. She would have to start wearing a coat; she shuddered at the mere thought.

"It's hard to believe that all the way up there"—Audrey pointed north, past the arch—"is where you live. A world away from here."

"Not that far. Same avenue."

"Hundreds of blocks."

"But still the same avenue, in the same city."

The waning light signaled the date's natural end. Audrey knew her parents would want her home before *Donny & Marie* started. It was a cherished family tradition, watching the show together every Friday night.

"I understand," said Bobby as they neared her apartment building. "I don't want to get in the way of family time."

"But this has been great," said Audrey, their arms swinging in tandem. "I really ... I had a wonderful time."

"Me too." Bobby stopped when Audrey did. "Oh. We're already at your building?"

"I'm afraid so."

Bobby surveyed the area, and Audrey wondered what it was like for him, seeing her neighborhood for the first time. What did he notice that she no longer did—that had just become commonplace for her?

"I like it here," he remarked. "It feels ... removed from things."

"Everyone knows everyone."

"That's nice. A sense of camaraderie, people looking out for each other."

"Sure, there's that. But also, a lot of busybodies. And weirdos. Next time, I'll tell you about Mrs. Adelson."

"Why don't you tell me right now?"

"Oh, I need at least thirty minutes to give you the whole backstory and everything."

Bobby laughed. "Well, then, I should let you go. I don't want to get you in trouble. If I'm the reason you're late, your parents might not let me go out with you again. And I wouldn't want that."

They stared at each other, neither wanting to be the first to look away. Her first date had been even dreamier than she could have imagined. She knew that as soon as she walked up those steps and entered her apartment building, it'd be over. And she wasn't yet ready to say goodbye.

Bobby pulled her into an embrace that lasted far too long to be platonic. Slowly, they parted, and Audrey looked up at him, her heart rate accelerating. An eyelash had fallen on his cheek, and Audrey instinctively reached up to brush it away. As her finger caressed his cheek, however, Bobby recoiled, his demeanor instantly stiffening.

"Oh." Audrey quickly lowered her hand. "I'm sorry. I just ... you had an eyelash. I was ... trying to get it."

Bobby blanched. "No, *I'm* sorry. I didn't ... I just ..." He shakily reached for her hand, to assure her. "I'm sorry. I didn't mean to react that way."

"It's okay. I don't want to make you uncomfortable or—"

"You don't. Trust me. I really like you a lot, Audrey. It's just ..." Bobby trailed off, sighing. "It's not you. I can promise you that."

"Okay. Good. Because ... I really like you too."

Audrey could sense his relief. The color returned to his face, and his posture relaxed once more. Desperately, Audrey wanted to kiss him, but she wasn't sure if a kiss on the first date was appropriate. She wished her parents had explained to her the dos and don'ts of dating; if they had, she wouldn't be standing here, wondering what the proper etiquette was. Luckily, she now knew that Bobby was also a novice at love's games, so maybe he was just as clueless as she was.

His eyes kept flickering between her eyes and her lips, as though he, too, were debating whether it was suitable to end the night with a kiss. Thankfully, he decided to lean in, and Audrey met him halfway. As their lips touched, fireworks exploded in her head, reminding her of every kiss at the end of a romantic movie, every happily ever after between a Disney prince and princess. Almost grudgingly, they pulled apart.

Audrey could feel the warmth of his breath against her cheeks, the electricity of his touch in her fingertips. She'd never experienced such stimuli before. Of course, she'd harbored crushes—small ones—but none of them had made her feel like this. Every graze from Bobby ignited a fire within her, one she hoped would never extinguish.

"Good night, Audrey."

"Good night, Bobby."

Bobby kissed her again. Audrey's lips screamed in silent protest when he pulled away. She watched him go, her spirits buoyed by the knowledge that she would see him in just a couple of days. When he reached the corner, he turned around one last time to wave goodbye before vanishing from her sight. Audrey stood stagnant for a moment or two, allowing her pulse to return to its resting rate before she faced her parents.

"Audie!" said Sophia as Audrey entered the apartment. "You're home!"

"How was it?" asked Alexander, rubbing his hands together.

Audrey had never been so grateful that her family's apartment didn't face the front of the building. If it had, her parents would have most likely been peering through the curtains, gawking at Bobby as one would a precious artifact in a museum.

"It was incredible," said Audrey. "We had a great time. We went for pizza, then I showed him around the Village. He's never been down here, so it was all new for him."

"He's taking you out again, right?" asked Alexander. "Maybe somewhere more ... his speed? Like ... Jean-Georges? Oh, the stories I've heard about that place."

Audrey furrowed her eyebrows. "Dad."

"I'm just saying—"

"Well, we can't wait to meet him!" said Sophia, her tone obliviously cheerful. "Now, come on, sweets. Get into your PJs. *Donny & Marie* starts in half an hour."

"And don't forget, Claire is staying over tomorrow night," Alexander added. "So, you know, if you threw anything onto her bed, make sure it's cleaned up before then."

Audrey put her hands on her hips. "I'm insulted, Dad. Do you really think I'd use my dear, sweet sister's bed as storage while she's at college?"

Alexander raised an eyebrow. "What, am I wrong?"

"Well, no. But still! I don't appreciate the third degree!"

Alexander laughed. "I just want to make sure Claire feels like this is still her home, that's all."

"Don't worry, Dad. I'll take care of it."

"That's my Audie."

Though Audrey loved *Donny & Marie*, her mind was shamelessly elsewhere during the whole program. Sophia noticed, as she pulled her aside afterward, asking what was wrong.

"Nothing's wrong," Audrey assured her, unable to stop smiling. "I just ... I had a great time with Bobby."

Sophia stroked Audrey's hair. "Yeah?"

"Yes! Oh, I *really* like him, Mom. A lot. He's so sweet and easy to be with. Honestly, it didn't feel like I was on a date with the son of one of the richest men in the country. Bobby's just a normal teenage boy. Dad'll be happy to know he likes baseball. And that weird robot movie."

Sophia smiled wistfully. "It's very cute, seeing you like this," she mused.

For some reason, Sophia's use of the word "cute"—and overall dismissive attitude—bothered Audrey. She'd just gone on her first date with a boy she really liked, and all Sophia could say was it was "cute." Audrey had wanted her mother to ask more questions, to probe, so Audrey could share she'd had her first kiss. Then, Sophia would tell her all sorts of stories about what it'd been like when she and Alexander had first started dating. After all, they hadn't been much older than Audrey was now when they'd met; they were both seventeen.

Indeed, Audrey had hoped that her parents—or, at the very least, her mother—would sit her down and give her that speech all teenagers seemed to dread about dating. Claire, for her part, had expressed relief when neither Sophia nor Alexander bridged the topic with her. But Audrey wanted that; she wanted to have an open dialogue with her parents, to feel comfortable sharing all her hopes and fears about dating.

Rather, Sophia kissed the top of Audrey's head, wished her good night, and headed off toward her bedroom, leaving Audrey alone in the hallway, all her excitement popped like a balloon. Slowly, Audrey made her way to her bedroom, her feet dragging along the floor.

Audrey knew she had to treasure this moment, where it was just her in the room, for tomorrow night, Claire was staying over. That meant that, once again, Audrey would be subjected to Claire's loud snoring and incessant teeth grinding.

No amount of thrown pillows, it seemed, ever quieted her; instead, they emboldened her, causing her to snore so loudly that, on a handful of occasions, Sophia had to come in and shush her.

But Audrey couldn't concern herself with Claire now. No, tonight, she would enjoy the quietness of the room, and tomorrow, she would grin and bear it, as she always did. It was only one night. Audrey had survived thousands of nights with Claire. One more couldn't be that bad.

She hoped.

CHAPTER 5

Audrey

MIXED OPINIONS

IT WAS ALWAYS A special occasion when the Nielsens went out for dinner. Sophia took it as somewhat of an insult when someone suggested eating out, thinking her family secretly hated her cooking. Of course, this was the furthest thing from the truth; Sophia was a whiz in the kitchen, able to whip up anything and everything with ease. As soon as she was old enough, Audrey had practically begged her mom to teach her how to cook, which had delighted Sophia, as Claire seemingly had no interest in ever learning. Audrey wasn't nearly as good as her mother, but she hoped that one day, she'd reach her level. Then, her kids would tell her how much they loved her cooking.

"So, we'll meet Claire at Monte's at six," Alexander announced. "She had a couple things to finish up, but she's very excited about seeing us, telling us all about her first few weeks at NYU."

Claire had chosen Journalism as her major. This didn't surprise Audrey; Claire had always been a strong writer, and she had no qualms about calling out injustice wherever it existed. Truly, Claire didn't back down or cower from a fight, no matter what. A few years back, a disgruntled customer had refused to pay Alexander for his services, and in retaliation, Claire had thrown a brick through his window, screaming that only scumbags didn't settle their debts. Though Claire's methods were unconventional—not to mention criminal—they, miraculously, worked; the next day, Alexander received the money he'd been owed. To this day, he and Sophia had no idea Claire was the reason why that money had shown up; Alexander still thought the customer had simply had a crisis of conscience and decided to pay up. Audrey, however, knew the truth; Claire hadn't been able to resist bragging about her triumph to someone. She'd made Audrey pinky promise she'd never tell another soul, and Audrey, understanding the sanctity of such promises, had kept her mouth shut all these years.

"One of our girls, a college student," said Sophia, shaking her head. "My, how the times have changed."

It was interesting, hearing Sophia boast about Claire's status as a college student. Audrey distinctly remembered how Sophia had questioned why Claire thought college was even necessary.

"I didn't go to college," Sophia had told her. "Why would you need to?"

"Because I want to," Claire had responded with her characteristic bluntness. "I have no interest in being a mom, staying at home."

"What's wrong with that?" asked Sophia, unable to hide her hurt.

"Nothing! It's great for some women, but ... I'm not one of them. I want a career."

Despite Sophia's continued objections, Claire applied to NYU, received a decent scholarship, and accepted the offer. Alexander had been skeptical too, but once he learned of the scholarship, he warmed up to the idea of one of his girls being an NYU-bound freshman. Though Sophia and Alexander did, of course, love their daughters and want what was best for them, they were also products of a generation that thought a man's place was in the office and a woman's was at home. Claire obviously didn't agree with this, and neither did Audrey. However, Claire was far more focused on her future career than Audrey was; indeed, Audrey was unsure whether she even wanted to go to college.

"You know, sometimes, I think you have no ambition," Claire had told Audrey once, her tone a bit too accusatory for Audrey's liking.

"I just haven't figured out what I want to do yet," Audrey had replied. "Is that really so hard to believe?"

Audrey knew it was difficult for Claire to understand, but Audrey had never felt drawn to a particular career path. Lots of things interested her—reading, cooking, baking, and gardening, just to name a few—but she didn't know how to harness those hobbies and turn them into a career. And, even more than that, she wasn't sure if she wanted to. The only thing Audrey knew for certain was that someday, she wanted to be a mother. And maybe that meant she'd stay at home for a few years, just like her mother had. Unlike Claire, Audrey didn't view that as a death sentence, but unlike her parents, Audrey didn't intrinsically believe that a woman should look after the house and a man should make money. For Audrey, it was all a personal decision, one that shouldn't be judged or made by other people.

"Yes," agreed Alexander, nodding, bringing Audrey back to the present. "We have much to celebrate tonight!"

Audrey, for her part, loved having a reason to dress up. She'd been tired of wearing the same, drab uniform to school, day in and day out. She decided that, for the occasion, she'd wear her best dress: a comely green tea dress Aunt Trina had given her for Christmas last year. Alexander, adorably, bragged about how beautiful his girls looked, insisting on taking a few photos to commemorate the night. Then, they made their way to Monte's, which had a good crowd, given it was a Saturday night. Audrey scanned the menu, trying to decide whether she was more in the mood for manicotti or a carbonara.

"There she is! Claire's here!" Alexander said, standing up.

Audrey turned. Yes, there was Claire. To Audrey's shock, she was now sporting bangs. Claire had vowed to never rock bangs again, after the infamous incident where she'd cut them herself—with disastrous consequences. But clearly, this time, she'd had a professional do her bangs for her, and she looked great. She seemed much older than before—more mature. Evidently, she no longer wanted to be seen as a teenager; she wanted to be seen as an adult.

"Mom! Dad!" said Claire, grinning as she neared the table. "Great to see you!" Then, with a patronizing air, she patted Audrey on her head, saying, "And good to see my little sister too!"

"You look different," said Alexander, his head cocked to the side. "Can't quite place it."

Sometimes, Alexander's lack of observational skills astounded Audrey. It wasn't that he didn't care; he just simply didn't notice things that were, in Audrey's estimation, glaringly obvious. For instance, one time, Claire had dyed her hair bright red, and it had taken Alexander two days to mention it. Godzilla could have been sitting next to him, and Alexander would've somehow missed him.

"It's probably the bangs," said Claire, claiming her seat. "Yeah, I had them done before starting at NYU. I figured, new school, new me!"

"Makes sense to me!" said Sophia. "And you look beautiful, by the way."

"Thanks, Mom. You too. Did Janelle do something new? Give you some layers?"

"She did, actually," Sophia said, patting her hair. "Why, what do you think?"

"You look ten years younger."

"Oh, that's so sweet of you."

Claire picked up her menu, her eyes immediately on the wines. Ever since she'd turned eighteen, she'd been obsessed with reminding anyone and everyone that she could drink alcohol. She was a "real adult" now, apparently—or so she believed.

"I could go with a red," Claire proclaimed.

"Yes, me too," Alexander agreed. "We'll do a bottle, then." He placed his menu on the table. "But Claire, tell us, what's it like at NYU? How are your classes going?"

"*Love* them. My professors are great, real geniuses. One of them thinks he can help me get an internship in the spring, which would be great."

"Oh, wow! An internship already!"

"Well, no promises, but ..." Claire crossed her fingers. "I'm hoping it all works out!"

"That's very impressive, sweetie," Sophia said, smiling warmly at Claire. "Who would it be with? Do you know?"

"No. Some paper company, I guess. I'd be in the mailroom, of course, but I don't mind the grunt work."

"Gotta start at the bottom," Alexander said, nodding knowingly, even though he'd never been a part of the corporate machine. "That's the way of it."

When the waiter came by, they all ordered their drinks and meals. Audrey decided she was in more of a manicotti mood, and as she waited, she willed her stomach not to make any noise. It was a unique kind of torture, watching other tables get their food, having to smell the wonderful aromas. What was even more torturous was watching waiters clean up plates that still had a fair amount of food on them.

"Audie, love," said Alexander, concern in his eyes. "You're very quiet tonight. Are you feeling all right?"

"Oh, I'm fine. I'm just hungry, that's all." Audrey leaned forward. "But that's really cool, Claire. I'm glad to hear things are going well for you."

"Thanks," said Claire with that signature bite to her voice.

"Audie's been doing us proud at Great Gray," Alexander boasted. "She's in the debate club. And she does lots of volunteer work. And she's getting good grades, to boot!"

"Well, mostly," corrected Audrey. "French and Geometry are tough."

"But you're still coming home with As and Bs!"

"And that's not all," Sophia piped up, reaching over to touch Audrey's hand. "Audie's also got a boyfriend."

"Mom," said Audrey, shaking her head. "You don't—"

"A boyfriend?" Claire smirked. "A bit young for that, aren't you?"

"You were thirteen when you had your first boyfriend," Audrey reminded her.

"That's different."

"How?"

Claire rolled her eyes. "I've always been more mature than you."

"Oh, right. 'Cause it was real mature when you put gum in my hair two Halloweens ago."

"Girls," said Alexander, glancing between the two. "Come on, now."

"Sorry, Dad," they said in unison.

After a few moments of silence, Sophia said, "But we're very happy for Audie. He's a sweet boy."

"You've already met him?" asked Claire, an eyebrow raised.

"No. Not yet."

"Then how do you know he's sweet?"

"Because he's Robert Dempsey's son," Alexander said, unable to stop himself.

Claire blanched. "You're dating the son of Robert Dempsey?" she asked Audrey.

Audrey did her best to bite her tongue. It bothered her, hearing her family refer to Bobby as Robert Dempsey's son. She wanted them to see him as his own person, not as a mere extension of his father. After all, Bobby was so much more than his surname, but it seemed that to her family, his most salient trait was he was a Dempsey.

"His name's Bobby," Audrey said. "But yes. And I really like him."

"Well, he's a Dempsey, so I understand."

"I don't care about that."

"Okay, little sister. Whatever you say."

Audrey took a deep breath, not wanting to ruin dinner for the family by blowing up on Claire. "So, NYU ... it must be fun living on your own, huh?"

"It is." Claire's mood instantly improved, now that she was once again the center of attention. "I mean, I have a roommate, but she's cool. And, you know, I really feel like I've found my niche. I think I ..."

Audrey managed to make it through the rest of dinner. When they returned home, they watched *Carter Country*, a show that all three Nielsen girls hated. Alexander, however, loved it, and none of them had the heart to tell him they didn't want to watch it with him. After, they started getting ready for bed. Claire was first in line for the bathroom once more, which Audrey only mildly resented. Claire was here for only one night, but she had no problem reclaiming her birthright, as the oldest child, to use the bathroom first.

"All yours, Audie," Claire said as she stepped out, her hair still damp.

Audrey, who had always preferred showering in the mornings, was in and out in a few minutes. Back in the bedroom, Claire was eyeing the various posters Audrey had taped onto the wall by their bunkbed.

"Little sister's growing up," Claire noted, gesturing at the Robby Benson and Parker Stevenson posters.

"Is that a problem?"

"No. Not at all. I just ... well, it's good to see you've finally caught up with the rest of us."

"What are you talking about?"

"Nothing." Claire crossed her arms. "I must say, though, I didn't expect you to bag a rich boy on your first outing."

"Bobby's more than just some rich boy."

"Oh, I'm sure. You must have a very ... special connection."

Audrey crossed her arms. She was not in the mood for Claire's sardonic comments. Claire, like their parents, had always believed that money would fix all her problems. Though Audrey knew, of course, that money could undeniably make things easier, she didn't think it equated to happiness, as many of her peers at Great Gray had illustrated. Indeed, in many ways, the students at Great Gray seemed more lost and depressed than the students at her old school.

"Good night, Claire," Audrey said, tucking herself into bed. It felt good, taking the high road.

Claire laughed, despite herself. "Good night, Audie. Sleep tight."

CHAPTER 6

Audrey

BIG STEPS

THE FOLLOWING WEEKS WERE nothing short of a teenage fantasy. Every morning, like clockwork, Bobby and Audrey met up before school, ducked into the empty auditorium, and spent half an hour or so making out. Then, they headed to their homerooms. Shamelessly, Audrey considered these early mornings to be her favorite part of the day. She and Bobby had been dating for a while now, and it had become increasingly difficult for them to keep their hands off each other. Audrey wasn't sure if it was chemical or hormonal or what, but she didn't care; she just loved being with him.

"We've been dating for, what, almost a month now?" asked Audrey one morning after a particularly intense make-out session, smoothing down her skirt and blouse.

"That sounds about right."

"And ... well, you know where I'm going with this, right?"

"Not exactly," laughed Bobby, adjusting his tie. "But go on."

"It's my parents. They've been begging me to bring you over. They really want to meet you."

"Meeting the parents." Bobby let out a low whistle. "That's a big step."

"A huge one. But they'll just get pushier and pushier."

"So, it's better to meet them sooner rather than later."

"Exactly."

Bobby ran his fingers through his hair. "Well, I'd love to. What about Thursday night?"

"Wow." Audrey's eyes widened. "You're braver than I thought."

"Why?"

"Because that's ... soon. Two days away."

Bobby laughed. "Aud."

Weeks ago, he'd stopped calling her Audrey and instead referred to her as Aud. It was simple but endearing, and Audrey adored the fact that Bobby had invented a new nickname for her.

"I feel great about us, about where we are, and I'm excited to meet your family," Bobby went on. "You've told me so much about them it's almost like I *do* know them."

"Well, in that case ..." Audrey pulled him in for a kiss. "I'll tell my parents tonight. They'll be thrilled."

"What do your parents like?"

"What do you mean?"

"Well, I want to bring them something. Do they like flowers, chocolates, *TIME* magazine?"

"They like all those things. But really, Bobby, you don't have to bring anything. You're the guest."

Bobby picked up his messenger bag. "I'll bring flowers," he decided, a smile on his lips.

"If you insist."

"I do." Bobby leaned down to kiss her. "Mmmm." He cupped her face in his hands, a playful glint in his eyes. "I love these mornings with you."

At the moment, everything was effortless and fun with Bobby—as it should have been. They slipped notes into each other's lockers, shared milkshakes, and sat in the back of the movie theater and made out. Introducing her parents into the equation, Audrey feared, would complicate things. But, on the other hand, Bobby's and Audrey's relationship would inevitably change. They were young, and they didn't yet know a great deal about each other. Every day, it seemed, Audrey was learning new things about Bobby. For example, just yesterday, she'd discovered that Bobby could play the piano.

"Is there anything you can't do?" she'd asked him.

"Plenty," he'd laughed in return. "But don't ever ask me to play the piano. I hate it."

"Why? It's such a beautiful instrument."

"You'd feel differently if you'd been forced to take lessons against your will."

Truly, Bobby and Audrey were in a great place, and Audrey wanted him to meet her parents. They'd been dating for only a month, but they were serious about each other. They were already talking about Christmas-themed things they wanted to do in the city. And though Audrey was worried about her parents potentially interrogating Bobby like he was some sort of criminal—they had always been protective of their girls—she was even more concerned they would simply ask him all sorts of questions about his father. She'd talk to them beforehand, to try and prevent that from happening.

Audrey's first three classes—French, Geometry, and Biology—were also, as luck would have it, three of her most dreaded. Fourth period, she received somewhat of a break, as she had History. But then, every other day, she shuffled off to Gym, her long-standing least favorite subject. This year, though, since she had a good friend with her—Florie—Audrey didn't detest it as much. She still didn't enjoy it, but most days, she could at least tolerate it.

Today, however, Mrs. Martin seemed hellbent on making Gym as miserable an experience as possible. In true form, Mrs. Martin demanded the girls start off by running laps outside, to "warm up," despite the already unseasonably warm weather.

"Torture," gasped Florie on their second lap. "Absolute torture."

"She hates children," Audrey agreed, pushing a sweaty strand of hair out of her face and remembering all the wonderful times when she hadn't felt as though she were about to pass out. She promised herself she'd never again take breathing for granted.

"At least it's mutual."

"All right, girls," said Mrs. Martin, blowing her whistle, lending further credence to Audrey's theory that people became Gym teachers only because they wanted a whistle. "Today, we're playing touch football. The rules are simple: no tackling. We need two teams. Let's count off." Quickly, Audrey moved so she and Florie would be on the same team. "All right. Team One, you're on offense first. Team Two, defense."

"I'm glad she specified," Florie said dryly. "I thought we were both on offense."

Since none of the girls were particularly skilled at football—or, quite frankly, interested in putting in the effort, given the heat—the game was mediocre at best. Mrs. Martin had taken to reading a *People* magazine. She didn't even notice that, while Audrey's team was on offense, Cassandra blatantly tackled Audrey, who didn't even have the football.

"Hey!" yelled out Florie, making a "T" with her hands. "What was that? No tackling!"

The wind had been knocked out of Audrey. She lay on the ground, her ears ringing, her head aching. Cassandra, for her part, didn't even offer to help Audrey up. She walked away, whispering with a bunch of her friends, none of whom Audrey had met before.

"Audrey!" Florie ran up to her. "You okay?"

"Yeah, I'm fine," Audrey lied, hoping she wasn't bleeding internally. Florie pulled her to her feet. "Just a little discombobulated, that's all."

"It was an accident," Cassandra insisted, her hands on her hips.

"Sure it was," Audrey muttered, brushing the dirt off her shorts.

"It was!" Cassandra placed her hand over her heart. "Promise! But honestly, Audrey, I thought you'd be better on your feet—you know, since your dad's a cobbler and all."

Cassandra practically spat the last three words, reveling in the power she so desperately wanted to have over Audrey. Jarringly, Cassandra's friends laughed, pointing at Audrey as though she were an alien among them. Mrs. Martin didn't even look up; she flipped a page of her magazine, blissfully unaware that the game had ended prematurely. Audrey wasn't sure how Cassandra had learned her father was a cobbler—or why she thought it was an insult. Clearly, Cassandra had incorrectly surmised that Audrey was embarrassed by her father's profession.

"You say that as if I should be ashamed of it," Audrey said, her head still spinning. "But I'm not. I'm not ashamed of my dad."

For the first time in twenty minutes, Mrs. Martin looked up. She blinked rapidly, her eyes adjusting to the sun.

"What's all this?" she yelled. "Get back to the game! Come on!"

Predictably, the remainder of the game was a nightmare. Cassandra continued to take cheap shots at Audrey, which Mrs. Martin either failed to notice or just deliberately condoned. Audrey wished she could have held it against her, but she knew Mrs. Martin was paid too little to involve herself in matters concerning the children of some of New York's most powerful families. The last thing she needed was Cassandra's no-doubt-overbearing father to come charging in, claiming his daughter had been treated unfairly.

"It was just so unnecessary," Audrey vented later at lunch, unable to shake the mental image of Cassandra and her friends laughing at her. "A few weeks ago, she basically told me I'm dead to her. Which, you know, that's fine, whatever, what do I care? But now, what, she's remembered I exist?" She shook her head. "I just don't get it."

"Cassandra hates everyone," Sarah assured her. "She still holds a grudge against me for not inviting her to my tenth birthday party."

"That's cold, Sarah," said Florie, jokingly tsk-tsking.

"She didn't invite me to hers! So, why should I have invited her to mine?"

"You still seem pretty hung up on it."

"Oh, get off it," said Sarah, playfully elbowing Florie. She turned to Audrey. "But really, Cassandra's ... she's the type who's always looking for drama. But if you want my opinion, I think she's just jealous of you. She's always liked Bobby, so she just hates the fact he's dating you, not her."

Audrey peeled her orange. "I guess. I just ... I hope the rest of the year isn't like that."

"It won't be. Sooner or later, she'll move on. Knowing Cassandra, though, it'll probably be later."

Audrey laughed. "Thanks. That's real encouraging."

"Don't let her get to you," Florie piped up. "Just think! This Friday, during the pep rally, Chordially Yours will be performing! So, you'll get to see me and Sarah in our element."

By all accounts, Great Gray's football team was abysmal, so they needed all the pep they could get. They had already lost every game they'd played this season, and it didn't seem like their luck would change anytime soon. Chordially Yours and the cheerleading squad had thus been booked to inspire school spirit and encourage the boys to play their hardest on Friday night. They would be facing off against their chief rival, Albrecht Academy, and morale had been high all week.

"Are you actually going to the game?" asked Audrey.

"Of course! Why, are you not going?"

Audrey shrugged. "I wasn't planning on it."

"But it'll be fun!"

"I don't know. I'll have to think about it."

"Sebastian and Bobby are going," Sarah informed her. "You could link up with them. They love commentating the games, poking fun at our team."

"Are you going?" asked Audrey.

"Oh, no," laughed Sarah, shaking her head. "No, as soon as I'm done singing, I'll be out of there."

"She's not very social," teased Florie.

Sarah raised an eyebrow. "Because I don't like sports, I'm not social?"

"That's pretty much what I said, yup."

"I don't like sports either," chuckled Audrey. "So, I don't—"

"Oh, come on!" Florie flashed Audrey her puppy dog eyes. "You don't want me to be there alone with the boys, do you? I'll be outnumbered."

"Oh, fine!" Audrey conceded. "I'll come! I'll need some guaranteed fun after Thursday, anyway."

"Why, what's Thursday?" asked Sarah.

"Bobby's meeting my parents."

"Oh, right! Right, he mentioned that in Calculus."

"And how'd he seem about it?"

"Nervous but excited." Sarah took a sip of her juice. "Why, are you worried?"

"Not really. I just ... Bobby's my first boyfriend, so I think Dad will be hard on him. I just hope he's not ... weird about Bobby's dad."

"Weird how?"

"I guess I'm just scared my parents will treat Bobby as a mini version of his dad, not as, you know, Bobby." Audrey sighed. "But we'll see. If all goes well, I'll get to meet his dad, and that ... well, that's both exciting and terrifying to think about."

"I wouldn't worry about it," Sarah comforted her. "Mr. Dempsey is a nice man. I'm sure he'll like you."

"I hope so. It just ... Bobby doesn't talk about his dad very much, so I don't ... I don't really know what to expect."

"They're a private family. And Bobby ... he's always been uncomfortable with people comparing him to his father. So, that's why he doesn't talk about him a lot. But try not to worry about it. I'm sure everything with Bobby and your parents will go well."

Desperately, Audrey wanted Sarah to be right. After all, if dinner with her parents went poorly, that would be the beginning of the end for her and Bobby's relationship. Audrey didn't want to date someone her parents disapproved of—or someone who disliked her parents. Everything, it seemed, was riding on what happened on Thursday night. Either she and Bobby would solidify what they had ... or fall apart.

"Yeah, me too," Audrey said, hoping that if she spoke it out into the universe, it would come to fruition.

CHAPTER 7

Audrey

MEETING THE PARENTS

AUDREY HAD NEVER SEEN her parents so on edge before. Sophia fluttered about the kitchen, repeatedly checking the oven and the stove to ensure that nothing had burned. Alexander, for his part, was, for some reason, dressed in his best suit and thumbing through *The Wall Street Journal* to learn the most recent stock numbers, as if that would give him and Bobby something to talk about. Audrey had tried to tell him that Bobby had no interest in stocks, but Alexander had brushed her off, unable to believe that the son of Robert Dempsey would be apathetic about such things.

"Audie, sweets, can you set the table?" asked Sophia, aggressively stirring the mashed potatoes to a disturbingly liquid consistency.

"I already did, Mom."

"Silverware, cups, plates, napkins, everything?"

"Yes."

"Oh." Sophia glanced over her shoulder, to see for herself. "Yes, you did. Very good."

Audrey pushed in all the chairs. "But why'd you choose *these* plates? They're not the ones we normally use."

"It's our wedding china. Thought we should use them sometime!"

"Wedding china?" Audrey put her hands on her hips. "The Queen of England isn't coming over for dinner. My boyfriend is."

"And your boyfriend is American royalty," Alexander said, returning his copy of *The Wall Street Journal* to the coffee table. "We want him to be impressed."

"He won't care about what plates you use or what you're wearing or any of that. He's just excited to meet you."

"And we couldn't be more excited to meet him!" Alexander looked down at his watch. "He should be here any moment now, right?"

"Dad, you're sweating."

"It's hot in here."

"Maybe that's because you're wearing a suit."

The intercom buzzed, and Sophia raced toward it, almost running headfirst into the wall. "Sophia Nielsen, Apartment 209!"

"Hello, Mrs. Nielsen. It's Bobby."

"Come on up!" Sophia slipped out of her apron and spruced up her hair. "He's coming! Everyone, stand up, look presentable."

When they heard a knock on the door, Sophia hastily opened it. Bobby stood on the other side, holding a bouquet of orange dahlias. Bobby's adult-like sense of fashion never ceased to charm Audrey. He wore a navy sweater vest over a white dress shirt, with a tie, slacks, and dress shoes. She couldn't help but wonder how he'd look in a pair of jeans—or a regular T-shirt.

"Welcome to our home!" Sophia announced.

"Thank you so much. It smells incredible in here."

"Why, thank you! I'm Sophia, by the way. Sophia Nielsen. You may have ... yes, I believe I said that over the intercom. Right." Sophia gestured to Alexander. "And this is my husband, Alexander."

"Hello," said Bobby, offering his free hand, which Alexander vigorously shook.

"We've been waiting to meet you for weeks," Alexander said, still shaking Bobby's hand, all the while making awkwardly direct eye contact with him.

"Forgive me for saying so, but you don't look anything like I thought you would. I guess I was ... well, to be honest, I was picturing a younger version of your father."

"I get that a lot," said Bobby pleasantly. "People always tell me I favor my mother."

"But it looks like you'll have your father's height," said Alexander, straining to see some Dempsey in him. "Now, your mom ... she was a ... a model, right?"

"Could have been, I'm sure. But—"

"No, right, I'm sorry, my mistake," Alexander sputtered, mentally cursing himself for having forgotten one of the talking points he'd memorized about the Dempsey family. "She was the Du Pont heiress. Right. Quite the looker. Shame that she ... well." Alexander cleared his throat, desperate to find a way out of the depressing conversation he'd initiated. "It's great to finally meet you! You already know Audrey, of course," Alexander went on, and Bobby—bless his heart—laughed. "We don't have Claire here tonight, unfortunately, but ... I hope we'll be good enough company!"

"Well, Aud's told me so much about you all, so I—"

"Only good things, I hope," Alexander said with a laugh, no doubt convinced he had invented the joke. "Soph, hon, could you take those flowers off his hands?"

"They're beautiful," Sophia said breathlessly, practically smooshing the flowers against her nose as she roamed the kitchen for an empty vase. Not finding one, she settled for the tallest glass they had. "And they smell *divine*, just *divine*."

Bobby's eyes fell upon a framed photograph of the family together, placed on the mantel. "Ah, this must be Claire."

Alexander nodded. "Yes. She's a busy college girl. She would've loved to be here, but ... well, maybe you'll meet her next time."

"But, you know, it's not the end of the world if you don't," Audrey chimed in, offering Bobby a knowing wink, which made him chuckle.

As Bobby surveyed the rest of the apartment, Audrey couldn't help but wonder what he thought of the place. She was acutely aware of how small everything was; it didn't take Bobby much time at all to cross from one side of the room to the other, and he had to duck to fit underneath the archway separating the kitchen from the rest of the room. Clutter claimed every available surface, and none of the furniture matched. To her dismay, her parents seemed keenly invested in Bobby's opinion of their home. Indeed, as Bobby wandered the living room, Alexander followed a bit too closely behind, like a hapless puppy. He had set up little vignettes around the room to make the family look more cultured and well traveled than they were; just for the occasion, he had purchased a map of France and placed it on an end table, seemingly trying to make Bobby believe they'd ventured outside the country.

"Have you, uh ... ever been to France there?" Alexander asked Bobby, gesturing at the map.

"Have *you*?" Audrey countered, and Alexander shushed her.

"Hmmm? Oh. Yeah." Bobby returned his attention to the mantel, reaching for one of the photographs. "This is a nice picture. Where was it taken?" he asked, holding it up to Alexander.

Alexander squinted at the photograph, then broke into a wide grin. "Oh, that was from this summer! We were in East Hampton for the Fourth. Took that on Audie's birthday."

"And made me wear that silly birthday hat," Audrey cut in, wishing Bobby had chosen a less embarrassing photograph.

"But it's tradition!" insisted Sophia, and Alexander sniggered.

Bobby glanced between Audrey and the photograph. "I like the hat. It suits you." He returned the photograph to its rightful place. "All these photographs ... looks like you have a lot of fun together."

"Oh, we do," gushed Alexander. "And see, when you have girls as pretty as mine, you like to show them off." He playfully nudged Audrey, who merely gave him an exasperated look.

"I love the photographs," Bobby said, almost wistfully. Clearing his throat, he added, "You really ... you have a beautiful family—and home."

"That's kind of you, but I'm sure it's nothing like what you're used to."

"It's lovely. Very homey. I love the windows."

"Well, we don't have a Central Park view or anything, but—"

"Dinner's ready!" Audrey practically blurted. "And I don't know about you all, but I *really* want to dig into that meatloaf."

In reality, Audrey had no interest in dwelling upon just how different her and Bobby's upbringings truly were. This was her home, and she was proud of it; she didn't want her parents to keep selling themselves short. So what they didn't have a Central Park view? That didn't mean they didn't have a lot to be grateful for.

"Then let's eat." Alexander nodded. "Yes, great idea, Audie." To Bobby, he noted, "I've always said, my Soph's meatloaf should be served in diners 'cross the city."

Bobby rubbed his hands together. "I haven't had meatloaf in ages."

Before Bobby's arrival, Audrey had instructed her parents to just be themselves and talk to him as they would any other teenage boy their daughter was seeing. Audrey wanted them to ask Bobby about his interests, hobbies, favorite subjects, and aspirations. She wanted them to see that he was so much more than Robert Dempsey's son. Instead, to her embarrassment—and annoyance—all her parents seemed to care about was his father.

"What does your father think of Mayor Koch?" asked Alexander.

Bobby wiped his lips with his napkin. "Well, my father doesn't share the mayor's party, but he certainly prefers him to Beame."

"Hmmm." Alexander nodded. "Yes, those were rough years. Your father did all right, though."

Bobby's eyes were glued to his meatloaf. "Right."

"He's an impressive man," Alexander went on, unaware he was the only one interested in continuing the conversation. "Has been very good to New York. You must be so proud, being his son."

Bobby shifted in his chair. "Well, I—"

"Now, I don't want to give in to hearsay or anything, Robert, but I've been hearing rumors your father is thinking of opening up a Dempsey Corp branch out west somewhere. Is that right?"

"I don't—"

"Dad," snapped Audrey, shooting daggers at him. "Bobby doesn't—"

"Ah. Keeping it a secret, are we?" asked Alexander, winking.

"I just really don't know, sir," Bobby said, his cheeks red.

"There will be none of that 'sir' talk." Alexander scooped more green beans onto his plate. "You can call me Alex."

The rest of dinner transpired similarly. Every question, it seemed, was rooted in Bobby's father—what it was like summering in the Hamptons, how many maids his family employed, how thrilled he was to be the sole heir to a billion-dollar fortune. Bobby's responses became briefer as the night wore on, which neither of her parents seemed to pick up on. He hardly touched the slice of vanilla cake Sophia had forced upon him. Audrey tried to cut in where she could, pushing her parents to ask more fun, personal questions, but they were too obsessed with learning all they could about Robert Dempsey.

"May I use your bathroom?" asked Bobby after being bombarded with questions about whom his father was voting for in 1980 and why.

"Yes, of course," said Alexander. "It's right over there, first door on the left."

Audrey waited until Bobby had closed the bathroom door before turning to her parents and saying, "I hope you're pleased with yourselves."

"What are you talking about, Audie?" asked Alexander, somehow taken aback by her frustration.

"Bobby has been here for almost two hours, and you haven't asked him one thing about himself."

"Of course, we have!"

"No! All you've been doing is asking about his dad! And you keep calling him Robert! His name is Bobby! And he's been so wonderful, just sitting there, answering all your questions, not complaining about how you're only interested in his dad, not him."

"Audrey." Sophia furrowed her eyebrows. "Watch your tone."

"I have been! I've been biting my tongue this whole time! I didn't bring Bobby over here so you could interrogate him about his dad. I thought you cared about who I'm dating and wanted to get to know *him*."

"We do. And we have been."

"Yes, he's a lovely boy!" Alexander insisted. "We like him a lot. He's very polite."

"Well, you two haven't been polite at all," Audrey snapped. "You've been rude. And I want you to know just how upset I am about all this."

When Bobby returned from the bathroom, the mood of the room had distinctly shifted. His eyes darted around the table, and he made his own silent judgments before sitting back down. Under the table, Audrey reached for his hand, and Bobby interlaced his fingers with hers, squeezing her hand. The gesture was small, but it relieved Audrey that Bobby didn't seem to blame her for her parents' zealous cross-examination.

"Dinner was delicious, Mrs. Nielsen," said Bobby, breaking the silence. "As was the cake and tea. Thank you so much."

"Oh, you're such a sweet boy," said Sophia, unable to contain her grin. The surest way to her heart was by complimenting her cooking.

"And I really appreciate you inviting me into your home, but I don't want to overstay my welcome."

"Nonsense!" said Alexander, waving a glib hand. "It's great to have another man in the house!"

"All the same, it's getting late, and I should be heading back."

"I'll walk you out," interjected Audrey, much to her parents' disappointment.

Bobby bade his goodbyes, then he and Audrey left. Once out on the street, Audrey heaved a deep sigh.

"I'm so sorry, Bobby," she said. "That was awful."

"No, it wasn't."

"Oh, come on! I saw how uncomfortable you were! You kept looking up at the clock, hoping more time had passed."

Bobby shuffled his feet. "It was a little overwhelming," he admitted. "But your parents are good people. They mean well."

"I'd told them to leave your dad out of it, to ask about you and what you like. But all that went out the window in the first five minutes."

Bobby offered her a smile that very nearly alleviated her frustration. "Don't worry, Aud. Your parents didn't mean to offend."

"But did they? Are you upset?"

"They're hardly the first people to ask me about my father."

"But it bothers you, doesn't it?"

Bobby shrugged. "It's just the way things are. Really, I swear, it didn't upset me. It was just a lot of questions, all in a row, so ... my head's still spinning a bit. But I'm happy we did this."

"Me too. And hey, look on the bright side. Me meeting your dad has to go better than that, right? I doubt he'll be interested in hearing about life in the Village."

Audrey had hoped that bringing the topic up lightheartedly would push Bobby into asking her when she'd like to meet his father. Instead, Bobby went quiet, his expression excruciatingly unreadable.

"Or, you know, maybe not," Audrey said.

"Aud." She knew that tone all too well. "He's just ... he's not an easy person to schedule things with."

"But he eats dinner, right? So, surely—"

"It's not like that."

"It's not like what? He doesn't eat dinner?"

"Not with me." Bobby clearly regretted saying it the instant he did, as he quickly added, "Because he's busy. Our paths just ... don't cross that often."

"But you could ... make them cross, right? Ask him what would work for him in a few weeks' time or something?"

"I ... I mean, I could. It's just ... I don't think it's really feasible."

Audrey crossed her arms. "If you don't want your dad to meet me, you can just say that."

"What? No, that's not the issue."

"Then what *is* the issue?" Again, Bobby was silent, purposefully avoiding her eyes. "Okay, you know what? We don't need to talk about this right now. It's fine."

Bobby rubbed the nape of his neck. "Aud, I ... I'd love for you to meet my father. But I don't ... it's not ... we don't do family dinners or anything like that." His shoulders slumped. "I'm not putting you off or embarrassed by you or anything like that. It's just ... my father and I don't have that kind of relationship. But, just so you know, I *do* talk about you a lot at home—just not with my father."

"You've told Charles about me?"

Charles Burke was the Dempsey family's long-serving butler. From what Audrey had gathered, Charles was highly involved in Bobby's life. Indeed, while Bobby had always been maddeningly tight-lipped about his father, he was very open about how close he was with Charles. They went to Yankees games together, and Charles was the one who had helped foster Bobby's early love for reading and writing.

Bobby grinned. "He's very excited to meet you, by the way."

"Well, make sure you tell him it goes both ways."

WHILE AUDREY WAS GONE, Sophia and Alexander had reflected on their actions, and when Audrey walked back into the apartment, they apologized profusely.

"I hope he can forgive us," Sophia said, her eyes glossy. "We didn't mean to ... well, we were just so excited, meeting someone who's ... but it wasn't fair—to Bobby or to you."

"It's okay, Mom," Audrey assured her, pulling her in for a hug. "Bobby had a great time. He loved all your food."

This relieved Sophia, who began cleaning up all the dishes, pots, and pans. Audrey had told her she would take care of it all, but Sophia had insisted, claiming it was part of her "punishment" for having been so focused on asking about Robert Dempsey.

"We'll be on our best behavior next time, Audie," Alexander promised. "We won't say a word about his father."

Audrey was grateful they'd seen the error of their ways. Though a part of her wanted to be petty and hold this against them for the next couple of days, she knew she wouldn't be able to do so. Her parents, as Bobby had said, were good people; they had simply gotten carried away, living vicariously through Bobby.

"I know you won't," Audrey said, kissing her father's cheek. "Now, come on. We can still catch *The Waltons*."

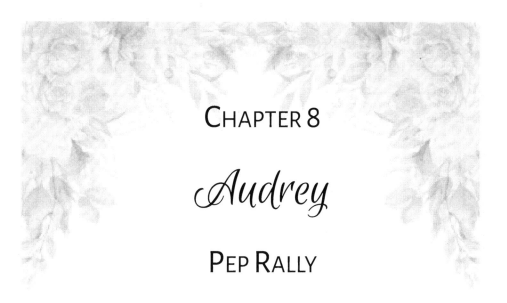

CHAPTER 8

Audrey

PEP RALLY

R ELUCTANTLY, ON FRIDAY, AUDREY attended her first pep rally. She wasn't a fan of sports—or forced camaraderie with classmates she didn't know or, to be frank, even like—but she was happy they got to skip out on the last class of the day to take part in the rally. More than that, though, Audrey was excited to see Florie and Sarah. She knew how important Chordially Yours was to them, and she wanted to make sure they both saw her up in the bleachers, cheering them on.

Chordially Yours sang the school song, a lovely if not boring tune. Florie had a small solo; she got to sing a line about "the great warriors of Great Gray coming to save the day." Audrey thought the lyrics were dreadful, not to mention melodramatic, but Florie's voice was melodious, imbuing the song with a sense of authority. The football team proudly stood, their hands over their hearts, gazing up at their team's banner. At the end of the song, everyone clapped, and the girls took their bows before they left the stage.

"Wow," said Coach Clayton, still clapping. "Let's hear it one more time for Chordially Yours—and, of course, our soloist, Miss Florence Washington!" After the applause died down, Coach Clayton went on, "I know these past few seasons haven't been the best, and we may have gotten off to a rocky start, but …"

"Florie better have plans to be a professional singer," Bobby whispered to Audrey.

"Oh, she does," Audrey responded. "She told me she's been singing since forever. It's her passion. She has dreams of being on Broadway."

After Coach Clayton's speech about how this year would be the best year in Great Gray's football history—a speech he'd most likely given every year, to little effect—the cheerleaders did a quick routine to invoke school spirit. Cassandra, in a predictable turn of events, was a cheerleader—as were Lisa, Shelly, and Barb.

"She had a go at me in Gym the other day," Audrey told Bobby.

"Who?"

"Cassandra Irvine."

Bobby nodded knowingly. "Sounds like Cassandra."

"Do you know her well?"

"Our fathers are close. But what'd she say to you?"

"Nothing much. She's just upset we're dating."

"Why?"

"Beats me. Sarah said she has a thing for you. Does that seem possible?"

Bobby shrugged. "It's hard to tell with Cassandra. She's kind of … cagey."

"Well, maybe we should put her in a cage! 'Cause she's a *beast* on the football field, let me tell you. I have the bruises to prove it. Maybe if the coach put her on the team, we'd actually win."

At last, the cheerleaders finished their routine, and after a few words of encouragement from Principal Waverly, who already appeared as though the school year had gotten the better of him, the pep rally was over. It had been built up as such a fun, lively event, but Audrey couldn't help but feel underwhelmed. In essence, the pep rally had boiled down to the school song and a couple of speeches. Bobby and Audrey raced to find Florie.

"Florie!" said Audrey, elbowing her way through the crowd. "You were amazing! Seriously, there isn't a word for what you were. No, there is—perfect! You were perfect!"

"Audrey!" Florie laughed as Audrey embraced her. "Oh, you're too sweet!"

"You were incredible, Florie," piped up Bobby.

"Thanks, Bobby!" Florie studied him for a moment. "Are we at that point in our friendship where we can hug?"

Bobby laughed. "I should think so."

"Good!" Florie pulled him into a hug. "Hey! You're a good hugger! I didn't think you would be."

"Well, thank you. I think."

"No, it's a compliment. I thought you'd be all stiff and weird."

"Sorry to disappoint."

"I've never been so happy to be disappointed." Florie looked between them. "So, are we ready to grab dinner or what? Need all the energy I can get to sit back and watch our boys lose."

The game was set to commence at seven thirty. To secure good seats, Bobby, Audrey, and Florie returned to the school around six thirty. They'd enjoyed a nice, casual dinner at a nearby restaurant before staking out their seats in the bleachers. Audrey made a quick trip to the bathroom, before the masses descended, and when she returned, Sebastian had joined Bobby and Florie. She could hear only snippets of the conversation as she neared. She heard Sebastian mention the Yankees, so Audrey assumed they were discussing baseball.

"Oh!" Bobby, ever the gentleman, stood up to greet Audrey. "Here, Aud. You can sit by me."

"Hold on a sec." Florie also stood up. "Did you happen to see if the concession stand is open yet?"

"It looked like they just opened."

"Perfect!" Florie linked her arm with Audrey's. "Me and Audrey are gonna grab a couple Cokes. Anyone else want anything?"

"A Coke would be great," said Bobby.

"I'll have the same," said Sebastian.

Audrey and Florie made their way down to the concession stand, which was already buzzing with activity. The mothers working the concession stand were clearly veterans, sending customers on their merry ways in a matter of seconds. Audrey and Florie each carried two Cokes as they hiked back up to the bleachers. Florie handed Sebastian one of her Cokes.

"Here you are," Florie said. "And yes, you are welcome."

"Thank you," laughed Sebastian.

"That was fast," added Bobby.

"Yes, well, the moms working the stand don't have time to chitchat," noted Audrey, sitting down between Bobby and Florie. "It's quite the operation down there."

Sebastian took a long sip of his Coke. "Still can't believe Alistair Amherst is the new quarterback."

"Hilarious, isn't it?" said Bobby.

"Ridiculous, more like. I've never known him to be the athletic sort."

"Well, I'd wager he only joined the team so cheerleaders would date him."

"I guess it worked," mused Audrey. "That is, if he's still dating Lisa Cargill."

"No, they broke up weeks ago," Florie enlightened her. "He's now dating Kimberly Fusco, who—if I'm not mistaken—actually dated his brother, Arthur, first. Brings a whole new meaning to 'keeping it in the family,' huh?"

Audrey grinned. "You've always got the scoop."

"I keep my ears open."

"You know, *The Bulletin* is always looking for new writers," said Bobby.

Florie laughed. "No way. I did my time with Mrs. Parker."

"That's the way you saw it? As 'doing time'?"

"Look, Mr. Dickens. You're different. You're her favorite. She'd always use your essays to show my class what A-quality work is. I was lucky to leave that class with a B. Only one kid got an A."

"Is she really that tough a grader?" asked Audrey, wide-eyed.

She had written a few papers for Mrs. Parker already—short ones—and she'd received high enough marks, but she and her classmates were now working on their semester-defining assignment: a twenty-page essay on *The Great Gatsby*.

"She has high expectations, sure, but I hardly think that's a bad thing," Bobby said. "Seb, wouldn't you agree?"

Sebastian whistled through his teeth. "I dunno. She made a couple kids cry last year. I wasn't one of them, but ... I could've been."

"He's joking," Bobby tried to assure Audrey, playfully nudging Sebastian. "Seb came away with an A-minus. But if you're really worried, I'd be more than happy to help. What's the essay on?"

"*The Great Gatsby*," said Audrey.

Bobby's eyes lit up. "Could you do Wednesday after school?"

"Sure."

"We'll go to my place. You'll get to meet Charles."

Audrey played it cool, but inside, she was elated. Bobby had never invited her to his house before. A part of her wondered what had changed—why he thought now was the right time—but she didn't want to have this conversation in front of their friends. Instead, she simply nodded, focusing her attention on the football field.

By no means was Audrey a football aficionado, but even she knew a bad game when she saw it. Albrecht Academy was absolutely decimating Great Gray. In the first half alone, Alistair threw three interceptions, two of which resulted in pick-sixes. (The others had given her a quick rundown of football terminology.) The Great Grays trailed the Albrecht Eagles by a whopping thirty points at halftime, having scored only three points.

"They can't get anywhere near the end zone," Bobby commented, unable to suppress his smirk. "This can't be good for Alistair."

"You're actually enjoying this," said Audrey.

"It's good for him to be put in his place. His parents have over-inflated his ego."

"They've got to bench him. They just have to," said Florie.

Shockingly, the coach refused to bench Alistair, and the second half of the game somehow managed to be even worse than the first. They ended up leaving in the middle of the fourth quarter, to avoid the embarrassment of being seen in their Great Gray uniforms after the game. Bobby and Sebastian walked the girls to the station before bidding them goodbye, heading back to their respective homes.

"Don't let that game ruin football for you," Florie told Audrey. "I swear, Great Gray is usually at least competitive. Well, actually, we're not. Not in recent years, anyway. Our baseball team, though ... that's where it's at. You'll get to see your boyfriend in action."

"I wasn't there for the game," laughed Audrey. "I just had fun, hanging out with you all. We should do it again."

"Oh, we will. Definitely." Florie squeezed Audrey's hand. "And hey, don't be stressing over that essay. Mrs. Parker is tough, but I'm sure you'll blow her out of the water."

When Audrey returned home, Sophia had already called it a night, but Alexander was in the living room, reading on the couch. His glasses—or "spectacles," as he always called them—had fallen to the tip of his nose, but he didn't feel the need to adjust them. Audrey's grandfather had been the same way, preferring to complain about how he couldn't read a menu instead of simply pushing up his glasses. Audrey remembered how humiliating it had been when, in public, her grandfather had refused to pull up his pants—or blatantly picked his nose. She vaguely wondered if, some twenty years in the future, Alexander would be that socially unaware grandfather for *her* children.

"Audie." Alexander pushed his glasses up with his forefinger. "You're home."

He proceeded to ask her about the game, and while Audrey assured him she'd enjoyed herself, she emphasized it wasn't because of the actual game.

"We were *destroyed*," Audrey admitted. "It was actually embarrassing to watch and be associated with."

"Oh, dear." Alexander kissed the top of her head. "I'm happy you're home safe—and that you had fun." He yawned, stretching for good measure. "But I'm gonna head in."

"Good night, Dad. Love you."

Before Audrey called it a night, she skimmed over her *Gatsby* essay, making sure it was presentable for Bobby's eyes. She didn't want to hand him a second-rate essay. Finally, a little before midnight, Audrey's eyelids started to droop.

Unable to stave off sleep any longer, she curled up on her bed, and within minutes, she was dead to the world. When she awoke the next morning, she again looked over her essay, and she was pleasantly surprised by how coherent her late-night edits were. Maybe she was more of a night owl than she had thought.

She knew she had a few days until Bobby would read her essay, but she couldn't help but obsess over it. It was the first major essay she had written for Mrs. Parker, and she was worried she'd be torn apart, like so many other students had apparently been. Furthermore, she was nervous about stepping foot inside Bobby's house. She knew he lived on Fifth Avenue, and she assumed his family owned a large apartment. She hoped she didn't do or say anything to embarrass him—or upset the staff. Because yes, Bobby's family had staff members who lived there full-time, something Audrey could hardly fathom. How big did a place have to be for an entire team to have to help clean and take care of it?

She spent the next few days alternating between worrying about the essay and her impending visit to Bobby's house. Finally, though, she wasn't able to put it off any longer. Wednesday had arrived, and as her last class ended, she knew she would soon be heading off with Bobby to his home.

"Are you ready to head out?" Bobby asked her, leaning against the neighboring locker. This had become a daily routine for them; Bobby always liked to chat with her by her locker before they went their separate ways.

"Ready," Audrey said, praying her voice didn't reveal her unease.

He reached for her hand. "Then let's go."

CHAPTER 9

Audrey

FIFTH AVENUE MANSION

"**Y**OU SURE THERE ISN'T a dress code or something?" asked Audrey as she and Bobby headed up Fifth Avenue.

She knew he lived close to Great Gray, but she hadn't been aware of just how close. He was only a few blocks up, right across from Central Park. Audrey wondered if his room had park views; for his sake, she hoped it did. It would be a disappointment, living right by Central Park but not being able to see it from your window.

"There's no dress code. Promise," said Bobby, leading her toward the door of his family's townhouse.

For some reason, it hadn't occurred to Audrey that Bobby might live in a townhouse. She had been picturing him in a penthouse, akin to the one Cassandra lived in and loved to boast about any chance she got.

Bobby stopped at the stoop, an endearing fear in his eyes. He held out his hand. "Are you ready?"

Taking his hand, Audrey teased, "You make it sound so serious."

Bobby laughed, then opened the door. He looked around, as though he were searching for something—or someone.

"Huh." He strained his neck and peered down one of the many lengthy hallways. "Charles is usually here."

Honestly, Audrey didn't pay attention to what he was saying. Instead, her eyes ricocheted around the room, trying and failing to absorb everything at once. Over-stimulated, she focused on the floor, momentarily shutting out the rest of the room. The floor was brilliant white marble, meticulously maintained and polished. If Audrey hadn't known better, she would have assumed that no one had ever stepped foot on it before. She slowly looked upward. The vaulted ceiling housed a glimmering chandelier that cascaded down, its colors seemingly altering depending on the angle from which Audrey looked at it. Paintings and tapestries adorned the walls—all originals, Audrey guessed. Despite the unmistakable grandeur of the room, the lack of personal mementos—not to mention the disconcerting absence of clutter—imbued Audrey with a sad sense of loneliness. It was like the house was on the market, and the family no longer lived here.

"This is where you live?" Audrey couldn't mask her incredulity.

To Audrey, the townhouse appeared less like a home and more like a museum. There were no marks on the floor or dust on the pottery, no imperfections on the walls or dirt on the rugs. It must have taken an army to keep this place in tip-top shape. She now understood why the Dempseys had staff members who lived here with them. Though Audrey couldn't, of course, verify this for herself, she would have bet good money there was not a single speck of dust on the crown molding, let alone any of the furniture.

Bobby sighed. "This ..." He gestured at the room, whose priceless artifacts and artwork had to be worth millions—more than Audrey's father would earn in several lifetimes. "... this isn't me."

"I know that." She squeezed his hand. "Money doesn't impress me. *You* impress me."

Bobby smiled. "Here, before we go upstairs, I want you to meet Charles." He approached the intercom. "Charles! I'm home! And there's someone here I'd like you to meet."

"Ah!" came a voice from the other end. "On my way!"

Audrey balked. "You have to call Charles with an intercom? Wait a second. Just how big is this place?"

"It's pretty big," Bobby said.

"How big?"

Bobby shifted on his feet. "Five floors."

"Five floors? What, does all of Fifth Avenue live here?"

"No," chuckled Bobby, feigning ease. "It's just me, my father, and the, uh ... main staff."

Audrey whistled through her teeth. "So, this is what my dad means when he talks about how the other half lives. It really is a completely different world up here."

"Believe me, I know this isn't normal. But—"

"Bobby!" Charles said as he entered the foyer. "Apologies for not being at the door to greet you! Your father had a large order of whiskey arrive today. I was sorting through it in the cellar, and clearly, time slipped away from me. I hope you can forgive me."

Charles looked almost exactly as Audrey had pictured him. He had a kind face, with laugh lines at the corner of each eye. His Afro and mustache were well groomed, and he had a warm, endearingly crooked smile. Dressed in an elegant black suit with coattails, Charles radiated timeless charm.

"Of course, Charles!" said Bobby.

Charles ruffled Bobby's hair. "It's good to see you."

The ever-fastidious Bobby made no attempt to fix his hair. "You too."

Bobby's and Charles's relationship was refreshingly casual. Audrey knew, of course, how much Bobby adored Charles—he talked about him all the time—but it warmed her heart, seeing that Charles seemed to equally care for Bobby. Their body language was more indicative of a father and son than a butler and employer's son. Charles, for his part, struck Audrey as the type of man who would have thrived as a grandfather. She could envision him sitting in a rocking chair by the fire, cradling his grandchildren and regaling them with stories of the past and hopes for the future. She wondered if he'd done that with Bobby when he was small—doting upon him as he would've his own child.

Charles turned to Audrey. "Hello, Miss Nielsen," he said, extending his hand. "It's so nice to finally meet you. Bobby has told us all so many wonderful things."

"Oh, thank you. Likewise." Audrey shook his hand. She was painfully aware she had no idea how to carry herself in an environment like this. "Um. This is a very beautiful home. I don't want to ruin the floors or anything, so ... do I take off my shoes?"

"Don't worry about it." Charles waved a glib hand. "The housekeepers are making their rounds, and they'll be cleaning the foyer shortly."

Audrey again surveyed the foyer. This room hadn't been cleaned yet? How was that possible? There was absolutely no sign of wear or tear anywhere around her. What were they cleaning? The air?

Charles continued, "May I ask where you two plan on being so I can tell them to steer clear of you?"

"In my room," Bobby answered. "Aud has a paper due, and she's asked me to look it over for her."

"I'll ask Benoit to prepare snacks for you, and I'll bring them up. Anything you like in particular, Miss Nielsen?"

"Not really," said Audrey. "But, uh ... if you don't mind, you can just call me Audrey. Being called Miss Nielsen makes me feel like I'm still in school."

Charles laughed good-naturedly. "Well, we don't want that. Now, how do you like your tea? Or would you prefer coffee?"

"Coffee?" Audrey's eyes lit up. "That's something my parents would never offer me."

"Well, I wouldn't want to—"

"Oh, no. Coffee sounds great. Thank you!"

"My pleasure." Charles smiled. "Oh, and one more thing, before I stop hounding you with all these questions. Benoit plans on having dinner ready by six thirty. And afterward, I've arranged for Felix to take you home."

"That sounds great," said Bobby. "Thank you so much, Charles."

"You're very welcome. I'll be up shortly with your coffee and snacks."

After Charles left, Audrey looked up at Bobby, an eyebrow raised. "Who is Felix?"

"He was my mother's chauffeur," Bobby explained. "When she died, my father didn't want to let him go, so he became my chauffeur. He's very nice. It just ... it still feels weird, having him drive me around. I'm not quite used to it."

"I can imagine."

But she couldn't. Audrey figured that Felix didn't get much action with Bobby. If Bobby could walk somewhere, he would, and even if he couldn't, he was more than fine hailing a taxi—or even taking the subway.

"But come on," Bobby said. "I want to see this essay of yours you're so worked up over."

Audrey panted as she followed Bobby up the seemingly endless staircase. He, however, was unaffected, bouncing up the stairs two at a time. She now understood why he was such a track star; he'd been training all his life, going up and down these stairs every day, multiple times.

"Good heavens, Bobby! Where is your room? On top of the Empire State Building?"

"It's not too much farther now," Bobby called over his shoulder. "Here we are. This is me, right over here," he added as he opened the door, immediately kicking his shoes off. He was oblivious that Audrey was still a few paces behind him, catching her breath from the long, four-floor climb. "Feel free to put your backpack wherever. And you can take your shoes off. Whatever makes you feel most comfortable."

As Bobby meandered over to his desk, Audrey finally reached his door. Bobby's bed looked like something out of the 1800s, with ornate carvings on the wood, a canopy, and gray drapes. Across from his bed was a wood-burning fireplace that had been used recently, as evidenced by the freshly charred logs and lingering scent of smoke. The nights had been getting cooler, something Bobby—a lover of the cold—relished. Audrey could picture Bobby sitting in the plush armchair during those cold winter nights, engrossed in a good book. The windows boasted unobstructed views of Central Park, and his desk was strategically positioned so as to take full advantage of the postcard-worthy scene. Bookshelves lined the other walls, no doubt methodically categorized. And, of course, a bedroom in a five-floor Fifth Avenue townhouse would not be complete without a full en suite bathroom and walk-in closet. Audrey wasn't interested in discovering whether Bobby's closet was, in fact, bigger than her entire apartment.

"Aud?" Bobby turned to face her. "Are you okay?"

"What? Oh. You mean the fact that I'm standing here like a statue? No, I'm fine." Audrey slipped out of her shoes. "See? Completely fine."

"Well, you can, you know, come into the room."

"I know. I just ... I was enjoying the view, that's all."

"The view's better over here, by the windows."

"I'll take your word for it."

"Aud." Bobby walked up to her. "I know this is ... I know it's a lot."

"It's a complete culture shock. Look, I'm sorry, Bobby, but ... I feel very out of my depth here."

"But you're not." Bobby cupped her face in his hands. "I want you to feel comfortable here—and with me. Okay?"

Despite her immobility, her heart rate increased, as though she were once again climbing the stairs up to his bedroom. "Okay," she said breathlessly, lost in his eyes.

"Good." Bobby kissed her. "Now, how about you show me this essay? I want to see what I'm working with."

"Right. One sec." Audrey opened her backpack and removed her essay from her English folder. "Here you are. Please forgive the smudged ink. And the handwriting. And the essay itself."

"I'm sure it's fine." He took the essay from her. "And what are you talking about? Your handwriting's great. Nothing to apologize for. Here, let's sit down."

Bobby sat down on the edge of his bed, and Audrey tentatively followed suit. The mattress was depressingly firm; Audrey uttered a silent prayer for Bobby's poor back. Being alone with Bobby in his bedroom was quite intimate—as was sitting so close to him on his bed. If they had been in her apartment, Audrey's parents would have insisted on the door being wide open, and they would have checked in on them every five or so minutes, just to make sure everything was under control.

"Okay, okay," said Bobby absently as he read her introductory paragraph, nodding. "Well, first, I want to say you're a very strong writer. From this opening paragraph alone, I get a great sense of your voice. So, I don't want you to leave here thinking I think you're a bad writer or anything."

"I promise, I'm not easily offended. If I didn't want your help, I wouldn't have accepted it. So, please, any advice would be really appreciated."

"Great. It'll just take me a couple minutes to read through the rest, and then we'll talk, okay?"

As Bobby read through her essay, he scrawled notes on a separate pad of paper. Audrey was entranced, watching as his eyes darted back and forth. Subconsciously, after reading a few sentences, he would run his fingers through his hair, muttering to himself. Audrey hoped this wasn't an ill omen, that her essay wasn't so painful to read. She remembered how fervently Bobby had been writing during the first day of school assembly. Young as he was, he had already found his talent. Audrey was rather envious; she was a couple of months older than he was, and she didn't yet know where she saw herself in ten or twenty years.

A knock on the door, however, jolted Audrey out of her thoughts. Bobby, for his part, didn't look up; it was entirely possible he hadn't even heard it.

"It's me!" came Charles's voice from the other side. "Is it okay for me to enter?"

"Yes!" Audrey stood up. Bobby finally reacted, lifting his eyes from Audrey's essay. "Here, let me get the door for you."

Before Audrey could reach the door, Charles opened it himself, and he entered, carrying a tray laden with two cups of coffee and an assortment of cookies, fresh fruit, crackers, and cheeses.

"Oh my gosh," gasped Audrey, taking it all in. "How do you expect us to have room for dinner after all this?"

Charles laughed, placing the tray down on Bobby's desk. "Take that up with

Benoit. This is his idea of a light snack."

"Well, he's right," quipped Bobby.

Charles wiped his hands on his pants. "If you need anything else, just let me know."

"Thank you so much," said Audrey.

"Yes, it all looks wonderful, Charles. Be sure to send our thanks to Benoit too," chimed in Bobby.

"Will do. Happy studying, you two," said Charles, closing the door as he departed.

Audrey walked over to the tray, helping herself to one of the cups of coffee and a cookie. "Do you want anything?" she asked Bobby.

"I'm good for now," he replied, his attention once again on her essay. "Sorry I'm taking so long. I just want to be thorough, make sure all my notes make sense."

"Don't worry about it. Take all afternoon, if you want. I'm more than happy just sitting here, eating these cookies."

Bobby laughed. "They *are* addictive. Please, take some of the food home with you. Benoit always bakes for an army."

"If I must." Audrey wrapped a couple of the cookies in a napkin and placed them in her backpack.

While Bobby finished reading her essay, Audrey explored the rest of his room. She discovered his books were arranged thematically and alphabetically by the author's surname. He was interested in all sorts of genres, from literary fiction to memoirs, historical accounts to poetry. No one Audrey knew came close to matching Bobby's passion for books. Despite all the bookshelves, he was somehow out of room, with neat piles of books perched on his windowsill, awaiting a new home.

Yet Audrey realized that his bedroom—like the foyer—was devoid of personal, homey touches. Everything was orderly—and unsettlingly adult. Indeed, that was the main problem with it; it wasn't the bedroom of a fourteen-year-old boy. There were no posters of celebrities on the walls; in contrast, the wall next to Audrey's bunkbed was covered in posters of her celebrity crushes. But nothing about Bobby's room hinted at his age. He should've had comic books or action figures, sports memorabilia or vinyl records. Instead, all the furniture matched, and everything in the room was a neutral color. Even the bedspread was a dreary gray.

"Okay. I've finished."

Bobby's voice brought Audrey back, and she sat down next to him on the bed, awaiting his critique. His hair had fallen into his face, which only served to further endear him to Audrey. He appeared more relaxed, with his tie dangled around his neck and his sleeves rolled up. Surely, he must have harbored some sort of inkling as to what the girls at school said about him, how they all thought—

"I think your thesis statement needs to be stronger," he started. "I get what you're saying—that the book dives into the differences between old and new money—but it'd help if you mentioned what, exactly, you'll be discussing. So, in your essay, you go on to talk about Gatsby, juxtaposing him against Tom. While Tom is more … subtle about his wealth, Gatsby flaunts it, with his grand parties, flashy car, all that. So, just make sure that's clear in your thesis—that that's your main argument."

"Right. No, that makes sense. I'll do that," she said, already forgetting half of what he'd just said.

"And there were just a couple other things—grammar things, word choice, that kind of stuff. We can go through point by point, if you want."

"Lay it on me."

For the next several minutes, Bobby relayed to Audrey his comments and suggestions. He gave Audrey quick lessons on how to use semi-colons, the difference between "that" and "which," and how to avoid splitting infinitives.

"I've been in school for, what, basically my whole life, and no one has ever told me any of that," Audrey remarked. "How did you learn all this?"

"I've been writing since I was a kid, so … I don't know." Bobby shrugged. "I think it came naturally to me, in some ways."

"Well, it's really impressive. In these past couple of hours, you've helped me make more sense out of this book than Mrs. Parker has in three weeks."

"You didn't like the book?"

"No! All the characters were so annoying! I didn't get what Gatsby saw in Daisy. None of it made any sense."

Bobby laughed. "But that's the point. It's a commentary on the shallowness of wealth, how it doesn't make people happy or complete in any way."

Audrey made a face. "I'm just glad we'll be done discussing it soon. Mrs. Parker keeps saying it's a classic, that it's an incredible book, but I just think it's incredibly overrated."

Bobby placed his pad of paper and her essay down on the bed. "Well, it's my favorite book."

"You're kidding."

"Afraid not." Bobby grinned, and Audrey was relieved she hadn't offended him. "I've easily read it over a hundred times. I go back to it all the time, in between other books."

"Oh. Well, I mean, when I say it's incredibly overrated, I don't … yeah, I guess I kind of dug my own grave there."

Bobby laughed, pushing the pad of paper to the side. "It isn't for everyone. I just hope this was helpful."

"It was. Very helpful."

"And really, I can do this anytime. I'd be more than happy to read over any of your other essays, offer you pointers."

Audrey smirked flirtatiously. "Well, you shouldn't keep helping me out without getting something in return."

"What do you mean?"

Without missing a beat, Audrey kissed him. At first, the kiss was soft and sweet, and Audrey worried that maybe Bobby hadn't expected her to be so brash. But when they briefly broke away and met each other's eyes, Bobby leaned back in, kissing her with a fervor she was all too happy to reciprocate. It was like they'd all at once felt the weight of the years they'd gone without the other's touch and were unable to stand one more second apart.

"Bobby? Audrey?" Charles's voice from the other side of the door caused

Bobby and Audrey to part, as though their closeness were forbidden. "Dinner is ready!"

"Dinner?" Audrey glanced over at the clock on the mantel, shocked to discover it was already six thirty. "Oh." Her face flushed, and she cleared her throat. "I guess we kind of lost track of time there."

"I guess so." Bobby stood up, pushing his hair out of his face. A puckish twinkle danced in his eyes. "But I can't say I minded."

Audrey thought of all the girls at Great Gray who would have gladly given away their Cartier necklaces to spend an afternoon with Bobby as she had. Come tomorrow, she would have to fend off her peers' intrusive questions about the Dempsey townhouse. She wouldn't answer them, of course; discretion was a virtue too frequently discarded amongst teenagers, and Audrey didn't wish to invite her classmates into her and Bobby's relationship.

"Me neither." Audrey's cheeks were burning. She wondered if Bobby could tell. "Um. I want to spruce up before dinner. Could I use your bathroom?"

"Sure. It's right over there. I'll wait outside the door, and we can walk down together."

Once in the bathroom, Audrey splashed cold water on her face. She was taken aback when she saw her disheveled appearance in the mirror. A casual observer would have assumed she had just returned from a run. Hurriedly, she brushed her hair with her fingers, to mitigate its wildness, all the while noting how impeccable Bobby's bathroom was, with his products all fastidiously arranged. There was a tube of concealer on the counter, which stood out amongst the Brylcreem and Yves Saint Laurent Pour Homme. Her first instinct was the concealer must have belonged to someone else, but if so, what would it be doing in Bobby's bathroom? She picked it up, her eyebrows furrowed.

Just then, she heard voices from outside the bedroom door—Bobby and Charles, by the sounds of it. Realizing how rude it was of her to be snooping around her boyfriend's bathroom, Audrey finished smoothing down her hair and joined Bobby and Charles.

As they escorted her to the formal dining room, Audrey pondered how many people had found themselves lost within the townhouse's several floors and winding hallways. There should have been a directory, indicating where in the house one was. It wasn't immediately evident to Audrey why Bobby's family lived in such a sprawling townhouse. Months must have passed without Bobby stepping foot in several of the rooms. Maybe there were even rooms he'd never entered before. At some point, clearly, one had to recognize there was far too much space.

The dining room table could host at least ten people comfortably, by Audrey's estimation, but she and Bobby elected to sit side by side so they could actually hear each other. Benoit had certainly cooked up a feast. Audrey hadn't anticipated multiple courses, but she enjoyed each one, making sure to lick her plate clean. Afterward, they asked Charles to thank Benoit for them, and Audrey packed up and prepared to leave.

"Thank you for letting me come over, helping me out with my essay," said Audrey as Bobby walked her to the door. "Oh, and I guess the making out was nice too."

Bobby laughed. "Happy to do that any time."

"The essay help or the making out?"

"Both, of course."

Before Bobby's hand could reach the doorknob, the front door opened. A short, frazzled man was on the other side, completely oblivious to Bobby's and Audrey's presence.

"Here you are, Mr. Dempsey," he said to someone still out of view.

A few moments later, a tall, well-dressed man stood in the doorway, his face briefly obscured by shadow. Concurrently, the foyer filled with musky cologne. Audrey couldn't quite place the scent, but it most assuredly smelled like money—*old* money, to be more specific. In fact, it was exactly the sort of cologne she could envision Tom Buchanan using.

In an instant, Bobby's demeanor shifted. He stiffened, swallowed hard, and directed his gaze upward, at the towering figure.

"Hello, sir," Bobby said, his tone uncharacteristically solemn; Audrey almost didn't recognize it as his voice. "Welcome home."

Audrey's brain could hardly compute she was standing in the same room as Robert Dempsey, one of the wealthiest men on the Eastern Seaboard. She didn't dare look at him directly, as though he were an eclipse. Even if Audrey had known nothing about Robert Dempsey, it was copiously clear he was a man of means. His hands were uncalloused, and he donned perfectly polished leather shoes and a brown three-piece suit that, no doubt, had been custom-tailored just for his six-foot-five, broad-shouldered frame. His shaggy gray hair was slicked back, and his Van Dyke beard was closely trimmed. In short, he looked like the sort of man who was used to attracting attention whenever he entered a room.

Robert nodded at Bobby. "Yes. It's good to be back in New York."

Robert's voice was deep, authoritative—exactly the sort of voice one would expect from a man so moneyed. His personal assistant—or whoever he was—remained in place, still holding open the door.

"Davis." Robert turned to the man by the door. "Meet me in my office, will you?"

"Yes, Mr. Dempsey," the man said, quickly retreating down some long hallway. Audrey was amazed he knew his way around so well—or maybe he was simply hoping he'd chosen the right hallway.

Robert adjusted his cufflinks. "I see you had company over," he said to Bobby, though his pointed gaze was fixed on Audrey.

"This is Audrey Nielsen," Bobby replied, his knuckles paper white. "We go to Great Gray together."

"Ah." Robert smiled warmly at Audrey. "Well, it's lovely to meet you, Miss ... Nielsen, was it?"

"Yes. And, um ... you too," Audrey said, a bit too hastily. "I've heard so much about you." She didn't mention, however that most of what she'd heard about him had come from her parents, not Bobby. Almost automatically, she added, "You have a beautiful home, Mr. Dempsey."

"Thank you so much." Robert, redirecting his attention to his son, said, "I see Felix is waiting outside. I assume he'll be taking the lovely Miss Nielsen home?"

"Yes, sir," said Bobby robotically.

"Very good." Robert again turned to Audrey. "I hope I'll see you again." Then, with a nod, he walked away, his footsteps ringing out on the marble floor.

Bobby watched him go, a strange look in his eyes. His hand was shaking, and the color had almost entirely drained from his face. Contradictorily, in the moment, Bobby appeared both older and younger than his age. His expression was wary, regarding the world with a suspicion atypical of one so young. And yet, his mannerisms were rather indicative of a child spooked by the monster under his bed. It concerned her, witnessing how deeply his father's presence had affected him, especially since, in her estimation, Robert had been perfectly polite—welcoming, even.

Bobby cleared his throat. "It's getting late. I don't want to keep Felix waiting."

They walked in silence for a few moments, then Audrey asked, "Why, um ... why do you call your dad 'sir'?"

"I, uh ... I guess it's just a habit, whenever guests are around. That's what I was taught, anyway—to be formal. But, um ... no, I don't ... usually call him that."

"Well, he seems really nice. Your dad, I mean."

Bobby didn't answer; he merely nodded, his eyes—and his mind, clearly—elsewhere. He neared a black car, which Audrey ascertained was Felix's, and he reached for the door handle.

"Bobby." Audrey stopped him. She searched his impassive face. "Are you okay?"

"I'm fine."

"Are you sure? Because ... when you saw your dad ... I don't know. I've never seen you like that before."

Bobby forced a smile. "I just didn't expect to see him, that's all. I thought he was out of town for a few more days. He took me by surprise."

"Okay," Audrey said, though she didn't quite believe that was the whole story. She didn't, however, want to pursue the matter any further and risk upsetting Bobby. "Well." She beamed up at him. "Thank you for a wonderful afternoon."

Bobby's eyes flickered to her lips, and he bent down to kiss her. Whenever she and Bobby kissed, Audrey lost all sense of the outside world. She existed in a heightened state, like she was on the brink of consciousness and unconsciousness, able to shut out the world around her but still know she was part of it. When she and Bobby at last pulled apart, Audrey returned to reality, disappointed that she was standing on a sidewalk in New York and not in her magical dream world.

"Mmmm." Bobby absently traced her lips with his finger. She was pleased to see the sparkle had returned to his eyes. "I think I've stalled as much as I can. Felix is probably getting impatient."

"Well, we don't want that," laughed Audrey, dismayed that Bobby wasn't going to kiss her again.

Bobby opened the car door for her, then relayed her address to Felix. "Thank you so much, Felix."

"Don't worry, Bobby," said Felix, nodding. "I'll make sure she gets home safe."

Once home, Audrey braced herself for her parents' barrage of questions. She knew they would be eager to hear all about Robert Dempsey's home, but she didn't feel comfortable divulging too much, as she didn't want to violate Bobby's privacy. She knew her parents meant well, but their questions bordered on invasive, and Audrey wasn't the sort to entertain such things. She opted not to tell them she'd briefly met Robert Dempsey; that might be enough to send her father into a tizzy.

"We had a great time, and that's all I'm going to say," Audrey said, feigning a yawn to end the interrogation early.

"Yes, of course. We're sorry, love. It's just exciting, that's all—you having your first boyfriend," Alexander said.

Audrey knew he meant it was exciting she was dating an Upper East Sider, but she decided to let that slide. She kissed both of her parents good night and headed into her room, finishing up some of her homework before she at last called it a night. As she drifted off to sleep, she thought again of that strange look on Bobby's face ... and his insistence that he simply hadn't expected his father to be home so soon. It still struck Audrey as odd, all these hours later. Perhaps she was reading too much into it; perhaps Bobby had, in fact, just been caught off guard by his father's premature arrival.

Nevertheless, Audrey couldn't help but think that something else was going on—something more worrisome. Most likely, it was just her mind running rampant; she was, after all, prone to overthinking. For all she knew, everything was perfectly fine, and she was just turning a small moment into something far bigger.

That was what she hoped, anyway.

CHAPTER 10

Bobby

THE FATHER AND THE SON

B OBBY STOOD ON THE sidewalk, watching as Felix's car vanished from his sight. He sighed, his hands deep in his pockets. He knew Audrey well by this point, and he could tell when something was bothering her. His reaction to seeing his father had troubled her, made her think something was wrong. He hoped he'd managed to explain himself well enough, that she wasn't at home worrying about him. Bobby had just never been good with surprises—particularly where his father was concerned.

After a minute or so, he reentered the townhouse. To his surprise—and delight—Charles was waiting for him in the foyer.

"She's a lovely young woman," Charles told Bobby. "I can see just how happy she makes you. I hope we'll be seeing more of her?"

"That's certainly the plan."

Bobby spent most of the evening in his bedroom, finishing up assignments and getting a head start on *Jane Eyre*. He'd always loved school and didn't mind the work. He knew that made him different—strange, even—but Bobby didn't care. Too many of his peers acted as though school was superfluous, unnecessary; clearly, they were relying on their surnames to get them whatever they wanted, both inside and outside Great Gray. They knew they didn't have to make good grades to get into the Ivy League school of their dreams; they only needed to ask their father to put in a good word for them, and their cushy future would be secured.

This mentality—not to mention unbridled conceit—irked Bobby. Even though he knew he could play the same games as these peers—Robert Dempsey was, after all, a force to be reckoned with in New York and beyond—Bobby didn't want anything he hadn't earned on his own merit. For as long as he could remember, he'd had his sights set on Columbia, which no doubt frustrated his father. For generations, the Dempsey men had attended Harvard. Forever beholden to tradition, Robert had expected Bobby to follow in their footsteps, and he'd been unable to hide his displeasure when Bobby told him he was most interested in Columbia. In Robert's eyes, Columbia was the weakest of the Ivy League schools, but Bobby didn't agree. Besides, Bobby loved New York, and he had no desire to leave. Above his desk hung the blue-and-white Columbia flag. He liked to look at it when he needed to be reminded of what he was working for: a way to carve a name for himself in the city he adored.

A little before ten, Bobby trekked down to the kitchen to brew himself a cup of chamomile tea, as was his nighttime ritual. The house was quiet, which was how he preferred it. During the daytime, he felt like he was constantly underfoot. His family had always been small—far too small to justify having so large a staff. Four people, including Benoit, worked in the kitchen, and four maids cleaned the townhouse top to bottom every day. Furthermore, there was a gardener who tended to the herbs, vegetables, and fruits on the rooftop garden, as well as two chauffeurs. Charles was in charge of the staff, doling out responsibilities and chores as needed. There used to be another staff member; Ava had served as the personal assistant for Bobby's mother, Margaret, but after Margaret died two years ago, Ava left the household in search of other employment. Though Bobby regarded the members of their staff as extensions of his nuclear family, he couldn't help but feel as though the whole thing was excessive—and antiquated. It wasn't like they had hundreds of acres of land that required maintenance, and ever since Margaret's passing, it had been only Bobby and his father, and they seldom entertained these days.

However, Robert saw it differently. He reminded Bobby they were employers, that their staff depended on them for their livelihoods.

"We take care of them, just as they take care of us," Robert had said once. "They're all paid very well for their work, and they know we'll always be here for them, no matter what."

This was true. A few years back, Rosita, one of the maids, had asked for some time off to visit her mother, who was dying from cancer. Robert and Margaret, in turn, had told her to take off as much time as she needed; they'd still pay her full salary, and whenever she was ready, she would have a home and a job to come back to. Gestures like this had endeared the Dempseys to their employees, and most of the staff had been working for them for as long as Bobby could remember. The Dempseys had exceptionally high retention rates—far higher than most Upper East Side households.

With his cup of tea in hand, Bobby headed back toward the front of the house, to the main staircase. As he stepped into the foyer, he saw movement from the opposing hallway. At first, he thought it was Charles making his late-night rounds, but from the sheer height of the shadow on the wall—and the sinking feeling in his stomach—he knew it was his father. Bobby had hoped he would be able to avoid Robert, who usually sequestered himself in his office until the early hours of the morning. Bobby hastened toward the staircase, but the shadow caught up to him.

Robert moved into the light, and Bobby froze. "You're up late," his father drawled.

"I was just getting some tea." Hands shaking, Bobby held up his mug, to prove he was telling the truth. "But, um ... I'm just heading up to my room, and I know you have things to do, so—"

"That girl you had over ... Miss Nielsen ..." Robert neared him. "I don't know a Nielsen."

Bobby had been dreading this moment ever since he and Audrey had run into his father in the foyer. He'd known his father would scour his memory banks, trying to determine where Audrey had come from—and, most importantly, whether she was, in his estimation, worthy of stepping foot in his home.

"Her family lives in the Village," Bobby replied.

"The Village." Robert spoke slowly, deliberately, as though he were saying these words for the first time. "And she's at Great Gray?"

Bobby heaved a sigh, mentally preparing himself for Robert's judgment. "She's a scholarship student."

Robert recoiled, as though he were allergic to every word Bobby had just uttered. And perhaps he was. At the end of the day, people like Robert didn't understand how privileged they were, how unimaginable their lives were to most people. The Dempseys had always gone to Great Gray, as far back as the school's founding. Thus, it was inconceivable to Robert that someone could enter Great Gray without that sort of pedigree, that someone could get in due to their own hard work and tenacity.

"And she's a ... friend of yours, is that right?" Robert prodded.

Bobby knew Robert wouldn't approve, but he wasn't about to downplay his and Audrey's relationship. "Actually, she's my girlfriend."

Robert nodded, taking this all in. "I see." His eyes were a sky threatening snow. "I'm sure she's a charming girl, but ... people talk, you understand. There are ... expectations for you, as my son. And a scholarship girl from the Village ... well ..." He spread his hands. "She doesn't fit."

"I like Aud. A lot."

"Yes, she's a very pretty girl," Robert acknowledged, "but she isn't ..." He trailed off, trying to find the perfect word. "... suitable. I'd say she's a ... a dalliance, at best."

"I don't agree. And maybe if you got to know her, you'd see why I feel that way."

Robert smirked. "So, that's how this will be. Well. I can't say I didn't see this sort of ... rebellion coming."

There was a slew of things Bobby wanted to say, retorts he wanted to fire off, one after the other, like rounds from a gun. Robert had gone Bobby's whole life acting ambivalent about his friends and hobbies. But now, having heard that his son had his first girlfriend—a girlfriend whose family tree wasn't as established as Robert would have liked—he was suddenly interested in Bobby's life. It'd been a great disappointment to Robert, learning his son had a personality and a will all of his own, that he wasn't moldable like clay. It was clear to Bobby that Robert had wanted him to be a carbon copy of himself, but instead, Bobby had shown, time and time again, that he wouldn't be like the Robert Damian Dempseys who'd come before him; he'd be someone new entirely.

"This isn't some sort of teenage rebellion," Bobby insisted. "I told you, I like Aud. And I'm going to keep seeing her."

Robert scoffed. "You're not a child anymore. You can't pretend you don't know how things work around here."

"People can say whatever they want," Bobby bristled. "I don't care."

"That's an ugly attitude to have. And an arrogant one, to think people don't matter."

"I never said—"

"I didn't raise you to be so inconsiderate."

"You didn't raise me at all! You let the nannies and the governesses do that *for* you."

Bobby spoke before he could stop himself. He knew he'd gone too far. His father never liked to be reminded of just how indifferent he'd been about his own son. Indeed, Bobby's parents would have loved it if after he'd been born, he'd magically turned eighteen. They hadn't known what to do with a baby, so they hadn't tried. Bobby's earliest memories centered around the team of women who'd taken turns tending to him, as well as Charles. Neither of his parents was even on the periphery of those memories.

When he was ten, they'd shipped him off to Ivy Hill, a premier boarding school in Connecticut. His tenure there was miserable and lonely, and though he sent weekly letters to his parents, they never responded. His depression reached its peak on his eleventh birthday, and in the aftermath, Charles, who had taken the train out to Connecticut to surprise Bobby, ended up bringing the desolate Bobby back to New York. Bobby knew his parents resented having him back in their home, but they hastily enrolled him in a local private school and did their best to explain their son's sudden departure from Ivy Hill. The classes were too easy; the teachers were subpar; the facilities were inadequate. Bobby, of course, knew the truth—as did the staff. Still, no one uttered a word about what Bobby had tried to do on his eleventh birthday, and though Charles had advocated on Bobby's behalf, arguing that Bobby should speak to a therapist, his parents had refused. To them, the optics of their son attending therapy far outweighed any benefit such sessions could have awarded him. That had always been their primary concern: appearances. Their son's mental well-being was simply collateral damage.

Robert stepped forward, his eyes stormy. Bobby preemptively flinched, bracing himself for what was to come. Just as quickly as Robert's demeanor had darkened, however, it returned to normal, and something akin to a smile graced his lips.

"Charles," Robert said, looking over Bobby's shoulder. "Done with your rounds?"

"Yes, Mr. Dempsey," Charles replied. "I'll see you in the morning. Good night, sir. And good night, Bobby."

Bobby turned and watched as Charles offered them both a nod before departing. Bobby started toward the staircase, praying he could escape his father's wrath by prematurely exiting the conversation. Robert, though, wasn't about to let Bobby get his way. He gripped Bobby's shoulder, wheeling him around. Most of Bobby's tea splashed onto the floor.

"You think you can say that to me and walk away?" Robert demanded in a low, menacing tone. "Do I really need to remind you, boy, that you've been given opportunities most would kill for? You'll never have to worry about things most people spend their whole lives worrying about—money, employment, stability. I've ensured you'll never want for anything. You'd do well to remember that."

Bobby nodded mutely, his fighting spirit ripped away from him. It never ended well when he tried to say something, to speak up for himself. His father would always have all the power. Too easily, Robert could put Bobby in his place by telling him just how fortunate he was, as though mountains of money made up for the lack of love, respect, and consideration he'd received—from either of his parents. In truth, Bobby would have gladly given up all the money in his trust fund in exchange for a happy, close-knit family—like the one Audrey had. A family who did things together, who had group photographs on their mantel.

"I know," Bobby muttered, his eyes on the floor. "I'm sorry."

"You're sorry what?"

"I'm sorry, sir."

Bobby didn't look up at his father, not wanting to give him the satisfaction, but he eventually heard Robert's retreating footsteps. He waited for a few moments, to make sure his father was well and truly gone. The sound of a closing door signaled that Robert had made it back to his office; the hallway was safe. Only then did Bobby's feet dare to move.

He returned to his bedroom and sat on the edge of his bed, sipping what remained of his tea, staring straight ahead at the unadorned wall. All sorts of thoughts ran through his head, thoughts he'd had hundreds of times over the years. His father was right; he had nothing to complain about.

It didn't matter to him that Robert didn't approve of Audrey. Robert hardly liked anyone who wasn't already in his social circle, and he'd always objected to all of Bobby's choices. Even if Bobby had brought Cassandra Irvine home, someone Robert doubtless believed would be a suitable partner for his son, Robert still would have protested; he would have been upset that Bobby had chosen Cassandra without any sort of push or prod—without his influence.

Bobby shoved these thoughts aside, deciding instead to focus on the positive. Charles liked Audrey, and Charles's opinion had always held more weight than his father's. Bobby had given his father far too much power over his life, allowing Robert's opinion to kill more than a single dream. He wouldn't let Robert ruin the best thing that had ever happened to him—or drive a wedge between him and Audrey.

If Bobby and Audrey didn't work out, it'd be for one of a million reasons—but it wouldn't be because his father told him she wasn't suitable.

CHAPTER 11

Audrey

THE RELUCTANT BIRTHDAY BOY

WORD QUICKLY SPREAD AROUND school that Bobby and Audrey were, indeed, serious. For months, Audrey knew, her peers had been convinced it was nothing more than an upstairs-downstairs fling that would fizzle out by the semester's end. Yet to their endless astonishment, as October bled into November, Bobby and Audrey had not broken up; in fact, they were stronger than ever.

Audrey didn't particularly wish to flaunt her relationship in others' faces, but she would've been lying if she said she didn't enjoy engaging in public displays of affection with Bobby, kissing at their lockers and holding hands down the hallway. She didn't care what her peers thought; she was happy, and she knew Bobby was too.

The day was going well, but then Mrs. Parker asked Audrey to stay after class to discuss her *Gatsby* paper. It had been a couple of weeks since she and her peers had turned their essays in, but Mrs. Parker had told them it would take her a while to grade them all; she liked to be thorough with her comments. Hence, Audrey had somewhat forgotten about the assignment—until Mrs. Parker brought it up, reigniting her anxiety.

Did Mrs. Parker think she had plagiarized? Did she think Audrey was a horrible writer? Was Audrey going to be expelled?

"This was a phenomenal paper," said Mrs. Parker.

"Oh." Audrey exhaled. "Thank you."

"Your argument was very persuasive, and you addressed all the concerns I'd raised in your rough draft—though, to be frank, there weren't all that many. Just a few grammar things, mostly. Small things."

"Your comments were very helpful. And I had another student read it over for me, to catch anything I was missing."

"That's very prudent of you. May I ask whom?"

"Bobby Dempsey."

"Ah." Mrs. Parker smiled—something Audrey hadn't known she could do. "He's a wonderfully talented writer. I'm sure he was a great help to you."

"Yes, he was."

Mrs. Parker leaned forward. "But I like your writing voice. It's witty without being informal. It's difficult to achieve that balance." She peered at Audrey over her glasses. "You're aware I'm the faculty adviser of *The Bulletin*, yes?"

"Yes."

"Well, Miss Nielsen, if you ever want to join our ranks, I think we'd be all the better for it."

"Thank you, Mrs. Parker. I'll consider it."

"I hope you do. In the meantime"—she handed Audrey back her essay—"well done."

At the end of the day, Audrey waited beside Bobby's locker, to ensure she wouldn't miss him. As if on cue, Bobby emerged from down the hallway, his hands thrust into his pockets, his eyes on the floor. When he neared his locker, he at last looked up, seeing Audrey. Something seemed off with Bobby's complexion; there was a slight discoloration around his left eye and cheek, which he had seemingly tried to hide with some sort of concealer. Audrey wasn't sure how she hadn't noticed it during their early morning meetup, but perhaps it had become more noticeable over the course of the day.

"Bobby," said Audrey softly. "Your face. It looks like you got in a fight or something."

"Oh. No, I just fell during practice yesterday."

Audrey remembered the tube of concealer she'd seen on Bobby's bathroom counter. It had struck her as odd at the time, but perhaps he used it to cover up sports injuries. Bobby was rather particular about his appearance—especially for a teenage boy—so it didn't seem out of character for him to want to conceal any facial imperfections.

"Well, are you okay?" Audrey asked.

"I'm fine. It doesn't hurt." Bobby's eyes drifted to the paper in her hand. "What's that?"

Audrey grinned. "It's my essay! I got an A!"

"No easy task in Mrs. Parker's class. Congratulations!"

"Thank you! It was pretty crazy. She held me back after class to talk about it. I thought she was going to tear into me or something, but she said she loves my writing voice."

"I told you what an amazing writer you are!"

"Yes, you did! And now, Mrs. Parker wants me to join *The Bulletin*."

"You should!"

"I don't know. I think I'd be over-extending myself."

"You don't have to write full-time. You could just do an Opinion piece every once in a while. And maybe next year, you'll want to do more."

"I'll think about it. How about that?"

"Sounds good to me." Bobby kissed her cheek. "I'd love to stay and chat, but I have to go. Practice is starting soon. So, I'll see you tomorrow, okay?"

Over the next couple of weeks, Bobby was perpetually busy, always prepping for a cross-country meet or an academic deadline. He and Audrey went out on fewer dates, but even when they did go out, Bobby wasn't his usual self. There was a persistent sadness in his eyes, and though Audrey didn't comment on it aloud, she noticed a handful of times when Bobby had once again used concealer to cover up some sort of minor injury on his face. He seemed anxious about something, but he didn't divulge anything to Audrey.

November 16, Bobby's fifteenth birthday, was a Thursday. Strangely, it was Sarah, not Bobby, who mentioned it to Audrey. It had only been an off-handed comment, but Audrey couldn't help but wonder why Bobby hadn't said anything. Still, that Thursday, Audrey wished him a happy birthday, which seemed to confuse him.

"How did you know it was my birthday?" he asked.

"Sarah mentioned it. So, I thought maybe we could do something."

Bobby shook his head. "No, I ... I don't think so."

"Oh, do you already have plans with your dad? Is he taking you out somewhere?"

"No. I ... I don't really do anything for my birthday. I kind of ... that's why I didn't tell you about it. Because it's not a big deal. It's just another day." No doubt noticing Audrey's bewilderment, Bobby quickly added, "But I'd love to go out with you this Saturday. We can go to the Met, make a day of it."

"I've never been."

"What? You can't be living here in New York, one of the cultural capitals of the world, and not visit the Met. I'll be your guide."

"Sounds like fun." Audrey paused, looking up into his eyes, straining to find the twinkle she so adored. "You'd tell me if something was wrong, wouldn't you, Gatsby?"

Ever since Bobby had told her that *The Great Gatsby* was his favorite book, she'd taken to using Gatsby as an affectionate pet name. At first, Bobby had jokingly expressed indignation, asking Audrey if she thought he was as desperate and clingy as the titular character, but she had assured him she just thought it was a nice homage to the book he loved more than any other.

"Aud." Bobby took her hands in his, absently stroking them. "I'm fine. It's just ... my birthday has always been kind of a rough time."

"Why?"

Bobby heaved a deep breath. "I just ... I kind of like to forget about it."

"I understand," Audrey said, though she didn't.

Audrey had always loved celebrating birthdays, both her own and others'. She wondered if Bobby's dislike for his birthday had to do with his mother no longer being around. She knew his mother had died in November; maybe she'd died close to his birthday, and he now associated the whole day with her. Though Bobby said he hadn't been close with his mother, he doubtless still missed her and wished she could be there to celebrate with him and his father.

"Thank you." Bobby brought her hands to his lips. "I know it's kind of weird, but ... that's just how I feel about it."

"No, it's okay. And I have to apologize in advance here, but ... since I didn't know about your birthday until yesterday, I didn't get you anything."

"I don't—"

"I know, I know. You say you don't need anything, but I still feel bad about it. I'm your girlfriend. I should get you something. Oh, wait! What's this?" Audrey opened up her backpack, pulled out an envelope, and handed it to him. "A birthday card, for the birthday boy!"

Bobby laughed. "You're so sweet." Audrey stared at him expectantly, and he asked, "You want me to open it now?"

"Yes!"

Chuckling, Bobby opened the envelope and removed the card. "Wow. Hand-made," he noted, delicately turning it over in his hands.

Audrey shrugged. "I'm pretty crafty."

"I didn't know that about you." As Bobby read the card's sentiments, his smile grew wider. "Thanks, Aud. This is ... this is really something."

For a moment, Audrey feared she had overstepped. Her fears were assuaged, however, when Bobby leaned down to kiss her forehead.

"I know the perfect place for it on my desk," he told her.

Audrey kissed him. "Happy Birthday, Bobby. I hope this year is the best one yet for you."

Bobby ran his fingers through her hair. "I have a feeling it will be."

The remainder of the week flew by, and at last, it was Saturday. Audrey rummaged through her closet, trying to find something suitable to wear to the

Met. She finally settled on a red sweater and faded blue jeans—a tried and true classic—and a light jacket. Bobby met her outside her apartment building, and she was surprised to see Felix's black car.

"I thought we were taking the subway," she said.

"Change in plans." Bobby held open the car door. "When I told Felix this would be your first time going to the Met, he insisted on driving us there in style."

"Oooo, fancy!" As Audrey slid into her seat, she told Felix, "This is much better than the subway. Thanks!"

Felix chuckled. "That's what I thought too. We should be there soon. Just sit back and relax."

During the drive, Bobby reflected on the first time he'd visited the Met. Charles had taken him when he was around six years old to see the *Harlem on My Mind* exhibit. A Harlem native, Charles was delighted to see his community celebrated in a world-class museum. He was aware the press—and prominent Black leaders—had criticized the exhibition, but he wanted to see it for himself, to form his own opinion.

"And yeah, like them, he was disappointed," Bobby mused. "He said it didn't capture the heart of Harlem, didn't showcase Black artists. He took me to his old neighborhood a few weeks later, to show me what it's actually like." He looked out the window, at the blurry landscape. "I guess that's the thing about museums," Bobby went on, more to himself than to Audrey. "They don't tell the whole story. They give you a place to start, but their view on the world ... it's so ... limited. Charles has always encouraged me to question my surroundings, to figure out for myself what's true and what's ... curated."

"That's a lot for a six-year-old to be thinking about," Audrey joked.

Bobby laughed. "Well, I guess I've thought a lot about it over the years. Don't get me wrong; I still love museums, but I see them a little differently these days." He took her hand in his. "And today, I'll get to see it through your eyes."

But he was wrong. It became evident to Audrey, upon entering the Met, that she would be seeing the museum through *his* eyes. Bobby's head whipped around; no doubt, he was noticing even the slightest changes since his last visit.

After placing his generous admission donation in the bin, Bobby stood immobile, unable to decide which wing to explore first. All directions, it seemed, equally enticed him.

"Where would you like to go first?" Bobby asked, bouncing on the balls of his feet. "What interests you the most?"

Audrey studied the directory, immediately overwhelmed by the sheer size of the place. "Oh, I love Ancient Egypt!"

"This way."

Audrey thought they would stick together, look at the pieces side by side, but she quickly learned she and Bobby had very different viewing strategies. Audrey was more of a fan of briskly walking through the galleries and stopping only when something really stuck out to her. Bobby, on the other hand, was compelled to give each piece of artwork his full, undivided attention, and he moved at a snail's pace. As a result, they didn't stay together for long. Nevertheless, at times, Audrey swore she could feel Bobby's eyes on the back of her head. She tried to brush it off, but she had a sinking feeling he was judging her for awarding a mere cursory glance at pieces he adored. Realizing how out of her element she truly was, she looked over her shoulder, to see what Bobby was doing. Bobby stopped at each piece, first studying it before reading the plaque, then regarding the art with fresh eyes. At one point, he turned to her, offering a warm smile, which Audrey returned.

"What do you think?" he whispered as he approached her.

"It's incredible. I had a whole Ancient Egypt phase when I was a kid, reading every book I could about it."

"We'll have to come back next month, then, when *Treasures of Tutankhamun* finally arrives."

Throughout the afternoon, Bobby explained the story behind some of his favorite pieces. He possessed a striking knowledge of the artists, their backstories, and the meaning behind their work. At last, they made their way to his favorite wing—Modern and Contemporary Art.

"I'm a big fan of abstract expressionism," Bobby informed Audrey, his demeanor reminiscent of a child on Christmas Day. "The reconciliation of man's darkest tendencies with his innate vulnerability ... the need to make sense of the world post-World War II ... it's all so beautifully tragic. And I see that struggle in their work, the mixture of rationality and irrationality. How do we heal ourselves from the wounds of two massive wars? How do we even begin to rebuild? I often think of how ..."

Though Bobby's understanding of abstract expressionism soared far above and beyond Audrey's head, she was enthralled by him. It was highly attractive, seeing how passionate he was about art; he was talking more quickly, using his hands more expressively, regaling her with information about important artists of the movement. Audrey, for her part, wasn't aware of the intricacies of each artistic school; rather, she was drawn to art that aesthetically appealed to her. She wasn't fond of searching for deeper meanings. To her, art was meant to be appreciated, not dissected. Still, she attentively listened as Bobby explained what abstract expressionism meant to him, all the while reveling in how happy he seemed. She hadn't seen him light up like this in weeks. Even though he didn't like to celebrate the day, she hoped he'd had a good birthday—and that her card had cheered him up, even if only a little bit.

"Sorry," said Bobby after a few minutes, his cheeks flushed. "I must be boring you. I tend to get a bit carried away."

"Don't apologize. I love how passionate you get about things. And, for the record, I wasn't bored at all. I was fascinated. I don't know any of this stuff. But you do. You really love it here, huh?"

Bobby nodded. "I come here a lot on my own, but being with you ..." He brushed his shoulder against hers. "I'm really enjoying myself."

They spent another hour or two strolling the galleries before they left. Bobby had his heart set on taking Audrey to Garden of Sweets, one of his favorite dessert spots. Since it was a short walk from the Met to Garden of Sweets, Bobby told Felix to pick them up in an hour. Chilly from the walk, Audrey ordered a hot chocolate, while Bobby, for some inexplicable reason, opted for a hot fudge sundae instead.

"Are you crazy?" asked Audrey, pulling her jacket tighter. "It's freezing out there."

"What are you talking about? It's fifty degrees."

"That's cold!"

"That's *comfortable*."

As they waited for their desserts, they chatted about the afternoon. Already, they were making plans for their next visit—which wings they'd missed and wanted to see, upcoming exhibitions that had piqued their interest, artwork they couldn't wait to view again.

"December is always my favorite time to go to the Met," Bobby said. "I love the way it feels around Christmas."

Audrey's hands gripped her mug, desperate for its warmth. "Oh, speaking of Christmas ... what do you do for Christmas? Any family traditions?"

"No. Not any family traditions, per se. My father always spends Christmas abroad—somewhere warm and sunny. My mother did as well. And I've always been here."

Audrey's stomach dropped. "You spend Christmas ... alone?"

"Oh, no. No, I spend Christmas with Charles at his sister's apartment in Harlem. But it's just me for the week or so beforehand, then the week after—up until New Year's. But I love Christmas. It's my favorite time of year."

"That must be awfully lonely."

Bobby shrugged. "I actually prefer having the place to myself for a while. And my father ... well, he's not big on the holidays, so ... it all works out."

Audrey leaned forward. "I know it's a month and some change away, but ... how would you feel about spending Christmas Eve with my family this year?"

"I don't know, Aud. That ... I don't want to impose."

"It wouldn't be an imposition! I'll ask my parents, of course, but ... I'm sure they'll say yes. Besides, our fridge isn't big enough to store all the food Mom whips up. We could use an extra mouth."

Bobby plucked the cherry off his hot fudge sundae and dropped it onto his napkin, as though he were repulsed by it. He then dug his spoon into the sundae with such gusto that some of the whipped cream splattered.

"What's Christmas like for *your* family?" he asked, his nose adorably speckled with whipped cream.

Audrey mimed for Bobby to wipe the whipped cream off his nose, which he did. "Oh, it's magical," she explained. "Mom always makes a roast chicken for Christmas Eve. We each ... sorry, can I have your cherry?" she asked.

Bobby laughed, handing Audrey the cherry, still coated in delicious whipped cream. "All yours."

"Perfect. Thanks." Audrey happily swallowed the cherry in one bite, placing the stem next to her mug. "Anyway, where was I? Ah, yes! We each open one gift on Christmas Eve. We put on the TV and watch whatever Christmas movie comes on. And oooo! How could I forget? We play charades. Not sure how that got started, but we've been doing it for as long as I can remember. I don't want to brag, but my team—me and Dad—we usually win. And, most importantly, we do a lot of baking and eat tons of gingerbread and sugar cookies. So, as you can see, you'd be missing out."

Bobby drummed his fingers on the table. "How about this? You ask your parents first, and then we'll see."

"I'm telling you, they'll say yes. They love you. Unless, of course, this ... hesitancy is your way of telling me you don't like my family."

"No! Your family is so wonderful. And loving. I just ... how would Claire feel about me spending Christmas Eve with you all?"

"She'll be fine with it. We're a pretty easygoing bunch, the Nielsens."

Bobby laughed, despite himself. "Not exactly the word I'd use to describe you, but—"

"Hey! I can be easygoing!"

Bobby teasingly smirked. "I didn't mean it as an insult. You've got a fire to you. That's one of the things I like best about you." His eyes averted to his watch. "Oh. Felix will be here soon." Bobby stood up, extending his hand to Audrey. "Shall we?"

Audrey happily took his hand, interlacing her fingers with his. During the drive to the Village, Bobby assured her—after some gentle prodding—that he did, indeed, have a good birthday. It seemed that even though Bobby wasn't keen on celebrating his birthday, that hadn't stopped his family's staff from making his day as special as possible. Benoit had baked him a chocolate cake—his favorite—and Charles had gifted him a Babe Ruth baseball card.

"From his own collection!" Bobby gushed. "He's been a Yankees fan since he was a boy. Big-time collector. He's the one who got me into baseball, actually. And for him to give me one of his best cards, of both our favorite player ... it was incredible. He saw Babe Ruth play, you know. He has a signed baseball too. I've seen it. He keeps it under lock and key, obviously." Seeing Audrey's blank expression, Bobby chuckled, saying, "I'm sorry. I know you don't like baseball."

"That's true. But"—Audrey scooted closer to him and patted his leg—"I will be at all your baseball games, cheering you on. I'm sure you look all dashing in your uniform."

Bobby grinned. "I'll try to hit a couple home runs just for you."

Though Audrey was happy to see Bobby back to his usual self, he hadn't mentioned what his father had done to celebrate his birthday. A part of her wanted to ask, but the other part didn't want to bring up a topic that Bobby obviously had no interest in discussing. Besides, it was entirely likely his father had been out of town for Bobby's birthday; it seemed he was gone quite a lot, and since Bobby hadn't mentioned him, she decided not to say a word.

After arriving in the Village, Bobby and Audrey took a few laps around the block. Bobby remarked how excited he was for the upcoming winter.

"I love this time of year. I just love the snow," he enthused, his eyes glistening. "I'm hoping for a snowy Christmas."

"Snow for the holidays is always nice," agreed Audrey. "But once it's March, and everything's all gross and slushy ... then, it's not so pretty."

"Fair enough."

He slowed, then, his grip on Audrey's hand still firm. Concerned, Audrey turned to him.

"Is everything okay, Bobby?" she asked.

"Everything's great. Better than great, actually." Bobby met her eyes. "These past few months have been the best of my life. You're one of the only people I've ever known who doesn't think of me as Robert Damian Dempsey the Fourth. With you, I'm just Bobby. And ... I love that. And ... I mean, I ... well, I, uh ..." He trailed off, swallowing hard. "What I'm trying to say is, I—"

Audrey quickly draped her arms around his neck, pulling him in for a passionate kiss. "I love you, Bobby," she said breathlessly.

He stared at her, blinking rapidly. It took him a few moments to process what she had just said, but once he did, he broke out in a boyish grin.

"I love you too," he said, kissing her again.

There was a new spring in their steps as Bobby walked Audrey to the front stoop of her apartment building. Audrey felt strangely adult, being in love. She'd heard dozens of songs and seen countless movies about the subject, but she'd never truly imagined what it would feel like to *be* in love. It was every bit as intoxicating and thrilling as she'd been told. In just a few months, Bobby had become one of the most important people in her life. Already, she had a difficult time envisioning what life would be like without him.

"Good night, Aud," he said, reluctantly releasing her hand.

"Good night, Bobby." Audrey gazed up into his eyes, dreamily wondering if someday, she and Bobby would no longer have to bid each other goodbye each night—if someday, they'd share a home, a life, a child.

Audrey knew others—her own parents included—would call her naive for claiming she'd met the love of her life at the impressionable age of fifteen, but she didn't care. Before, her conceptions of the future had been vague, undefined. But now, her future husband had a face and a name—both of which were Bobby's. The simple thought of someday not being with him, of them one day falling out of love with each other, was enough to send Audrey reeling. She couldn't imagine looking into his eyes and feeling something other than passion and love; she couldn't imagine feeling anything other than safe, treasured, and content in his arms.

"I love you," he said again, his forehead pressed against hers.

And, most of all, Audrey couldn't imagine responding to those three words with anything other than:

"I love you too."

CHAPTER 12

Bobby

THE DAGENHARTS

F OR AS LONG AS Bobby could remember, he and Sebastian had been best friends. Even though Sebastian was almost three years older than Bobby, that had never stopped them from being close. Indeed, Bobby had always gravitated toward people who were older than he was. He partly blamed this on his parents, who'd enrolled him in preschool as soon as he was eligible. Consequently, Bobby had always been one of the youngest students of his year, and to fit in, he'd had to mature a little faster than he was perhaps ready for. It had all worked out for the best; Bobby was well on track to be the valedictorian of his class, and Columbia was within reach.

Sebastian's father, Darius Dagenhart, worked in finance, and he'd made quite the name and fortune for himself, as evidenced by the Dagenhart family's impressive Park Avenue apartment and Montauk mansion. Darius and Robert were both admired in their respective fields, and because they didn't work in the same industry, there wasn't a sense of competition between the two men. Thus, their friendship had always been easy, natural, steady.

At least once a month, all the Dagenharts—including the children who'd since moved out and started their own adult lives—ate dinner at the family's apartment together. Sebastian and his five older siblings—Edward, Sybil, Lillian, Dean, and Grant—weren't blood-related; they had all been adopted. Bobby, of course, knew it must have been a difficult thing for Sebastian and his siblings to come to terms with, but he wasn't exactly sure why Sebastian had been so bothered by it; at least Sebastian could content himself by knowing his parents had chosen him, wanted him. The only reason Bobby existed was so his father could have an heir. He would have much preferred to know his parents had gone out of their way to provide him with a loving, happy home.

"It's just hard, that's all," Sebastian had explained to Bobby a few years ago, at the height of his identity crisis. "It makes me feel like I ... well, like I don't deserve what I have, like I should be—was *meant* to be—somewhere else. Some*one* else."

Bobby could empathize with Sebastian's dilemma, as he'd also struggled greatly with his place, his purpose. He knew what he was supposed to do—carry on his father's legacy and eventually take control of Dempsey Corp—but it wasn't the future he dreamed about. In truth, Bobby envied Sebastian's freedom; his father had never tried to shoehorn his children into a certain career path. Looking at the Dagenharts, Bobby saw everything he wanted for his future family.

Eventually, Sebastian accepted his place in the family, and he managed to walk the fine line between confident and cocky. All the Dagenharts possessed a sharp wit; it was never a dinner with them unless there was a lively debate of some sort. Tonight, they were all under the same roof once again, and the hot-button issue was whether zoos should be outlawed.

Sybil, forever the animal rights activist, insisted that zoos inhibited animals' autonomy, stole them from their natural habitats. Dean, on the other hand, argued that zoos helped educate the masses about the importance of conservation. They went back and forth, as they always did, with everyone chiming in with their thoughts on the matter. Sebastian sided with Sybil, noting how psychologically damaging it was for animals to be forced to live in an artificial, human-controlled environment.

"And you, Bobby?" asked Eugenia, the matriarch of the family. "What do you think?"

All eyes immediately focused on Bobby. He had known this was coming, so he'd been mentally preparing his talking points. Up until now, he hadn't been able to get a word in edgewise.

"I think both sides have merit," Bobby began, "but, if I had to choose one, I guess ... well, we'll never get rid of zoos, will we? So, I guess we should do everything we can to make sure the zoos we do have are, you know, ethically sound."

"Ever the diplomat," Sebastian laughed.

"He makes a good point, though." Darius nodded at Bobby. "Just for that, you'll get first dibs on dessert."

After dessert, Bobby and Sebastian retreated to Sebastian's room. Now that he was the only Dagenhart child still living at home, Sebastian had the largest bedroom—after the master, of course. He was grateful for the extra space—before, he and Grant had shared a room—and he immediately put his own mark on the place, decorating it with Yankees memorabilia and *M*A*S*H* posters.

"I have to say, Bobby, it's nice to see you." Sebastian sat down on the bay window bench. "Weirdly enough, I've been seeing Audrey more than I've seen you. Every Wednesday, it's like she's a glutton for punishment, sitting there as my team crushes hers in The Great Debaters. But you ... you've been a ghost."

Bobby laughed, his hands in his pockets. "Sorry. I guess I just ... I've been spending lots of time with Aud."

"Me too. Didn't you hear what I just said?"

Bobby laughed again. "You know what I mean."

"Yeah, I know." Sebastian smiled. "You really like her, huh?"

"More than that." Bobby sat down next to Sebastian, drawing a deep breath. "We said we love each other."

Sebastian let out a low whistle. "Sorry, that's just ..." He chuckled, shaking his head. "... it's hard to believe there's a girl out there who, you know, would actually say that, be interested in you."

Bobby knew Sebastian was joking, that he didn't mean it, but he had inadvertently hit upon one of Bobby's main insecurities. Bobby had always been stunned by—and, quite frankly, jealous of—the open, affectionate relationship Sebastian had with his family. They would say they loved each other all the time, without any prodding or difficulty. It came naturally to them, instinctually, like breathing.

But Bobby's parents ... they'd never said that word to each other, let alone to their own son. When he was younger, Bobby had told his parents he loved them, desperate for that connection, but they never responded; instead, they simply stared at him, as though he'd just announced his intention to join a traveling circus. After a while, Bobby had stopped trying; their silence had pained him more than any critique they'd ever fired his way, any insult, any lecture. At least when they were yelling at him, they were *seeing* him, *noticing* him, *acknowledging* him. At least then, he wasn't invisible.

Neither Robert nor Margaret had ever been comfortable with emotional displays, be they private or public. Bobby could count on one hand the number of times he'd ever heard his mother laugh, the number of times he'd ever seen his parents touch. Their emotional reticence should have made them perfect for each other. And yet, for some reason, there had always been a distance between them, a simmering resentment, an unspoken rancor. When he was younger, Bobby had assumed he was the one who had created that chasm. Surely, his parents must have been happy once, and if they'd never been happy with him around, then he must have been the reason why—the one responsible for their quiet dinners, separate bedrooms, and endless string of lovers. As he aged, however, Bobby realized their marriage had simply been one of convenience, a union of the massive Dempsey and Du Pont fortunes. It was likely they'd never cared for each other at all—not even platonically.

Charles and the rest of the staff had never seen this side of his parents—or if they had, they most assuredly wouldn't have dared to comment on it. Still, even though they were all on his parents' payroll, they had always gone out of their way to make Bobby feel appreciated. Notably, though, none of them—not even Charles—had ever said they loved him. Bobby didn't hold this against them; it would've been odd—inappropriate, even—for any of them to say such things to their employers' son.

Audrey was thus the one who ended the fifteen-year-long drought, the first person to tell Bobby she loved him. And when she said it ... she hadn't hesitated at all. With those four glorious words—"I love you, Bobby"—she had changed Bobby's world, proved he wasn't as unlovable as he'd been made to believe.

"I know," Bobby said, hoping his tone was as lighthearted as he'd intended. "I really ... I'm acutely aware of just how lucky I am to be with her."

Besides being the most beautiful woman he'd ever seen, Audrey was also exceptionally vivacious. She made everything fun—even mundane activities like waiting in line at the movie theater. And her laugh ... that had to be one of Bobby's favorite sounds in the world. He loved her energy, her zest for life, her quick wit. And she loved him for *him*, for all his idiosyncrasies, all the things he'd tried to mediate or change. She loved how meticulous he was about his appearance, how he never wore a crinkled shirt or creased pants. She didn't think he was pretentious for liking art and literature, and she didn't think he was merely showing off by using big words. With her, he could just be himself, and he'd never felt so safe and accepted.

"You know, I don't think I've ever seen you this happy before," Sebastian noted.

Sebastian was someone Bobby could intrinsically trust—he had been Bobby's primary confidante since they were boys—but Bobby still didn't feel comfortable waxing lyrical about his and Audrey's relationship. He wasn't sure why that was, exactly—self-consciousness, fear, introversion, maybe something else entirely—but he wasn't about to tell Sebastian how alive he felt when he was around Audrey, how much he missed her when they were apart, how often he fantasized about what their life could be like together.

"I don't think I've ever *been* this happy," Bobby admitted. "I really ... look, I know she's my first girlfriend and all, but ... she's special."

Sebastian patted Bobby on the back. "I have to say, it's nice seeing you so ... well, let's just say, I would've thought you'd have tried to talk yourself out of this by now—you know, being Mr. Logic and all."

"Maybe. But with Aud ... I don't want to do anything that might jeopardize what we have."

"Just don't overthink it."

"Oh, that's real helpful. Thanks, Seb."

"You know what I mean. You're always at your best when you're just yourself. And besides, you already got over the first hurdle. Her folks liked you, right?"

Bobby clenched his teeth. "I think they liked the son of Robert Dempsey more."

"Well, it was only the first time meeting them. I remember when I met Julie's parents for the first time, they asked me about *my* dad. Maybe it's just, you know, a way for them to try and figure you out—asking about your family, seeing where you come from, all that. Next time, it'll be more about you."

"I hope you're right."

"Aren't I always?" Sebastian asked, a spirited glint in his eyes.

"I guess. But didn't you and Julie break up a month later?"

"Semantics! Look, the point is, you and Audrey aren't like me and Julie. I'm sure it'll all work out for you."

Before Bobby could respond, they heard a knock on the door. It was Sybil, asking if they'd be interested in joining the rest of the family for a game of Monopoly. Apparently, the dinner debate hadn't satiated their competitiveness; they were eager to crush one another in a classic game of risk, rivalry, and reward.

Sebastian jumped up. "We'd love to! Come on, Bobby. Nothing gets the mind off prying parents like a good, friendly game of Monopoly."

Bobby laughed. "All right. Just don't get too upset when I beat you."

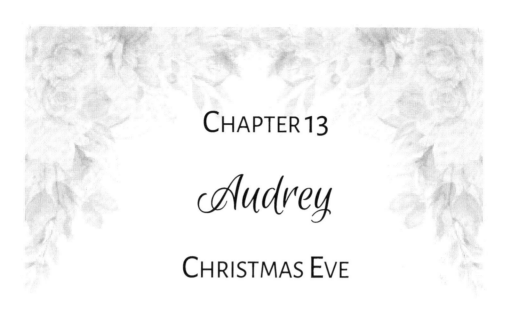

CHAPTER 13

Audrey

CHRISTMAS EVE

OVER THE NEXT COUPLE of weeks, Audrey found herself overwhelmed with final examinations that all her teachers wanted to fit in before Christmas Break. It seemed evil, putting this sort of pressure on students right before the longest break of the school year. Everyone was already mentally checked out for the rest of the calendar year, but because of these exams, they had to refocus and play the role of students for a little while longer. Audrey and Florie spent many afternoons together, preparing for their examinations, taking turns cursing out a different teacher.

"There has to be some kind of law against having a test in three different classes on the same day," Florie complained, hitting her head against her Geometry textbook.

Audrey nodded, all the numbers on the page blurring together. "But just think, come Friday, we'll be free for a couple weeks. So, the end is in sight."

"Sure. But do you actually understand Geometry? Because ... I really don't know what the point of a proof is."

"No idea. I think we're just trying to ... prove things."

"But *what*? And *why*?"

"You can't think about it, Florie. You just have to do it."

Florie scrunched her nose. "You sound like Mr. Keller."

Audrey made a face. "How dare you."

Florie laughed, raising her hands in mock surrender. "Sorry. I take it back." She momentarily stared at her textbook before closing it, heaving a deep sigh. "Friday can't come soon enough. That's for sure."

"Excited for Christmas?"

"We're going Upstate, spending it with Grammy. She has this cozy house in the Adirondacks. Great hills for sledding." Florie leaned back against Audrey's bed. "What's it like having Claire back in the apartment?"

Audrey placed her pen down. "She's been trying to get Mom and Dad to start the SlimFast diet."

"Why on Earth would she do that?"

Audrey shrugged. "Apparently, she thinks we need to cut back on things. Like food—and happiness."

Alexander knocked on the door. "Hey, girls. Sorry to interrupt, but it's getting close to six. Florie, I thought I'd walk you to the station. Whenever you're ready."

"Thanks, Mr. Nielsen." Florie started packing up. "Well, come Monday, it'll be our trial through fire."

Luckily, the last week of classes before break passed quickly. The days were monotonous, filled with exams and pointless busywork. Audrey knew it wasn't her teachers' fault; if they had it their way, they would have stopped classes a week ago and thrown a big party for the holidays, but they were forced to keep the students "engaged" and "working." As soon as she finished her last exam, it was like a huge weight had been lifted off Audrey's shoulders. She was finally free. Florie, Audrey knew, was heading Upstate immediately after classes ended on Friday. Audrey made sure to say goodbye to her before she left.

"How do you think you did on the exams?" Audrey asked.

"You know what? Not too bad, actually." Florie grinned. "Well, have a great Christmas, Audrey! See you next year!"

Like the rebel she wasn't, after Audrey returned home, she immediately conked out on the couch, with *Match Game* on in the background. When she came to, Claire was home. Her semester had ended a few weeks ago, but she'd been spending most of her time out and about with her friends, rubbing it in Audrey's face that she had endless leisure time. Audrey didn't mind, actually; the less time she had to spend with Claire, the better.

Audrey asked her parents if Bobby could spend Christmas Eve with them, and they readily agreed, as she knew they would. Even Claire seemed interested in getting to know Bobby—and no doubt passing judgment on his and Audrey's relationship. But Audrey was just happy that Bobby would get to spend Christmas Eve with her family.

Christmas Eve was every bit as magical as it always was. Bobby was due to arrive in the early afternoon, and Audrey waited outside, wanting to secure a few private moments with him. She saw him approach, wearing a handsome black trench coat that he left unzipped in the unseasonably warmer weather. Underneath, he donned a red sweater over a white dress shirt, with a black tie, slacks, and dress shoes. Outside of cross-country practice, she'd never once seen him in a shirt without a collar, and he never wore jeans or sneakers. She assumed his closet was akin to the Scooby-Doo characters—multiples of the same sort of outfit. In his left hand, he was holding a shopping bag.

"Bobby!" Audrey greeted, running toward him. "You're here!" She pulled him in for a kiss. "Merry. Christmas," she said in between kisses.

"Merry Christmas, Aud!" Bobby grinned, kissing her again. "I've missed you."

"I've missed you too." Audrey gestured to the bag Bobby had placed on the ground. "What's that?"

"Christmas gifts for your family."

Audrey put her hands on her hips. "Bobby."

"No, I know, you said not to get anything. I swear, I didn't go overboard. Just one gift for everyone."

"That's still too much! But I guess I can't do anything about that now."

Bobby looked up at the sky. "It's too warm," he said, his brows furrowed. "Call me traditional, but it's hard to be in the Christmas spirit without snow. We got rain but no snow."

"Well, I can't make it snow, but I know we've got lots of fun things for you upstairs, so ... follow me!"

For the next few hours, Bobby was treated to a Nielsen family Christmas. He helped them finish decorating the tree, joined in on the baking fun, enjoyed Sophia's legendary roast chicken, and watched *The Nutcracker*. Throughout the day, Audrey was pleasantly surprised to see Claire making a real effort to include and get to know Bobby. Audrey knew she had been unhappy at the prospect of a practical stranger spending Christmas Eve with them, but she appreciated how Claire didn't make Bobby feel like an outsider. As was tradition, each family member opened one gift before calling it a night.

"Thank you so much for letting me celebrate Christmas Eve with you all," Bobby said to Sophia and Alexander.

"Of course, Bobby!" said Alexander. "We were happy to have you! As we said earlier, you're more than welcome to crash on the couch if you want."

"Thank you, but I'll head back home."

"If you insist." Alexander kissed Audrey on the top of her head. "Don't stay up too late, love, or Santa won't come."

"Okay, Dad," laughed Audrey.

Bobby and Audrey sat in the living room, in front of the dying fire. Claire was already going about her nighttime routine, darting between the bedroom and the bathroom, taking care to avoid Bobby and Audrey. Audrey had to admit, Claire had been a great sport all day. Maybe Sophia had spiked her eggnog with an extra dose of Christmas spirit.

Bobby pulled her closer. "You know, I was kind of hoping you'd open the gift I got for you right now."

"Right now?"

"I know it's breaking the rules, opening more than one gift on Christmas Eve, but ... I want to be here when you open it." Bobby dug around in the shopping bag for her gift. "Here you are," he said, handing her a small black box.

Audrey opened the box, and inside was a gorgeous rose-gold necklace. She blinked rapidly, struggling to take it in. She'd seen necklaces like this in Fifth Avenue storefronts, but she could scarcely believe she was now holding one in her hands—and that it was hers.

"Oh, Bobby." Audrey looked up at him, wide-eyed. "I mean, it's beautiful, absolutely beautiful, but … it must have been so expensive."

"Don't worry about the price, Aud. I thought of you as soon as I saw it."

"And really, that's so sweet of you. But … I don't want you to think … these aren't the sorts of gifts I expect from you, you know."

"I know." He smiled. "That's kind of why I got it—to surprise you, give you something special. Would you, um … maybe like to try it on, see how it fits?"

He looked so hopeful she couldn't say no. "Of course. Thank you." She pulled her hair to the side and turned so Bobby could fasten the necklace behind her. "Well?" she asked, facing him. "How does it look?"

"Beautiful." He beamed.

Audrey kissed his cheek. "Well, since I opened your gift, you should open mine."

"That's fair." Bobby watched with anticipation as Audrey handed him his present. "Let's see …" He opened it, unveiling a picture collage.

"I've been working on it for weeks," Audrey explained. "Your room is so … well, boring … and I wanted to give you something to brighten it up. I've been going through old newspapers and magazines, looking for things that remind me of us. See, the Met, over here, and Zabar's … Great Gray. And then, of course, these adorable pictures of us."

"I love how crafty you are." He kissed her. "Thank you. Not only for this but for asking me to spend Christmas Eve with you and your family. I really … I had the best day." He noticed the clock on the mantel, sighing knowingly. "But I should be heading back."

After Audrey walked Bobby out, she returned to the apartment, quickly going about her nighttime routine. As soon as her head hit the pillow, Audrey was overcome with exhaustion; her eyes drooped, and she found herself being slowly lulled into—

"Did he leave?" asked Claire.

Audrey's eyes opened, adjusting to the dark. "Yes, he's gone."

"Huh. Well, I have to say, Audie, he was ... different than I thought he'd be."

"Different how?" asked Audrey, turning on the light, much to Claire's chagrin.

"Dunno. Just ... different. He seems really nice."

Audrey didn't even try to mask her incredulity. Was Claire actually complimenting her boyfriend? She did a double take, to make sure she was, in fact, in the right bedroom—with her actual sister.

"I have to say, Claire, I'm surprised. I thought you'd be telling me how I should enjoy it while it lasts, how all young love is doomed to fail."

Claire laughed, despite herself. "I guess I thought I'd be saying that too, but ... you two look good together—happy." She cleared her throat. "But just so you know, if that boy breaks your heart, he'll have to answer to me."

"I'd expect nothing less." Audrey hugged Claire. "Merry Christmas, Claire."

"Merry Christmas, Audie. Now, turn off that light! I need my sleep."

Audrey wasn't sure how long Claire's supportiveness would last—Claire was known to change moods on a dime—but Audrey couldn't concern herself with that right now. All that mattered was her parents—and now Claire—approved of Bobby. Her parents hadn't been difficult to convince; before they'd even met him, they'd been adamant this relationship would work out.

Audrey could hardly believe how natural everything with Bobby felt, how right. He fit in with her family so well; he chatted with her father about New York's hidden gems, helped her mother by offering to plate all the various appetizers, talked to Claire about their favorite authors and books. She could see them doing this, year after year.

As she climbed into bed, Audrey once again looked at her necklace. She already knew she'd never be taking it off—not as long as she and Bobby were together. She loved how elegant it was, how adult; it was a tangible symbol of their relationship, proof of Bobby's love. Now, every time she touched the necklace, she would think of Bobby, of the way his eyes had lit up after he'd fastened it around her neck.

She wasn't sure how 1979 could even begin to top this year. She had such a good group of friends, and she'd fallen in love with the boy of her dreams. In just a few months, her entire worldview had shifted—for the better. She was the happiest she'd ever been, and although it would be difficult to say goodbye to such a wonderful, momentous year, she had a gut feeling that 1979 would be the best one yet.

CHAPTER 14

Bobby

MISS LORETTA ABERNATHY

B EFORE BOBBY KNEW IT, the holiday break was over, and they were back at school, about to start the spring semester. The first week back was always a bit of a culture shock. It was difficult, trying to reacclimate to classes, homework, and after-school activities. Bobby had gotten used to having some downtime, catching up on reading and getting some writing done. Though he loved school, he knew it would be increasingly challenging to find time to write for fun. But he'd manage to fit it in; he always did.

To their credit, the teachers tried their best to corral the rowdy students, who were all gushing about their vacations and Christmas presents. When asked about his Christmas, Bobby played coy, not wanting people to know he'd spent Christmas Eve with Audrey's family. He and Audrey had agreed beforehand that they would keep it to themselves, as they didn't particularly feel like adding any more grist to the Great Gray rumor mill. People talked about them enough as it was; they didn't want to invite their classmates into something they had no business being a part of.

That Friday, after school, Bobby and Audrey met up at a café near Great Gray, and they properly caught up. They'd seen each other here and there throughout the week, but they had both been busy with their various extracurricular commitments, so they hadn't had a chance to exchange more than just a few sentences. Bobby wanted to sit down with Audrey and tell her something—something he had learned about only a couple of days ago.

"You look like there's something on your mind," Audrey said as she stirred some cream into her coffee.

Bobby hadn't even said a word, but already, she knew he had something he wanted to get off his chest. Sometimes, Audrey could surprise him with just how intuitive she was. Perhaps Bobby wasn't as unreadable as he liked to believe he was.

He heaved a deep breath. "My father ... he ... well, he met someone. I guess that's where he went for Christmas—to see her—and ... I'm supposed to meet her tomorrow night."

"Oh." Audrey nodded slowly. "So, it's ... serious, then."

"My father doesn't date. If he's introducing her to me, that means he's going to marry her."

"Marry her? Isn't it a bit fast for something like that?"

Bobby shrugged. "You would think, but ... my father seems to think they're compatible."

"How can he know that? He hardly even knows her!"

"Financially compatible." Bobby smiled wryly. "I don't know much about her, but ... I know she's wealthy—and a widow. So, they have that in common."

Audrey leaned forward. "And how do you feel about that?"

"About ...?"

"About your father dating again. Or ... I guess ... marrying someone else."

Bobby sipped his tea. "It's not like it'll change anything. I'm sure she and I will hardly ever speak."

Audrey reached out, touching Bobby's hand. "You never know. Maybe she'll want a relationship with you. And ... maybe she'll make your dad happy."

Bobby laughed, despite himself. "It's not like this is some magical love story, Aud. They compared assets and realized they were a good fit. It's not a love match but a financial arrangement."

"That sounds—"

"Horrible? Cold? Impersonal?" Bobby sighed. "It's just how it is for people like my father. That's certainly how it was with him and my mother."

He hoped he didn't sound as bitter as he felt. Neither of his parents had tried to hide their affairs from each other—or Bobby. More than a handful of times, Bobby had seen his parents with other people. He knew this should have upset him—that he should've been angry his parents were cheating on each other—but instead, all their indiscretions had made him realize what he didn't want in a relationship. When Bobby married, it wouldn't be for money or social capital. On the contrary, he would marry because he was blissfully in love with a woman who made him happy.

Audrey met his eyes. "Still. This could be different. I mean, your dad already has enough money to found his own country. It's not like he needs more. So, maybe this *is* about love for him."

"Maybe," Bobby said, trying to sound as optimistic as she did. He cleared his throat. "I'll be sure to let you know how it goes."

THE NEXT EVENING, BOBBY stood in front of his mirror, trying to decide which tie to wear. Then, rather unceremoniously, his bedroom door opened, and in his peripheral vision, he saw his father, one hand still on the doorknob. It was rare for Robert to cross the threshold into Bobby's bedroom, but whenever he did, he didn't knock. Instead, Robert liked to remind Bobby this was *his* house, and Bobby was but a guest. There was no privacy, no place Bobby could go to ever truly be unreachable.

Robert didn't say a word. He walked deeper into the room, then stood behind Bobby. When they were next to each other, it was clear how little resemblance there was between the two. Robert had, of course, named Bobby after him, hoping he'd follow in his footsteps, just as Robert had followed in his father's footsteps, but Bobby had been a letdown from his birth. Physically, Bobby heavily favored his mother, which Bobby considered a blessing, given his father's sharp, angular features. The only physical characteristic Bobby shared with his father, other than his height, was his aquiline nose—something Bobby used to be insecure about until Audrey told him how cute she thought it was.

Robert watched as Bobby entertained a couple of different ties. He'd never understood Bobby's love for fashion, his attention to detail. Robert's suits came in one of two colors—brown or tan—and his dress shirts were all the same bland shade of white. His ties were just as boring: either solid black or solid brown. Bobby would have loved to go shopping with his father, to liven up his wardrobe, but Robert was nothing if not impervious to change.

"I don't need to remind you how important tonight is," Robert said at last.

"I know." Bobby met his father's eyes in the mirror.

Robert glanced at the ties in Bobby's hands. "You're not seriously considering that blue one, are you?"

Bobby looked down at the tie in question. "Aud helped me pick it out."

"You're still seeing her?"

"Yes."

Robert scoffed but decided not to give his opinion on the matter. Bobby knew his father didn't approve of Audrey. Though he'd put on a wonderful show for her a couple of months ago, making her think he was fine with her spending time with his son, Bobby knew better. Robert had done his research on Audrey, and he'd been dismayed to learn her pedigree wasn't up to his superficial standards. Consequently, for the past few months, Robert had been unsubtly trying to push Bobby toward Cassandra, reminding him how much better it would look for a Dempsey to be seen with an Irvine.

"Her father and I are quite close, you know," Robert had told Bobby, trying but failing to sound unrehearsed. "And we happen to think it'd be a good match."

"And you're welcome to think that," Bobby had replied. "But I have no interest in Cassandra. I'm very happy with Aud."

Though displeased with Bobby's answer, Robert had, mercifully, dropped the subject. Bobby, however, knew his father wasn't done—not by a long shot. Most likely, Robert assumed Bobby's and Audrey's relationship would implode all on its own, without any outside help or intervention. Then, Robert would once again bring up Cassandra and all but force Bobby to be with her. But that day would never come. Even if Bobby and Audrey were to break up, Bobby would never want to be with someone he had no interest in.

"Wear the black one." Robert looked down at his watch. "She'll be here in ten minutes, so make sure you're downstairs before then."

After Robert left, Bobby tossed the black tie onto his bed and chose the blue one. Subsequently, he made his way downstairs, mentally preparing himself for the painful small talk that would ensue. No doubt, this woman—whoever she was—would briefly pretend to be interested in Bobby's life, to try on the role of a stepmother, then, of course, inevitably, she and Robert would enter their own world of conversation, completely excluding Bobby and making him wish he had just stayed in his room.

When Bobby entered the foyer, he saw Charles standing at the front door. Charles was wearing one of his best tuxedos; clearly, he wanted to make a good impression on the woman who would, in all likelihood, become the new lady of the house, the new Mrs. Robert Dempsey.

"Bobby!" Charles said. "Don't you look dashing?"

"Thanks, Charles. Where should I be?"

"Your father's already in the drawing room, so you can meet him in there."

Bobby nodded, then headed down the hallway, his heart thudding in his chest. As he neared the drawing room, a million thoughts ran through his mind. Maybe he should have worn the black tie after all. He didn't want to incur Robert's wrath unnecessarily, tonight of all nights. Maybe he still had time to—

"She's here!" Bobby heard Charles call out.

Bobby froze in the hallway. Should he go into the drawing room and wait there, or should he go back to the foyer to greet this woman? Just then, Robert came out of the drawing room, running his fingers through his hair. For once in his life, Robert actually looked nervous. Perhaps this woman meant more to him than Bobby had thought. In fact, Robert was so on edge he almost ran into Bobby in the hallway.

"What are you doing?" Robert asked. "She's here."

Bobby was grateful Robert hadn't noticed his silent rebellion—or if he had, he'd chosen not to mention it. Silently, Bobby followed his father back into the foyer. Charles opened the door, and a woman entered, along with a person who Bobby assumed was her personal assistant.

Bobby hoped his shock wasn't plastered all over his face. She was far more glamorous than he had anticipated; indeed, she looked more like an actress than a widowed socialite. Bobby couldn't help but think that she, just like his mother had been, was far out of his father's league, with her perfectly manicured bob, impeccable fashion sense, and confident air. Bobby wouldn't have been at all surprised to learn she was related to Diahann Carroll; both women shared the same timeless elegance and beauty. It was obvious she'd be a real asset to his father; with her on his arm, he'd make a statement—one New York society wouldn't be able to ignore.

"Loretta." Robert stepped forward, greeting her with a kiss on the cheek. "So wonderful to see you."

"And you, Robert." She had a lovely Southern drawl. Her eyes fell on Bobby. "And this is your son, I presume?"

"Yes. Bobby." Robert gestured toward Bobby.

Bobby reached out his hand. "It's a pleasure to meet you."

Loretta laughed. "Oh, no need for handshakes. That's far too formal." She pulled Bobby in for a hug. "My, you're a handsome boy."

"Yes, he takes after his mother, thankfully," Robert cut in.

Robert played it off as a joke, as he usually did, but Bobby knew how greatly it bothered his father, being reminded of his late wife every time he looked at Bobby. It wasn't that Robert missed Margaret; rather, he didn't like to think about the woman he hadn't loved, the woman he'd been forced to marry, whenever he was with his son.

With her hands on her hips, Loretta said, "Now, don't be selling yourself short. You're not so bad-looking yourself."

"You're too kind." Robert held out his arm for her. "Shall we?"

Bobby didn't quite know what to say—or do. He'd never seen his father act so playfully around a woman. With Margaret, he'd hardly ever cracked a smile, and as for his lovers ... Robert had treated them more like business associates. Maybe Audrey was right; maybe this *was* a love match.

"Bobby." Robert's voice broke Bobby out of his thoughts. "We'll have drinks and chat a bit more in the drawing room before dinner."

Bobby found his voice. "Right. Of course."

"Drinks?" Loretta's eyes glinted. "Is he old enough for that?"

Robert chuckled. "He'll have sparkling cider."

Bobby followed them, watching as Robert and Loretta laughed about something Bobby didn't understand. They already had inside jokes, it seemed. Maybe they'd been courting each other for far longer than he'd assumed. Bobby hadn't expected it to be this way. In truth, Bobby strained to remember whether he had ever witnessed even a single ounce of romantic chemistry between his parents. Their relationship had always been so detached, like they were nothing more than indifferent roommates sharing the same house.

Loretta, Bobby soon realized, was very different from Margaret. Margaret had been poised and reserved, and her face had never betrayed any sort of emotion—good or bad. She had been the ideal wife for someone like Robert Dempsey, able to stomach small talk, remember names, and host glitzy events with seeming ease. Margaret hadn't been gregarious, but she didn't need to be; she knew her role was to look graceful and support her husband. Loretta, on the other hand, wasn't so austere. Instead, Loretta was exceptionally charming, and everything she said oozed with warmth and sincerity. Her smiles weren't coerced; her mannerisms were relaxed. Bobby learned she was from Houston, and her deceased husband had been some big power player down there in oil. To be honest, most of that conversation had gone far above Bobby's head, but he took away the most important part: Loretta was now a very wealthy, powerful, and eligible woman. By marrying her, Robert would further shore up the family's future—and fortune.

"How long have you been in New York?" Bobby asked her.

"A little over four months now."

"And do you miss Houston?"

"Sometimes. But there are also things I don't miss. Summers down there were brutal, absolutely brutal."

Robert laughed. "Well, New York can get hot. But that's why we usually leave the city in the summer."

"And go where?"

"To the Hamptons."

"Oh, I've heard it's beautiful out there."

"It is. We have a house in Montauk, right on the ocean. Stunning views. You'll love it."

"Will I, now?"

"How could you not? Waking up and looking out at the Atlantic Ocean ... it's heaven on Earth."

Vaguely, Bobby wondered how many times they had met before. They seemed comfortable with each other, but there was obviously still so much they didn't know. Or perhaps this conversation was just a show, a way to make Bobby feel like he was actually important, like his opinion mattered. They chatted more about New York and its many wonders. Loretta had never tried a black-and-white cookie, but she promised she would, and she'd report back to them with her thoughts.

"There's just so much to take in," Loretta mused. "It must be overwhelming for y'all at times."

"I've lived here almost my whole life," Robert said. "I went to Harvard, but I always knew I'd come back to New York. To be honest, I can't see myself anywhere else."

"Well, I'm starting to see why."

They had dinner, and the conversation continued to flow. While Bobby ate dessert in the dining room, Robert and Loretta, full from the scrumptious dinner, returned to the drawing room to talk some more, just the two of them. As Bobby polished off his slice of vanilla cake, he thought about how lovely Loretta seemed. Maybe she was exactly what Robert needed. She seemed to bring out a more lighthearted side to him; around her, he wasn't so uptight. Bobby sincerely hoped his father wouldn't let her slip through his fingers.

After Loretta and her personal assistant left, Bobby met Robert in the drawing room. Bobby prayed he'd performed well, that he hadn't unintentionally embarrassed his father.

"I know you don't need my approval," Bobby started, gauging his father's mood, "but just so you know, I do approve of her."

"Hmmm." Robert casually examined his nail beds. "That certainly makes things easier."

He looked over at Bobby, his expression infuriatingly indiscernible. Bobby had always thought his father would have been a superb poker player, given his masterful ability to mask his emotions. Maybe that was just something people in his position learned to do, to prevent anyone from taking advantage of them. Bobby hoped that wouldn't be him someday, that his children wouldn't spend so much time trying to read him, trying to figure out what he was thinking or feeling.

Robert went on, "Loretta had nothing but glowing things to say about you, you know. And I ... well, I wanted to apologize."

Bobby had never heard his father say those words before. In truth, Bobby had been under the impression that his father was physically incapable of accepting fault—or issuing a legitimate apology. He'd always had an excuse for every curt word or insult. Long ago, Bobby had accepted he'd never hear his father admit any wrongdoing. But now, it seemed that Robert was metamorphosing before Bobby's very eyes.

"Apologize?" Bobby asked, his mouth agape. "For what?"

"For being so hard on you. You were wonderful with Loretta, and ... I just wanted you to know how much I appreciate it. I know it can't be easy for you, letting someone new in, and ... you could have tried to sabotage this, to make her question whether this is what she really wants."

"Why would I do that? I like Loretta. And I think she'll be a great addition to the family."

"So do I. That's why ... we'll be married by the summer. She's thinking June."

Bobby's eyes widened. "That soon?"

"It's been in the works for a while."

"Oh. So, you already proposed, then?"

"We discussed it a few weeks ago. She was curious to meet you, though, so here we are."

"What if she didn't like me?"

"I knew that wasn't a possibility."

Again, Bobby was baffled. His father was actually complimenting him? Had Bobby entered an alternate universe? Was this the real Robert, or was this someone else masquerading as his father? Maybe his father had an identical twin whom Bobby had never heard about or met—until now.

Robert placed his hand on Bobby's shoulder. "I want to make things right between us, Bobby. I know that you and I ... we haven't been as close as we should be. But Loretta ... she wants us to be a family. And I want that too."

"You do?"

"You're my son, my only son. And maybe it's too late to try and—"

"No, it's not too late. I want that too, sir."

Robert shook his head. "You shouldn't have to ... from now on, why don't you call me Dad?"

"Okay. Dad." The word felt foreign to Bobby's tongue, but it was a language he wished to become fluent in.

"Well, it's getting late. I should head up. Don't stay up too much longer."

"I won't. And Dad?" Bobby swallowed hard. "Thank you."

In response, Robert nodded, then disappeared down the hallway. Bobby stood there, his mind racing. It seemed Loretta had inspired Robert to change, evolve into a better man. Bobby couldn't wait to tell Audrey. She'd be beside herself—assuming, of course, she wouldn't first give him a look and say she'd told him so. Even if Audrey jokingly rubbed it in, reminding Bobby how cynical he had been about his father's and Loretta's relationship, Bobby knew she would, at the end of the day, be happy for him.

He finally had what he'd been craving for so long: a real family.

CHAPTER 15

Audrey

A LONG-AWAITED MEETING

T HOUGH AUDREY WASN'T USUALLY excited to watch Sunday meld into Monday, she was eager to hear what Bobby thought about his soon-to-be stepmom. They hadn't had a chance to talk all weekend, as they'd both been busy, but she knew Bobby would tell her all about it first thing Monday morning. And sure enough, as Bobby walked Audrey to her locker, he giddily gave her the rundown on what had happened. He'd been apprehensive at best about meeting Loretta, but clearly, she had won him over.

"She's incredible, Aud," Bobby gushed. "I really ... I feel like Loretta and my father ... they might actually be happy together."

"That's great, Bobby! I'm so happy to hear that!"

Bobby leaned against the neighboring locker as Audrey rifled through her textbooks and notebooks. "And my father ... he told me he wants us to be a real family—you know, actually doing things together, that sort of stuff. In fact, he's taking me and Loretta to see *The Kingfisher* this week. Can you believe that? I didn't even know my father liked Broadway."

"You've never done that sort of thing before?"

"No, never. He and I have never ... it's always been Charles who takes me out to shows on his days off. But I guess ... it seems like my father wants to change that."

"And how do you feel about that?"

"That's all I've ever wanted from him—for him to see me."

"I'm sure he's always seen you. It's just—"

"No, I know. He's got a lot going on. But he's promised to make me more of a priority. And ... I mean, I don't want to think too far ahead, but ... I've always wanted him to come to one of my games or ... or read one of my articles for the paper. And maybe ... maybe that'll be a real possibility."

Though Audrey was delighted to hear that everything had gone well with Loretta, it pained her to see how desperate Bobby was for a relationship with his father. She didn't know Robert at all, but she did know that he worked long hours and traveled a lot, which perhaps explained why he and Bobby didn't spend a lot of time together. Still, Audrey couldn't help but wonder why Robert hadn't tried to develop a closer bond with Bobby years ago. Why were things different now? Was it simply because of Loretta? Had she helped Robert see there was more to life than the office? Maybe because of her, he'd step back from Dempsey Corp and let someone else take the helm so he could be more involved in Bobby's life. Audrey knew that would make Bobby happy—so, of course, it would make her happy as well.

Bobby continued, "I'd like you to meet my father—properly, this time. And Loretta. Before they get married."

"When are they getting married?"

"June."

"That soon?"

"That's what I said too, but ... they seem keen on getting everything finalized as quickly as possible. And ... well, I was hoping you'd be my date to the wedding."

Audrey grinned. "I'd love that! I'll have to do some shopping, but ... I'd love to go with you."

Over the next few weeks, Bobby kept Audrey updated on how everything was going with his father and Loretta. They'd become much more of a family unit. At least a couple of times a week, they had dinner together, just the three of them, and Robert and Bobby continued showing Loretta around New York. Bobby would have been an excellent tour guide, as he seemed to know everything about anything in New York. He loved pointing out buildings to Audrey and telling her their histories. Audrey knew how much Bobby loved New York—he'd told her time and again how it was the only place he could ever see himself living—and through him, she'd grown fonder of the city as well. She wasn't sure if it was her forever home—she'd always pictured herself somewhere warm and sunny—but for the foreseeable future, she wanted to be where Bobby was.

It took a while, but finally, in the middle of February, Bobby and Audrey managed to find a date when Audrey would be able to come over and meet Robert and Loretta. Though she'd seen Robert a handful of times since their first meeting, it'd always been brief. Audrey was nervous about actually sitting down across from him. He was, after all, one of the most powerful men in the nation. If she embarrassed herself in front of him, she'd never be able to get over it; truly, it would haunt her for the rest of her life.

"You won't embarrass yourself," Bobby had assured her earlier at school. "They'll love you."

"Is there anything I should be aware of? Any conversations I should try and steer clear of?"

"As long as you don't say we should kill the rich, you'll be fine."

Audrey had told her parents she was going to meet Robert—officially, this time—and they offered her their full support, reminding her just how fabulous she was. They were biased, of course, seeing as they were her parents, but she was still grateful for their words of encouragement; unmistakably, they could tell how on edge she was, and they wanted her to feel as confident as possible.

Sophia in particular didn't miss a beat. Together, she and Audrey had gone shopping to find a dress that was both suitable for meeting American royalty and fiscally responsible. They managed to find one: a stunning blush-colored dress. As soon as Audrey saw it, she knew it was perfect for the occasion; indeed, it was almost as though the dress had been made just for her. Audrey hadn't been aware of just how good she looked in pink, as she'd usually opted for more earthen colors. She'd have to do some more shopping to correct this oversight.

"You look beautiful, sweets," Sophia commented as she helped Audrey zip up the back of her dress. "You'll knock 'em dead."

"Hopefully not literally. I want them to like me, you know."

Sophia chuckled. "If they have any sense at all, that won't be a problem."

Bobby seemed to second her mother's sentiments. He was standing outside his townhouse, awaiting her arrival. As usual, Bobby was dressed to the nines, wearing a handsome light-gray suit with a plum tie and matching pocket square. When he saw her, his eyes widened, and he ran up to her, picking her up and twirling her around.

"You are perfect," he told her after he kissed her. "Absolutely perfect."

"You don't look so bad yourself." Audrey smiled up at him, thankful she hadn't opted for lipstick, as it would've smeared all over his face. "I'm not late, am I?"

"No, not at all. You're right on time. Here. Come on. I'll walk you in."

It flattered Audrey, how proud Bobby was to have her on his arm. There were a few other couples at Great Gray who were challenging the class system. In those pairings, the more affluent student seemed almost humiliated to be seen with their less affluent partner, and as such, they chose to keep their relationship a secret—or as secret as a high school romance could be, given teenagers' propensity for gossip. Audrey was relieved Bobby had never been that way. Instead, he'd been more than willing to let everyone know, in no uncertain terms, that he and Audrey were an item.

"They're in the drawing room," Bobby explained as he led Audrey down one of the many hallways. Someday, maybe, Audrey would be able to figure out where she was in this labyrinth. "I just ... did I mention how beautiful you look?"

"You did. But I don't mind hearing it again."

A boyish smirk appeared on his face. "Okay. Here we are. Ready?"

"Ready! Wait." Audrey kissed his cheek. "Now, I'm ready."

When Audrey entered the drawing room, she saw Robert and Loretta standing by the fireplace, chatting away. There was a natural chemistry to them, as though they had known each other for years. They each had a glass of some kind of liquor in their hands—Audrey assumed red wine—and they seemed entirely absorbed in their conversation. Neither, it seemed, had noticed Bobby's and Audrey's presence.

"Dad. Loretta." Bobby cleared his throat. "Aud's here."

"Oh!" Loretta was the first to react. She placed her glass on the mantel, then walked over to Audrey, pulling her in for a hug. "It's wonderful to finally meet you! Bobby's told me so much about you."

"You too," said Audrey, smiling. "Thank you so much for inviting me over."

"It's been long overdue, long overdue." Loretta turned to Robert. "Come here, Robert. Be social. Say hello."

Robert chuckled, stepping forward. "Hello, Miss Nielsen. Nice to see you again." He motioned toward the couches. "Shall we sit? Dinner should be ready in an hour."

Bobby and Audrey sat across from Robert and Loretta. Audrey couldn't believe how stunning Loretta was. She carried herself with such poise and regality. Margaret, Bobby's mother, had been the same way; indeed, Sarah had described Margaret as arrestingly beautiful. Perhaps that was Robert's type—women who were not only easy on the eyes but also wealthy beyond anyone's wildest imagination. Robert wasn't unattractive, per se, but he certainly wasn't the parent Bobby had inherited his looks from. Of course, Audrey knew there was more to a relationship than physical appearances; for all she knew, Robert could be the most charming, gregarious man in New York.

"Bobby has told us you'll be attending our wedding," Robert said, cradling his glass.

"Yes," Audrey answered. "Is that ... okay?"

"The more, the merrier. In fact, Loretta and I ... we want the rest of your family to come too."

"Really?" Audrey was flattered. "That's very generous, but ... you haven't even met them yet."

"Well, we're hoping to correct that. Clearly, you're a big part of Bobby's life, and ... I'd like to meet the people who raised a young woman such as yourself."

"Oh." Audrey could feel her cheeks redden. "Thank you."

"So, if it's not too much trouble, we'll need your address—so we can send your parents an invitation. And I believe you have a ... a sister, yes?"

"Yes. Claire."

"She's welcome too." Robert glanced at Loretta. "It'll be nice, won't it? The Nielsens and the Dempseys together."

"Very nice," Loretta agreed. To Audrey, she asked, "Your parents will want to come, right?"

"Absolutely." Audrey nodded for emphasis. "They'd be honored."

Audrey thought it was best to downplay the situation; in truth, her parents would be over the moon to receive invitations to the most high-profile wedding of the New York social season—maybe of *any* social season. A year ago, Audrey's life had been completely different. Now, here she was, sitting in the drawing room of one of the richest families in the nation. It was strange, really, how drastically her life had changed. Back in August, she'd been afraid that going to Great Gray would be a mistake. But now, she couldn't imagine what would have happened if she'd gone to another school, if she hadn't met her new, wonderful friends—and, of course, Bobby.

It was surprisingly easy, talking with Robert and Loretta. They seemed genuinely interested in getting to know Audrey, as they asked her all sorts of questions about her family and interests. She remembered how overly zealous her parents had been, peppering Bobby with all sorts of questions about his father. Robert and Loretta were much more laidback, and neither made Audrey feel as though she were being interrogated.

"You should be proud, Miss Nielsen," Robert said. "It's no small feat, getting into a school like Great Gray."

"It's all because of my parents. They're the ones who believed in me, who made this possible."

"They sound like marvelous people."

"They are. The best. They've always put me and Claire first."

"As they should." Robert took a sip of his wine. "Now, I'm even more interested in meeting them. You said your father is a ... cobbler, correct?"

"Yes. It's been the family trade for generations. He's very proud of it."

"I'd imagine so. It isn't easy work. I actually ... I could send some business his way. Many of my friends could utilize his services."

"I'm sure he'd appreciate that, but ... you really don't have to go out of your way or—"

"Please." Robert waved a flippant hand. "I'm more than happy to do it."

Dinner was just as pleasant. Benoit once again outdid himself by preparing a feast. At times, Audrey wasn't even sure what she was eating, but it was delicious all the same. She asked if she could take some food home to give to her parents, and Benoit personally brought out a few Tupperware containers for her. He'd even added in a few slices of his mouthwatering chocolate cake.

Before leaving, Audrey thanked Robert and Loretta for their hospitality, and they told her she was welcome anytime. As Bobby walked her out, Audrey resisted the urge to skip down the stairs. She couldn't believe how swimmingly everything had gone. Robert and Loretta had been even lovelier than she'd anticipated, and they'd made her feel so at home. For months, she'd agonized over sitting across from Bobby's father and engaging him in conversation, but her worries had been unfounded. Robert had been perfectly agreeable.

"I'd say that went well," Bobby said.

"Me too. Very well. I mean, I don't want to toot my own horn or anything, but ... I think they liked me."

"They definitely did. But ... that's not exactly a surprise. I mean, it *is* you we're talking about. I think they like me more now because I'm dating you."

"Then I guess my job here is done."

Bobby laughed, leading her over to Felix's car. He held the door open for her, and as Audrey climbed inside, Bobby started relaying her address to Felix, but Felix stopped him, saying he already had it memorized.

"You know, I spend more time with Miss Audrey than I do with you, Bobby,"

Felix teased.

Bobby good-naturedly countered, "Are you complaining or—?"

"Oh, no, no. I much prefer her company. In fact, I was thinking ... maybe I should become *her* chauffeur."

"I wouldn't mind that!" Audrey piped up from the back.

Bobby chuckled. "Be careful what you ask for, Felix. She'd be much more demanding than I am."

"Demanding? Miss Audrey? Never," said Felix, winking at Audrey in the rearview mirror.

"Well, regardless, thank you for taking her home. And here." Bobby pulled out some cash from his wallet. "A little extra for all the back and forth. And for having to put up with Aud."

"Hey!" said Audrey, her arms crossed.

Felix smiled, pocketing the money. "I'd drive Miss Audrey for free. You know that."

"Oh. Well, in that case ..." Bobby held out his hand, acting as though he were interested in getting his money back.

Felix laughed, shaking his head. "Sorry, Bobby. No takebacks."

The whole ride, Felix and Audrey chatted away. Over the last few months, Audrey had gotten to know Felix rather well, and she looked forward to these rides. Audrey asked him if he'd become Loretta's chauffeur, once Robert and Loretta were married.

"I know it'd probably be a big step up for you, but ... I have to say, I'd miss you," Audrey was saying.

"No, I'll still be Bobby's chauffeur. Miss Loretta—the soon-to-be Mrs. Dempsey—she has her own chauffeur, you see, so he'll get to drive her around." With a melodramatic sigh, he added, "And I'll still be stuck with Bobby."

"I'm so sorry." Audrey put her hand over her heart. "That's a fate worse than death."

Felix laughed heartily. "No, I'm happy where I am. So, I'm afraid I'll be driving you around for the foreseeable future, if that isn't too much of an inconvenience."

"Well, I guess we all have to make sacrifices."

Audrey decided not to tell her parents they would be attending Robert's and Loretta's wedding. She wanted them to be surprised when they received the invitation in the mail. Within a week, their invitation arrived, and they both stared at it, as though they had received a Golden Ticket to Willy Wonka's chocolate factory.

"Is this real?" asked Sophia breathlessly. "We really ... we're invited?"

"Yes!" Audrey grinned from ear to ear. "We'll all be there! Even Claire—if she wants to, that is."

"Of course, she'll want to!" Alexander enthused. "How could she not? Oh, what will we get them? What can you get someone like Robert Dempsey?"

"You don't have to get them anything," Audrey told him. "Mr. Dempsey explicitly said—"

"We can't just show up empty-handed. We have to ... we have to get them something!"

"No. You really don't. They're not accepting gifts. Didn't you read the invitation?"

"No, I ... I guess I didn't. I stopped at 'cordially invited.'" Alexander chuckled. "Well, still, we ... we'll need to do some shopping! To look our best!"

It was adorable, seeing her parents so excited. Still, Audrey didn't want them to break the bank trying to keep up with the other guests. She reminded them they had nothing to be ashamed of, that the Dempseys didn't expect them to dress like they were Rockefellers.

"No, I know," Alexander said, bobbing his head distractedly. "But you don't need to worry about money, love. You know, we're not as destitute as you may think."

"I don't think we're destitute," Audrey said, hoping she hadn't unintentionally insulted her father. "I just ... we don't have anything to prove. That's what I'm trying to say. We can just be us."

"We will be. We'll just be ... a little more well dressed than usual, that's all."

"Okay. But only a *little* more well dressed. We don't need to go overboard here."

Alexander laughed. "We'll stay firmly on the ship. I promise." He kissed the top of her head. "I knew going to Great Gray would be the best thing for your future. I just knew it."

Audrey could not help but agree.

CHAPTER 16

Bobby

ON THE TOWN

I T WAS A FRIDAY night, and Bobby didn't have any plans. Sebastian was out with Melissa, his new girlfriend, and Audrey was busy volunteering for Helping Hands. Bobby could've tried to meet up with some of his baseball teammates, or even some of his track friends, but if he was being honest, he just wanted to kick back with a pizza, watch whatever was on TV, and fall asleep on the couch. It'd been a long week, and he was looking forward to a restful start to the weekend.

"Bobby!" Charles greeted him at the front door, as he usually did. "Great to see you! How was your day?"

"It was good. I had a pop quiz I wasn't really ready for in Physics, but ... I think I did okay."

"I'm sure you did better than okay." Charles beamed at him. "Now, I don't mean to put you on the spot or anything, but ... do you have any plans for the night?"

"No, actually. I was just going to hang out here."

"Yes, that's what I thought. And you're more than welcome to do that, but ... see, your father and Loretta are out for the evening, and I actually have the night off, so I was wondering if you'd like to join me for a Broadway show."

Bobby's eyes lit up. "I'd love to!"

"Ah, I was so hoping you'd say that! Excellent! Then I don't have to give these tickets to anyone else."

Charles reached into his pocket and pulled out two tickets to *Sweeney Todd*. Bobby's eyes widened. The show had opened up just a few weeks ago, but it was already receiving rave reviews. It was a miracle Charles had been able to purchase tickets at all.

"And I don't mean to rush you or anything," Charles went on, "but we do have reservations at Sardi's in a little over an hour, so ..."

Bobby laughed. "What would you have done if I'd said no, that I already had plans?"

"Well, that's why I've been asking you all week, just to make sure this would work out. I was almost positive I must have been annoying you with all my questions."

"No, not at all."

"Oh, good." Charles clasped his hands. "And I know you don't really like surprises, that you were probably going to just get some pizza and settle in here for the night, but—"

"This is way better than that. Really, Charles, I ... you've made my whole day!"

"Just meet me down here when you're ready, okay? Then we'll take off."

Bobby bounded up the stairs with a newfound energy. He had known his father and Loretta were spending the night together, just the two of them. Everything was still rather new with them, and they had been more than generous, inviting Bobby to all sorts of events and going out of their way to do things as a family unit. But it had been far too long since Bobby and Charles had had a night out on the town.

Quickly, Bobby hopped into a shower, then changed into something fit to see a Broadway show: a cobalt sweater and khakis. Satisfied with his choice, Bobby returned downstairs, and he saw Charles in the foyer, wearing his favorite cardigan. The yellow, brown, and white geometric pattern was busy, but on Charles, it worked. It was always somewhat odd, seeing Charles in street clothes, as more often than not, he was dressed in his coattails. On nights like these, though, Bobby got to see a little more of Charles's fun-loving personality shine through, and he loved it.

Charles motioned toward the grandfather clock. "You were quicker than I thought you'd be."

"I didn't want to leave you waiting."

They took the subway down to 42nd Street, then walked to Sardi's. Over the years, Charles had taken Bobby to many Broadway shows, and they always ate at Sardi's beforehand. It had become their unspoken ritual. Without even asking, Charles would go ahead and make them reservations. He knew how much Bobby loved consistency; it was a rare day, indeed, when Bobby decided to venture outside of his comfort zone and try some new restaurants.

"Let's see, when were we last here?" Charles asked, stroking his chin. "It was a little before your birthday, I think—sometime in early November."

Bobby hung his head. "I'm sorry, Charles. Things have been so busy, and I—"

"No, no. Don't apologize. I didn't mean it like that, like an accusation. I just ... I know how things have been for you, and, to be frank, I've been quite occupied myself. The staff and I, we've all been doing everything we can to make sure the house is in good shape for Mrs. Abernathy. After all, I mean, in just a few months, she will be moving in, and ... well, I guess we'll be calling her Mrs. Dempsey at that point."

"A few months." Bobby let out a low whistle. "Time's moving so fast."

Charles met Bobby's eyes. "Tell me honestly, Bobby—and I swear, this stays between us. How do you feel about Mrs. Abernathy—about having a stepmother?"

"I really like her. She's nice, easy to talk to, funny. And she and my father ... they make each other happy. I mean, I really ... I don't think I've ever seen him like this before."

"No, me neither. They *do* seem like a good match. But I just ..." Charles rolled his shoulders. "I know it was sprung on you so quickly, back in January, and ... you didn't really ... even if you didn't like her, it wasn't like you could just ... say that. And I guess I just ... I wanted to check in with you, make sure you're okay with it—really okay with it. Because I know you've told me how much you like her, but that was in the house, and I didn't ... I wanted to ask you somewhere neutral—somewhere no one could overhear us."

Charles's compassion never ceased to amaze Bobby. No part of his job description said he needed to look out for Bobby, make sure he was okay, ask him how he was doing; he didn't have to take Bobby out to Yankees games, Broadway shows, or exhibits at the Met. And yet, Charles had always done these things so willingly, so merrily, without any sort of resentment or reluctance. Tonight was his night off, for goodness' sake, and he wanted to spend it with his employer's son. He could've done anything, gone anywhere in the city, but here he was, treating Bobby to a night out on Broadway.

"I really appreciate that, Charles. But I promise you, I'm okay. In fact, I really ... I don't think I could've asked for a better stepmother than Loretta."

"That's good to hear. And truly, I'm relieved you feel that way because ... well, I was really wrestling with it for a while there. See, your father ..." Charles cleared his throat. "... he told us about Mrs. Abernathy after Thanksgiving, but he asked us not to say anything to you, as he wanted to wait until things were more ... settled. But I really ... I wanted to tell you, to at least give you a heads-up. And maybe I should've, but I didn't—"

"It's okay. You were just doing your job. I understand that."

"But you're very dear to me, Bobby, and I ... I never want you to think I'm hiding anything from you. Because that wasn't my intention. If I'd had things my way, I would've told you the same night I found out, but ... I couldn't go against your father."

"I know." Bobby smiled at him. "Really, Charles, you don't have to apologize. I guess a part of me ... I kind of figured my father and Loretta must have known each other for a lot longer than he'd let on. But none of that matters because ... it's all worked out, right?"

"Right." Charles nodded.

"How do *you* feel about her?" Bobby asked, a little worried Charles perhaps had a different view of his soon-to-be stepmother. "Do you like her?"

"I do. When your father told us he was thinking of getting married again, I didn't ... well, I didn't expect to see a woman like Mrs. Abernathy walk through the door. I mean, ten years ago, something like this couldn't have happened—would've been illegal, even. I'm sure people will talk—they always do—but change doesn't rely on talk; it relies on action. And I've always known your father to be a man of action."

Yes, Bobby thought; that was certainly true—in more ways than Charles realized.

With a sigh, Charles added, "I just hope New York society doesn't scare her away."

"She's from Texas. I'm sure she'll be just fine."

Charles chuckled. "You're far too wise for your years. You know that?"

"Well, lucky for me, I've had some good role models—you know, teaching me all about art and books and the Yankees."

"You should've said the Yankees first. Because obviously, that's the most important."

"Obviously."

Charles laughed. "Well, speaking of art ... what do you know about *Sweeney Todd*? Have you read anything about it?"

"Just the basic summary. I guess a crazed barber starts murdering people?"

"That's what I've gathered as well. I didn't want to read too much about it, as I was planning on taking you and didn't, you know, want the critics' opinions coloring mine. But ... yes, a little macabre, isn't it? Hmmm. Well. I'm sure there's more to it than that. And hey, if the story isn't that good, then I hope the music at least is catchy."

They finished up their meals, then made their way over to Uris Theatre. Charles had gotten them excellent seats, just a few rows back from the stage. Though undoubtedly macabre, Bobby and Charles agreed that the musical was quite extraordinary—certainly different from anything else they'd seen in the last few years. The whole subway ride back, they chatted about the story, sharing their favorite moments and songs.

"Thanks again, Charles," Bobby said as they entered the townhouse. "Tonight was amazing. Maybe I'll try not having plans on a Friday more often."

"Thank *you* for coming with me. I really ... I think I enjoyed the musical more than I thought I would. Hope that doesn't say anything too bad about me."

"Not at all. It was a great story! And just so you know, next time's on me."

"Not a chance." Charles ruffled his hair. "Now, off to bed with you. It's late."

"All right." Bobby headed toward the staircase. "See you in the morning."

"Yes, of course. And Bobby?" Bobby turned to face Charles, and with a wistful smile, Charles said, "I really missed this."

"Me too."

Charles shifted on his feet. "And I know you're busy with school and clubs and Audrey, and I have a lot on my plate as well, but ... we should really do this more often."

"Absolutely. At least once a month."

"It's a deal."

CHAPTER 17

Audrey

TWO WORLDS COLLIDE

B EFORE AUDREY COULD EVEN process it, her sophomore year was almost
over. The past few months had been a haze of essays, tests, group projects,
and baseball games. She had opted to step away from The Great Debaters, as she'd
found it too difficult to keep up with the group's schedule. In her excitement,
she had over-extended herself, and to ensure her grades didn't suffer as a result
of being spread too thin, Audrey decided to focus solely on her coursework and
Helping Hands for the time being.

"I knew you couldn't take the heat," Sebastian teased her. "What, you didn't
like always being on the losing side?"

"Maybe I just got tired of seeing you every Wednesday afternoon," Audrey
quipped, hands on her hips.

"Well, that can't be true. I'm certainly easier on the eyes than your boyfriend
here," Sebastian said in mock indignation, slinging his arm around Bobby's
shoulders.

Bobby laughed. To Audrey, he said, "But I think that's a good idea, stepping
back. It's important to know your limits."

"Thank you." She blew Bobby a kiss, then told Sebastian, "But I'll still debate you anytime, anywhere."

At the start of June, Audrey had the dreaded end-of-the-year meeting with her guidance counselor, Mr. Barlowe. She feared he'd chastise her for her mediocre Gym grade—why did Gym give out grades, anyway?—but he instead informed her she was in the top thirty percent of her class.

"It's very impressive, Miss Nielsen—especially since you only joined our ranks this year," he said. "Now, to prepare for next year, I thought I'd show you the list of electives we have for the fall semester, see what appeals most to you."

Audrey struggled to take in the long list of available electives. Great Gray offered everything under the sun, from foreign language courses to business classes to film studies. Just by looking at the list, she could tell what Florie, Sarah, and Bobby would go for. Florie, the future singer, would enroll in music theory, while civically minded Sarah would opt for political science. And, of course, Bobby would take creative writing. Though a part of Audrey wanted to ensure she'd be in a class with one of her best friends, she also knew their interests weren't hers. No, instead, she found herself drawn to electives such as family studies, early childhood development, and women's studies.

"And, um ... how many should I pick?" asked Audrey.

"Well, that depends. You can choose up to three, but keep in mind that'd mean you won't have study hall or a lunch period."

Audrey certainly wasn't willing to give up her lunch period. Bobby had, as he was one of those crazy people who wanted to take as many classes as physically possible, but Audrey needed guaranteed downtime during the school day.

"Okay." Audrey underlined family studies and early childhood development. "I'd like to take these."

"Very good." Mr. Barlowe made a note of her choices. "May I ask ... what are your career goals at the moment?"

"To be honest, I don't really know, but ... I know I'd definitely love to work with kids. I've been babysitting since I was twelve, and I think I'd ... I guess I could see myself as a nanny or a social worker—maybe even a teacher."

"That's fantastic to hear. Now, I don't want to overwhelm you"—he lowered his glasses—"but, you know, I should just let you know that next year, I'll be asking you about your post-Great Gray plans."

"Of course."

"And I guess I want to know ... is college part of your plan?"

"I don't think I want to go right into college after I graduate. I'd like to work for a year or two, find my footing, before I go back to school."

Mr. Barlowe jotted something down in his notebook. "Thanks for letting me know. It just helps me out so I'm not, you know, pestering you about college if it's not something you're planning to do right away. Well, that's all I have for you right now, Miss Nielsen. Finish out the year strong, and have a great summer!"

The last baseball game of the school year was against Albrecht Academy, Great Gray's archrival. Luckily for Great Gray, Bobby was in top form, lodging balls up and down the field, preventing Albrecht from making much headway. Thanks in large part to his herculean efforts, Great Gray scored twelve home runs, while Albrecht Academy scored only three. Even though Audrey had been attending these games all semester, she still didn't know what Florie was talking about when she said, "Throw him a chair!" If she was being honest, Audrey still didn't get the appeal of baseball—it went on for *far* too long—but she loved seeing Bobby in his element. Besides, it didn't hurt that Bobby looked dashing in his uniform—especially when it was all stained with grass and dirt.

Over the last few months, Audrey had gotten to know Loretta more—and Robert—and at least once every two weeks, she joined the Dempsey family for dinner, much to her parents' delight—and envy. Their envy melted away, however, when they were invited to dine with the Dempseys in their Fifth Avenue townhouse a little over a week before Robert's and Loretta's impending nuptials.

Alexander and Sophia were beside themselves; it would be their first time meeting Robert and Loretta—and, perhaps more notably, entering their home. Audrey knew what a big deal this was for her parents—she, too, had been wrought with nerves when she first visited the Dempseys' townhouse—but she didn't want them to be consumed with anxiety.

"They know we're not like them," Audrey reminded her parents. "And they're not going to judge us for that."

"No, I know." Alexander laughed uncomfortably. "You know, I've, uh … I've actually been itching to, uh … to have an excuse to wear that old tuxedo of mine!"

"Oh, please!" Sophia cut in. "Like that would fit you now!"

"It'll fit if I do this!" Alexander sucked in, holding his breath until his cheeks turned red. "Ooof!" He struggled to catch his breath. "That actually … that really took it out of me."

"Dad." Audrey gave him a look. "You can just wear your suit. I swear, Bobby's family … they're not that fancy."

"They don't wear tuxedos?"

"Not for a casual dinner, they don't."

"I see. Well, I don't want to stick out, do I? So, I … I guess I'll just wear my suit, then. Very good."

Bobby had asked Felix to pick Audrey and her parents up and bring them to his family's townhouse. Whereas Audrey walked right up to the car, greeting Felix with a smile, Alexander and Sophia stood back apprehensively.

Audrey turned and waved them over. "Come on!"

Slowly, her parents approached the car, arm in arm. Audrey knew what a big deal this was for them, but she wanted to do what she could to make them feel as comfortable as possible.

"Mom, Dad, this is Felix. Felix, these are my parents, Alexander and Sophia."

Felix nodded. "Nice to meet you, Mr. and Mrs. Nielsen."

"Oh, please … just call me Alex," Alexander said, a bit too hastily. He started to reach for the car door.

"I'll get that for you," Felix said.

"Oh, I … right. Thank you."

The whole car ride, Alexander and Sophia were uncharacteristically quiet, their eyes glued to their respective windows. Their nervousness was not only palpable but also contagious; Audrey's shoulders tensed, and she fanned herself, suddenly overcome with heat.

"Everything okay back there?" asked Felix, meeting Audrey's eyes in the rearview mirror.

"We're good. Thanks, Felix." Audrey looked at her parents. "Right? Everything good?"

"Huh?" Alexander turned to her. "Oh. Oh, yes. Everything's fine. Couldn't be better." He patted her hand, to try and comfort her, but Audrey could feel how shaky he was.

Audrey had already met Robert and Loretta before, so the pressure was off, but her parents ... this was a moment they had been mentally preparing themselves for since Audrey had announced she was dating the son of Robert Dempsey.

"Here we are." Felix stopped the car.

Alexander stared at the townhouse, his mouth agape, and Sophia leaned over Audrey to get a better look at it. Both were silent, their minds no doubt racing with a million thoughts, fears, and insecurities. Alexander glanced back at Sophia and Audrey, a wistfulness in his eyes. Audrey knew what he was thinking—what he was *always* thinking whenever he was confronted with such immense wealth: *"I'm so sorry I couldn't give this to you."*

Audrey, who was sitting between her parents, grabbed their hands and squeezed them. She never wanted either of them—particularly her father—to ever think she was anything but proud of the life they'd provided for her and Claire.

"We're more than enough," Audrey assured them, nodding for emphasis. "We don't have anything to prove."

"More than enough," Alexander agreed, though not as confidently as Audrey had hoped.

Felix came around the side of the car and opened the door for them—something that clearly embarrassed Alexander, who apologized profusely for being so slow. As Audrey and her parents exited the car, the front door of the townhouse opened, and Bobby descended the staircase, arms outstretched.

"Welcome!" He hugged Audrey's parents first before pulling her in for a warm embrace. "We're so happy you could come."

"We're happy to be here." Alexander again looked up at the townhouse, exhaling. "Beautiful place you have here."

"Oh, thank you." Bobby gestured to the staircase. "After you."

Gripping each other's hand, Alexander and Sophia headed up the staircase, and Bobby and Audrey followed close behind. Once out of view of her parents, Bobby leaned over and kissed Audrey's cheek.

"I love that dress," he whispered to her. "Is it Kelly green?"

"I don't know. Maybe?"

Bobby laughed. "Well, it's beautiful—really suits you."

Robert and Loretta were standing in the foyer. There was an unmistakable regality to them; in fact, they would have been at home among the portraits Bobby had shown Audrey in the Met of kings and queens. Meanwhile, her parents looked like they'd walked out of a Vermeer painting.

"Alexander. Sophia." Robert was the first to break the silence. He stepped forward, offering his hand to Alexander. "We're honored to finally meet you."

Alexander shook his hand. "I rather think the honor's ours," he replied, struggling to maintain eye contact with a man he'd admired for so many years.

Robert then politely bowed his head to Sophia, and Sophia, in response, offered a quick curtsey. Audrey fought the urge to pull both of her parents into a bear hug; she knew how wildly out of their depth they were, and she wanted them to know it was okay, that they didn't need to put on airs or pretend to be someone they weren't. The Dempseys were well aware this wasn't the Nielsens' world, and they wouldn't hold that against them. Her parents seemed so stiff, so robotic, terrified by the prospect of doing or saying the wrong thing.

Loretta, all smiles, walked up to Alexander and Sophia. "I'm Loretta."

"Sophia." Sophia turned to Alexander. "My husband and I ... we wanted to thank you both for inviting us to your wedding."

"Yes," piped up Alexander, nodding, his eyes flickering between Robert and

Loretta. "You have no idea how much it meant to us, receiving an invitation."

"Well, you're very welcome," Loretta responded, and Robert nodded sagely. Glimpsing over at Bobby and Audrey, Loretta added, "I have a feeling our families will be spending a lot of time together."

After a little more small talk, Robert and Loretta led them on a tour of the first two floors, skipping over Robert's office. Audrey, for her part, wanted a better sense of the townhouse's layout. Even though she had been to the Dempseys' home a handful of times by this point, there were still tons of rooms she hadn't seen. For example, she hadn't been aware there was a legitimate ballroom, like the ones she'd seen in all the fairytale movies.

"Golly." Alexander gawked at the cathedral-style ceiling, hand-painted murals, and gilded gold paneling. "The parties you must have in this place ..."

"Yes, we really should entertain more," Robert said, his eyes on Loretta. "If you'd like, that is."

"Don't have to twist my arm," Loretta chuckled. "I love a good party."

Audrey scanned the ballroom, taking it in. It was a stunning room, to be sure, but something about it felt ... odd. Maybe it was the musty scent, or maybe it was the fact that the room looked like it belonged more in Victorian England than modern-day New York. Most of all, she struggled to picture Bobby in this environment, schmoozing with his father's friends and employees. He would have been much more at home in the cozy library, curled up with a cup of tea and a good book.

The tour concluded in the dining room—just in time for dinner. Robert, Loretta, and Bobby sat on one side of the table, while Alexander, Sophia, and Audrey sat on the other. Alexander and Sophia had loosened up over the course of the evening; they no longer seemed so on edge, and the conversation flowed much more naturally. Benoit had prepared a three-course meal for them, and just when Audrey thought she couldn't eat another forkful, the staff brought out a champagne cake.

"You have a lot to be proud of," Robert told Alexander and Sophia as they ate their cake. "You have raised an exceptional young woman—*two*, if I'm not mistaken. Claire is your oldest daughter, yes?"

Alexander, who had just taken a bite of his cake, bobbed his head. "She just finished up her first year at NYU."

"What's she studying?"

"Journalism, but she's also working toward an English minor. She loves to write."

"A commendable choice. We could always use more writers."

Across the table, Audrey saw Bobby tighten his grip on his fork. He'd been giddily digging into the cake, but his hand was now frozen in midair. Slowly, he looked up at his father, an almost doleful expression in his eyes. Audrey remembered what Bobby had told her, back on their first date. It was his dream to become an author, but his father expected him to take the helm of Dempsey Corp. For Bobby's sake, Audrey hoped that had changed, that Robert was no longer pushing him down a path he didn't want to pursue. Audrey tried to meet Bobby's gaze, to convey to him she was on his side, but he didn't notice; his eyes were locked onto his father.

The conversation continued as they all finished up their desserts. At last, Audrey managed to make eye contact with Bobby, and he offered her a wink. Relief flooded over her; perhaps he wasn't as affected by his father's statement as she'd assumed.

"Well." Robert leaned back in his chair. "This has been a most wonderful evening."

"Thank you so much for inviting us, for your hospitality," Alexander said.

"It was our pleasure, Alexander. I mean that."

Afterward, they all retreated to the foyer. Audrey's parents once again thanked the Dempseys and congratulated Robert and Loretta on their upcoming wedding. Before she joined her parents outside, Audrey lingered on the doorstep, hoping to secure a few moments with Bobby.

"My parents had a great time," Bobby assured her. He interlaced his fingers with hers. "Are you excited for the wedding?"

"I love weddings! I got the perfect dress." Before he could ask for further clarification, she got on her tiptoes to kiss his cheek. "Call you tomorrow, okay?"

During the car ride, Alexander and Sophia couldn't stop gushing about how perfectly the evening had gone. It was adorable, really. They acted as though they'd been confident the entire time, as though they'd never questioned how well they would get on with Robert and Loretta. Audrey decided not to remind them how slowly they'd walked up the front steps, how tightly—almost desperately—they'd been gripping each other's hand ...

Alexander now seemed more than comfortable referring to Bobby's father as Robert, when just hours before, he'd called him Mr. Dempsey. Audrey had always heard people shouldn't meet their heroes, but it had clearly worked out for Alexander; somehow—unbelievably—his opinion of Robert Dempsey was now even higher than it'd been previously.

At least now, there wasn't a sense of distance between the Dempseys and the Nielsens, an aching reminder that the two families would never truly be equal. Robert and Loretta had greeted Alexander and Sophia with open arms, and despite their vastly different backgrounds, it seemed the four of them had a great deal in common.

"The Nielsens and the Dempseys," Alexander murmured, more to himself than to anyone else. "Who would've thought?"

Who, indeed? And yet, Audrey couldn't imagine what her life would be like now if she'd never met Bobby, if he'd never sat down next to her at the assembly on the first day of school—or asked her out. Maybe she would've still been stuck at the table with Cassandra and her posse; she shuddered at the mere thought.

"And who knows?" A spirited glimmer appeared in Alexander's eyes. "Maybe someday, our two families ... we'll be here talking about you and Bobby's wedding."

Audrey laughed, trying to play her father's comments off as a joke, but she would've been lying if she said she hadn't been thinking the same thing. And, to be even more honest, she didn't care if people thought she was being delusional. At the moment, everything with Bobby felt so right, and even though they were teenagers, that didn't mean what they shared wasn't real. Audrey's parents, for their part, had met when they were seventeen, just a couple of years older than she and Bobby were now. Hence, it didn't seem too far-fetched for Audrey to think she and Bobby had found that same sort of connection—just a little bit earlier.

"Oh, don't put pressure on them," Sophia told Alexander. "Let them be."

"Yeah, Dad," Audrey cut in, chuckling. "Let us be."

"Fine." Alexander smirked, despite himself. "We'll just have to wait and see, won't we?"

CHAPTER 18

Audrey

THE WEDDING OF THE CENTURY

ROBERT'S AND LORETTA'S WEDDING began in the early afternoon on June 23. Though it was a gorgeous, warm day, the wedding was held indoors, at Cipriani 42nd Street, one of Manhattan's most exclusive venues. As soon as Audrey entered the building, she could see why. The place radiated Old World charm, with stoic marble columns, glittering chandeliers, and inlaid floors. The color scheme for the wedding was blush and gold—a truly timeless choice—and the low lighting added to the romantic atmosphere. Clearly, Robert and Loretta had spent a sizable fortune on the event; in the corner, there was a string quartet, and a stunning floral archway had been erected at the altar. By the looks of it, well over 500 people would be attending the ceremony. Audrey was floored; Bobby had told her it would be an intimate wedding, but perhaps the Dempseys had a different definition of "intimate."

"Wow." Sophia's eyes wandered around the room. "This is *beautiful*."

"But not as good as our wedding, right?" Alexander joked.

Sophia laughed, kissing his cheek. "Of course not. Nothing could top that."

"This could be your wedding someday," Claire teased Audrey. "You know, if you and Bobby stay together."

"We wouldn't have this kind of wedding," Audrey responded.

"I don't think people like him have much of a choice."

Audrey and her family sat down in their respective seats. They had arrived a bit earlier than they needed to, as they didn't want to miss a thing. The processional started at two o'clock on the dot. All the men were wearing gray suits with blush pocket squares except for Robert, whose pocket square was gold. Audrey managed to make eye contact with Bobby, who offered her a quick wink. He looked so handsome, standing up there as one of the groomsmen. Finally, he had the family he'd been longing for.

Then, the music changed, and the doors swung open. Everyone stood up in anticipation of Loretta's arrival. As Audrey had expected, Loretta was the star of the show. She was wearing a lace A-line gown with bell sleeves, intricate beading, and floral embroidery—the epitome of grace and glamour. Her and Robert's vows were simple but heartfelt, and more than once, Audrey found herself dabbing at her eyes.

Afterward, everyone was ushered into the reception hall for refreshments, while the wedding party posed for photographs. There was a wide array of food choices, from fondue to meatballs to quiches to shrimp cocktails. They were also serving something called Texas caviar, which Audrey had never heard of before, but it looked delicious. To Audrey's delight, Alexander, Sophia, and Claire were keen on mingling. Audrey directed them toward people she knew would be agreeable—such as the Dagenharts—and she told them to stay away from the Irvine brood.

"And how will we know who they are?" asked Sophia, genuinely concerned. "It's not like they're wearing name tags."

"Oh, easy," Audrey explained. "Cassandra's parents look just like her. All the Irvines have dark-brown hair, brown eyes, and permanent expressions of superiority on their faces."

"Oh, dear."

"I think I see them," Alexander noted. "And don't worry, Audie; I'll be sure to steer clear of them."

"Cassandra." Claire said the name slowly. "That's the girl who tried to stop you from seeing Bobby, right?"

"Claire." Audrey put her hands on her hips.

"Don't worry. I won't do anything to get us thrown out." Claire gestured toward one of the younger Dagenhart boys. "Who's he?"

Audrey struggled to remember the names of all of Sebastian's brothers. "I don't know. Maybe Grant? Or Dean? Why?"

Claire cocked her head to the side. "I think I'll go introduce myself, see if he can handle a Nielsen."

As Claire walked away, Sophia wrapped her arm around Audrey. "You'll be okay on your own for a bit, sweets?"

"Absolutely! You two go have fun, make new friends." Audrey waved as Alexander and Sophia disappeared into the crowd.

Audrey scanned the hall, straining to find someone she knew. Sarah and her family were here, of course, but she couldn't see them in the immediate vicinity. Sebastian was deep in conversation with a young woman—probably his new girl-friend, based on their proximity. Claire seemed to be doing well with whichever Dagenhart boy she'd cornered; he was laughing at something she said.

"Audrey." The unmistakable voice of Cassandra came from behind her.

Audrey turned around. "Cassandra. Hi."

Cassandra stared at Audrey's lilac dress, no doubt judging Audrey for wearing something so simple to such a grand affair. She bit the end of her thumbnail, deep in thought.

"You look nice," Cassandra said at last.

"Thanks. You too. I love that shade of blue."

"It's an Oscar de la Renta," Cassandra said, knowing very well Audrey had no idea what any of those words meant.

"Well, it looks lovely on you."

Cassandra glanced around. "No Bobby yet, huh?"

"He's still taking photos with his family."

Cassandra absently bobbed her head. "Mr. Dempsey's made quite the statement, you know—marrying that woman.”

Audrey's jaw instinctively clenched. “Her name's Loretta.”

“Right. Because you know her.” There was a subtle malice to Cassandra's tone.

“I do. And let me tell you, she's one of the nicest people I've ever met.”

“I'm sure! But she's very ... different from the former Mrs. Dempsey. You didn't know her, of course, but I did, and ... she was much more ... traditional.”

Audrey shrugged. “I've always thought that tradition's overrated.”

Cassandra smiled—though it looked more like a wince. “Maybe you're right. As long as they're happy, right? That's all that matters.”

“Aud!” Bobby practically ran up to her. “Sorry it took me so long to find you. It's like a zoo in here.” He then noticed Cassandra. “Hi, Cassandra.”

“Hi, Bobby!” The abrupt change in Cassandra's tone was disarming. “Me and Audrey, we were just saying how beautiful the ceremony was.”

“I thought so too. And hey, I'm glad you and your family could come.”

“Wouldn't have missed it for the world.” Cassandra smoothed down her hair. “Well, um ... I'll let you two chat.”

As soon as Cassandra was out of earshot, Audrey heaved a deep breath. “Thank you for saving me from that conversation.”

“Was it really that bad?”

“It's Cassandra.”

“Fair point.” Bobby cupped her face in his hands and kissed her. “You are so beautiful.”

Audrey beamed, tugging on his suit jacket. “Well, *you* are so handsome! It was difficult not just looking at you the whole time.” She kissed his cheek. “But that was quick! I thought you'd be gone longer.”

“The photographer's a pro. And they only needed me for a few shots, anyway. This is Loretta's and Dad's day.”

Audrey gestured at the crowd of people around them. “I thought you told me this was an intimate wedding.”

“Well, you know, Dad and Loretta have a lot of close friends.”

"Wait. These are just the *close* friends? How many people would have been here if all their friends were invited?"

"Probably double."

Audrey whistled through her teeth. "Well, let me tell you. My wedding will be nothing like this."

"Oh?" Bobby crossed his arms. "And what, pray tell, will your wedding be like?"

"Small. I'd only want people there I know and love. But ... I do love the idea of a summer wedding. Maybe I'll get married in a park or something—somewhere outdoors, for sure."

"That sounds ... nice."

"Try not to sound too enthusiastic."

"Well, I just ..." Bobby made a face. "There'd be lots of bugs, wouldn't there? In the summer. And it'd be hot."

"It'll be perfect. You'll see. Maybe. If you're lucky."

Before everyone was seated for dinner, Bobby and Audrey managed to catch up with Sebastian and Sarah. Sebastian had brought his new girlfriend, May, and though she seemed lovely, Audrey knew—based on Sebastian's track record—that she would soon be out of the picture. In the time since she'd known Sebastian, his longest relationship had been a month.

"That's, like, a year in high school time!" he'd told Audrey back in April, after he and Francine broke up. "Look, I just ... there's always something, isn't there? Some reason to break it off. And maybe I'm too picky or shallow or whatever, but I don't want to waste my time—or her time—if I'm not into it. And, for the record, I'm not always the one to end things. Julie broke up with me."

"Which one was Julie?"

"You didn't know her."

"But I think I remember Bobby mentioning her. He said you were pretty serious about her. I guess you two lasted, what, two months?" she teased, and in response, Sebastian had thrown his pencil at her.

"It's nice to meet you, May," Bobby was saying, snapping Audrey back to the present. "And thank you for coming."

Sarah, for her part, was staying on the outskirts, trying her best to avoid all the people who were milling about. She was excited to see Bobby and Audrey, though, and she flagged them down.

"I'm so happy for you, Bobby," Sarah said, hugging him. "Your father and Loretta are a lovely couple. And Loretta ... I think she'll change how things are done around here—for the better."

Bobby laughed. "Yes, she is certainly a force to be reckoned with."

"I think Loretta ... maybe she's exactly what your father needs. Just watching them say their vows ... I don't think I've ever seen him smile that much before."

"Loretta's really ... she's brought that out of him."

Remarkably, Robert and Loretta had invited all their staff members to their wedding. Audrey would have loved to hear what people like the Irvines had to say about that—but, of course, they'd never dare question the Dempseys. Bobby and Audrey chatted with Charles and Felix for a good while, then Bobby formally introduced Audrey to Benoit. Though Audrey had eaten many of his delectable meals, she'd never actually seen him before.

"You are every bit as divine as Bobby has said," Benoit said, kissing Audrey's hand. He had a delightful French accent. "It's a true pleasure to meet you."

"You too."

"Benoit's a bit upset he didn't get to cook the food," Bobby told Audrey. "We all tried to tell him he's a guest, that he's off the clock, but—"

"I could've cooked up something far better than *this*." Benoit pointed at the nearby food table.

Bobby surveyed the food on the table. "I think those are called cheese dreams."

"What?"

"Cheese dreams. One of Loretta's favorites."

Benoit's face contorted. "I don't know what they're doing in Houston, but it's a travesty."

Bobby laughed, picking up one of the cheese dreams and popping it in his mouth. "They're pretty good, actually."

"Bah!" Benoit looked to Audrey for support. "You agree with me, yes? The food here ... it's not good. Not fitting for the Dempseys."

"Don't worry, Benoit," Audrey said. "Your food is much better."

Finally, dinner was served. The menu celebrated Robert's and Loretta's backgrounds, and for each of the three courses, guests had two choices: one that was more classically Southern and one that was more classically Northeastern. For an appetizer, guests could have either a fish cake with tarragon mayonnaise or pasta primavera. For an entrée, guests could opt for either pork chops, rice, and cornbread or a strip steak, mashed potatoes, and baguette. And finally, for dessert, guests could eat either a slice of pecan pie or a personal-sized New York-style cheesecake.

Before the desserts were brought out, Robert stood up and addressed the ballroom. "Good evening, everyone. Thank you so much for spending your day with us, for sharing in our joy. Today has been even more perfect than I could've imagined. And believe me, I have been looking forward to this day for a long time." He paused for a moment, his eyes on his bride. "I knew from the moment I met Loretta that she was the woman I wanted to spend the rest of my life with. Many of you have gotten to know Loretta over the last few months, and you are well aware of how impressive she is. She never forgets a name or a face. She genuinely cares about people, wants to make a difference. Now, I know you don't need to hear me wax on about all her wonderful attributes, or else we'd be here all weekend." Robert paused as the crowd laughed. "But what I *do* want to say—what I *need* to say—is that ever since she came into my life, everything has seemed ... brighter. Easier. Better. And I will do everything I can to make her every bit as happy as she has made me." Loretta beamed up at him, and he leaned down to kiss her cheek, then raised his glass. "To Loretta Dempsey!"

"To Loretta Dempsey!" everyone chorused.

Loretta spoke next. "Thank you, everyone. Thank you. Now, I haven't been in New York very long, and I have to tell y'all, I was ... well, I was nervous! I'd heard stories about New Yorkers, about how rude y'all can be, but ... that hasn't been my experience. No, instead, I was greeted with open arms. I don't really know what I fell in love with first—Robert or the city. But ... I know this is where I belong—here, with my wonderful husband and his delightful son, Bobby." Loretta beamed at Bobby. "Bobby, I can't even begin to explain how much I've loved getting to know you these past few months. You've been so kind to me, so welcoming. You are, in short, the perfect stepson, and I can't wait to see all the great things you'll do in the future." She blew Bobby a kiss, and he grinned. "Well, I know we're all waiting for that pecan pie—or, you know, the cheesecake, if you're into that—so let me just finish off by saying how grateful I am to be a part of this family—and of this city. And I better see all y'all out there on the dance floor!" In response, the crowd laughed.

As soon as their empty dessert plates were taken away, everyone poured onto the dance floor, including Bobby and Audrey. Before the wedding, Audrey hadn't been aware of just how incredible a dancer Bobby was. This realization made him even more attractive to her—something she hadn't thought was possible.

It'd been a long time since Audrey had attended a wedding, and she savored every moment of it. She couldn't help but fantasize more about her future wedding as she saw Robert and Loretta make their rounds, talking to all the guests. Audrey smiled at Bobby, who was sitting to her right. They'd been dancing almost all night, and they would have kept dancing if Audrey's feet hadn't turned against her. She had made the mistake of wearing somewhat new heels to the event, and she was now paying the price. To recuperate, she and Bobby sat on the sidelines, watching as the crowd slowly thinned out.

Bobby must have sensed her eyes on him, as he turned to her. "Is everything okay?"

"Everything's perfect," she replied, squeezing his hand. "Absolutely perfect."

She and Bobby were young, of course, and they hadn't even been dating for a year, but she could see their future so vividly. As she thought about her dream wedding, she realized she didn't care so much about the venue or the décor, the food or the music. She didn't even really care about the dress. Well, that wasn't exactly true; she still wanted to wear a striking off-white dress that would make her guests audibly gasp—and her father shed a sentimental tear. But truly, the most important thing was the man waiting for her at the end of the aisle, the man she'd be spending the rest of her life with. And no matter how many times she tried to tell herself not to dupe herself into thinking she'd met the man of her dreams in high school, she couldn't help it. She wanted that man—her future husband—to be Bobby.

"It was such a beautiful wedding," Bobby observed. "I've never seen my father look so happy."

"They seem like a good match—your dad and Loretta."

Bobby nodded. "You know, sometimes, I ... I try to imagine what my parents' wedding must have been like, but ... I don't know. They never really talked about it."

"Why do you think that is?"

"Because they didn't love each other."

Bobby's quick, blunt response would have disarmed Audrey six months ago, but she was now well aware of how strained Robert's and Margaret's marriage had been. Indeed, when Loretta had first entered his and his father's lives, Bobby had told Audrey how different the dynamic was between Robert and Loretta, how genuine their relationship seemed. In just a few months, Loretta had changed the atmosphere of the Dempsey household—and helped bring Bobby and his father closer together.

Bobby went on, "I feel bad that my mother ... she never got to experience ... *this.*" He gestured around the emptying ballroom. "She never got to be happy."

Audrey was never really sure how to respond when Bobby talked about his mother. Margaret wasn't a topic he tended to bring up, so whenever he did, she wanted to ensure he felt as safe and supported as possible. She knew Margaret had died only a couple of years ago, and it was clear Bobby was still struggling with the loss. Audrey could see his latent grief resurface sometimes when she talked about her mother, about how they loved to cook and bake together, pop in and out of shops, sing along to the Bee Gees. Though Bobby always managed to shake it off, reminding Audrey he and his mother weren't all that close, Audrey never wanted to be the person responsible for reigniting his pain, for making Bobby relive the darkest period of his life.

Audrey rubbed his arm. "She had *you*. I'm sure you brought her a lot of happiness."

Bobby sighed. "I think she would've been happier if she could've ... she was obsessed with Europe—especially Paris. Everything she wore was straight from *L'Officiel*. Maybe she would've ended up there, in Paris. Maybe not, though."

Audrey drew a deep breath, praying she didn't unintentionally upset Bobby. "Do you and your dad ever ... talk about her? I mean, with each other."

Bobby shook his head. "No. And now that he's with Loretta ... he's always believed in keeping the past in the past."

"That must be difficult for you."

"Sometimes. But I don't really like to ..." He trailed off. "Anyway." He rolled his shoulders, clearing his throat. "I guess you could say this marks the true beginning of our summer." A smile formed on his lips, dispersing the dark cloud that had been hovering above him. "We'll have a lot of fun."

Though Audrey wanted to continue asking about his mother, encouraging him to talk about his feelings on the matter, she didn't want to push him. Over the last nine months, Audrey had learned it was never a good idea to keep harping on a subject Bobby had no interest in discussing anymore. If she asked more about his mother, he would shut down on her, which she most assuredly didn't want—especially not at his father's and Loretta's wedding. Besides, Audrey didn't think it was her place to force Bobby to talk about his mother. What she did know about the subject? Her mother was still alive. How could she possibly help Bobby deal with his complex emotions surrounding Margaret's death?

So, instead, Audrey smiled in return, resting her head on his shoulder. "It'll be the best summer ever."

CHAPTER 19

Audrey

ANOTHER SCHOOL YEAR

THE SUMMER WENT BY quickly—far too quickly for Audrey's liking. When she wasn't with Bobby, she was with Florie, getting up to all sorts of mischief. Most memorably, Florie showed Audrey the songs she had been working on since she was a kid. Part of the reason why her parents had applied to Great Gray on her behalf was because the school had a reputable, award-winning music program.

"So many alumni have ended up doing sold-out tours," Florie explained. "And I'm hoping to be one of them!"

It was admirable, Audrey thought, how certain Florie was about her future. Bobby was the same way; he'd always known he wanted to attend Columbia and pursue writing. In truth, Audrey had only vague ideas about what she wanted to be—or where she wanted to end up. She contented herself by knowing she didn't need to make any of these decisions right away; she still had time to figure it out. At the very least, she would be spending the next few years in New York. Audrey hoped inspiration would hit her, that she would wake up one day and magically be instilled with a sense of direction. Luckily, Bobby didn't judge her for her uncertainty.

"Whatever it is you end up doing," Bobby comforted her, "you'll be the best at it."

In late July, the Nielsens, sans Claire, spent a week in Boston, taking in all the historical sites and eating the best seafood Audrey had ever had. Claire would have loved to join them, of course, but she was interning for the *Post*. It wasn't Claire's ideal internship, given the paper's penchant for sensationalism, but she was grateful to have a job that was in her field. They all wished her well, and though they missed Claire's presence and jokes, Audrey and her parents still had a great time in Boston.

Sadly, though, summer once again came to a close, and Audrey found herself back at Great Gray—this time as a junior. She thought it would be depressing, starting another school year, knowing that her fun-filled days were far behind her, but to her surprise, she was ready to get back into the swing of things. She was more confident than she had been last year, and she was much happier knowing she had a steady group of friends. Additionally, the culture shock had worn off. Audrey was now used to the way things were done at Great Gray, for better or worse, and she wasn't as easily intimidated by her peers. She was proud of how far she'd come.

Strangely enough, on the first day of school, while Audrey was making herself at home in her new locker, Cassandra came up to her. The two hadn't spoken since Robert's and Loretta's wedding, and though a part of Audrey wanted to pretend Cassandra didn't exist, she remembered her father's sage advice: "Don't burn bridges."

"How was your summer?" Cassandra asked.

"It was great. Spent some time with my family and friends. It was nice to be off for a few months. What about you?"

"It was fine. We were traveling all around Europe, which, you know, can be a lot, but I got this tan and a whole new wardrobe, so ... it wasn't all bad."

Audrey could hardly understand how Cassandra could be so blasé about a summer spent traveling around Europe, but she held her tongue. She wasn't about to start her junior year off by telling Cassandra just how spoiled she sounded.

Cassandra awkwardly gestured at Audrey's outfit. "Bobby's track jacket looks good on you."

"Oh. Thanks." Audrey tightened the jacket around herself. "Yeah, he gave it to me over the summer. I guess they're getting new ones for the season, so ... this was a birthday gift."

Cassandra smiled, and, to Audrey's surprise, it seemed genuine. "I'm really happy for you. Honestly, I ... look, I know I gave you a hard time last year, and things were kind of weird at Mr. Dempsey's wedding, but ... I just wanted to clear the air, make sure we're good. We *are* good, right?"

"I don't see why not."

Cassandra exhaled a sigh of relief. "Good. Because I wanted you to know that the whole thing with Bobby ... I actually have a boyfriend now, and he's really amazing, so ..."

Cassandra waited for Audrey to ask questions about this mysterious boyfriend of hers, but Audrey was too busy putting up pictures of her and her friends in her locker. She wanted to make sure her locker was decorated as early as possible to add some jolt of happiness to her school day.

Clearing her throat, Cassandra went on, "His name's David. David Bettencourt. He's a senior. Star of the polo team. Super tall and handsome. He's got that gorgeous, long blond hair. You must know him."

"Right." Audrey nodded along, feigning familiarity. "Well, that's great, Cassandra. Happy to hear it."

Cassandra dreamily leaned against the neighboring locker. "Yeah, David's taking me to all the senior events, so ... I probably won't be seeing you around too much."

"That's too bad," Audrey lied, wondering how she could politely exit this conversation.

Cassandra lazily turned to face her. "Anyway, I just wanted you to know—so there isn't any weirdness between us."

"I appreciate that. And really, Cassandra, it's all good. Water under the bridge."

Later, once Audrey caught up with Florie, she told her all about her bizarre encounter with Cassandra. Neither of them was really sure what to make of it, but they decided there was no sense in stressing over whether Cassandra had some sort of ulterior motive. Besides, there were much more important things going on. For one, Florie was over the moon that the drama club was doing *Grease* for their upcoming musical. Audrey could hardly believe it. She'd seen *Grease* last year and absolutely loved it. Florie thought she had a good chance at nabbing one of the lead roles, and Audrey agreed.

"They're holding open auditions this Friday," Florie informed Audrey as they walked to Trigonometry. "I'm hoping to knock their socks off!"

"Will they allow people to watch? Because I'd love to sit in the back of the auditorium and cheer you on!"

"I'm sure they will. They usually do, anyway. But I've been doing the grunt work for the past two years, you know? And, of course, I know nothing's guaranteed, but ... I feel it in my bones this time. I'm going for either Sandy or Rizzo. Sandy, as you know, is the lead, so that'd be great, but Rizzo is the better part, I think. Still, I can't be picky."

"Well, they'd be hard-pressed to find someone half as talented as you to play either of those roles. But, for the record, it's easier for me to see you as Rizzo."

Florie laughed. "Me too."

Sarah, meanwhile, was back at work on Student Council. She'd been elected class president, and she was already advocating on her peers' behalf. Her first order of business was demanding reduced fees for the juniors' winter formal. Great Gray, of course, couldn't be like other schools; instead of a prom at the end of the school year for juniors and seniors, the juniors and seniors had their own events. The juniors' winter formal was held in January, and the seniors' spring formal was held in April. When Audrey learned they'd have to pay thirty dollars apiece for the winter formal, she was floored. All the school dances she'd gone to in the past had been free. Granted, they'd been horrible, bordering on tragic, but at least she hadn't been expected to shell out money to attend.

"Has it always been that way?" Audrey asked Sarah, trying not to sound as perturbed as she actually was.

"Unfortunately. It's ridiculous they make us pay," Sarah lamented. "Social events are bad enough as is, having to pretend to like each other. And sure, most of us can afford it, but ... it's just a way of further alienating a good swath of the student body. They say about thirty percent of our students are here on some sort of scholarship—so, you know, a significant minority. We can't keep acting like everyone here comes from the same background."

Audrey agreed—and not just because she was one of the less affluent students at Great Gray. It bothered her, the idea that students could be barred from participating in something simply because they couldn't afford it. High school was political enough, with all the cliques and hierarchies. But for some reason, Great Gray wanted to be a high school on steroids, injecting class into the discussion. Bobby assured her he'd cover the fee for her, which was sweet, but it didn't address the root of the issue.

"It's not like the school needs my thirty dollars that badly," Audrey vented to Bobby. "It's just ... I don't know. It feels like a reminder that some of us will never truly be on equal footing."

"Well, look on the bright side. Sarah's doing all she can to change that."

"And what do you think the chances are of her doing that?"

"Knowing Sarah? Rather high." Bobby took Audrey's hand in his. "Try not to worry about it. The dance is a couple months away. A lot can happen between now and then. Let Sarah work her magic."

Audrey looked up at him. "I hope you know I'll be expecting you to properly ask me to the dance. You can't just assume I'll be your date because I'm your girlfriend."

Bobby laughed. "I wouldn't have dreamed of it."

For the rest of the week, Audrey helped Florie become more familiar with the material for her audition on Friday. Florie was what they in the showbiz world called a triple threat. Audrey had known what a talented singer Florie was, but she hadn't been aware that Florie was also a formidable dancer and actress. By

Thursday, one thing had become abundantly clear: Florie was destined to be up on that stage.

"You're just biased," Florie laughed as she and Audrey entered Great Gray that Friday morning.

"I am not! Their socks are going to be knocked across the room. That's how impressed they'll be by you."

Florie laughed again. "Thanks, Audrey. You've been a real help, going through the material with me, giving me some pointers. You know, you'd be a great Doody."

"Yeah, right. You think this school is progressive enough to do a gender reversal like that?"

"Well, I'm hoping they're progressive enough to cast a Black lead."

"They'd have to be crazy not to cast you."

After classes let out on Friday, everyone who was interested in auditioning for the musical—or simply watching the auditions—gathered outside the auditorium. Out of solidarity, Audrey stood beside Florie, scoping out Florie's competition. To her confusion, Cassandra and Shelly were two of the interested students. According to Florie, neither of them had ever auditioned for a play or musical before.

"Can they even sing?" Audrey whispered to Florie.

"Shelly can carry a tune all right. I've heard her singing in the bathroom. Weird, I know, but not the point. Cassandra, on the other hand? Not that I know of. But maybe she's, you know, interested in being part of the ensemble."

"Oh, please. Like Cassandra would ever be okay not being the center of attention?"

Florie shrugged. "Maybe she'll surprise us. She could be a great singer."

She wasn't. She wasn't a bad singer, by any means, but Cassandra wasn't nearly as talented as the other girls who were auditioning. She couldn't sight-read, and it was obvious she hadn't prepared for her audition. She stumbled through the song and didn't enunciate her words all that well. When she finished, she thanked the director for his time.

"Thank *you*, Miss Irvine," he responded, jotting down notes.

Shelly was good, if not a little over the top with her facial expressions. Florie, of course, was the standout; she was calm, cool, and collected up there, and when she sang a bit of "There Are Worse Things I Could Do," literal chills ran down Audrey's spine.

"All right!" the director said after the last audition concluded. "Thank you all so much! We'll have the cast sheet up bright and early on Monday."

"You nailed it!" Audrey told Florie as soon as she saw her. "I can't imagine them not giving you Rizzo."

And yet, that Monday, Audrey and Florie made their way to the auditorium to see the cast list, and they were stunned by what they saw. Florie hadn't gotten Sandy or Rizzo; in fact, she hadn't gotten any main role at all. Instead, she was cast as an ensemble member. Adding insult to injury, Cassandra nabbed the part of Rizzo, and Shelly would be playing Sandy. It was an outrage. Worse than that, it was unfair. By far, Florie had been the best of the female hopefuls. It didn't make any sense.

"That's okay." Florie tried to remain positive. "At least I'm in the show."

"No, something's wrong. There's no way—"

"It's *okay*."

"No, it's not! You should be playing Rizzo, Florie. Cassandra—"

"Audrey." There was a sternness to Florie's tone that Audrey had never heard before. "Don't worry about it. I'm in the show. That's the most important thing." Something—or someone—behind Audrey caught Florie's attention. "Cassandra. Hi. Congratulations."

Audrey wheeled around to face Cassandra. She knew she should keep her mouth shut—more for Florie's sake than anything else—but she couldn't.

"Your parents must be *so* proud," Audrey snapped.

It was obvious to Audrey that the only reason why Cassandra had gotten the role of Rizzo was because of her parents—more specifically, her powerful father. Everyone knew how much money the Irvines contributed to the school, so it made sense that the director, desperate for a hefty donation, would kowtow to their only daughter. He couldn't snub such an important family by offering one of the lead roles to someone else—and a Black woman, at that. The injustice made Audrey sick to her stomach.

"Thanks," Cassandra said slowly.

She looked like she had more she wanted to say, but Audrey wasn't in the mood for her gloating. She linked her arm with Florie's.

"Come on, Florie," said Audrey. "Let's go."

"Okay." As Audrey pulled her down the hallway, Florie whispered, "Where are we going? My homeroom's that way."

"I just needed to get us away from her, that's all." Audrey stopped. "Are you still going to do the musical?"

"Of course! Look, Audrey, I meant it when I said I'm happy to be in the show. Would I have loved to be one of the leads? Absolutely! But I'll be the best ensemble member *Grease* has ever seen! You'll see!" She laughed, reaching out to touch Audrey's arm. "It'll all be fine. If there's one thing I've learned at Great Gray, it's to lower your expectations. And change won't happen overnight—if ever. Not that that means we should give up."

"No, you're right." Audrey nodded absently. "You'll make them regret their decision. That's for sure."

Florie grinned mischievously. "That's the plan."

CHAPTER 20

Bobby

BRIGHT NEON DREAMS

SUNDAYS HAD BECOME BOBBY'S and Audrey's day. The staff, minus Benoit and the rest of the kitchen crew, always had Sundays off, so they spent their days out and about in the city, enjoying their free time. For the past couple of months, Robert and Loretta had been in the habit of spending weekends out in the Hamptons, returning to the city late Sunday night. Thus, for the most part, the townhouse was empty on Sundays. Audrey would come over in the morning, and she and Bobby would go out somewhere for brunch—usually a café on Madison—before settling in for the afternoon.

While Bobby finished up an essay for his History class, Audrey wandered around his bedroom. This had become a habit of hers. She'd commented a few times on how boring Bobby's room was; consequently, over the past few months, she'd been gifting him things to brighten up his space, such as posters, handmade cards, and figurines. She took great joy in seeing all these items spread across the room. As she made her way over to the desk, where Bobby was currently sitting, Audrey stepped on a loose floorboard.

"Oh!" Audrey looked down at her feet. "Did you know you ...?" She trailed off, her eyes on what lay beneath the uprooted floorboard. "Bobby." She crouched down and picked up a stack of faded pages. "What's this?"

"It, um ..." Bobby heaved a deep breath. "It's *Bright Neon Dreams.*"

"What's that?"

"It's my book."

"Your book?" Audrey furrowed her eyebrows. "Why is it under a floorboard?"

Bobby wasn't sure how to answer that question. He decided in the moment it would be too complicated, telling Audrey about how his eleven-year-old self had written a novel and proudly shown it to his father, hoping it would somehow impress him. Instead, Robert had laughed before unceremoniously tossing the manuscript into a roaring fire, telling Bobby that his writing would never amount to anything.

"Your future is already mapped out for you," Robert had lectured, seemingly oblivious that his son was in tears, struggling to salvage his ashen story from the grate. "You'll never be a writer."

Bobby, however, didn't listen to his father. Over the next couple of years, he painstakingly rewrote *Bright Neon Dreams* as best as he could remember. After every writing session, he hid it under a floorboard in his room, to ensure his father would never find it. It was a safe bet; Robert hardly ever entered Bobby's bedroom, but even when he did, he never walked over to the desk. *Bright Neon Dreams* had remained hidden all this time, never seen by anyone—except for Bobby, obviously, and now Audrey.

"To keep it safe," Bobby replied.

It wasn't a lie. At some point, Bobby wanted to tell Audrey the whole story, but now wasn't the time. Besides, the person Robert had been five years ago was so far removed from the person he was today. He'd softened, become much less critical and splenetic. It didn't seem fair, dredging up old history, painting Robert as a villain he no longer was.

"Oh." Audrey glanced between the manuscript and Bobby. "I'll just, uh, put it back, then," she said, moving as slowly as she could.

"You don't have to." Bobby stood up. "Actually, I ... I'm glad you found it. And ... it'd mean a lot to me if you were to, you know ... read it."

"Really?" Audrey grinned. "You trust me with it?"

"Of course. And there's no rush or anything. Take your time with it. I really ... I'd appreciate any feedback, good or bad."

"Have you ever shown it to anyone before?"

Again, Bobby thought back to the horrible image of his beloved story burning in the fire. In a certain respect, he *had* shown it to someone else, though Robert hadn't read a single word of it—not even the title. But Bobby didn't think that counted.

"You're the first," he told her.

"Well, I'm honored." Audrey held the manuscript close to her chest. "I'll read it as quickly as I can. Promise."

Later, after Audrey left, Bobby made his way downstairs. He could hear laughter and conversation floating up the staircase, signaling that Robert and Loretta were home. He saw them in the drawing room, each with a glass of wine in their hand; they hadn't yet noticed Bobby's presence. Bobby didn't mind, nor did he blame them. They were newlyweds; he wanted them to have time to themselves, to enjoy each other's company. He tried to slip past the drawing room, to avoid being seen, but Loretta saw him and waved him in.

"Bobby! Join us!" she insisted.

"That's okay. I really don't—"

"Please! We haven't seen you all weekend! Come in here. Sit down!"

"All right," Bobby acquiesced, chuckling, sitting on the arm of the couch. It was impossible to deny Loretta anything.

He filled them in on how he'd spent his weekend. He didn't, however, tell them about how Audrey had discovered *Bright Neon Dreams* and taken it home with her. His father had changed in many ways since meeting Loretta—all for the better, it seemed—but Bobby didn't know how Robert would react if he heard that his son still harbored dreams of someday being a published author. Now wasn't the time to test the limits of Robert's fatherly love.

Bobby stood up. "Well, I'm going to go out and grab some dinner," he said, not wanting to overstay his welcome.

"You don't want to join us?" asked Loretta, unable to mask her disappointment.

"Well, I ..." Bobby looked over at Robert. "I thought you two would want your space."

"We've had our space. We'd love for you to join us. Wouldn't we, Robert?"

Robert set down his wine glass and clasped his hands together. "I've already asked Benoit to prepare a seat for you."

"I can hardly say no to Benoit," Bobby replied.

"No, you certainly can't. Come on, then. Benoit's been cooking all day."

Dinner was as delicious as always. Benoit outdid himself, presenting a feast fit for at least half a dozen people. Bobby loved these family dinners. They'd been exceedingly rare when his mother was alive. Back then, Bobby had ended up eating alone in his bedroom most nights, as his parents' schedules had made it difficult to schedule dinners. Bobby had tried to convince himself he didn't mind, that dinners in his room were better than the awkwardly silent ones he and his parents had been subjected to before, but he still dreamed of what it would be like, having a family who liked spending time together—a family like the Dagenharts or the Nielsens. Now, he had that. Loretta had brought out a side of his father Bobby hadn't known existed. Maybe this was what his father could have been like all along, if he'd been permitted to marry for love right from the onset.

After dinner, Bobby excused himself, knowing very well that Robert and Loretta would be retreating into the drawing room, where they would be served after-dinner drinks. He knew they would have been more than happy to accommodate him, but Bobby told them he still had some reading to do before tomorrow's classes.

"What, a smart boy like you?" teased Loretta. "I'm sure you know all your stuff."

"I just want to be prepared, in case there's a pop quiz."

"Very well." Loretta sighed, kissing the top of Bobby's head. "Good night, honey. Sleep well."

"You too, Loretta." Bobby turned to his father. "And you, Dad."

Robert simply nodded in response, his eyes on the dancing fire. A part of Bobby wondered whether every time Robert looked at a fire, he thought about what he'd done, all those years ago. Had that incident been burned into his brain the way it'd been burned into Bobby's? Or had he forgotten all about it? It had been a defining moment of Bobby's childhood, an image he'd never been able to dispel, no matter how hard he tried. But perhaps it hadn't been all that memorable for Robert—just another example of Bobby's immense shortcomings.

As Bobby entered his bedroom, he thought about Audrey. Had she started reading *Bright Neon Dreams* yet? He'd told her there was no rush, and he meant it, but it was too tantalizing, wondering whether she'd met his characters yet, been introduced to his carefully crafted world. He knew the story wasn't perfect—nothing was—but he would've been lying if he said he wasn't nervous about her potential critiques. Would she say something that would hit a bit too close to home, something that would make him wish he'd hidden it somewhere else, somewhere no one would ever find it?

He shook his head, pushing these thoughts aside. If he wanted to be an author—which he did—he needed to learn how to accept criticism without becoming riddled with insecurities or doubts. Audrey, more than anyone, would be gentle, as she knew all about Bobby's literary aspirations and had no desire to discourage him. More than anything, Bobby was excited that he'd finally have someone to talk to about his work, someone who knew how much this book meant to him. Yes, despite his fears, Bobby knew he'd made the right decision, asking Audrey to read it.

Bright Neon Dreams would be safe with her.

CHAPTER 21

Audrey

CLOSE TO THE CHEST

A UDREY KNEW BOBBY HAD told her to take her time, to not feel obligated to read *Bright Neon Dreams* in one go, but she couldn't resist. She stayed up well into the early hours of the morning, poring over it, her eyes racing across the pages. She and Bobby had been dating for over a year at this point, and they'd become comfortable sharing their thoughts, dreams, and insecurities. But after reading Bobby's novel, his own work, Audrey gained even greater insight into who he was—and what he was compelled to write about.

His novel seemed autobiographical in some ways. After all, *Bright Neon Dreams* centered on a young man who loved New York—and all the opportunities it presented. But the novel also delved into darker topics like depression and loneliness, topics that—to Audrey—seemed removed from Bobby's life. Yet he wrote about them so masterfully, so intimately, as though he'd experienced them himself. And maybe he had. Maybe there was still so much about Bobby that Audrey didn't know. She hoped it wasn't true—that Bobby's past wasn't so dark—but his childhood could have been much different than she'd presumed.

On Monday, Audrey waited for Bobby by his locker, with *Bright Neon Dreams* under her arm. As soon as she saw him, she broke out into a grin, and he did the same as he neared her.

"You didn't finish it already, did you?" he asked, right away noticing the manuscript.

"I couldn't stop myself! Once I started, I couldn't put it down." Audrey got on her tiptoes to kiss his cheek. "I loved it."

Adorably, he couldn't contain his relief. "You did?"

"Of course! It drew me right in. I loved your characters, the way you write ... I can tell how much this story means to you."

"It does. I mean, it's not ... there's a lot of work I need to do to make it ... when you were reading, did anything ... stick out to you? Anything that should be changed?"

"I actually do have some notes—mainly about the female characters. I think I could help you make them sound more ... well, real."

Bobby laughed good-naturedly. "I'd love that. Any sort of feedback would be a great help."

Audrey handed him the manuscript. "Thank you for letting me read it."

"Thank *you* for reading it."

Audrey wasn't exactly sure how to ask him about the more personal parts of the book—the parts that very well may have been inspired by his own life. She didn't want him to feel as though he had to divulge things he maybe wasn't ready to share. Still, she couldn't help but wonder whether the sad, lonely boy who watched the world from his window was, in fact, him—if he, too, had ever wrestled with feelings of ineptitude, abandonment, or melancholy.

"You know, I ..." Bobby sighed. "It's fiction, but ... parts of it ..." He trailed off, no doubt trying to determine how best to phrase it. "... aren't."

Hearing those words pained Audrey more than she could explain. She'd feared that was the case, that Bobby had inserted more of himself into his novel than she'd wanted to see. Nevertheless, she was grateful Bobby had volunteered this information on his own, without any sort of push from her.

Audrey squeezed his hand. "You don't have to tell me anything you don't—"

"No, I know. And ... it's not ..." Bobby ran his fingers through his hair, avoiding eye contact. "Look, I want to tell you. I just ... I thought you might ... well, when you were reading, you might have ... had questions. And I'll answer them, but ... you should know, I ... I wrote it a while back, and right now ..." He caressed her hair. "I'm really, really happy. And I'm relieved you liked the book."

"Someday, it'll be in every bookstore, read by millions of people. And I'll be able to say I was the first to read it—your first fan."

Over the next few weeks, during what little downtime they had, Bobby and Audrey workshopped *Bright Neon Dreams*. Bobby was receptive to Audrey's suggestions, and together, they reworked parts of the book, to make it as polished as possible.

"I think you should show it to Mrs. Parker," Audrey told Bobby. "She'd be able to give you better feedback, help you turn it into something that could be published someday."

"You think it's in good enough shape to show her?"

"Bobby." Audrey gave him a look. "You know you're a great writer. Mrs. Parker told me herself she thinks you're the best writer who's ever come through Great Gray."

"She did?"

"Yes. And, as you know, she doesn't hand out compliments lightly."

"Wow, I ... that means a lot, coming from her."

Audrey flipped her hair. "Just for the record, I *know* you have what it takes—just, you know, in case my opinion means a lot too."

"Your opinion means more to me than anyone's." He kissed her. "I owe you for this, you know. You've been so helpful."

"Well, I am a super generous person, so ..."

"No disagreements here." He rested his hand on her thigh. "I should start calling you Thalia—my beautiful muse."

"I don't know who Thalia is, but ... she sounds very ... regal."

"She's the muse of comedy and bucolic poetry."

"I'll take your word for it."

Bobby smiled. "So, I know this isn't ... I was planning on asking you in a better way—with flowers and a card and all that—but I guess now's as good a time as any." He met her eyes. "Aud. My lovely Thalia. Would you do me the honor of accompanying me to the winter formal?"

Audrey placed her hand over her heart. "Yes! A million times yes!" She pulled him in for a kiss. "I was starting to wonder whether you'd forgotten."

"Never." Bobby winked. "By the way, how's everything going with Florie? Is she excited for the musical?"

"She is. I mean, she was robbed, absolutely robbed. Rizzo should have been hers, but ... she's much less salty about it than I am." Audrey sighed. "But she'll be great."

"I can't wait to see it."

Audrey glanced up at the clock. "I actually ... I promised Florie I'd help her with some of her choreography this evening."

"Oh, of course. Go ahead. I didn't mean to keep you."

"No, this was fun." Audrey kissed him again. "Now, I can officially start planning my outfit for the winter formal—you know, since I have a date and all."

Endearingly, Florie wasn't confident in her dance skills, despite her natural dexterity, and she had asked Audrey to help her master some of the more complicated moves. Audrey was flattered. She'd always loved dancing—she'd even taken classes when she was younger—and she was more than happy to impart some of her knowledge—however minimal it was—onto Florie.

"There you go!" Audrey was saying as Florie performed a near-perfect pirouette. "Much better!"

"I could actually feel the difference!" Florie couldn't contain her delight. "All right! I think I'm getting the hang of this!"

"And it all feels good, makes sense?"

Florie nodded. "You have no idea how much this has helped me out. I didn't want to be making a fool of myself anymore in rehearsals."

"Oh, come on. You have talent—and rhythm. I think you were just letting your nerves get the best of you. You'll be the one in the ensemble everyone's watching. Guarantee it."

Florie downed her glass of water. "It's a lot to keep up with, but ... I think the show's coming together."

To thank her for all her help, Florie took Audrey to Comfort Corner, a new restaurant in Hell's Kitchen. Everything on the menu looked delicious. They both enjoyed hearty bowls of gumbo, then scanned the dessert menu.

"Hey, what's good here?" Florie asked their waiter, Mark.

He heaved an exaggerated sigh. "I don't know."

"Well, what do you usually get?"

"I don't eat dessert."

"You don't eat dessert?"

"That's what I said."

"Okay." Florie studied the menu. "Could we do one slice of the peach cobbler, please?"

"Sure."

"With ice cream!" Audrey piped up.

Mark fought the urge to roll his eyes. "Whatever."

"Not very friendly, is he?" Florie said, watching as Mark stomped off to the kitchen.

"Maybe he's had a long day," Audrey offered.

"Or maybe he just hates us."

"Could be that too."

"You know," Florie started, leaning forward, "I sometimes find it hard to believe that you and me ... we might not be sitting here if Cassandra hadn't tried to stop you from seeing Bobby. Crazy, right? And who knows? Maybe you would've still been eating lunch with her and those weird friends of hers."

Audrey laughed. "Speaking of Cassandra ... how's she been? Is she as much of a diva as I've been imagining?"

"You know what? She's really not too bad. She actually ... she's been pretty nice, on the whole."

"Huh." Audrey scrunched her nose. "Maybe she got Scrooged over the summer."

"The hell is that?"

"You know, like in *A Christmas Carol*, where the three ghosts visit Scrooge to get him to change his ways?"

"Oh, right." Florie laughed, shaking her head. "Forgive me, I just ... I didn't know Scrooged was a verb."

"It probably isn't, but ... maybe I'll make it a thing."

"You should. It's fun to say—Scrooged." Florie smacked her lips. "I'll have to start using that. But yeah, I'm just as surprised as you. She was always standoffish before, but in rehearsals ... she's actually kind of shy sometimes, sort of ... uncomfortable. And she's been asking me for advice on how to sing without straining herself."

"That's a relief. Honestly, when I saw she and Shelly were in the musical, I was worried it'd be a whole cliquey thing."

"Oh, you don't have to worry about that. I've been a theater kid since I was a freshie. I'm *part* of the annoying clique. They'd be the ones on the outside."

Audrey laughed. "But you were telling me how seriously the director's taking it."

"Oh, yeah. He brought in a real vocal coach to help us out. I'm talking a professional voice coach, the kind that works with Broadway stars. She's a little intense, but ... she really knows her stuff, I gotta say. She's helped me develop my chest voice. I mean, I've been going to voice lessons since I was a kid, but she's been pushing me to improve my technique. And you know what? It's been helping! And you know what else? She says I have spunk and pizzazz."

"Well, she's right. Hey, do you think they'll let me sit in on any rehearsals so I can see you in action?"

"No, unfortunately. Only the dress rehearsal. That's weeks away, though. Thank goodness. We still have a lot of work to do before then, so don't be stressing me out like that."

"Well, you have a little less to stress about now—you know, now that I've helped you with your moves and all that."

"True." Florie held up her glass of Coke. "I'm so grateful our paths crossed—at Great Gray, of all places."

"Who would've thought?"

"Who, indeed?" Florie laughed, despite herself. "The most privileged school in Manhattan. But I guess it all worked out the way it was supposed to. And hey, we've done pretty good for ourselves. Just two scholarship girls making their way in the world."

"Damn straight." Audrey nodded for emphasis. "And someday, when you're up there on stage, I'll be cheering you on!"

"And whatever it is *you* end up doing, *I'll* be cheering *you* on too!"

Audrey took a long sip of her Coke. "I'm hoping I get some clarity on that soon."

"You'll figure it out. You just gotta be kind to yourself."

"Yeah, I know. That's what my parents keep saying. It's just hard, seeing you and Bobby and Sarah know exactly what you want to do. And now that we're juniors ... it's all becoming very, very real."

"Hey." Florie took Audrey's hand in hers. "No matter where we go, no matter what we end up doing, we'll always have this. So, don't get all weird about the future, about life after graduation. And look, I know you, and I know nothing I say will get you to stop all your fretting, but you don't ever have to worry about us. All right? We'll be good."

Audrey could feel her eyes tearing up, so she quickly blinked. "Yeah, we'll be good," she managed, offering Florie a smile. Clearing her throat, she added, "And *you'll* be better than good up there on that stage!"

"Damn straight!" Florie winked.

Mark, with a strange pep in his step, handed them a generous slice of peach cobbler and vanilla ice cream. "Here you go, ladies," he said, smiling. "Enjoy!"

"Thanks!" Audrey exchanged a look with Florie. "I guess dessert cheers him up!"

"He said he doesn't eat dessert," Florie reminded her.

"But maybe it makes him happy."

"Or maybe he got Scrooged." They both laughed at that. "But let's dig in before all the ice cream melts!"

"Don't have to tell me twice!"

CHAPTER 22

Bobby

A NEW WAY FORWARD

B OBBY COULDN'T REMEMBER THE last time he'd entered Dempsey Corp. It wasn't a place he frequented, as he didn't exactly like to be reminded of the life his father had always been pushing on him. Many times, Bobby had tried to explain his desire to pursue a different path, but his father had elected not to hear it. Thus, for most of his life, Bobby had done all he could to avoid Dempsey Corp, viewing it as a symbol of everything he had grown to resent.

But after school on November 9, Bobby made his way to Dempsey Corp to surprise his father. Loretta was out of town, visiting her parents back in Houston, so Bobby had thought it would be a nice gesture to take his father out to dinner. They hadn't had a lot of time together in recent months, given Robert's busy schedule. Charles, however, had hinted to Bobby that Robert's evening was clear, and Bobby knew he had to seize this opportunity while he could.

As he walked through the imposing doors of Dempsey Corp, he was confronted with that strange mixture of black pepper and cinnamon: the signature aromas of the building. The smell unlocked a myriad of memories, all flashing through Bobby's mind, fighting for dominance. Various emotions accompanied these memories: dread, anxiety, guilt, dejection. Nevertheless, he shook these feelings off; he was determined to start anew.

At the front desk, Bobby introduced himself, and he was allowed upstairs. Almost immediately after exiting the elevator, he saw Eileen, Robert's long-serving secretary.

"Hi, Eileen," Bobby said as he walked up to her. "I'm here to see my father. Is he in?"

Eileen furrowed her eyebrows, studying him carefully. "Oh!" A flash of recognition crossed her face. "Little Robert! It's been so long! Well, I guess I can't really ... you're not so little anymore."

Bobby chuckled, trying his best to seem unperturbed. "It's Bobby, actually."

"Oh. Sorry." She offered him a tight-lipped smile. "Well, your father isn't in his office, but his last meeting for the day is just finishing up. You're more than welcome to wait for him in there."

"Thank you so much."

Robert's office was exactly as Bobby had remembered. The wenge-wood floors had been recently polished, and the black couch still appeared as though it had never been sat on. When he was a child, Bobby had tried to sit on the couch, and Robert had swiftly reprimanded him, telling him the couch wasn't for lounging. Bobby was thus left to wonder what the couch was for, if not for sitting, but he slowly learned that it was there for appearances, to make the office seem homier than it was. Robert's desk—also made of wenge wood—faced the wall, not the windows, which Bobby had always found to be odd. If this had been his office, he would have situated his desk as close to the windows as possible, to look out upon the New York skyline.

There were very few personal effects. This didn't surprise Bobby, as Robert had never been a sentimental man. He didn't keep anything that wasn't of practical use—or, more importantly, anything that didn't highlight his professional achievements. Most of the photographs in his office were of him and his business associates. Notably, though, a photograph of Robert and Loretta was in a place of honor on Robert's desk. Bobby smiled as he looked at it. He'd never seen his father look so happy. There was another photograph on the bookshelf, one of Robert,

Loretta, and Bobby. Loretta had given the photograph to Robert as a birthday present, back in February. However, to Bobby's confusion, a vase was obscuring him, making it seem as though it was just a picture of Robert and Loretta. He started to move the vase when he heard the door open and close behind him.

Bobby turned around and saw his father. "Hi, Dad." He gestured at the bookshelf. "I was just, um … admiring your photos."

"Yes, they're quite lovely, aren't they?" Robert stood beside Bobby, his eyes on the family photograph. With a heaved sigh, he picked the vase up, positioning it on the far side of the shelf. "When they dust, they forget to move things back to their rightful place."

Bobby wondered if Robert had sensed his disconcertment. A part of Bobby had feared that Robert had placed the vase there intentionally, but it seemed it had just been a harmless mistake. All at once, Bobby's tenseness dissipated.

Robert rested his hand on Bobby's shoulder. "This one's my favorite, you know."

"It is?" Bobby looked up at his father, wide-eyed.

Robert nodded. "You've always favored your mother, but … as you've gotten older … it's been … healing, looking at you and seeing her. I just know she would've been so proud of the young man you've become."

Bobby hadn't heard his father speak so admiringly about his mother since her funeral. In fact, over the past few years, he'd barely heard him utter two words about Margaret. After they buried her, it was like she'd ceased to exist. Within weeks, Robert had donated all her clothes and jewelry, turning her bedroom into a sterile guest room. When Bobby entered the room for the first time after her death, it was nearly impossible to believe it was Margaret's old room. Everything was white, bland, generic. He didn't smell the powdery notes of her Bal à Versailles perfume in the air; he didn't hear the rhythmic ticking of the Black Forest cuckoo clock she'd purchased in Germany; he didn't see her hideous floral bedspread that had always been far too busy for Bobby's tastes.

It'd been difficult for Bobby, watching all the traces of his mother disappear so suddenly. After she died, Bobby had hoped he and Robert would talk about her, keep her memory alive. Wasn't that what people were supposed to do? Robert, though, had never bridged the topic with Bobby, and whenever Bobby asked questions about Margaret, aiming to learn more about the woman he hadn't been able to spend enough time with, Robert blew him off.

Now, though ... now, Robert seemed ready, for whatever reason, to discuss Margaret. Did he feel guilty, now that he was in a relationship with a woman he genuinely loved? Did he wish that Margaret had been able to experience a love like he and Loretta shared? Did he at all feel as though he'd wasted Margaret's life, prevented her from achieving true joy? All these questions swirled in Bobby's head, making him dizzy.

Robert studied Bobby carefully. "I know I haven't ... talked about her enough. And I know you have questions about her. I'd like to answer them for you, give you a better sense of who your mother was. And you know, Bobby ... grief works in mysterious ways. For me, it was easier to move on, but you ... you needed more. And I didn't give you that."

"You did your best."

"But I could've done better." Robert's posture straightened. "And I *will* do better."

Bobby shifted on his feet. "What's brought all this on?"

"Well, as you know, the third anniversary of her death is on Sunday, and ... I guess I've been thinking about her more, going back over how I handled everything. It's made me realize I made mistakes—mistakes I hope I can still fix." He met Bobby's eyes. "What I'm trying to say, Bobby, is ... I want you to ask me about her."

Bobby had known, of course, that the anniversary of his mother's passing was coming up, but he hadn't expected his father to mention it—or, quite frankly, to even remember it. Bobby had always assumed—perhaps unfairly—that Robert hadn't loved Margaret, that her death had been a blessing for him. With her out of the picture, he no longer had to feign pleasantries or act as though he and Margaret were the picture-perfect couple they'd always tried to emulate. He could more brazenly spend nights with his women, shower them with all kinds of gifts and attention. But maybe Margaret's death had been harder on Robert than Bobby had thought.

"Anyway," Robert said, his tone instantly lightening, "I'm assuming you didn't come here to talk about your mother."

"No, I … I was actually … I was wondering if you'd like to go out to dinner, just the two of us. I figured with Loretta out of town, we could do something."

"I know just the spot."

Robert led Bobby down the hall, stopping at a few cubicles along the way, introducing him to some of his employees. Bobby had always hated these forced introductions, knowing very well his father was trying to signal that these people would all be working for him someday, but this time, Robert seemed more interested in boasting about his son. He mentioned that Bobby would, if all went according to plan, be attending Columbia in two years' time. Bobby was dumbfounded. Had Robert finally accepted that Bobby wanted something different for himself?

Bobby continued to ponder this as they left Dempsey Corp and made their way to Sparks Steak House, one of Robert's favorite restaurants in the city. Bobby vaguely wondered whether Robert was so enamored with the place because of its connection to the Gambino crime family. Robert had always been fascinated with Mafia history—something he'd passed on to Bobby. Both men ranked *The Godfather* as one of their favorite movies. It had, until recently, been the only thing they could talk about besides the weather.

"Dad." As they sat down, Bobby placed his napkin on his lap. "I know you didn't like the idea of me going to Columbia, but … have you … changed your mind on that?"

Robert took a thoughtful sip of his water before answering. "Columbia is a great school," he started. "It's not Harvard, but … it has a strong business program. It'll prepare you for what's to come."

Bobby's stomach dropped. It'd been ignorant of him to think that Robert was now also on board with the idea of Bobby pursuing writing as a full-time career. Columbia, Robert could accept; after all, Columbia, like Harvard, was part of the Ivy League. But Robert had never been supportive of Bobby's more creative endeavors. The flickering candle on the tabletop brought Bobby back to the night he'd watched *Bright Neon Dreams* turn to ash right in front of his very eyes. He blinked, looking away.

"What's wrong?" asked Robert, no doubt noticing Bobby's squirminess.

"I just ..." Bobby summoned all his bravery. "I really wish you'd take me more seriously when I tell you that I don't want to take over Dempsey Corp."

Bobby braced himself for his father's reaction, expecting the worst. Robert wasn't the type to make a scene in public, but Bobby could very easily see him standing up and walking away, refusing to finish his meal—or their conversation. Instead, Robert's expression was unchanged. Something akin to a smirk formed on his lips.

"I know you don't," Robert said evenly. "That's not what I was talking about."

"But ... you were talking about Columbia's business program, and at Dempsey Corp ... I don't know. I guess it seemed like you were trying to—"

"I know you want to be an author, open your own publishing house someday. And all I'm saying is Columbia will help you with that."

Bobby blanched. "You ... you're okay with that?"

"Why wouldn't I be?"

"Because ... it's always been your dream for me to take over Dempsey Corp. You ... you're okay with it ... going to someone else, someone who isn't ... a Dempsey?"

Robert leaned back in his chair and folded his hands across his stomach. "Dempsey Corp will be fine. It isn't something you need to worry about—not anymore. Maybe I should have told you this earlier, but ... there you go. You're free to do as you please."

If Bobby hadn't been sitting directly across from Robert, looking into his eyes, he wouldn't have been able to believe these words were coming out of his father's mouth. What had changed? Why was Robert now singing a completely different tune?

"I ... I don't know what to say," Bobby said at last, struggling to form a coherent response. "I guess I just ... has something happened to ... change your mind?"

"Nothing you need concern yourself with. Loretta and I talked about it, and ... you should do as you wish." Seeing Bobby's agape mouth, Robert chuckled, adding, "What, were you expecting me to say something else?"

Bobby swallowed hard. "I just ... I didn't think ... I always thought you were ashamed of me for wanting to do something else with my life."

"You're my son. How could I ever be ashamed of you?"

Tears formed in Bobby's eyes. Hurriedly, he blinked them away, not wanting to cry in public—or in front of his father. Despite his amended stance on Columbia, Robert was still a man who detested any sort of emotional displays—particularly from other men.

"Thank you," Bobby said, clearing his throat.

Robert raised his wine glass. "To a new beginning—for both of us."

CHAPTER 23

Audrey

A RISING STAR

*G*REASE WAS OPENING IN a few days, and Florie was on pins and needles. She and the rest of the cast had been working around the clock to make the production as professional as possible, but now that the show was right around the corner, nerves had started to kick in. Adding to their anxiety, Cassandra hadn't been in school for the past week.

"I don't know what we'll do," Florie told Audrey and Sarah at lunch. "The dress rehearsal is tomorrow night! If Cassandra doesn't show up, we don't have a show."

"No one's heard from her?" asked Sarah.

"No! She's just ... gone."

Audrey took a sip of her juice. "Why don't *you* play Rizzo?"

"What?"

"Yeah! I mean, you know all the lines and songs and everything. And, let's be honest, it should've been yours from the get. If Cassandra doesn't show up tomorrow, you should tell the director you can be Rizzo."

Florie shook her head. "He'd never go for it."

"What if I go with you? As moral support. You said people can sit in on the dress rehearsal, right?"

"Right."

"So, that's what I'll do! I mean, what's the alternative? No show?"

Florie stroked her chin. "Cassandra could show up to the dress rehearsal."

"But what if she doesn't?" Audrey reached across the table and touched Florie's hand. "This could be your moment. And like I said, I'll be right there in the audience, cheering you on!"

The next night, Audrey showed up to the dress rehearsal and sat toward the back of the audience. The cast was all standing on stage, and the director was waving his arms around erratically. Right away, Audrey could see that Cassandra was nowhere in sight.

"We open in two days!" the director was saying. "Where is Cassandra?"

"No one's seen her all week," one of the students said.

"She's really sick," interjected Shelly.

"But she's our Rizzo! She can't just ... not show up!"

Audrey's eyes were on Florie. Slowly, Florie stepped forward, clearing her throat. Excitedly, Audrey rubbed her hands together.

"I could play Rizzo," Florie offered.

"What?" The director stared at her. "No, you ... that's not ... that won't happen."

"I know the part. I can do it."

"You're in the ensemble."

"No one will even notice one ensemble dancer missing, but I think they'll notice if there's no Rizzo." Florie gestured at the other students on stage. "We've all worked so hard on this show. It can't just ... not happen."

The director pondered this. "You really ... you think you can do it?"

"I *know* I can," Florie assured him, hand to her heart. "The show must go on, right?"

He smiled, despite himself. "Okay, everyone! Places!"

It took everything inside Audrey not to stand up and applaud. She made eye contact with Florie, who winked at her. Finally, it was Florie's moment to shine.

Audrey was on the literal edge of her seat, anticipating Florie's debut as Rizzo. And, as expected, Florie did not disappoint. If Audrey hadn't known better, she would've assumed that Florie had been Rizzo all along. She effortlessly exuded the same sort of coolness that Stockard Channing had in the movie.

Afterward, the cast and crew congratulated Florie, telling her how incredible she was. The boy who was playing Kenickie seemed particularly smitten with her; he couldn't stop singing her praises. It warmed Audrey's heart, seeing Florie receive the attention and acclaim she so deserved. She would certainly be the talk of the school, once the musical officially opened.

And she was. On opening night, a few people in the audience murmured amongst themselves, unable to believe that Florie, a Black woman, now had a prominent role in the show. Audrey wished she could say she was surprised by their racism and ignorance, but she had expected there to be some backlash. Nevertheless, no one could credibly discount Florie's talent. She was one of the highlights of the entire show, and Audrey made sure to clap as loudly as she could for Florie during the bows.

After the show, Audrey waited in the lobby with Florie's parents, Kenneth and Kay. Kenneth and Kay were absolutely beside themselves; Florie hadn't told them she would be playing Rizzo, as she'd wanted it to be a surprise.

"Our little girl, up there on that stage!" said Kay. "Never thought I'd see it."

Kenneth turned to Audrey. "Did you know she'd be Rizzo?"

Audrey shrugged, chuckling. "Maybe."

They looked up whenever they saw someone emerge from backstage. Finally, Florie came out from one of the side hallways. Audrey managed to wave Florie down, and Florie ran over to them.

"How'd you like the show?" Florie asked them.

"We loved it!" Audrey replied. "You were amazing, absolutely amazing!"

"Oh, honey!" Kay pulled Florie into a hug. "You were so good!"

"Thanks, Momma!" Florie gripped her mother's hands. "I'm so glad you made it!"

"We wouldn't have missed it for the world," Kenneth piped up. "And knowing you had a leading role … that just made it even better. We always knew you'd be a big star someday!"

"It's just a high school production, Poppa," Florie reminded him, her cheeks red.

"That's where it starts. But just you wait and see where it takes you."

"Hey, Florie." Cassandra walked up to them.

"Cassandra." Florie cocked her head to the side. "What are you doing here? Shelly said you were sick."

"I was. But Shelly told me you were going to be Rizzo, and … I didn't want to miss it." She offered Florie a smile. "You were really great."

"Oh. Thank you!" Florie smiled in return. "And hey, I'm sorry you didn't get to be up there. I know you worked real hard."

Cassandra waved a flippant hand. "You are a far better Rizzo than I ever was." She nodded at Florie's parents. "Your daughter's really talented."

Kenneth wrapped his arm around Florie. "We certainly think so."

"Well, I should go congratulate Shelly. But great job, Florie." And with that, Cassandra left.

"Wow." Audrey's eyes widened. "Didn't see that coming!"

"You're telling me." Florie let out a low whistle. "People keep getting Scrooged left, right, and center!"

Kenneth grinned. "Let's take you out somewhere to celebrate. Audrey, you wanna join us?"

"I'd love to!" Audrey said.

They ended up eating burgers at Jack's, and Kenneth, Kay, and Audrey all took turns telling Florie their favorite part of her performance. Florie, in turn, shared some backstage secrets.

"I can't wait for the next few nights," Florie gushed. "I was real nervous tonight, but … I think I'll find my groove."

"That was you nervous?" asked Audrey. "You seemed confident to me!"

"It's called acting, honey."

Audrey laughed. "Right. Sorry."

Florie grinned. "You'll come tomorrow night, right?"

"I'll be at every show. You can count on that!"

Each night, Florie's performance improved. She was much more comfortable during the Sunday matinee than she'd been on opening night, and she seemed like she was having more fun with the role. Audrey loved seeing her best friend in her element, living her dream.

Indeed, Florie was a rising star, and Audrey couldn't wait to see her shine.

CHAPTER 24

Audrey

THE WINTER FORMAL

T HIS YEAR, BOBBY SPENT Christmas with Robert and Loretta in the Hamptons, but he and Audrey wished each other a happy holiday over the phone, and they promised to exchange gifts once school resumed. Florie, for her part, stayed in the city, and Sarah and her family traveled to San Francisco, where most of her extended family lived.

On New Year's Eve, Audrey and her family tuned in to *Happy New Year, America*. They preferred watching the ball drop from the comfort of their own home. Alexander always said the ball drop was a tourist trap, and real New Yorkers knew to stay as far away from Times Square as possible. As usual, Sophia fell asleep on the couch before midnight, and Claire was more than a little tipsy. And then, somehow, it was 1980.

Audrey and her peers returned to school for the spring semester of their junior year. Before school began on that Monday, Bobby and Audrey met up in the auditorium, as they usually did, but this time, they were swapping Christmas gifts. It had been odd, not seeing Bobby for so long, but they'd compensated by calling each other almost every day—something that had driven Claire crazy.

Bobby cupped Audrey's face in his hands, kissing her. "I missed you so much," he said.

"I missed you too."

Audrey pulled him in for another kiss, but she quickly broke away, knowing very well that if they started down this path, they wouldn't have enough time to exchange gifts. Promptly, Audrey composed herself and opened the small box Bobby had given her. It was a rose-gold ring.

"It's a promise ring," he explained. "I know we're young. But I wanted to give you something to show you just how serious I am about you."

"Oh my goodness!" Audrey rotated the ring in her hand. "It's gorgeous! And look, it looks so good with the necklace you gave me last year," she added, holding the ring up to her necklace.

"That's why I got it."

"I love it." Audrey slipped on the ring, then kissed him. "Thank you, Bobby. It's perfect."

"You're very welcome." He took her hand in his, caressing the ring with his thumb. "You know, I can hardly believe I've only known you for two Christmases. It feels so much longer, doesn't it? Like I've known you for forever."

"I know what you mean." Audrey tightened her grip on his hand. "I love you so much."

"I love you too." He slowly pulled his hand away, reaching for her present. "Now, let's see what's in here, shall we?" He picked up the box, which was rather sizable. "It's got a bit of weight to it," he noted.

"Just open it already! We don't need the play by play."

"All right," he chuckled, opening the box. He stared in disbelief at what was inside: a cornflower-blue cable knit sweater. "Aud." He looked up at her, wide-eyed. "You didn't ... you didn't have to buy this for me."

"I didn't buy it. I made it!"

"You made this?" He blinked rapidly. "I ... how? When?"

"It's just a little something I've been working on for the past few months. I feel I know your style pretty well, and I thought ... well, I thought you'd look super handsome in it. And you'll see on the left cuff, there's a tiny, little heart sewed on there, with the letter A in the middle—you know, so you'll think of me whenever you wear it."

He held the sweater up, shaking his head. "This is better than most of the sweaters they have in stores. And knowing you made this ... that just makes it even better. Thank you." He kissed her. "You're the best."

"I *am* pretty amazing."

He laughed. "I've really got to step up my game here. You've been showing me up."

"No way. I love all your gifts. They're so sweet." She once again admired her ring. "I put this on the right hand, right? 'Cause I don't want people to get the wrong idea and start thinking we're engaged or anything."

"That's the right hand," Bobby assured her. "And hey, it's literally the right hand! How's that for coincidence?"

Audrey made a face. "I see why you and my dad get along so well. You both love those awful, punny jokes."

"They're great jokes." Bobby smiled coyly, tucking a loose strand of hair behind her ear. "Are you excited for the winter formal?"

"Obviously! I already have my dress and everything. And I know you keep saying you'll pay for both of us, but—"

"That actually won't be necessary."

"What do you mean?"

"Sarah did it. Over the break, she was able to convince the committee to eliminate the fee for the winter formal."

"Really? That's fantastic!"

"I told you she'd work her magic." Bobby met her eyes. "But I'm looking really forward to it. We'll have fun."

"Don't we always?"

T HE WINTER FORMAL WAS held on January 12 in The Plaza Hotel. Audrey couldn't believe how decked out the space was. Evidently, the party committee had an enviable budget, one that allowed them to book The Plaza and decorate the ballroom with fairy lights, streamers, and balloons. The color scheme, as always, was blue, purple, and white, and students were encouraged—or, more accurately, forced—to wear those colors, unless they wanted to be turned away at the door.

"They run a tight ship," Audrey said to Sarah, who, ironically, was involved in planning the affair, despite her hatred for all social events.

"They like the idea of everyone wearing similar colors. I don't know why. Maybe they think it puts us all on the same playing field or something," Sarah said.

In keeping with the winter formal tradition, Audrey wore an amethyst Grecian dress with spaghetti straps, a mock wrap bodice, and a matching tie around her waist. Bobby, for his part, donned a navy-blue tuxedo with a velvet collar, satin lapels, and an amethyst bowtie. As they entered the ballroom, Audrey was imbued with a strange sense of invincibility. With Bobby on her arm, nothing could go wrong.

Paul Knight, the boy who'd played Kenickie in *Grease*, had asked Florie to the winter formal—as friends—and she'd happily accepted. She'd told Audrey how much she was dreading attending such a year-defining event alone—or even worse, with someone she didn't like—so Audrey was relieved that everything had worked out. Bobby and Audrey stood on the side, surveying the room, and Audrey nearly squealed when she saw Florie. Florie was wearing a white pleated skirt halter dress, while Paul sported a white tuxedo.

"Florie!" Audrey ran up to her, grabbing her hands. "You look amazing!"

"You too!" Florie grinned. She looked up at Paul. "You know Audrey, right? My best friend?"

Paul nodded, saying, "We met after one of the shows. I can't believe you came to all four performances."

"Of course!" Audrey said. "You were fantastic, by the way."

"Well, thank you. But all the credit goes to the lady here on my left."

"Oh, stop it!" Florie playfully smacked his arm. "You were a great Kenickie before I ever became Rizzo."

"You both did a remarkable job," Bobby piped up, stepping forward.

Paul studied him carefully. "Bobby, right? You wrote the piece about our show in *The Bulletin*."

"Guilty as charged."

"That was a great article. My mom actually ... she's thinking of getting it framed. Says it can count as my first positive review."

Bobby laughed. "The first of many, I'd say. You were a natural on that stage."

The two couples chatted for a while. Then, they went their separate ways. Paul and Florie were more interested in the social scene, talking with anyone and everyone, while Bobby and Audrey were more interested in sneaking away to make out behind the balloons. It had always been like this with them: fun, flirty, and exciting. They were like magnets. Whenever they were alone, they were all over each other, and it was a genuine struggle to not take things further. Their willpower had been tested many times over the past sixteen months, but so far, they had managed to avoid temptation. They both knew they wanted to take that next step—at some point—but they also wanted to make sure the timing and location were right.

"I had a lot of fun tonight," Audrey said as Felix drove them back to her apartment.

"Me too." Bobby kissed the top of her head. "I hope I'll be able to feel my feet tomorrow, what with all the dancing we were doing."

"Hey, I was the one dancing in heels!"

Bobby laughed. He then looked out the window, sighing. "Looks like we're here." He took Audrey's hand in his. "I'll walk you to your door."

Slowly, Bobby and Audrey walked to the front door of her apartment building, neither wanting the night to end. It had been a perfect, fairytale-like night, and she wasn't yet ready to bid her prince goodbye.

"Aud." Bobby stopped, his thumb caressing her promise ring. "I just ... I want you to know ... when I gave you this ring ... it doesn't mean ... I don't want you to feel pressured into anything. I'm really happy the way things are, and I ... I don't want you to feel—"

"I know." Audrey stroked the back of his hair.

"Because ... I love you so much. And I never ... I'd never want you to feel like ... like I'm pushing you for more. Because really, I ... I'm more than happy just doing this." He grinned impishly, leaning in to kiss her.

Audrey laughed, grasping his hair and pulling him closer. "I love you, Bobby," she said as they parted. "Thank you for tonight."

She kissed him one last time before she headed up to her apartment. As she'd expected, her parents were still awake, wanting to make sure she arrived home safe and sound. They were delighted to hear she'd had a magical evening, and she promised she'd tell them more about it in the morning.

"But right now," she said, "I just want to sleep."

And yet, despite her exhaustion, Audrey couldn't sleep. She'd been hit with a second wind. She ended up staring at the ceiling for hours, images of the night playing on repeat in her mind. It had been so perfect—even more perfect than she could have imagined.

Already, 1980 was off to a fantastic start.

CHAPTER 25

Bobby

A FAMILY MATTER

W HEN BOBBY ENTERED THE townhouse, he didn't expect to see anyone else up and about. It was rather late, and at this hour, Loretta was usually upstairs, and Robert was in his office. To Bobby's surprise, however, he saw a light on in the drawing room, and he could hear muffled voices through the ajar French doors. Curious, he poked his head in, to see who was still awake.

Both Robert and Loretta were sitting on the couch, each holding a glass of sherry. They always seemed so at peace with each other, so comfortable. To announce his arrival—and ensure he didn't scare them by simply walking into the room—Bobby knocked on the door.

Loretta was the first to look up. She stood up and waved Bobby over.

"Bobby! We actually ... we were waiting up for you." She pulled him in for a hug. "How was your night? Did you have fun?"

"I did."

Loretta straightened his bowtie—and his tousled hair. Her gaze lingered on the lipstick marks on Bobby's face and neck, but thankfully, she elected not to say anything. That was something Bobby greatly appreciated about Loretta: her discretion.

"You look dashing," Loretta said. "I'm so happy we got all those photos of you and Audrey beforehand."

Bobby smiled. "Well, I was just going to head up to bed, and I don't want to—"

"Actually, Bobby," started Loretta, "your father and I ... there's something we wanted to talk to you about." Loretta made eye contact with Robert, who stood up and walked over to her. "Do you want to tell him, or shall I?"

"You can tell him," Robert said.

Bobby nervously looked between the two of them. "Tell me what?"

"Well," drawled Loretta, an unmistakable zeal in her voice, "your father and I ... we've been talking about it, and we think—I mean, as long as you're okay with it, of course—we're thinking of ... expanding our family."

Loretta looked positively giddy, with Robert's arm wrapped around her waist. Robert, too, seemed happy, though he, of course, was much more subdued than Loretta. Their joy was practically infectious; Bobby could not help but smile himself.

"That's great news!" Bobby said.

"Really?" Loretta couldn't hide her relief. "You're really okay with that?"

"Of course! I mean, I always ... I've wanted a sibling for as long as I can remember."

"And it wouldn't be weird for you, being so much older? Because ... well, this is all hypothetical right now, of course, but ... your father and I just wanted to make sure you wouldn't be ... well, you've been an only child your whole life, and you'll be in college soon, so this might be—"

"I promise you, I'm more than okay with it." Bobby turned to his father. "What changed your mind?"

Loretta furrowed her eyebrows, glimpsing between the Dempsey men. "Changed his mind?"

Seeing his father's eyes darken, Bobby hastily replied, "It's just ... my parents always said they only ever wanted one child."

Loretta looked up at Robert, a mischievous twinkle in her eyes. "What, was

Bobby such a bad kid he scared you out of ever wanting any more?"

Robert laughed, despite himself, and Bobby was grateful he hadn't angered his father. The light returned to Robert's eyes, and he pulled Loretta closer.

"No, nothing like that," Robert said. "It was just never in the cards for me and Margaret." He kissed Loretta's forehead. "But with you, it's a different matter altogether."

This satisfied Loretta, and to Bobby, she said, "We just wanted to let you know ahead of time so that nothing ... we didn't want you to be surprised is all."

"And I appreciate that." Bobby tried to fight back a yawn but couldn't. "Well, I'm spent. I'm going to head on up."

"Yes, good idea. It's getting late." Loretta broke away from Robert to kiss Bobby's cheek. "Love you, honey. Have the sweetest dreams."

As Bobby made his way up to his bedroom, he thought about what life could possibly look like a year or so from now. If everything went as Robert and Loretta planned, there could be another Dempsey in the family. Would he have a brother or a sister? He didn't care much either way; he'd do everything he could to make sure his sibling felt all the love and affection he'd lacked in his childhood. He hoped he'd be a good big brother, the kind his sibling could come to for moral support.

More than anything, he wanted everything to work out for Robert and Loretta. Though Bobby had never been the religious sort, he found himself praying for Robert, Loretta, and their future child. He knew nothing was guaranteed, of course, that anything could happen, but he held out hope that Robert and Loretta would get their happy ending.

CHAPTER 26

Audrey

SPRING BREAK IN MONTAUK

FOR SPRING BREAK, BOBBY invited Audrey, Florie, and Sarah to his family's house in the Hamptons. They'd have the place to themselves, as Robert and Loretta were staying in the city. To Audrey's shock, Alexander and Sophia had no qualms about her and her friends hanging out in a mansion without any adult supervision.

"We trust you," Sophia said. "Just know we'll be calling every night, to make sure you're okay."

Sarah's parents were the most difficult to convince, but because they knew Bobby so well, they eventually conceded. It helped that they knew the Dagenharts' house was just down the road, and Sebastian, who was off on break from Columbia, promised them he'd swing by the Dempseys' house to check in on them.

"Just girls, huh?" Florie asked Bobby, an eyebrow raised. "You know how that looks, right? You asking a bunch of girls to your house?"

Bobby laughed. "A lot of my track and baseball friends will be in Montauk too. They'll come over and hang out. I think you'll like them! They're a good time."

"If you say so." To Audrey, Florie whispered, "You sure he has other friends?"

"Yes!" laughed Audrey, hitting Florie's arm. "They just have places to stay out there, that's all."

They all met up outside Bobby's townhouse after school on that Friday, and Felix drove them to the Hamptons. Audrey had never been to the Dempseys' Hamptons house before. As Felix pulled into the long driveway, with old-growth oak trees on either side, Audrey audibly gasped. She couldn't believe Bobby had referred to it as a house; it was, unmistakably, a mansion, straight out of *The Great Gatsby*. It was a Georgian-style manor, with blue shutters framing the windows. The mansion looked like it had three floors, including a basement. She could just see the edge of a pool off to the right; it was mostly obscured by the hedges. Beside the pool, there was a guest house, which looked like a miniature version of the mansion.

"We're here!" Bobby said as he hopped out of the car. "Thank you, Felix. You're going to stay the night, right?"

"Well, I don't want to impose," Felix protested. "I know you kids have plans, and—"

"Nonsense! It's getting late. I'd feel better if you stayed. Besides, we have more than enough room."

"If you insist."

"I do. And don't worry about the bags. We've got them."

While they unloaded the bags, Felix pushed open the gate to the backyard and started walking toward the beach, eager to stretch his legs after the long journey. It'd been a stressful one, with heavy traffic, but he'd done a masterful job of keeping them all safe. They'd made it to Montauk in just under four hours, which, according to Bobby, was great timing—especially for a Friday evening.

"Okay." Bobby stood on the front stoop, looking down at Audrey, Florie, and Sarah. "I figured you ladies would want to check out all the guest rooms, see which one you like best. Most of them have ocean views, if I remember correctly, so you won't have to fight over that. But other than that, come on in! And please, make yourselves at home."

Bobby unlocked the absurdly large front door. Skilled artisans had crafted the door, as evidenced by the detailed carvings of flowers and cherubs. Bobby led them into the foyer, which boasted blue-and-white tiled floors and a sweeping staircase. The side of the staircase was intricately engraved with vines and birds. A lot of nature going on with these design choices: flowers, vines, and birds. The cherubs were a curveball, but for some reason, rich people seemed to like having cherubs in their homes. Toward the back of the foyer, windows looked out onto the backyard, with unobstructed vistas of the Atlantic Ocean. Audrey could see Felix, returning to the house.

"Here, if we put our bags down, I can give you a tour of the place first," Bobby said, waving them farther into the foyer.

Bobby showed them all the highlights: the kitchen, the dining room, the terrace, the living room, the library, the parlor. At some point, Audrey lost track of where they were in the house. Before they went upstairs, they retrieved their suitcases. Bobby told the girls they could choose which rooms they wanted for the week.

"Any preference?" Sarah asked Florie and Audrey, not wanting to be the first to claim her room.

"Are you kidding? I still can't believe I'm here!" Florie closed her eyes and spun around in a circle, pointing at a random door. "There! I'll take this one!"

"Excellent choice," Bobby laughed. "Sarah? Which room would you like?"

"I'll take the one by Florie," Sarah decided, high-fiving Florie.

The two girls darted into their respective rooms, excited to unpack, leaving Bobby and Audrey alone in the hallway. Even from the other side of the door, Audrey could hear Florie's squeals of delight as she made herself at home in the room.

Bobby's eyes fell on Audrey. "And you?"

"The one down the hall's really nice," Audrey said, pointing for good measure.

"I was hoping you'd say that."

"Why?"

"Because that one's next to my room." Audrey could feel her cheeks redden. Bobby picked up her suitcase. "Let's get you settled in."

Bobby led Audrey down the hallway and used his elbow to open the door to her room. Her room looked out on the side of the house, facing the pool, but she could still see the ocean. When Bobby had given them the grand tour, she'd felt drawn to this room's sage, cream, and white color scheme. It was one of the most calming rooms she'd ever been in.

"Here you are." Bobby placed her suitcase next to the closet. "I'll give you some time to unpack. And then, I figure we can all have some dinner and hang out."

Audrey draped her arms around his neck. "Thank you for inviting us. It's beautiful out here. I can see why you love it so much."

Bobby kissed her. "I've been looking forward to this for a long time. There's tons to do, both around here and in town. I can't wait to take you all to the Montauket. It's my favorite. Everything on the menu is fantastic."

Audrey ran her fingers through his hair, tousling it up. "I don't think I've ever seen you this giddy before. Clearly, the sea air does wonders for you."

Bobby laughed. "Montauk has been my stomping ground for years." He kissed her again. "But like I said, I'll let you unpack. Come downstairs when you're ready, okay?"

Quickly, Audrey freshened up, wanting to appear somewhat presentable for dinner. She knew she didn't have to impress anyone, but she could still smell the car ride on her. She changed into comfier clothes, then headed downstairs. Luckily, she wasn't the last one down; Sarah was still unpacking. Bobby and Florie were sitting in the dining room, chatting away, while Felix was outside, looking out at the ocean. Audrey stood back for a few moments, watching Bobby and Florie. She couldn't remember them ever having a one-on-one conversation before. She wasn't sure what they were discussing, but she assumed it had something to do with sports.

"... better than last year," Florie was saying.

"I think they're in a good position this season," Bobby said. "I mean, with Randolph and Jackson—" He cut himself off when he saw Audrey. "Aud! Hey!"

"I didn't want to interrupt," Audrey said, sitting down next to Florie. "What were you talking about?"

"What else? The Yankees," Florie said with a laugh.

"How ... fascinating."

Florie shook her head, jokingly upset. "It should be illegal for New Yorkers to not love the Yankees."

"Agreed." Bobby winked at Audrey; she, in turn, stuck her tongue out at him. Laughing, Bobby went on, "Well, the pizzas are in the oven. Dinner should be ready soon."

Within a few minutes, Sarah joined them, and the four teenagers and Felix ate their pepperoni pizzas. Afterward, Felix excused himself, telling them he'd be setting off bright and early tomorrow morning. They wished him a safe journey before they moved the party into the parlor. Audrey decided, perhaps prematurely, it was her favorite room in the house. During the day, the sun-soaked parlor would be the perfect place to curl up and stare out at the ocean, lost in its spellbinding beauty.

Despite their best intentions, they all found themselves fading fast, so they retired to their rooms for the night. Audrey couldn't believe how serene it was out here. She didn't hear any sirens or car horns—only the waves lapping along the beach. She drifted off to sleep, knowing the week ahead would be full of fun in the sun.

And it was. During the day, the house was a revolving door, with teenagers coming in and out at will. Audrey knew most of them, as they also attended Great Gray, but some of them were from other private schools. As he'd promised Sarah's parents, Sebastian popped in every day to make sure everyone was okay. Audrey had met most of Bobby's teammates before, but one of them—Rick—was somehow unaware that she and Bobby were dating, as he took every opportunity he could to hit on her.

"You gotta give him points for persistence," Florie said as she and Audrey lounged by the pool, sipping lemonade.

"I don't know how many ways I can say no." Audrey rolled her eyes. "Some guys just don't get it, I guess."

"I think you'll find *most* guys don't get it. You got lucky with Bobby. He's one of the good ones. And from what I can gather, there are very few of them out there."

Audrey watched as the boys played soccer in the backyard. She knew how athletic Bobby was, but she hadn't expected him to be able to hold his own against his friends, some of whom were also on Great Gray's soccer team. Nevertheless, Bobby kept pace with them; he even scored a goal for his team.

"Great. Now, they're gonna be all sweaty and gross when they come back," Florie said, sighing melodramatically. "Our peace and quiet will be ruined."

Audrey peered at Florie over her sunglasses. "You make it sound so torturous, spending our days lazing around this gorgeous mansion."

Florie laughed, placing down her glass. "No, it's been a blast. Their music room is amazing. Bobby said I can go in there whenever I want to work on some music." She leaned back, basking in the sun. "Really, Audrey, he's a keeper—a perfect, little peach."

"Don't have to tell me twice."

As if on cue, the boys bounded back toward the pool, yelling and jumping on top of each other. Audrey could hardly fathom how they had so much energy. She and Florie had spent the better part of an hour doing nothing but sitting by the pool, but Audrey could hear a nap calling her name.

"Mark my words," said Florie, sitting up. "They're gonna be pushing each other into the pool, and then they're gonna expect us to jump in with them." She slipped on her swim cap, securing it behind her ears. "Just in case one of them grabs me, I gotta be prepared."

Bobby broke away from the pack, running up to them. Audrey absently bit her straw. He somehow managed to make his navy-blue tracksuit, which was covered in dirt and grass stains, look good. If Audrey hadn't known better, she would've assumed he was posing for an Adidas ad; his sweaty, messy hair had perfectly fallen into his sun-kissed face.

"Who won?" called out Florie.

"We did," Bobby said proudly.

"Well done." Florie gripped her lounger. "You're not here to pick us up and throw us into the pool, are you?"

Bobby laughed, shaking his head. "No. I was actually going to jump into a quick shower. I just, you know, wanted to say hi." He met Audrey's eyes. "Having fun?"

"Oh, absolutely," said Audrey, nodding. "You boys put on quite the show for us."

"I wasn't sure if you were watching."

"I was."

Bobby grinned. "I'll be right back down. Make sure the guys stay out of trouble."

"Oh, so now, we're their babysitters?" asked Florie with a groan.

While Bobby was gone, the boys set up the volleyball net in the pool. They asked Audrey and Florie if they wanted to play, and they said they would. They needed Sarah to make the teams even, so Audrey darted into the house to find her. As she'd expected, Sarah was in the library, getting ahead on her schoolwork. With some gentle prodding, Sarah agreed to play water volleyball with them. By the time they reached the pool, Bobby was already back. To Audrey's disappointment, unlike the other boys, Bobby was wearing a T-shirt. The teenagers divided themselves into teams, then jumped into the pool to play.

Sensing Rick's eyes on her, Audrey made sure to be obvious, bordering on annoying, about her affections. Every chance she could, she was touching Bobby, jumping on his back. It seemed to work; after the game, Rick, in an attempt to be sneaky, asked Florie if Bobby and Audrey were an item, and Florie told him they were.

"But I think you already knew that. You just ... didn't *want* to know," Florie said. She patted his shoulder. "Sorry, Rick. But, you know, there's lots of fish in the sea, all that."

Audrey, who had overheard the whole conversation from her vantage point near the pool house, mouthed "Thank you" to Florie, who, in turn, gave her a thumbs-up.

"You were unbelievable," Bobby said as he wrapped a towel around Audrey. "And here, I thought you didn't like sports."

"I don't. But it was fun." Audrey looked up at him, pulling the towel closer for warmth. "I like being on your team."

Bobby leaned down to kiss her. They could hear the exaggerated groans of some of Bobby's friends, but they didn't care. Slowly, they parted, and they watched as the sun at last slipped behind the horizon.

"Another beautiful night," Bobby mused, resting his chin on Audrey's shoulder. "I just love it out here—especially at this time of day."

"I can see why. It's straight out of a postcard."

"Aud." His breath tingled the hairs on her neck. "I was wondering if you'd—"

"Come on, everyone!" one of the boys said, corralling the group together. "Let's eat!"

"Oooo! Food!" Audrey grabbed Bobby's hand. "Let's go! Before they eat it all."

After dinner, the boys dispersed, heading back to their respective houses, and Sarah, Florie, Audrey, and Bobby retreated to the music room, where Florie played some of her songs for them. Bobby listened for a while, then told them he was going to turn in for the night. The girls stayed up for a bit longer before they also called it a night, knowing they'd need to be well rested for tomorrow's activities.

As she made her way to her room, Audrey passed Bobby's room. The light shone from underneath his door, signaling that he was still awake. Gently, Audrey knocked on the door, and from the other side, Bobby said it was open. She'd caught a glimpse of Bobby's bedroom earlier in the day, as he'd left his door open, but she hadn't wanted to trespass in his space without his permission. Adorably, Bobby was sitting cross-legged on his bed, reading a well-worn copy of *Their Eyes Were Watching God*. He was wearing a dark-gray sweatshirt that had "NEW YORK" embroidered on the front in big, black lettering. When he heard the door open, he looked up.

"Aud!" He marked his page, then placed the book on his bedside table. "Come on in."

Audrey surveyed his room, noting how much more decorated it was than his bedroom in New York. Travel posters lined the walls, giving Audrey greater insight into the kinds of places Bobby wanted to go—mostly Northern European countries that were famous for their natural beauty and cooler temperatures. A shiver ran down her spine, as though she'd been transported to these snowy landscapes just by looking at the posters.

Bobby slid off his bed and approached her. "Florie's going to make an incredible album someday," he said. "The stuff she was playing for us was so good."

"Oh, I know! She'll become a household name, for sure. I'd put money on it." Audrey motioned to the posters. "You really like the cold, don't you?"

Bobby shrugged. "I am what I am."

"Well, if we ever go on vacation together, we're going to have to compromise. Because I'd rather be on a beach than in a snowy cabin."

"I'm sure we can make it work." Bobby wrapped his arms around her waist, pulling her closer. "But what's up, Aud? Is everything okay?"

"Everything's great! I just wanted to see you, that's all—spend a bit more time with you." She met his eyes. "What were you going to ask me earlier? Out by the pool."

"Oh." Bobby chuckled. "I was just wondering if your parents would be okay with you spending some time out here this summer. They're welcome too, of course, whenever they want, but ... I thought this would be more up your alley than the city." He jerked his head toward the window. "There's a beach after all."

"Mmmm. You know how much I love a beach."

"Is that a yes?"

"I'll ask them when I get home. How's that?"

"That's good enough for me."

Audrey ran her fingers through his hair. "You're really amazing, you know that? Me and the girls were saying how much fun we've been having."

"Well, I'm happy to hear that. And the best part is, we still have a lot more days of fun ahead of us." He smirked flirtatiously. "And nights."

That was all the lead-up Audrey needed. She pulled him in for a passionate kiss. They clumsily stumbled over to Bobby's bed, where they continued to make out. It was like they were lost in their own world, as they often were. Audrey had no sense of time until she happened to see the clock on Bobby's mantel; it was almost one in the morning.

"Oh my God!" Flustered, Audrey broke away, smoothing down her hair. "I didn't, uh ... realize how late it was."

Bobby, too, saw the time, and his eyes widened. "Or early, I guess."

They looked at each other, then laughed. Audrey kissed him again before she headed toward the door.

"Aud." Bobby's voice caused Audrey to turn around. "Come by tomorrow night."

"You mean tonight?" joked Audrey, pointing to the clock.

The rest of the week was much the same; they had fun horsing around in the pool, playing on the beach, and exploring Montauk. They popped into the shops, ate at the Montauket, and biked along the coastline. And each night, like clockwork, Audrey sneaked into Bobby's bedroom, where they made out for a few hours before finally calling it a night.

Then, to everyone's dismay, it was the last day of spring break. Grudgingly, they packed up their bags and awaited Felix's arrival. Still, they were determined to keep their spirits up, and the whole ride back, they reflected on the week's events, telling Felix all about their many adventures around Montauk. Felix dropped Audrey off first, as she was the farthest away from his ultimate destination, Bobby's townhouse. They all bade their goodbyes to each other, making loose plans to spend more time in Montauk over the summer.

"Remember to ask your parents," Bobby said to Audrey as she stepped out of the car.

"I will. I promise." Audrey kissed his cheek. To the group, she said, "See you all tomorrow! Bright and early!"

In response, Florie groaned, and everyone laughed. Audrey waved as Felix pulled away, then climbed the stairs up to her apartment. Excitedly, Audrey told her parents all about her week before she bridged the subject of spending a few weeks out there over the summer.

"There would be adults around," Audrey assured them. "Bobby says Loretta is planning on spending the whole summer out there, and his dad will be in and out. Felix, Bobby's chauffeur, will also be out there, and I'm assuming Charles will come out with Mr. Dempsey."

Alexander laughed. "How long have you been working on this sales pitch?"

"The whole car ride back."

"I can tell." Alexander smiled. "I don't see any problem with you staying out there—as long as you're home for the Fourth of July and your birthday."

"Deal!"

Audrey hadn't expected her father to give in so easily; she'd thought he would need to hear more about what she and her friends would be doing all day. Later, when Audrey expressed her bafflement to her mother, Sophia chuckled, shaking her head.

"We trust you, Audie," Sophia said. "And we trust Bobby. We know his family, and … look, you're a smart young woman. I know you'll stay vigilant. Just promise me you won't walk anywhere in town alone—not even in the daytime."

"I promise." Audrey raised her right hand.

"Good. That's what I wanted to hear." Sophia kissed the top of her head. "Sleep well, sweets."

For the first time in over a week, Audrey set an alarm. She knew it'd be difficult, getting back into the swing of things at Great Gray, but on the bright side, she had only a few more months of school left. Then, it'd be summer. And not just summer—the summer before her senior year.

She could hardly wait.

CHAPTER 27

Audrey

A DREAMY SUMMER

DURING THE SUMMER OF 1980, Audrey was happier than she'd ever been. She spent most of the summer in the Hamptons, taking full advantage of her proximity to the beach. Summers weren't like this in the city; they were hot and crowded, with far too many people and not enough fresh air. But out here, Audrey could enjoy the heat without feeling stifled by it. Her bedroom window was perpetually open so she could breathe in that glorious ocean air. She had always known she loved the beach, but as she walked along the shore, gazing out at the ocean, she realized this was where she was meant to be. Wherever she ended up, she wanted to be within walking distance of a beach.

Periodically, their friends would stop by. Florie was busy working at her neighborhood record shop, but she took the bus out to Montauk almost every weekend. Sebastian also dropped by the house every once in a while, and he introduced the group to his new girlfriend, Mavis. Audrey wanted to make a joke about how similar the name Mavis was to May, the last girlfriend of his she'd met, but she decided against it. Besides, Sebastian and Mavis seemed like a good fit; she had no problem putting him in his place, which he relished, and he made her laugh. Sarah, for her part, was busy touring schools on the East Coast, trying to figure out which one best suited her ambitions. She seemed to have set her heart on Yale, due to its world-class political science department, but Sebastian and Bobby were trying to convince her to attend Columbia so they could all be together. Audrey appreciated their efforts, as she selfishly wanted Sarah to stay in the city too, but she knew Sarah had already made up her mind. They'd have to learn how to be content with seeing her only a handful of times a year, unless she decided to move back to New York after college.

Alexander and Sophia had told Audrey they wanted her to be with them for the Fourth of July and her birthday, but after hearing about how much fun Audrey was having out in Montauk, they decided to hop on the bus and spend the holiday weekend out in the Hamptons as well. Robert and Loretta were more than happy to accommodate them, and the two families celebrated together.

"The birthday of America, followed by the birthday of our baby girl," Alexander said, beaming at Audrey. "I just ... I can't believe you're turning seventeen. It feels like only yesterday, we were watching you go off to kindergarten."

"Don't worry, Dad. I'll always be your little girl," Audrey assured him.

For her birthday, Bobby gave her a sewing machine, which pleasantly surprised Audrey. She joked that he'd been gifting her beautiful jewelry for the past couple of years, and it was nice to see him branching out.

"Oh, I'll keep getting you jewelry," Bobby said, "but I thought a new sewing machine could really help you out."

Audrey kissed his cheek. "I love it. Thank you."

Throughout the summer, they enjoyed pool parties, bike rides, campfires, and barbecues. As they did during spring break, Bobby's teammates regularly came by the house, and they brought along some of their friends as well, giving them more than enough people to play games such as capture the flag. At night, Bobby and Audrey met up, acting as though they were forbidden from seeing each other. It added an illicit nature to their late-night make-out sessions, and on more than one occasion, Bobby even climbed the trellis up to Audrey's bedroom, to add an extra layer of excitement.

"You don't have to do that, you know," Audrey told him one night with a laugh. "Our bedrooms are right next to each other."

"But it makes this"—Bobby passionately kissed her—"all the more enjoyable."

Audrey loved these meetups with Bobby. Throughout the summer, it had become increasingly difficult to keep their clothes on during these rendezvouses. Up until July, the furthest they'd gone was making out, but they'd both agreed they were ready to take their relationship to the next level. They hadn't slept together yet, but they'd done everything else. And though they were keen on consummating their relationship at some point, they didn't want to do so under Robert's and Loretta's roof.

"So, we'll wait," Audrey said, hands in her lap. "No big deal."

"Yeah." Bobby stared at her, biting his lip. "Yeah, it'll be easy."

It wasn't. It was nothing short of a struggle, but somehow, they managed to stand strong. Audrey attributed their success to the cold showers she and Bobby had integrated into their daily schedules. And, on more than one occasion—particularly when their hormones were at a peak—they surrounded themselves with family and friends so they wouldn't be tempted to slip into Bobby's bedroom and lock the door behind them.

As July melted into August, gloom permeated the air, reminding them all that their days of unbridled leisure were numbered. Before they knew it, they'd all be back at school, and they would no longer have the freedom they had now. Audrey, however, refused to mope around. She was determined to enjoy her summer until the very end.

And she did. But, as it always did, the last weekend of summer vacation eventually reared its ugly head. As a last hurrah, the Dempseys threw an end-of-summer barbecue. All the doors and windows were open, and the salty ocean air filled the house. All sorts of people stopped by. Audrey recognized most of the adults, as they'd attended Robert's and Loretta's wedding last summer, but she didn't know their names. Still, it was nice to have so many people milling about.

"This is going to be the best year yet for us," Bobby told Audrey.

"Everyone seems to say senior year is the most fun. I hope they're right, that they're not just lying to us."

"I have a good feeling about it."

Audrey turned, taking him in. Somehow, he'd become even handsomer over the summer. For one, he'd grown an inch or two; he was now only slightly shorter than his father. And Bobby was more comfortable with himself than he'd been when they first met, which imbued him with an attractive confidence. He no longer kept his short hair slicked back with Brylcreem; instead, he favored a more natural look, allowing his hair to fall into his face. He'd also taken to sporting light stubble. Audrey loved all these changes, even though they'd undoubtedly make him even more alluring to the girls at school. She knew she'd have to get used to women fawning over Bobby, especially as he continued to mature and come into his own, but she couldn't help but feel a pang of jealousy when she thought about other women ogling her boyfriend. She'd have to learn how to deal with these feelings. After all, it wasn't like she was worried about Bobby falling out of love or expressing an interest in someone else.

"I'm just really happy the way things are," Audrey said, reaching for his hand. "It kind of scares me, thinking of things changing, everyone growing apart."

"That won't happen with us."

"You sound so certain."

"I am. You know how much I love you, right?"

"Of course. And I love you too. But ..." Audrey shrugged. "I don't know."

Bobby scooted closer to her. "Has something brought this on?"

Audrey sighed. "Everything seems to be moving so fast. Sarah's looking at Yale, Florie's working on her music, you'll be at Columbia next year. I just ... I don't want to lose *this*." She squeezed his hand. "And I know there are no guarantees, but with you ... it's not just a high school thing to me."

Bobby kissed her. As they parted, he brushed his nose against hers and said, "For the record, it's not just a high school thing to me either. I really ... when I think of the future, I see you."

After he uttered those simple but comforting words, it was like all her anxiety disappeared into the night. Audrey rested her head on Bobby's chest, breathing in his cologne that smelled like safety and love. With him, the future didn't seem so daunting.

And so, she allowed herself to relax and enjoy these last few hours of summer with the man she loved—the man she wanted a future with.

CHAPTER 28

Audrey

HITTING THE GROUND RUNNING

AUDREY HADN'T EXPECTED THE start of her senior year to be so chaotic, though, in hindsight, she recognized this was woefully naive. Most of her peers—including Bobby and Sarah—were stressed about college applications. Audrey knew Bobby and Sarah didn't have anything to worry about; they were practically shoo-ins for their chosen schools, given their impressive transcripts and extracurricular activities. In fact, Bobby was on track to be the class's valedictorian, while Sarah would most likely be the salutatorian. Nevertheless, they were both on edge, trying to prepare themselves for the worst-case scenario.

One Friday night, Audrey babysat for the Paulsens, who lived directly across the hall from her and her family. Their kids, Brian and Rebecca, who were nine and seven, respectively, were usually well behaved; they could entertain themselves for hours on end with coloring books. Consequently, Audrey invited Florie over so they could hang out.

"It's kind of scary, everything being so unknown, but ... it's also exciting," Florie shared. "I just ... I know I want to be a singer. That's the goal. So, I was talking with my parents, and they ... they think I should really try and pursue that."

"And how will you do that?"

"After graduation, I'm going to start knocking on some doors, showing people my music, getting my name out there. I know it's a long shot, but ... I'll never know if I don't try."

"That sounds like a great idea!"

"You think?"

"Yes! I've always told you how talented you are, and I know you'll make it big."

"That's sweet of you to say. But ... I'm so new to all this, obviously, and I guess ... I want to make sure it all works out, that's all. And I know everyone says that, that everyone has these big dreams, but ... I really think I can do it. Or, you know, I *want* to believe I can do it."

"You can! It won't be easy, and it won't happen overnight, but it'll definitely happen. You have to believe that."

Florie sighed. "I guess I'm just in my head about it. All the doubts start creeping in, all the voices telling me I'll never make it, that I'll fail, that it'll all be for nothing."

"And believe me, I get that. But aren't you the one always telling me not to overthink things?"

Florie's eyes widened. "Are you saying we've somehow reversed roles?"

"Well, if that were the case, I'd be able to sing without breaking windows."

"And I'd be dating Prince Bobby."

"Perish the thought!"

Audrey looked over at Brian and Rebecca, who were sitting on the floor. They were completely absorbed in their coloring books, as she knew they would be.

"Hey, do you two need anything?" Audrey asked.

Brian shook his head. "We're good, Audie! Thanks!"

Florie leaned back into the couch. "You're really good with them."

"What, because I asked if they need anything? That's kind of my job," Audrey joked.

"You know what I mean! The way you played with them, got them their dinner, set them up with their coloring books ... you're a real natural."

"I've been doing this for years. I love it. I love kids."

"And *they* love *you*. Please tell me you're seriously considering the whole teaching thing. Because we need more teachers like you—teachers who are fun and cool and approachable."

"Maybe down the line. Whoa, whoa, whoa!" Audrey quickly slipped off the couch and pulled a crayon out of Rebecca's mouth. "Let's not chew on these, yeah? These are for coloring only. If you want something to chew on, try ... this." She handed Rebecca one of her plush toys, then returned to the couch. "I was actually talking with Loretta a couple weeks ago, and she was saying she knows some families who'd be interested in hiring a nanny."

"And since they're Loretta's friends, you know they'll pay *good* money."

Audrey laughed. "That's definitely a plus. But I think it'd be good to get some real-world experience before I maybe go back to school."

"Girl, you're preaching to the choir." Florie pointed at herself. "I'm really hoping this whole singer thing works out for me because I have no fallback." She whistled through her teeth. "I *do* feel bad for Sarah, though. She's been stressing with all the college stuff. Today in study hall, I tried to talk to her, and she shushed me, told me she was too busy going over her essay for the zillionth time."

"Bobby's been the same way. I've tried to tell him he'll be fine, but ... I guess that's easier said than done."

Florie conspiratorially rubbed her hands together. "Speaking of your boyfriend ... what are you doing for his birthday? That's coming up in a few weeks, right?"

"It is, yeah. Geez. Hard to believe it's already the end of October." Audrey shook her head, unable to process how swiftly the fall semester was flying by. "I'm taking Bobby out to brunch. Loretta told me she has something special planned for him in the evening, so I want to make sure he's back home before then."

Florie absently stroked her chin. "I'm happy for Bobby, that it's all working out with Loretta. Can't be easy, losing your mama so young, then finding out your papa's marrying again so soon. Well, maybe it wasn't soon to him—to Mr. Dempsey—but for Bobby ... it was, what, only a couple years after?"

Audrey nodded solemnly. "I think it was hard on him. I mean, he doesn't talk about his mom that much, but … when he does …" Audrey trailed off, sadness washing over her. Clearing her throat, she went on, "But I think … if Bobby didn't like Loretta, it'd hurt a lot more, but he really loves her, so that makes it … I don't know … easier, I guess? Not that it's easy to get over his mom, but … you know what I mean. And Loretta … his dad's just obsessed with her. You should see them together. They're surprisingly cute."

Florie let out a low whistle. "If Loretta can make Robert Dempsey look cute, then she must be magic or something. 'Cause let me tell you … that man … let's just say, you're lucky your Bobby takes after his mama."

Audrey laughed, despite herself. "That's horrible!"

"But true."

"Still horrible!"

"Still true."

Audrey laughed again. "The point is, Loretta's one of the best things that's ever happened to Bobby."

"As are you."

"Oh, that's sweet. Excuse me as I go vomit."

"Oh, come on! You must think about it, right? About what life will be like for you and Bobby after graduation?"

"I do." Audrey twiddled her fingers. "Probably more than I'd care to admit."

Florie smiled. "Just, you know, in case I haven't made this obvious over the past few years, I'm rooting for you and Bobby. I think you two are just … you look annoyingly good together, like Paul Newman and Joanne Woodward. You have to work out; you just have to."

"Thanks, Florie." Audrey squeezed her hand. "And just so *you* know, I'm rooting for you too."

Florie placed her free hand on top of Audrey's. "You're the best friend I could've ever asked for."

"I feel the same way about you."

CHAPTER 29

Bobby

A CHANGE IN THE WIND

For Bobby's seventeenth birthday, Audrey took him out to brunch. Though Bobby still wasn't a fan of celebrating his birthday, he also knew Audrey's intentions were good, and she just wanted to make sure he felt loved and appreciated. Besides, it wasn't like she'd pushed him into it; she'd asked if he wanted to do anything, and he was the one who'd brought up the idea of going to brunch.

"It's kind of weird, isn't it?" Audrey was saying as she cut into her omelet. "This is your last birthday before you're an official adult."

"I guess I never thought about it that way."

"It just kind of puts it all into perspective, doesn't it? Makes you realize how fast things are moving."

Bobby stirred his tea. "Not fast enough. Take Columbia, for instance. I mailed in my application weeks ago, but ... a part of me wishes I could just fast forward to the day when I learn that I've either been accepted or rejected."

Bobby knew it hadn't been a particularly wise decision to go all in on Columbia, forsaking all other schools, but he couldn't help it. It was the only school he could see himself attending. For as long as he could remember, he'd been dreaming about what it'd be like to be an official Columbia Lion, and if luck were on his side, in a few weeks, he'd find out whether or not his dreams were coming true.

"If they reject you, then something's seriously wrong," Audrey told him. "I mean, you're basically the poster child of what a Columbia student should be—smart, dedicated, hardworking. Super handsome. Really, I can't see them turning you away."

"We'll see." Bobby sipped his tea. "I know I've been driving you crazy with all my Columbia talk."

"Not crazy, per se, but ... I know how you are. You're an overthinker." She smiled coyly. "I guess you could say that's something we have in common."

"But from now on, I swear, I won't say another word about it."

Audrey scoffed. "I'll believe that when I see it—or hear it."

"But you *won't* be hearing it. That's what I'm saying."

"All right," Audrey laughed. "Then what would you like to talk about instead?"

Bobby placed his mug on the table. "Remember at the end of summer, when you were saying how scared the future makes you, how you wish there was some way to know how things will turn out?"

"Yeah." Audrey slowly looked up at him. "What, are you saying you have some sort of crystal ball that can tell us where we'll be five years from now?"

"Unfortunately, no." Bobby leaned forward. "But I just ... I want to make sure you know ... I love you so much, Aud. And ... I think we're really compatible. I mean, we make so much sense together. We both want to get married someday, make a real difference in our community, have kids ..."

"How many kids do you want?"

"Is this a trick question? Do you have a specific number in mind, and if I don't say the same number, then that's it? We're finished?"

"Maybe." Audrey smirked flirtatiously. "But no, seriously, how many do you want?"

"I don't ... well, definitely more than one. I've always wanted a big family."

"How big is 'big'?"

"At least three? Maybe?" Bobby shrugged. "I don't know. But I really ... I want my kids to, you know, remember me reading to them, playing with them, saving them from the monsters under their bed."

Bobby may as well have just said he wanted to be the exact opposite of what his father had been. For Bobby's childhood, Robert had stood back and allowed the nannies, maids, and governesses to tend to his son's needs. Not that Margaret was any better; she probably would have combusted on the spot if she'd had to change a diaper or clean up after Bobby. That wasn't the sort of childhood Bobby wanted for his children. He wanted to be right there beside his wife, doing everything they could to make their children's lives as happy as possible.

Bobby hoped it would be different with Robert's and Loretta's child, that Robert would step up and assume the role of a proud father. Neither Robert nor Loretta had said much on the subject lately, but Bobby knew these things took time. Besides, Loretta was only in her early thirties, which seemed young to Bobby, even if society considered women in their thirties to already have one foot in the grave.

Audrey rested her chin on her hand. "You'll be an amazing dad. But just, you know, as a caveat: I bet you'll spoil those kids rotten. You won't be able to tell them no."

"Well, maybe you can be the one to, you know, put your foot down."

Audrey's eyes widened. "So, we're having these kids together, are we?"

Bobby flushed. "Well, I ... I mean, I was just, um ... I ... well, maybe. Someday." Clearing his throat, he asked, "But what about you? How many kids do *you* want?"

"Oh, I'd love a small army." Her eyes lit up. "And, um ... I'm not saying this to scare you or anything, but ... because I want a big family, I ... well, I want to be a young mom. Not as young as *my* mom was when she had Claire but ... still young."

Audrey had told Bobby that her parents were nineteen when they had Claire. Though Claire was a surprise, she was a happy, welcome one, and Alexander and Sophia had considered the news to be more of a blessing than a hindrance. Consequently, they'd gotten married as quickly as possible, and the rest, as they said, was history.

"I'd love to be a young father," Bobby said. "And I know some people will say that's crazy, that you should see everything the world has to offer before you settle down, but ... that's just not for me. I don't need to see what else is out there because ... well, I know that this—what we have—it's real. In fact, I ... do you remember what you said to me on my birthday two years ago?"

Audrey pondered this for a moment, then said, "I think I said ... it was something along the lines of, 'I hope this is the best year yet for you.'"

"Exactly. And you know what? These past two years ... I've been the happiest I've ever been. And you're a big reason why."

Audrey reached across the table, taking his hand in hers. "I love you so much, Bobby. And ... I mean, you already know this, but ... I'm really happy with you too."

Bobby leaned forward to kiss her. "You always know how to make my birthday feel less ... depressing."

"Well, I'm glad. Birthdays shouldn't be depressing." Audrey clasped her hands together. "So, what do you say? Do you want to go for a walk, watch a movie, what? Loretta asked me to make sure you're home by five, so ... we have a couple hours."

"Both of those sound perfect." Bobby reached for her hand. "Let's go."

W HEN BOBBY RETURNED HOME, no one was in the foyer. That wasn't a surprise, as he hadn't given them an exact time when he'd be back; he'd just said he'd be home before five. It didn't take long, however, for his arrival to be noticed.

"Happy Birthday, Bobby!" Charles said. "You were out so early this morning

I didn't even see you."

"I'm sorry. I went out for a walk, to see the sunrise, and I guess I ... I kind of lost track of time. And then, Aud and I had brunch, so—"

"No apologies necessary! I just felt bad is all. I'm usually the first to see you on your birthday, but I guess Audrey beat me to it."

"That's okay." Bobby scanned the foyer. "Where are Dad and Loretta?"

"Mrs. Dempsey is in the drawing room. And Mr. Dempsey ... I'm afraid he had some things to take care of in the office."

"On a Sunday?"

"On a Sunday." Charles smiled wryly.

Bobby nodded absently. "Right."

For the past couple of months—at least since the start of the school year—Bobby hadn't seen his father all that much. This wasn't entirely odd, as things at Dempsey Corp always picked up once summer was over, but it was almost like ... like Robert had stopped making an effort. Last year, Robert had made sure he was home before six every weeknight, and he, Loretta, and Bobby would have family dinners at least four times a week. But for the last two months, they'd averaged two family dinners a week.

Of course, Bobby knew how busy his father was, but he had been under the impression that the family dinners were here to stay. Lately, however, Robert and Loretta seemed much more interested in having dinner just the two of them. And yes, Bobby knew they were husband and wife, that they wanted to spend quality time as a couple, but he just wished they'd include him more. Next year, he'd be at college, and he wouldn't be able to partake in these dinners as frequently. Couldn't they wait until next year to box him out?

Bobby jumped into a quick shower, then headed back downstairs. Even from the staircase, he could hear Loretta's voice coming from the drawing room. She was talking to someone—most likely Charles. When Bobby poked his head into the drawing room, he couldn't help but wonder whether he'd been transported to another room in another house. The room was filled with blue and white balloons—the Columbia colors—and streamers were hanging from every window and archway. Presents had been placed next to the fireplace, which was lit, and a banner that read "HAPPY BIRTHDAY, BOBBY!" hung above the mantel.

Loretta must have seen him in her peripheral vision, as she turned to him. "Bobby! Happy Birthday!"

Bobby stayed in the archway, too overwhelmed to move. "What's all this?"

"It's your birthday, silly! We wanted to do something special for you." Loretta slung her arm around his shoulders. "Can you guess what our theme is?"

"Columbia?"

"Correct!" Loretta kissed the top of his head. "You're such a smart boy. Now, what would you like first? We got the presents in here, but if you want to wait and open those after dinner, we can."

"What's for dinner?"

"Your favorite, of course! Chicken parm and penne."

Bobby's eyes lit up. "And that'll be ready soon?"

Loretta laughed. "Just about. Do you want to head into the dining room, then?"

"Sure! But, um ... should we wait for Dad?"

Loretta sighed. "Unfortunately, your father's tied up at the office. I know he'd rather be here, but ... some emergencies just can't wait until Monday." She pulled him closer. "But don't you worry. You still got me! And I hope I'm good enough company."

"You're the *best* company."

After dinner—which was absolutely delicious—they retreated into the drawing room, and Bobby opened his gifts. Charles had bought him an Aurora fountain pen, and Loretta had bought him a first-edition copy of *The Great Gatsby*.

"You're always saying it's your favorite book," Loretta said. "So, you know, I did some searching."

"I can't believe this!" Bobby didn't dare touch the book with his bare hands. "Thank you so much, Loretta! And thank you, Charles, for this pen!" He held up the pen. "You always know when I'm running low."

Charles chuckled. "You're the most voracious writer I know, Bobby. And someday, I hope you know I'll be expecting you to give me your autograph with that pen."

"You got it."

The night winded down, and Bobby went down to the kitchen to brew his cup of chamomile tea. When he returned upstairs, he saw Charles in the foyer.

"Bobby." Charles neared him. "I just ... I wanted to ... well, I wanted to make sure today wasn't too much for you. I know you don't like doing anything for your birthday, but Loretta was so excited about it, and I didn't have the heart to tell her no. I hope that was okay."

"I had a great time."

"You did?" Relief flooded over him.

Bobby nodded. "And thanks again for the pen. I really love it."

"You're very welcome."

Bobby took a sip of his tea, to ensure it wouldn't spill on the walk up. "Well, good night, Charles."

"Good night, Bobby. And Happy Birthday." Charles pulled him in for a hug.

Bobby waited until Charles disappeared down the hallway before he craned his neck to see if the light was on in his father's office. It wasn't. Bobby furrowed his eyebrows. Surely, Robert wasn't still at Dempsey Corp? It was almost eleven. Had he already gone up to bed? But if that was the case, then why hadn't he sought Bobby out first, said good night to him? Was Robert ... avoiding him?

All these questions swirled in Bobby's head, making him nauseous. It reminded him of what life had been like before Loretta; back then, he and his father had never spent quality time together. Were those days returning? If so, why? What had Bobby done wrong?

Perhaps he was overthinking. His father was, after all, the CEO of one of the largest conglomerates in the country; there were always fires for him to put out. Most likely, his absence had nothing to do with Bobby. As usual, Bobby was probably just reading into things, seeing problems where there weren't any.

Everything would be fine. There was nothing to worry about.

CHAPTER 30

Bobby

IN LIKE A LION

EVERY DAY IN DECEMBER, Bobby waited for the envelope that would change the trajectory of his entire life. Would he become a Columbia Lion, or would he have to scramble to apply to other universities in New York? With each passing day, his anxiety increased, and he wondered how long he would have to wait. Then, finally, the envelope arrived.

Audrey sat with him on his bed, watching as Bobby stared at the unopened envelope. He was nervous—far more nervous than he could properly articulate. Yes, this was the moment he'd been waiting for, but now that the envelope was actually in his hands … he wasn't sure if he could open it. What if he didn't like what it said?

"You do it," he told Audrey, handing her the envelope.

"Why me?"

"Because … I don't know. But I can't." He covered his eyes. "Just … if it's bad news, don't say anything. But if it's good news … you can tell me."

He could hear Audrey opening the envelope and removing its contents. It felt like he'd been sitting there with his eyes closed for an eternity, but then, finally, Audrey gripped his hand.

"You're in," she whispered.

"What?" Bobby opened his eyes.

"You're in!" Audrey showed him the letter. "You did it!"

Bobby laughed out loud, pulling Audrey in for a tight embrace. "Oh my God! I'm in!"

She laughed, kissing him. "Congratulations, Bobby!"

"Thank you!" He kissed her again. "Oh, I finally feel like I can breathe again! This just ... oh, I'm so relieved!"

"Your dad and Loretta will be so happy for you. And Charles, of course."

"I'll tell them tonight." Bobby's hands were shaking. "I just ... I can't believe this. I'm going to Columbia!"

"You're going to Columbia!"

That night, Bobby told Robert, Loretta, and Charles he was officially a member of the Columbia Class of 1985. Loretta and Charles were beside themselves. They showered Bobby with congratulations and hugs, telling him how proud they were of him. Robert, on the other hand, was far more subdued. Of course, he was happy for Bobby—at least he said he was—but something seemed ... off. While Loretta and Charles peppered Bobby with all sorts of questions about which neighborhood he'd want to live in and which classes he'd be taking, Robert stood off to the side, sipping his wine and staring out the window.

This distance between Robert and Bobby became even more conspicuous over the Christmas Break. Bobby could count on one hand the number of times he and his father had a conversation during the two weeks he was home. He didn't understand. Last year, he, Robert, and Loretta had spent Christmas in the Hamptons, and they'd had a wonderful time together. This year, however, Robert seemed colder, more detached. They ate Christmas dinner together, but there was no sparkle in Robert's eyes, no warmth.

"He's just been so stressed at work," Loretta assured Bobby. "They've had to lay off so many people over the past year, and your father ... he takes that hard. And with inflation the way it is ... he's just doing all he can to keep Dempsey Corp afloat."

Bobby, of course, understood the dire state of the economy, but he wished his father would be more open about that. Bobby wasn't a kid anymore; Robert didn't need to exclude him from real-world problems. Indeed, Bobby would have been more than happy to lend an ear, to listen to his father gripe and groan about the flailing economy.

"I just wish …" Bobby heaved a deep breath. "I mean, we hardly ever have family dinners anymore, and … I know Dad's busy at work, but … we can still have dinner together, right?"

"Bobby." Loretta caressed his hair. "I'm so sorry. We didn't … we didn't know you felt this way. Your father and I kind of … I guess we just assumed that, you know, you're a senior now, and … we didn't think you'd want to be stuck having dinner with us all week."

"But I don't think of it as being 'stuck.' I … I love the family dinners. I love spending time with you and Dad as a family, and … I don't want to lose that."

"You're not going to lose us. We'll always be a family. That isn't going to change."

"But next year, I'll be at Columbia, and … it won't be like it is right now. And I know you and Dad like your space, and I don't want to get in the way of that, but … maybe we can, you know, try and have the family dinners at least three times a week? Would that be okay?"

Loretta pulled him in for a hug, kissing the top of his head. "Absolutely."

Before the break, Mrs. Parker had asked Bobby for a copy of *Bright Neon Dreams*, and she'd assured him she'd finish it before school started back up in January. She was intent on helping him turn *Bright Neon Dreams* into something that could be shopped around to agents and publishers in the city.

"It's a fantastic story," Mrs. Parker told him after school on the first Monday back from break. "Your setting, your characters, your world … it's all so vivid, so real. And the stakes! You've done a great job of pulling at the reader's heartstrings, making them care. I just have a few things—mostly pacing issues, things like that. But if you're willing to put in the work—"

"That's why I'm here."

"Fabulous." Mrs. Parker pushed her glasses up with her forefinger. "Let's start from the beginning, shall we?"

Audrey, of course, was thrilled that Bobby had finally handed his manuscript over to Mrs. Parker. She'd been telling him for months that it was in good enough shape to show her, but Bobby had been scared. The last time he'd given an adult his story, it'd been thrown into the fireplace. Thankfully, Mrs. Parker had enjoyed the story, and Bobby appreciated her expertise. She was a published author herself, so she knew what she was talking about.

"I'm so happy for you, Bobby," Audrey told him. "Everything seems to be falling into place. Columbia, *Bright Neon Dreams* ... but, um ... how are things with your dad? Is he still being kind of distant?"

Bobby nodded. "Loretta says work has been really stressing him out. I've hardly seen him. And I know things are rough, that he's got a lot on his plate, but ... isn't that what family's supposed to do? Help you feel better? Cheer you up?"

Audrey rubbed his arm. "Maybe it's just difficult for him to ask for help. Your dad ... I mean, he seems like a pretty stubborn guy."

"But if he let me in, I ... maybe I could help. I don't know." Bobby hung his head. "I just wish there was something I could say to make him smile."

"Why don't you tell him about your book?"

"What?"

"Your book! Surely, that will make him happy—hearing his son is well on his way to being a published author!"

Bobby shifted on his feet. "I don't know if my father ... if that's something he wants to hear about."

"What are you talking about? It's a huge accomplishment! He'll be so proud of you." Audrey interlaced her fingers with his. "You and Mrs. Parker have been working on the book for the past couple of weeks. It's in a great spot. You said so yourself."

"Maybe you're right," Bobby said, bobbing his head. "Maybe it will cheer him up."

THAT FRIDAY NIGHT, THE Dempseys had dinner together as a family. While Robert and Loretta chatted about upcoming engagements they had to attend, Bobby tried to gauge his father's mood. He didn't seem angry, per se, but there was an unmistakable darkness in his eyes. He hadn't looked Bobby's way once.

"And what about you, Bobby?" Loretta asked, turning to him. "What have you been up to?"

"Well." Bobby cleared his throat. "School's started up again, so ... that's been good. But, um ..." He took a sip of water. "I actually ... I have something I want to tell you—both of you."

"Oh?" Loretta clasped her hands together. "Do tell!"

"I actually ... see, I've been, um ... working on a story for the past few years. It, um ... it's called *Bright Neon Dreams*, and ... well, Mrs. Parker—she's the faculty adviser for *The Bulletin*—she's been helping me make it, you know, publishable. And she seems to think ... she really thinks it has potential."

"Oh, Bobby!" Loretta covered her mouth. "That's wonderful news! Robert, isn't that the most incredible thing you've ever heard?"

Slowly, Robert looked up. Bobby swallowed hard, praying he hadn't made a mistake. He hadn't said a word to Robert about his writing since the first version of *Bright Neon Dreams* had gone up in smoke, but back when Bobby and Robert had eaten dinner together at Sparks Steak House, Robert had seemingly expressed his support for Bobby's creative endeavors. Was that no longer the case? Had something changed?

"This Mrs. Parker ... what sort of experience does she have?" asked Robert.

"Well, um ... she's actually ... she has four published books—all fiction. So, I really ... I think she can help me out," Bobby said.

"Hmmm." Robert drummed his fingers on the table. "I didn't know you had a book."

Bobby stared at his father, struggling to determine whether he was being sarcastic. It was always difficult to tell with Robert. Perhaps Robert thought this was a new book Bobby was working on, completely different from the one Bobby had shown Robert all those years ago.

"I've been working on it for a while," Bobby responded, "but … I guess I didn't … I didn't want to tell you about it before it was … well, good."

"We're so proud of you!" Loretta piped up. "Please say you'll let us read it! Before it becomes a bestseller!"

"Of course. I mean, it's not ready yet, but when it is, I'll let you know."

"Yes. Do that." Robert's voice betrayed no sort of emotion. Then, to Loretta, he said, "We have dinner with the Agnellis next week. Tuesday."

"Oh, right. Remind me, are they coming here, or are we going over there?" asked Loretta.

"They're coming here."

Loretta looked at Bobby. "Will you be okay on your own, honey?"

"I'll be fine," Bobby lied, wondering why he had never heard of the Agnellis before. "I'll probably eat dinner with Aud and her family."

"That's good. But we'll be able to do dinner the three of us on Wednesday," Loretta said. "And Thursday too."

Bobby nodded, his eyes on his plate. He wasn't sure why, but he had a sinking feeling those family dinners wouldn't happen. Maybe it was for the best. As Loretta had said, he was a senior now, and soon enough, he'd be living on his own. Maybe he was too old for family dinners. Maybe they weren't something he needed after all.

"That sounds great," Bobby said automatically, offering Loretta a smile. "I can't wait."

CHAPTER 31

Audrey

A BIG DECISION

THE SPRING FORMAL, WHICH would be held on April 10, was only weeks away. Clearly, the budget for the event was massive, as they had booked one of the ballrooms in The Plaza. Bobby and Audrey had been talking about it for what felt like months at this point, and they agreed that after the spring formal, they would spend the night together. Bobby would reserve them a room at The Plaza, and they'd have complete privacy.

"What do you think?" Bobby asked.

Audrey smiled, pulling him in for a kiss. "I think that sounds perfect."

"Really?" Bobby couldn't hide his excitement. "Because ... there's no pressure, Aud," he assured her, his gorgeous eyes gazing into hers. "If you decide you don't want to ... or aren't ready—"

"I don't see that being a problem."

"But if it is—"

"Then I'll tell you. But ... I'm ready, Bobby. I want to be with you."

He took her hand in his, kissing it. "What will you tell your parents?"

"The truth. Well, I'll tell my mom, and she'll tell my dad. I don't want to lie to them."

"And how do you think they'll take it?"

"They'll be understanding. They were teenagers once too, you know, so they know what it's like. But more than that, they love me—and you—and they know how serious we are, so it's not like you're some random guy. You're my boyfriend, and I love you."

Bobby smiled. "I love you too. But I also love your parents, and I just want to make sure they won't ... hate me."

"They could never hate you."

"Good." Bobby heaved a sigh of relief. "And I think it's good that you'll tell them. I don't want you to feel any sort of guilt about it."

"Will you tell your parents?"

Bobby's face flushed. "I don't know. That ... that'd be uncomfortable."

"Of course, it's uncomfortable! But won't they notice if you're out all night?"

"Dad and Loretta will be in the Hamptons that weekend, so they won't even be there."

"But what about Charles? Won't he notice?"

"That's true." Bobby nodded absently. "I guess I'll have to say something, then." He groaned. "It's going to be so awkward."

"But necessary. After all, I don't want you feeling any sort of guilt about it," Audrey teased.

"Right. No, you're right." Bobby ran his fingers through his hair. "Just gotta rip the Band-Aid off, I guess."

"It won't be that bad. And besides, it's all for a good cause, right?"

Bobby laughed, despite himself. "I'd say so." His eyes twinkled in the light. "It'll be the best night of our lives."

CHAPTER 32

Audrey

A NIGHT TO REMEMBER

I T WAS EVERYTHING SHE had hoped it would be—and more. Attending the spring formal with Bobby was something Audrey had been looking forward to since the beginning of the school year—maybe even earlier. She and Bobby had such a wonderful time at the winter formal last year, but this year would be even more fun and memorable—for a variety of reasons. Most obviously, of course, Bobby had secured them a room, and he and Audrey had decided that tonight would be the night they'd finally consummate their relationship.

Audrey wasn't sure what their peers thought of her and Bobby. Most of them—other than their close friends—probably assumed that Bobby and Audrey had been sleeping together for months at this point. After all, they were hardly shy about their affections, and they were the steadiest couple in their class.

"It doesn't matter what people think," Bobby had told her once. "Let them talk. It won't change anything between us."

Sometimes, Audrey was struck by just how mature Bobby was. He wasn't bothered by the minutiae of high school life, the drama, the gossip. Audrey was aware of how toxic the male locker room could be; in fact, Bobby had told her that his peers were constantly asking him about her, demanding that he give them all the prurient details of his and Audrey's relationship. But Bobby remained tight-lipped, much to their annoyance.

"Most of them are lying, anyway," Bobby had brightly remarked. "But even if they aren't ... I just don't care what they're doing with their girlfriends. They're not me ... and their girlfriends aren't you."

A few days before the dance, Audrey sat down with her mother and told her that she and Bobby were planning on spending the night together after the spring formal. To her surprise—and confusion—Sophia didn't ask any follow-up questions. She simply nodded, gave Audrey her permission, and told her to enjoy the dance. Thinking that her mother had misheard—or tuned out—Audrey reiterated that she and Bobby would be staying at The Plaza.

"Yes, you mentioned that," Sophia said, chuckling. "And I said it's fine."

"But ..."

Audrey wasn't sure how to play this. She was relieved that Sophia wasn't putting her foot down, but it just felt odd, how flippant she was about the whole situation.

"But what?" asked Sophia, her head tilted to the side. "What's wrong, Audie?"

"It's just ... Bobby and I ... we haven't ..." Audrey trailed off, trying to think of how to phrase it.

"Oh." Sophia seemed taken aback by that statement—shocked, even. "I, um ... I guess I just assumed ..." She leaned forward, taking Audrey's hands in hers. "We love Bobby, you know—me and Dad. He's a wonderful young man, and ... I know he'll always be there for you, to take care of you." She squeezed Audrey's hands. "You didn't have to tell me, but ... I'm glad you did."

"I wasn't going to lie to you."

"And I appreciate that." Sophia kissed the top of her head. "I love you so much, Audie."

"I love you too, Mom."

Audrey waited for her mother to impart some wisdom onto her, but Sophia had nothing more to say on the topic. Audrey's parents had always been uncomfortable talking to their daughters about sex—they had visibly reddened when Claire and Audrey obliviously sang along to Marvin Gaye's "Let's Get it On"—but Audrey had hoped that before she had sex for the first time, her mother would tell her what to expect. Indeed, it would be a whole new experience for Audrey. What if she messed up? What if it wasn't at all what she'd thought it would be? But Audrey, it seemed, would have to figure this out for herself.

Nevertheless, she was relieved that she was off the hook. She didn't have to concoct any stories or tell her parents she was crashing at Florie's place. Frankly, she couldn't believe she'd managed to pull the whole thing off, but she was proud of herself for being so open with her mother. She knew Sophia would eventually tell Alexander—which was mortifying to think about—but Audrey couldn't let that bother her. At the moment, the only thing that mattered was that she would be able to enter that hotel room guilt-free.

And then, it was April 10. While the color scheme for the winter formal was white, purple, and blue, the color scheme for the spring formal was white, pink, and green. Consequently, when Bobby picked Audrey up outside her apartment, he was dressed in a handsome light-gray suit with a pink pocket square. Audrey, for her part, was wearing an off-the-shoulder pink dress and sparkly heels.

Bobby reached out his hand. "Are you ready?"

Audrey nodded, taking his hand. "More than ready."

The decorating committee had once again outdone themselves. The whole ballroom was decked out in white, pink, and green balloons and streamers, and there were fresh flowers everywhere. Daffodils, hyacinths, lilacs, irises ... they'd spared no expense on the bouquets and garland. There was a wonderful energy in the room; all the seniors were well aware of what a rite of passage tonight was, and they were ready to have the time of their lives. Bobby and Audrey, of course, were no exception. For most of the night, they were a staple on the dance floor, stepping aside only a few times to pour themselves some punch or get some fresh air. Then, finally, as the ballroom thinned out, Bobby leaned over to her, his lips tickling her ear.

"Do you want to go upstairs?" he asked her, his voice little more than a whisper.

Audrey met his eyes, unable to calm her racing heartbeat. She'd been anticipating this night for weeks—months, really—but now it was becoming real. She'd read so many books about how monumental this moment was. She didn't like the term "loss of virginity"; that made it seem like something was being stolen, taken away, and that wasn't how she felt at all. Instead, she was excited—and, admittedly, a little scared—to take this step with Bobby. Tonight would be a night they'd never forget.

"Let's go," Audrey replied.

Bobby led her to their suite. The room was large—far larger than Audrey had imagined—and the windows looked out on Central Park. They made small talk for a bit, commenting on all the furnishings and amenities. When Audrey saw just how anxious Bobby was, she, perhaps contradictorily, relaxed. A part of her had been worried she was overthinking things, allowing herself to get worked up over nothing. But Bobby was just as nervous as she was. He kept wandering around the room, making sure everything was immaculate. After he smoothed down the bedspread for the third or fourth time, Audrey walked up to him, looping her arm with his.

"I'm pretty sure you can bounce a quarter off that," she told him, leaning her head against his arm and kissing it.

"I know. I just ..." He heaved a deep sigh. "I want this night to be perfect."

"It already is."

In response, Bobby cupped her face in his hands, pulling her in for a kiss. Quickly, the kiss became passionate, and they fell back onto the bed, where they continued to make out. They'd done this hundreds of times before, but this time, they were both acutely aware of where this was leading. Regardless, they knew this was a safe space, that they wouldn't be judged for their inexperience. Expectedly, there were awkward and uncomfortable moments, but they laughed them off, knowing very well their first time was more of a trial run than anything else.

"I'm really happy," Audrey told him afterward, kissing his cheek.

"Mmmm." Bobby absently played with her hair. "Me too." He propped himself up on his elbow. "You know, I really ... I can't believe how beautiful you are."

"Bobby."

"No, I mean it." He moved his hand down her back, and all the hairs on Audrey's neck stood up. "You are so beautiful."

In response, Audrey kissed him. Predictably, they didn't get much sleep; hormones were running high, and they wanted to make the most out of the expensive hotel room. Audrey couldn't believe how lucky she was, sharing such an important moment with a man she loved, with a man who had been her first everything: her first date, first kiss, first boyfriend, first love. Now, they'd experienced another first together.

"I love you, Aud," Bobby whispered, half-asleep, his arms wrapped around her.

Audrey snuggled up to him, unable to wipe the silly smile off her face. "I love you too."

CHAPTER 33

Audrey

A QUESTION

THE NEXT MORNING, BOBBY and Audrey ate breakfast in the hotel before going for an early stroll through Central Park. To Audrey's relief, the previous night's events hadn't changed their dynamic. A part of her had been worried that things would be awkward between them, but if anything, Audrey felt even closer to Bobby now than she had before.

"Should we stop here for a sec?" Bobby asked, motioning toward a nearby bench.

"Oh, my feet thank you!"

They sat down on the bench and looked out across Turtle Pond. The park was quiet; only a handful of people were out and about, enjoying the gorgeous spring weather. No doubt, the park would fill up more as the day progressed; it wasn't even nine yet.

"So," Bobby said at last, turning to her, "about last night ... how are you ... how do you feel?"

Audrey chuckled. "You're so cute." She kissed him. "It was perfect. Wouldn't have changed a thing."

Bobby smiled. "I thought so too." He caressed her cheek. "I just ... I'm really happy, Aud. And not just because we ... well, I mean, yes, last night was amazing, but ... that's not why I—"

Audrey pressed her finger to his lips. "I'm going to stop you right there, before you say something you regret."

Bobby laughed. "I know I'm stumbling over my words, but ... no, you know what? I'll take your advice and stop."

"Probably for the best." Audrey scooted closer to him.

They sat in silence for a while, enjoying each other's company. The city seemed so peaceful at this hour. Bobby, like Alexander, loved New York—especially in the early morning—and his love for the city was infectious. Audrey had never thought of New York as her forever home, but through Bobby, she had grown to appreciate the city's many wonders and charms. It didn't seem so daunting, staying in New York. Maybe she could be happy here.

Audrey stared at Bobby's profile, wondering—not for the first time—how she'd gotten so lucky. She thought about all the alternate scenarios, about everything that could have gotten in her and Bobby's way. What if she'd never been accepted to Great Gray? What if Bobby had never sat down next to her at the assembly? What if Audrey had listened to Cassandra and not gone out to Jack's with Bobby and his friends? She was so grateful she was sitting here, beside her handsome boyfriend, without a care in the world.

"But it was really nice, waking up with you," Audrey went on. "It's something I could get used to."

"Someday, we'll have it."

Bobby met her eyes, and images of last night flashed through Audrey's mind. She wondered whether Bobby's thoughts were just as titillating as hers, if he, too, was thinking about how much he wanted to relive that night and—

"And maybe ..." Bobby's face reddened. "Maybe we won't have to wait too long."

Bobby's eyes flickered between her eyes and her lips, and he swallowed hard. Heaving a deep breath, he stood up, never once looking away from Audrey, then got down on one knee. For some reason, Audrey's brain stopped working, and she couldn't understand what Bobby was doing—or why. It became clear to her only when he took her hands in his, his eyes gazing up into hers.

"Bobby," she gasped, her eyes wide. "I—"

"I love you, Aud," he started, his eyes twinkling in the morning light. "And nothing would make me happier than spending the rest of my life with you. When I think of the future, I don't just see me; I see us, and ... and I think in terms of 'us,' of where we'll be and what we'll be doing. And I know we'll have our ups and downs, and life won't always be as easy as it is right now, but ... I know we'll make it through all of that. Because we'll have each other, and ... that's all I want—to be with you." He took a deep breath. "Aud ... my beloved Thalia ... will you marry me?"

"Yes." It took Audrey a moment to process what had just happened. "I mean yes! Yes, I'll marry you!"

Bobby grinned. "Yes?"

"Yes!" Audrey kissed him. "Oh, I love you, Bobby." She kissed him again, then laughed, despite herself. "This is crazy! I mean, it's wonderful ... but my parents ... they're going to be so surprised."

"I don't think so."

"What do you mean?"

"I kind of ... well, I bridged the topic with them a couple weeks ago, and ... they gave us their blessing."

"They did?" Audrey's mouth was agape. "You mean they've known? All this time? And they didn't say a word?"

"They promised they wouldn't. I wanted it to be a surprise."

"Well, you certainly accomplished that."

Suddenly, everything made sense. If Bobby had asked her parents for their blessing weeks ago, then that explained why Sophia had been so blasé about Bobby and Audrey spending the night together; she knew Bobby would be asking Audrey to marry him, so Sophia didn't have to worry about her youngest daughter having her heart broken.

Audrey ran her fingers through his hair, trying to compute the fact that he was now her fiancé. "How long have you been planning this?"

"A while. I wasn't sure when I'd ask you, but ... I don't know." He shrugged. "This felt like the right time. And I swear, I'll buy you a ring. I just ... well, I was so focused on everything else I sort of ... forgot about that part."

"I already have a ring," she reminded him, pointing at her promise ring.

"I know, but ... I want you to have a proper ring, an engagement ring. One that's beautiful and one of a kind—just like you."

Audrey jokingly rolled her eyes. "Just don't go spending a lot of money on me, okay?"

"I won't. I promise."

When her parents found out that she and Bobby were engaged, they were over the moon, as Audrey had assumed they'd be. They revealed how difficult it had been, keeping the secret. Claire, however, was dumbstruck, unable to comprehend why Bobby and Audrey would tie themselves down so young. Claire told Audrey it was a big mistake, but Audrey didn't allow her sister to dampen her mood. Bobby's and Audrey's friends, for their part, were surprised but supportive, expressing their love for the couple.

"I knew you two were serious, but ... I didn't think you were *that* serious," Florie joked. "But no, in all honesty, I'm really happy for you, Audrey—for both of you. You and Bobby are great together. And you'll invite me to the wedding, right?"

"Of course! But it's not like we're getting married tomorrow. It'll be years from now, after Bobby's done at Columbia."

Florie eyed her carefully, shaking her head. "It'll be sooner than that. No way you two are waiting that long. Mark my words."

A few weeks later, Bobby gave Audrey her ring: a rose-gold princess-cut ring. The ring looked expensive, but Bobby assured her it wasn't; he'd paid for it himself, without having to dip into his savings account.

"The most important thing is, do you like it?" he asked, his eyes glinting boyishly.

"Are you kidding? I love it! It's beautiful!"

Audrey held it up to the light, to see it shimmer. This ring solidified the fact that she was no longer Bobby's girlfriend; she was now his fiancée. The word sent a shiver down her spine. She felt so adult, so grown up.

At this moment, everything was perfect. Bobby and Audrey were in their own little bubble, perpetually high on a mixture of serotonin and adrenaline. They couldn't keep their hands off each other; every chance they could, they'd duck into Bobby's room. Neither of them was in a hurry to tie the knot; they agreed they'd get married once Bobby graduated from Columbia. That was years away, almost a lifetime away. They had nothing but time to savor their engagement and plan their dream wedding.

At least ... that was what they thought.

CHAPTER 34

Audrey

THE BEST LAID PLANS

AUDREY WASN'T EXACTLY SURE how she knew. Maybe it was a gut feeling. Maybe it was ... maternal instinct. But by early May, Audrey was almost positive she was pregnant. She had missed her period, and Audrey was almost never late. This revelation, however, didn't send her into a downward spiral. It wasn't that she was happy about it, per se, but she also wasn't upset. Indeed, she and Bobby had always said they wanted to have children, but they obviously hadn't expected to be entering the world of parenthood so soon—or so young.

First, she told her parents. They took the news remarkably well. Of course, they weren't jumping up and down for joy, but because they loved Bobby—and because he and Audrey were already engaged—they were less distressed than they probably would have been. Besides, they could empathize with Bobby and Audrey, as they had been teenage parents themselves. Even though they told Audrey this wasn't what they'd wanted for her, they promised her they'd always love and support her—and Bobby.

"You're not alone in this, Audie," Sophia said. "Dad and I ... we're going to be right next to you—through all of this."

"Absolutely," Alexander agreed. "You never have to worry about that."

Claire was less supportive—at least vocally. She made a snide remark about how Audrey was throwing her life away by doing "that marriage and babies thing," but Audrey knew that was Claire's fear talking more than anything else. Deep down, Claire was just scared of her sister being forced into a role she wasn't yet ready for. Truly, when it came down to it, Audrey knew Claire would be there for her—just like she would be there for Claire if she needed her. In fact, Claire took it upon herself to learn everything she could about pregnancy, and all her little quips and comments—"You know, you should be eating more"—showed just how much she loved Audrey.

After she told her family—and was informed by a doctor that she was, indeed, pregnant—Audrey reached out to Bobby. She hadn't wanted to tell him until she was sure she wasn't just late. In her estimation, it wasn't worth worrying Bobby over something that might not even be true. She knew he'd be there for her, no matter what, but she didn't want him to make any rash decisions or do anything he'd later regret. For example, if he hastily dropped out of Columbia to support her and their baby, only to learn there wasn't a baby at all, she'd never be able to forgive herself.

After school on Friday, Bobby and Audrey met in Central Park, at the bench where he'd proposed only six weeks before. Audrey tried to play it cool at first, to make casual conversation before telling him she was pregnant, but she couldn't do it. It was clear he knew something was wrong; no doubt, he could feel her hand shaking, and it wasn't like Audrey at all to avoid eye contact with him.

"Aud." In her peripheral vision, she could see him craning his neck, struggling to meet her eyes. "Is everything okay?"

"No. I mean, yes. Well ... it's complicated." Audrey finally looked up at him. "Bobby, I ... I don't know how to say this."

"Say what?"

Audrey heaved a deep sigh. "I'm pregnant."

Bobby was silent as he digested this news. Slowly, he bobbed his head. Then, after a few moments, he reached out, resting his hand on her thigh.

"I'm so sorry, Aud," he said. "I didn't ... I should've known better, done better.

I—"

Audrey shook her head. "Don't blame yourself. I'm certainly not blaming you. Neither are my parents."

"Your parents ... how did they, um ... take it?"

"They love us. And they'll help us through all this."

Bobby nodded absently. "I just ... sorry it's taking me so long to ... I'm trying to ... to process this, that's all."

"It's okay. Take your time."

Bobby took her hand in his. "I love you. I should've said that first. I love you, and ... this isn't ... I mean, we both knew we'd have children someday, right? It's just happening a bit ... earlier than we thought, that's all. And just so you know, I ... I'll do everything I can for us—and our baby."

"I know you will." Audrey swallowed hard. "And I know we didn't plan on—"

"It's okay, Aud." Bobby pulled her into a warm embrace. "It's okay. We just ... we're moving our timeline up. We'll get married after graduation, and ... and we'll find a place of our own. And during the summer, I'll work, and ... we'll figure it out."

Audrey looked up at him. "How, um ... how are you going to tell your dad and Loretta?"

"I'll wait until Loretta gets back. She's coming home tomorrow."

"Do you want me there with you?"

"No, I ... I'll tell them myself. I reckon they'll be like your parents; they won't be thrilled about it, but they'll understand and give us their support." Bobby wiped her tears away with his thumb. "Don't cry, Aud. This isn't something to be sad about. It's ... it's a blessing, having a baby." He smiled. "Being a father ... that's not something I could ever regret—especially not with you."

Audrey blinked, trying to stop herself from crying. "How is it you always know just what to say?"

"Maybe it's the writer in me." He kissed her forehead. "Don't worry, my love. We'll be all right. I promise."

CHAPTER 35

Bobby

TRUE SELF

B
OBBY KNEW IT'D BE easier to tell Charles first. Charles had always been
there for him, through everything, and he'd never once cast any sort of
judgment on Bobby's mistakes. It wasn't easy, sharing the news, but Charles took
it better than Bobby could have hoped.

"I know how much you love Audrey—and how much she loves you—and ...
I know you'll take care of her—and your child," Charles told him.

"You're not mad?"

"Bobby." Charles touched his arm. "It's not like you've just told me you've
killed someone. You're going to be a father. And though I don't have any children
of my own, from my understanding, that's often viewed as a positive thing."

"When you're older and married."

"But sometimes, things happen the way they were supposed to. And maybe
you and Audrey ... maybe this was meant to happen now. We can't know. But
what I *do* know is you're going to be a great husband—and father. And don't
worry; before you move out, I'll be sure to teach you some practical skills—you
know, how to do your own laundry and all that."

Bobby laughed, despite himself. "Thanks, Charles. You really ... you have no idea how much your support means to me."

"I'll always be here for you, Bobby. You know that." He took a deep breath. "When will you tell your father and Mrs. Dempsey?"

"Tomorrow, I think—after Loretta gets back. It'll be easier to tell them at the same time." Bobby bit his thumbnail. "How do you think they'll take it?"

"They love you. They'll do everything they can to help you and Audrey. Just ... try not to worry about it."

That was easier said than done. All night, Bobby stewed in his bedroom, pacing back and forth. He hated feeling like he was hiding something. But he had a plan; he'd tell Robert and Loretta together, after they'd had a nice meal, and hopefully, they wouldn't be too upset with him. He could see them being disappointed in him, but after the initial shock wore off, he hoped they'd come around and express their support, just as Audrey's parents and Charles had. That was all he could really ask for.

Bobby sneaked downstairs to brew himself a cup of chamomile tea, but when he came back up to the main floor, he ran into his father, who was heading into the drawing room.

Robert eyed him warily. "Where are you off to in such a hurry?"

"I was just, um ... going to my room."

"Well, could you spare a few minutes? There's actually something I wanted to discuss with you—something rather urgent."

"There is?"

A lump formed in Bobby's throat. Had Robert found out? How? There was no way Charles would have told him; he would never go behind Bobby's back like that. But what else would Robert want to talk to him about? They'd barely said two words to each other for weeks, but now, suddenly, Robert had things to say?

"Loretta and I were looking at apartments on the Upper West Side for you—for when you're at Columbia—and, as you know, it's better to get a start on these things sooner rather than later, so ..." Robert gestured toward the drawing room.

"Right." Relief flooded over Bobby, though he knew he wasn't out of the woods yet.

Robert led Bobby over to the coffee table, which was covered in newspapers. Various apartments were circled—all with only one bedroom. Bobby gulped. He had no idea how he was going to get out of this. Robert wanted him to choose an apartment tonight, but how could Bobby tell him he'd need a two-bedroom apartment instead, that this time next year, he'd have a child?

"Bobby?" Robert furrowed his eyebrows. "Which one?"

"Oh. Um." Flustered, Bobby ran his fingers through his hair. "I don't... I can't really make a decision right now."

"Why not?"

"Because ... I mean, Columbia's so far away, and it's not like—"

"We figured you'd want to move in as soon as possible—after graduation."

"But maybe I ... can we do this another time? I really don't—"

"Just pick one."

"I can't!"

"It's not that difficult. They're all—"

"Aud's pregnant."

Silence hung in the air—the most uncomfortable silence Bobby had ever experienced. Robert refused to make eye contact with Bobby; instead, he was engaged in a staring contest of sorts with the newspapers—and losing.

"What did you say?" he asked, his voice barely a whisper.

"Aud's pregnant."

"I see." Robert reached for his glass of whiskey, which was perched on the edge of the coffee table. He took a sip. "How much do you need to make this problem go away?"

Bobby hadn't expected that to be his father's response. It took him a few moments to recover from the initial shock.

"No, we ... she's going to have the baby. And ... we're going to get married—this summer, we think ... after her birthday."

Robert was deathly quiet. He crossed his arms and stared at Bobby, as if he were seeing his son for the first time. Bobby squirmed under his gaze.

"I know it's a lot to take in," Bobby went on, "but I love her, Dad. And I'm going to do everything I can to provide for her and our baby."

"How?" Robert's tone was eerily even.

"What?"

"How will you do that?"

"Well, I … I'll get a job over the summer. And while I'm at Columbia, I'll work part-time. I'll find something; I know I will."

Robert scoffed. "You've never worked a day in your life."

"That doesn't mean I can't—or won't."

"You can't be a teenage father. And you're far too young to get married."

"But we're already engaged."

"Engaged? Since when?"

"Since last month. I asked her after the formal."

"After you spent the night with her, you mean." Seeing Bobby's bewilderment, Robert sneered, adding, "You didn't think I'd see the bill?"

"I … no. I guess I didn't."

"And you didn't think to tell me about this … engagement?"

A part of Bobby wanted to mention that Robert hadn't told him about Loretta until after they were already engaged, but he knew this wasn't the time to provoke his father. Right now, he needed to placate his father as best as he could.

"I was going to," Bobby said, "but … I didn't think you'd approve."

"At least you were right about one thing." Robert smirked. "I'll sort this out. Tomorrow, I'll go talk to the Nielsens. I'm sure they don't want their daughter doing this. It was a mistake, and—"

"That's not your call to make."

"Bobby—"

"We're going to have this baby—and be parents."

"No, you're not."

"Yes. We are."

"Enough!"

Robert's pleasantness evaporated so swiftly it disarmed Bobby. He threw his whiskey glass against the wall, shattering it. Bobby flinched as his father neared him, a dangerous glint in his eyes. Bobby hadn't seen his father like this in years—not since before Loretta. All at once, he wondered whether this had been the right decision after all, telling his father about the baby when they were all alone. He knew he should've waited for Loretta to come home before—

"I know it may seem like I'm giving you a choice here," Robert started, his fury still simmering, "but this isn't up for debate. You'll do as I say. Tomorrow, you're going to break things off with that slut and come back to your senses."

Bobby shook his head. "No, I won't. And Aud isn't a—"

"You really think you can make it on your own? Because that's what you'd be doing. If you go through with this, if you marry that girl, then you're on your own. This won't be your home anymore. You won't be my son. Do you understand?"

Bobby bit his lip. "I don't ... I knew you'd be upset, but I didn't think—"

"You didn't think what? That I'd disown you for disgracing my family name, for diluting my family line by fucking some commoner?" Robert was visibly shaking. "Your life has been so easy, so comfortable. Everything has been laid out for you—since before you were born. You impregnating some whore from the Village ... that wasn't part of the plan. You can't marry that girl, Bobby. You can't be a teenage father."

"Aud isn't a whore." Bobby stared at his feet, his heart racing.

"Look at me when I'm talking to you!"

Quickly, Bobby looked up. His father was very close to him now. In the dim light, Robert appeared almost as though he were possessed; his eyes were glazed over, and he was glaring at his son with an intensity Bobby had never seen before. Suddenly, Bobby became acutely aware of how much bigger his father was, how much broader his frame was, how much larger his hands were ...

Robert grabbed Bobby by his hair. "I've done everything I could to make you a worthy successor," he snarled. "All those years ... all the money I spent trying to mold you into someone you could never be ... it makes me wonder why I even bothered with you in the first place, why I didn't just leave you there at Ivy Hill."

He shook his head, pushing Bobby away. "Such a fucking waste. This is why ... Loretta and I ... with her, I'll have a son I can be proud of, a son who will honor the Dempsey name."

"I'm so sorry, Dad." Bobby didn't know what else to say. "I know this isn't what you wanted for me, but—"

"It doesn't matter what I wanted for you, does it? It never mattered to you. You always wanted to have things your way. Well, now you can. From this day on, you're on your own. Don't come asking me for money when things get rough. You wanted this life? Then it's all yours. Oh, and just so you know ... your apartment?" He shoved the newspapers to the floor. "Find one yourself. Your trust fund? Frozen. You'll see just how dismal things are out there without any money to lean on." His eyes narrowed. "So, tell me, Bobby. Do you want to be with that girl, or do you want a life?"

"I love Aud," Bobby started, "and I'd never—"

Before Bobby could finish, Robert punched him. More accurately, he decked him, sending Bobby stumbling backward, struggling to maintain his balance. Without relenting, Robert advanced, continuing to assault Bobby with a barrage of stunningly powerful punches. Each one hit its mark, causing blood to pour out of Bobby's nose and mouth.

"Dad! Please!"

Bobby raised his hands in self-defense, but he knew from past experience that Robert wouldn't heed him. Once he'd started, it was like he couldn't stop. Then, mercifully, a sound outside the room forced Robert to stop. He pushed Bobby back onto the nearby armchair, then situated himself on the other side of the room, casually surveying the albums near the phonograph.

"Sorry to disturb you." Charles had entered the room. "But ... I thought I heard something fall, and I ... I just wanted to make sure everything was okay."

"Everything's fine," Robert said, his tone uncannily cheery. "We were just trying to decide which album to listen to."

Bobby didn't dare look up; he couldn't meet Charles's eyes. He did his best to obscure his face by turning toward the fireplace, resting on his left hand. He could feel Charles's eyes on him, but he remained focused on the fireplace, praying Charles wouldn't walk up to him.

"Okay." Charles cleared his throat. "Well, I just, um ... I'll head up, then."

"Very good, Charles. Thank you."

As soon as Charles was out of earshot, Robert walked back over to Bobby and grabbed him by his hair, pulling him to his feet. The room was spinning; Bobby wished Robert had just left him in the armchair. He was almost certain his father was going to kill him. It was unclear how Robert would explain Bobby's death to Loretta or the staff, but he'd find a way. And he'd get away with it. Men like Robert always did.

"Get out of my house," Robert ordered, his tone a baleful whisper. "And don't ever come back."

Bobby's suitcase was open on the bed. He couldn't pack everything, obviously, but he would take the essentials. Maybe he'd enlist Sebastian's help at some point in the future; he'd be allowed to cross the threshold and retrieve the rest of Bobby's belongings.

It was an out-of-body experience. Bobby didn't even feel like himself. He was just going through the motions, filling up his suitcase with as many clothes as he could fit. He was still bleeding, but he didn't care; now wasn't the time to wallow. Occasionally, he wiped his face with his sleeve, but that didn't stop his packing.

"Bobby." It was Charles, knocking on the door. "May I come in?"

Bobby sniffled. "Not now, Charles."

Slowly, the door opened, and in his peripheral vision, Bobby saw Charles standing in the doorway. Bobby was over by his closet, and his back was to Charles. He closed his eyes, hoping Charles would just go away. He couldn't talk to him—not now. Not when he looked like this.

"Bobby, I ... what's all this?"

He must have noticed the suitcase on the bed. Bobby pulled another polo out of his closet and tossed it to the side. He'd find a way to jam it in later.

"I'm leaving," Bobby said flatly.

"Why?"

"Because that's what my father wants."

He wasn't Dad anymore; he'd made that abundantly clear. Bobby was so sure his father had changed, that he'd never hurt him again. He thought Loretta had inspired him to be a better man, one who was more involved in his son's life. He'd believed all the promises his father had made him, all the flowery words. How naive he'd been.

"Did you tell your father about Audrey?"

Bobby mutely nodded. Why couldn't Charles just leave him be? Why did he feel the need to ask him how he was?

"I'm sure he'll calm down," Charles went on. "Maybe he's upset right now, but by the morning … he'll be more understanding."

"I don't think so."

Bobby could hear Charles's footsteps; he was coming closer. Damn it. How could he get out of this situation? There was nowhere to run—or hide. He was cornered.

"Bobby." Charles touched his shoulder, and Bobby instinctively jolted. Quickly, Charles removed his hand. "Will you … will you please look at me?"

"I can't."

"Please, let's just … let's talk about this. Like I said, I'm sure your father—"

"He doesn't want anything to do with me."

"He loves you. You're his son."

All of a sudden, the strength Bobby had been exhibiting vanished, and he crumbled to the floor, sobbing uncontrollably. Charles immediately dropped to his knees, wrapping his arm around Bobby's shoulders. Bobby, in turn, buried his head into Charles's chest. It reminded him of his eleventh birthday, when Charles had held the inconsolable Bobby in his arms, telling him over and over he was here, that everything would be okay, that he'd take him back to New York. Bobby thought he'd left that wretched boy behind, but apparently, he was just as broken now as he'd been six years ago. How could he have expected Robert to change when he himself was still the same scared boy he'd always been?

"Oh, Bobby." Charles kissed the top of his head. "It'll all be all right. Okay? It'll all be all right. I—" He stopped, then, and Bobby could feel Charles's arm shaking. "Bobby." His tone was more serious now, more concerned. "Why are you bleeding?"

Through tears, Bobby sputtered, "It was him."

"Who? Your father?"

Charles lifted Bobby's chin, to observe his injuries, and at once, the damage was clear. Bobby hadn't even seen it for himself yet; as soon as he'd entered his room, he'd made a beeline for the closet, and he'd started packing. He hadn't looked in a mirror. Maybe he'd been too afraid of what would look back at him.

"Oh, Bobby." Tears welled in Charles's eyes. "Your father did this?" Bobby nodded, and Charles pressed on, "I ... I don't understand. How could he ...? Oh, my dear, sweet boy. Come here." Charles pulled Bobby in for a hug, stroking the back of his hair. "I'm here. You're safe with me."

"I know." Bobby wiped his nose, flinching from the pain. "That's always how I've felt."

"Always?" Charles met his eyes. "Bobby. This is the first time your father's ever ... he's never done this before, has he?"

A knot formed in Bobby's stomach. He knew this would be almost impossible for Charles to hear, but Bobby was done protecting his father, making excuses for him. If Robert was so intent on severing all familial ties between them, then so be it. There was nothing holding Bobby back anymore, no sense of misplaced loyalty.

"Before Loretta, he ... he hurt me. All the time."

"What?" Charles appeared as though he'd seen a ghost. "All the time? How? I ... how did I not ... why didn't I know about this?"

"I'm sorry."

"No, Bobby, I'm not ... it's not your fault. That's not what I'm saying. I ...

it's *my* fault. I should've ... I should've known. I'm in charge of this household. I should've—"

"You couldn't have known. They told me if I ever said anything—"

"Who's 'they'?"

"My parents. Ava. The maids."

"They all knew about this?"

Bobby wiped away tears. "I don't want to talk about it."

"And you shouldn't have to. I'm sorry. I just ... I never ..." Charles gripped Bobby's hands. "No one's ever going to hurt you again. Do you hear me? No one." Bobby appreciated Charles's conviction, but his trembling hands lessened the overall impact. "Here's what we're going to do. You're going to stay here for the night; you're not going anywhere. And then tomorrow, bright and early, you and I ... we're going to go pick Mrs. Dempsey up from Teterboro, and we'll tell her all about what happened tonight, okay?"

Bobby vehemently shook his head. "I can't. I can't be the one to ... I can't ruin their marriage."

"Bobby—"

"Loretta is so happy with him, Charles. And they're thinking of having a child together."

"All the more reason she should know! What if he does this to their child, your sibling ... her? Bobby, I know how difficult this is, and I'm not trying to ... I don't want to push you into anything. But Mrs. Dempsey has a right to know."

"She'll never believe me over him."

"Why would you say that?"

"Because he's Robert Dempsey! No one would take my word over his. And he's her husband. She loves him." Bobby again shook his head. "I can't do it, Charles. I can't."

"Sleep on it. Maybe in the morning, you'll feel different. Can you do that for me?"

"I'll try."

"Good." Charles heaved a deep breath. "Now, let me help you ..." He couldn't finish his sentence.

"I have a first aid kit in the bathroom," Bobby told him.

"And who gave you that?"

"The maids."

Charles's jaw clenched. Anger flashed in his eyes, alarming Bobby, who'd never seen Charles like this before. He was always so mellow, so sanguine. But now, he looked like he was prepared to go to war.

Under his breath, Charles muttered, "All this time, and they never ..." He cleared his throat, then said, more loudly, "I'll take you to the hospital. But I don't want you worrying about anything, okay? I'm right here. And I'm not going anywhere."

CHAPTER 36

Bobby

SOMETHING LOST, SOMETHING GAINED

C HARLES AND BOBBY SLIPPED out of the townhouse as quickly and quietly as possible, as they didn't want Robert to know what they were
doing—or, more importantly, where they were going. Bobby had been worried
about this, knowing very well that once Robert found out what Charles had
done, he would fire him.

"That's why I placed my letter of resignation on his desk this morning,"
Charles told Bobby.

"You're leaving?" Bobby's eyes widened. "Charles, I ... I don't want you to lose
your job, your home. Not for me."

"I can't stay here and knowingly work for a man who hurts his own son."

"But—"

"No. I won't hear it. I've made my choice, and I'm not going back."

Baptiste, Loretta's chauffeur, was supposed to pick her up from Teterboro,
so Charles and Bobby hitched a ride, telling him they needed to talk to Loretta
about something. Baptiste, thankfully, didn't ask any questions, and he allowed
them to sit in the back of the car.

During the car ride, Bobby's eyes were glued to the window. He didn't know how to tell Loretta the truth about her husband. A part of him was afraid she wouldn't believe him, that she'd take his father's side over his. That would hurt most of all—more than any of the bruises or cuts on his face.

"I can tell her," Charles said. "You don't have to say anything you don't want to."

"I ... I feel I should say something."

"Not if you don't want to. It's enough that you're here. She ... she'll be able to see you aren't ... that what we're saying is true."

Late last night, Charles had taken Bobby to the emergency room, and the doctors informed him his nose was broken. That wasn't a surprise; he hadn't been able to touch his nose without wincing. His facial injuries, though painful, would heal in time, and the doctors said there wasn't any nerve damage around his black eye. All in all, Bobby had gotten lucky; if Charles hadn't interrupted Robert when he did, things might have escalated even further.

Finally, they pulled up to Teterboro. The private jet had landed just a few minutes ago, and Loretta was standing outside, chatting with the man who was carrying her luggage.

Charles turned to Bobby. "Are you ready?"

"As ready as I'll ever be."

Loretta was pleasantly surprised to see Charles and Bobby. As she neared them, however, her smile evaporated, and her eyebrows furrowed.

"Honey, what happened?" she asked Bobby. "You look like you've been in a brawl. I know you're playing football in Gym, but no one should be hurting you like this."

Charles stepped forward. "We need to tell you something," he said. "It ... won't be easy to hear."

"I know about Audrey."

"What?"

"Robert called me last night. He was a right mess about it." Loretta looked at Bobby. "But don't worry, Bobby. I'll talk to him, and—"

"It's not about that," Bobby cut in. "Well, I mean, it sort of is, but ... there's something you should know—something about my father."

Loretta glanced between Bobby and Charles, and Charles simply nodded in response. "Okay." She smoothed her skirt. "Let's, um ... let's get in the car. Don't want to keep Baptiste waiting."

Charles, thankfully, took the lead and did most of the talking. He told Loretta about what he'd witnessed last night, and Loretta sat in stunned silence, blinking rapidly.

"No." She shook her head. "No, I ... not Robert. He's never ... I've never seen him ... how can this be?"

Bobby's stomach dropped. His worst fear had been realized; Loretta didn't believe him. She would stand by his father through all of this, and he would be left without any parental figure. He had felt so close to Loretta, had truly thought that one day, he would end up calling her Mom. Did she think he had made all of this up to deflect from his and Audrey's predicament?

"Loretta." It was the first time Bobby had ever heard Charles refer to his stepmother by her first name. "I know it's difficult to hear. But Bobby ..." Charles placed his hand on Bobby's shoulder. "... look at him. He clearly ... this isn't some injury from Gym class."

"But Robert ... he isn't ... he would never hurt Bobby. He loves him. Bobby, I ..." Loretta looked at him imploringly. "Tell me it isn't true."

"I can't," Bobby sputtered, tears in his eyes. "But I know there's nothing I can say to make you ..." He turned to Charles. "I told you she wouldn't believe me."

Loretta reached for his hand, but he shook his head. "It's not ... I don't ... it's just ... your father ... I have to see him for myself, talk to him, before I can—"

"You don't believe me."

"I never said I—"

"If you believed me, you wouldn't ... you wouldn't have to ..." Bobby trailed off, rubbing his eyes. Everything was blurry. "I knew I shouldn't have ... that this was a mistake."

Charles inched closer to him. "No one thinks you're lying. She just—"

"She believes him over me."

"That's not true." Loretta again shook her head. "I just ... I'm trying to take this all in. I ... I didn't ... this isn't what I expected to hear. I'm ... processing it."

Bobby hung his head. "I'm sorry."

"What are you sorry for?"

"For telling you this, for ... I never ... I thought it was over. I thought ... I thought he'd changed. And I know how happy you two are, and I ... I didn't ... I'm so sorry."

Loretta bit her lip. "Oh, my darling boy. Come here. Let me hold you."

"No." Bobby looked away. "No, you ... you're on his side."

"I'm not on his side. I just ... oh, Bobby, I ... I'm so sorry, honey. I didn't ... I didn't mean to ... please, will you look at me?" Slowly, Bobby met her eyes. "I'm not on his side," she reiterated. "I just need time. Can you give me that? Can you give me time?"

In response, Bobby nodded, and for the rest of the car ride, the three of them sat in silence. Guilt ate away at Bobby. He was the one responsible for Loretta's misery—and Charles's unemployment. He was the one who had put them in this position. Because of him, they could lose everything. It wasn't fair. Neither of them deserved this.

When they returned to the townhouse, Loretta slowly ascended the front staircase, and Charles and Bobby followed close behind. Charles had promised Bobby he wouldn't let him enter the townhouse by himself; he would stand beside him. Bobby knew he would never be able to properly thank Charles for all the sacrifices he had made, but he would do everything in his power to make sure that Charles didn't suffer; he would help Charles find other employment.

It was odd, standing in the foyer, knowing that not twelve hours before, Robert had essentially banished Bobby from his home. Charles protectively placed his arm around Bobby, and they stood to the side, watching as Loretta paced back and forth, trying to summon her bravery.

"Robert!" she called out at last. "I'm home!"

A few moments later, they heard movement from the drawing room. Bobby drew a quivering breath. He hadn't seen his father since their confrontation last night. He wasn't sure if he was ready for this.

"Loretta!" Robert offered her a warm smile as he entered the foyer. "You're back! I—" He then saw Charles and Bobby, and his eyebrows immediately furrowed. "What's going on here?" he asked.

"I know." Charles's voice was steady, firm—as was his hand on Bobby's shoulder.

"You know what?"

"What you did. What you've always done. Bobby told me everything."

"I don't understand. What did he tell you?"

Robert seemed genuinely perplexed; his head was cocked to the side, and his mouth was agape. He had always been a phenomenal actor, able to mask his emotions with ease, but Bobby had never seen his father try to act like the victim before. Vaguely, Bobby wondered whether Robert had seen Charles's letter of resignation yet.

"They, um ..." Loretta cleared her throat. "They ... told me some things."

Robert's attention returned to Loretta. "Like what?"

"They just ..." Loretta's eyes fell upon Robert's bloodied, bruised knuckles, and she swallowed hard. Pointing at his knuckles, she softly asked, "What happened?"

"Oh." Robert laughed, despite himself. "Boxing injury."

"Boxing injury." Loretta's tone was uncharacteristically flat.

"Yes, I ... what is this about?"

Tears formed in Loretta's eyes, and she turned back to face Bobby. Bobby had never seen her look so helpless before. He wanted to rush over to her and comfort her, but he had no interest in standing so close to his father.

"I'm so sorry," she said. "Oh, my sweet boy. I should've—"

"What did he tell you?" Robert's geniality had now been replaced with defiance. He pointed an accusatory finger at Bobby. "Because whatever he said ... you know he's lying, that he's only trying to—"

"You hurt your own son?"

"What? No! I—"

"Then explain the injuries on his face! Explain why Bobby—"

"I don't know! But I can tell you that I certainly didn't—"

"You weren't boxing at the gym. You were—"

"I have never laid a finger on him, Loretta! Look, I don't know what they told you," Robert said, making it clear that in his view, it was now him and Loretta against Charles and Bobby, "but it's not true. You have to believe me."

Loretta studied him carefully, tears still streaming down her cheeks. "I don't," she said with finality. "I don't believe you."

"I'm your husband. How can you believe that boy over me?"

"Because Bobby isn't lying. You are."

It was oddly cathartic for Bobby, seeing his father so hapless. He begged and pleaded with Loretta, tried to make his case, but she wouldn't hear a word of it. In real time, Bobby watched as Robert's authority was pulled away from him. Loretta was the one in control now; she held all the power.

"From now on," she told Robert, "I'll be the one making the decisions around here."

"Loretta. Please. You don't—"

"Unless you want a full-blown scandal on your hands, you'll do exactly as I say."

Ever so briefly, Robert's eyes found Bobby's. The only word Bobby could use to describe the look in his father's eyes was hatred. Bobby knew Robert wanted to say something, but there was nothing he could do. The damage—both figurative and otherwise—had already been done. No amount of flowery words or apologies could repair what he'd destroyed. All he could do now was try and minimize the fallout.

"What do you want me to do?" he asked through gritted teeth.

Loretta neared him. "Right now, I just need you to listen very carefully to what I say next."

CHAPTER 37

Audrey

SHOCK AND FURY

AUDREY HAD NEVER BEEN so angry before. When Bobby told her about what his father had done, the world around her stopped. She couldn't breathe. She couldn't even see straight. Everything had blurred, and all she could focus on was Bobby, who was sitting beside her on their favorite bench in Central Park. He'd told her everything, every horrible detail.

She couldn't believe she'd never seen this side of Robert Dempsey. She thought back to when she'd first met Robert. He'd been so welcoming, and Audrey had been under the impression—the mistaken impression, as it turned out—that he was a kind man, that he'd support her and Bobby's relationship. Now, she was hearing about how dismissive Robert had been, how he'd done his research on her family and come to his own conclusions about their apparent worthiness. It made her skin crawl, how easily he'd duped her. How could she have been so blind? On the day she met Robert, Bobby had been standing beside her, shaking, and she'd somehow chalked it up to him being surprised to see his father. She thought back to the times Bobby had shown up to school with concealed facial injuries, how reluctant he'd been for her to meet Robert, how the protagonist in *Bright Neon Dreams* had a difficult, tense relationship with his father. How hadn't she put the pieces together?

More than anything, though, Audrey hated how Bobby had been pressured to hide the abuse, to defend his father, to concoct stories about how he'd gotten his wounds. She couldn't understand how a parent could hurt their own child. It was the worst kind of evil Audrey could imagine. And despite everything, despite all the years of abuse, Bobby had still been willing to give his father the benefit of the doubt, to have a relationship with him. Robert had convinced Bobby that he was a changed man, that he'd never again lay a finger on him.

For the first time in her life, hatred, true hatred, bubbled up inside her. There were so many things she wanted to say to Robert, so many things she wished would happen to him. She'd never wished ill on someone before, but Robert ... he deserved to suffer for what he'd done.

"I just ... I hope you don't ... that you don't think I ..." Bobby swallowed hard, studying her carefully. "I hope you still feel safe with me."

Audrey gripped his hands. "I love you, Bobby," she said. "And I know you're nothing like him. I know you'd never ... you'd never do anything like that."

In response, he squeezed her hands, then said, "I ... I know I've been talking a lot and haven't given you the chance to speak, but ... I just ... I wanted you to know everything, in case it ... changes things for you."

"Nothing could change the way I feel about you."

"Good. Because ... nothing that's happened ... it hasn't changed my mind on anything. And ... I mean, things won't ... they won't be easy. I know that. But at least we know we're not alone in this. We have your family's support, and Loretta and Charles ... I know they'll help us out too. But ..." He trailed off, sighing. "Aud, I ... everything I've told you ... I want it to stay between us. I don't want anyone else to know."

"Not even my family?"

"Not even them." He met her eyes. "This isn't the sort of thing I want broadcasted around the city. It's personal, and ... look, I know I can trust your parents, but ... I don't want this getting out."

"But my parents love your dad. I think they'd want to know if he—"

"Maybe we can tell them someday, but right now, it's just ... it's not something I'm ready to deal with."

"Okay." Audrey squeezed his hands. "I won't say anything. I promise."

"Thank you." He kissed her hands. "For everything. You really ... I know it's a lot, what I've told you, but ... you've made me feel so safe, so ... heard."

"You'll always be safe with me." She kissed his cheek.

For Bobby's entire life, Robert had taken him for granted. He knew that no matter what he did, his son would still love and forgive him. It didn't matter how many times Robert broke Bobby's trust or went back on his word; Robert knew how greatly Bobby craved his approval, how desperately he wanted to make him proud. Robert didn't deserve Bobby, and Audrey would make sure he didn't get him. She'd help Bobby get as far away from his father as possible.

Together, they'd build a new life—one that wouldn't involve Robert Dempsey.

CHAPTER 38

Bobby

THE HOUSE OF CARDS

F OR THE NEXT COUPLE of weeks, Bobby stayed with Sebastian. He didn't tell Sebastian the whole story; he simply said things were tense with his father at the moment, and he needed a place to live for a while. Thankfully, Sebastian was more than happy to have Bobby act as his temporary roommate, and he even offered to go to the townhouse and retrieve the rest of Bobby's belongings. Bobby was grateful, as he'd left in a hurry, and he had no desire to step foot in that townhouse ever again.

Meanwhile, Loretta had found a sprawling four-bedroom apartment for Bobby and Audrey on the Upper West Side, but they told her it was far too large and expensive for them.

"But I'll be the one buying it for you," Loretta insisted. "So, it's not like—"

"We want a place that's within our means—a place we can afford on our own," Audrey replied. "We really appreciate everything you've done for us, Loretta, but this ... this is something we need to do ourselves. And ... well, right now, we won't ... buying a place isn't really realistic for us, so we'll find an apartment we can rent."

"I understand." Loretta nodded slowly. "Then at least let me give you a check for the first and last month's rent. Please, will you let me do that?" Bobby and Audrey exchanged a look, and Loretta quickly added, "I know I'm posing it as a question, but really, I ... I won't take no for an answer."

Bobby laughed good-naturedly. "Thank you."

"You're very welcome." Loretta beamed. "So, have you found a place yet?"

"We're still looking."

A couple of days later, Audrey informed Bobby she'd found an affordable two-bedroom apartment in Morningside Heights. She took him to see the apartment, and her giddiness was practically infectious.

"I know it's not ... well, let's be honest: it's not what you're used to," Audrey laughed as they neared the door to the apartment, "but I can really see this being our first home together. So ... have an open mind."

Though the apartment was, admittedly, a little dated—the once-cream carpet was now a brownish color, and the galley kitchen hadn't been renovated since the 1950s—Bobby could clearly see why Audrey had fallen in love with it. There was so much character. To Bobby's delight, the living room windows let in a lot of natural light, and he didn't have to duck to fit under the doorways. Both the bedrooms were a decent size, and Bobby loved how convenient the location was. He would be able to walk to Columbia, and the nearest subway station was right down the street.

"What do you think?" Audrey asked, rubbing her hands together. "Isn't it perfect?"

Bobby turned to her, a smile on his lips. "I love it," he said. "I'll call Loretta, and she can help us fill out the paperwork."

By the first week of June, Bobby was able to move in, and he and Audrey began purchasing furniture for their apartment. Audrey would move in once they were officially married, but she frequently visited the apartment to see Bobby and help with the decorating. It was a surreal experience, for many reasons. Bobby still hadn't digested the fact he was now living on his own, and within a month or so, he'd be married. Even more mindboggling, in six or seven months, he would be a father. He hoped he'd be a good one, that he was as far removed from his father as physically possible, but he couldn't help but worry about it.

"You're going to be a great father," Charles assured him one evening.

"But how do you know that?"

"Because I know you. And I know what a gentle, loving soul you are." Charles placed his hand on Bobby's shoulder. "You're going to love your child with all your heart."

It comforted Bobby, hearing Charles's affirmations. After all, Charles had known Bobby since he was a baby; he'd watched him evolve into the young man he was today. Charles believed in him, and that helped alleviate some—but not all—of Bobby's concerns about his impending fatherhood.

Bobby sipped his tea. "How, um ... how's the job search going? Did my father end up writing you a recommendation after all?"

"He did." Charles absently drummed his fingers on the table. "I wasn't sure if he would, but ... I think he just wants me to go quietly." He laughed, despite himself. "Never thought I'd be here, looking for another job, but ... actually, I have an interview at The Carlyle Hotel next week, so ... we'll see how that goes."

"Charles." Bobby shifted in his chair. "I really ... I'm so—"

"No." Charles raised a hand. "I won't hear any of that. I don't regret my decision to leave, Bobby. My only regret is that I wasn't able to ... that I couldn't save you from that man."

"But you couldn't have known—"

"I *should've* known. That's the thing. I *should've* known." Charles heaved a deep breath. "I know I can't ... I can't change what happened, but ... I'll do everything I can to make sure you and Audrey ... that you're safe and happy, that you don't ever have to worry about him."

Over the next month or so, Robert and Bobby communicated mainly through Loretta, as Bobby refused to be in the same room as his father. Reluctantly, Robert gave Bobby his permission to marry Audrey, and while he would attend the wedding, he would keep to himself. Bobby would have been lying if he said he didn't relish his father's fall from grace. Robert was now at Loretta's and Bobby's mercy; all too easily, they could cause his pristine reputation to come crashing down around him, possibly taking Dempsey Corp down with it. Consequently, Robert had no choice but to acquiesce to all their demands—no matter how much he detested them.

One night, Bobby asked Loretta whether she planned on staying with his father, given all she had learned about him. It couldn't be easy, having to look at his face every day, knowing all the things he was capable of.

"I don't believe in divorce," Loretta started, "and neither does your father. No, we'll stay together—until death do us part."

"But why? Why stay with him?"

"It's just the way it is."

"But you deserve so much better than him. You ... you shouldn't be—"

"Don't worry about me, Bobby. I can handle myself—and your father." She smiled wryly. "And I know he's told you you're on your own, that he won't help you and Audrey out, but he doesn't have a say over how I spend *my* money."

"About that." Bobby clasped his hands together. "I really ... I appreciate everything you've done for me and Aud, but I don't want you thinking ... see, I'm going to get a job, and I'll—"

"I know you are. But it'll take you a while to get on your feet. In the meantime, I'm not going to let you and Audrey live on crumbs. You're my family, Bobby. I love you. You know that, right? That I love you?"

Bobby nodded. "I love you too. And I promise, I'll pay you back. Every cent."

"This isn't a loan. It's an investment in you and Audrey's future."

"I'll pay you back."

"Tell you what. How about instead of paying me back, you promise me something else?"

"Anything."

"You'll let me come over and have dinner with you and Audrey whenever I want. And I'll be there in the hospital when she's giving birth. And I'll be at your place all the time to spend time with you, Audrey, and my grandchild. How about that?"

Bobby smiled. "I wouldn't have it any other way."

"Good." Loretta kissed his forehead. "I just ... I don't want you worrying about your father anymore. He can make all the threats he wants, but he's never ... he'll never hurt you again. And ... I figure you already know this, but ... your father and I ... we won't be having a child together."

Bobby bit his lip. "I'm sorry. I know how much you wanted to—"

"I wanted to have a child with the man I thought I married, but clearly ..." She trailed off, clearing her throat. "It wasn't meant to be."

"I really ... I'm so sorry, Loretta. It was never my intention to ... to ruin your marriage."

"Ruin my marriage?" Loretta leaned forward. "Is that what you think? That everything that's happened is somehow your fault?"

Bobby hung his head. All his life, Robert and Margaret had told him he was the one to blame for their truculence. They couldn't control themselves, it seemed; the only way to force Bobby into submission was by beating him senseless and hurtling verbal abuse his way. The physical wounds eventually healed, but the mental ones ... those had found a permanent home inside Bobby's mind, and they always materialized when he was at his lowest. But that wasn't even the worst part. The worst part was that his parents had made him believe he was the problem, that he was the instigator.

"It's not your fault," Loretta assured him. "None of this is your fault."

"But I should've told you when I met you. If I'd said something, maybe you wouldn't have even married him. Maybe you—"

Loretta shook her head. "I don't play those sorts of games. You can't live your life in the past, Bobby, thinking about all the things you did wrong, all the times you should've said this or done that. You'll drive yourself crazy. Yes, things with your father didn't work out the way I'd planned, but that doesn't matter now. I have you. And you ... you have been the greatest gift of all."

Bobby took her hands in his. "I was wondering ... if it wouldn't be too weird for you ... would you mind if I maybe ... if I call you Mom?"

Loretta's eyes glistened. "Nothing would make me happier."

CHAPTER 39

Audrey

DAYTIME NIGHTMARE

G RADUATION WAS ONLY A couple of weeks away. Her last semester of high school had flown by, but Audrey was ready to leave Great Gray. Now that finals were done, she could focus her attention on other matters, such as her and Bobby's upcoming wedding. Their wedding would be small, which neither of them minded, and Alexander and Sophia would host the wedding in their apartment. Only a handful of people would be attending, so it wasn't like they needed a lot of space. Bobby and Audrey had agreed to this, thanking Alexander and Sophia for their support.

"Someday," Bobby promised Audrey, "when we're older, I'll make sure you have your dream wedding."

"I'm marrying you," Audrey reminded him. "It *is* my dream wedding."

Everything was going well, but one Friday afternoon, when Audrey approached her apartment building, she saw a parked black limousine. Her heart lodged itself in her throat. It was Robert Dempsey's limousine. What was he doing in Greenwich Village? She quickly entered her apartment, and to her horror, she saw Robert sitting at the dining room table with her parents, laughing away. Every muscle in her body tensed; her jaw instinctively clenched, and she balled her hands into fists.

"Audie!" Alexander was the first to see her. "We have big news!"

"Do you?" Audrey slowly stepped into the room, purposefully avoiding eye contact with Robert.

"Robert here has offered to pay for the whole wedding! Can you believe that? There'll be catering, flowers, everything! And, even better, you won't have to get married here. He said we can hold the wedding at his house in Montauk. An oceanside wedding! Does it get any better than that?"

"No, it certainly doesn't." Audrey forced a smile. To Robert, she managed, "That's very generous of you."

"Happy to do my part." He stood up, reaching across the table to shake Alexander's hand. "I'm glad this all worked out."

"I'll say!" Alexander beamed. "Thank you again."

"Of course." Robert walked over to Audrey. "Actually, it's a good thing you showed up when you did. There are some things I'd like to discuss with you—in private, if you don't mind."

"That's okay," Audrey said. "Anything you want to say to me you can say in front of my parents."

"Oh, but I'd like it to be a surprise for them." He turned back to Alexander and Sophia. "You like surprises, don't you?"

"Love them!" Sophia piped up.

"Fantastic." Robert gestured toward the door, telling Audrey, "Please, if you would, join me for a walk around the block?"

Against her better judgment, Audrey took Robert up on his offer. They walked in silence for a few minutes. Audrey was acutely aware of Robert Dempsey's physicality; he was built like a football player, with wide shoulders and massive hands: hands, Audrey now knew, he used to hurt his own son. She fought the urge to push him into oncoming traffic.

"I'm not a verbose man, so I'll keep this brief," Robert began, his expression as vacant as a church parking lot on a weekday. "I assume my son has told you some inane stories about me."

"Stories?" Audrey couldn't hide her incredulity. "I saw for myself what you did."

"He's always had a puerile love for fiction. It used to be endearing, but now ... now, it's become rather ... piteous."

For someone who claimed to lack verbosity, Robert sure knew a lot of big words—*inane, puerile, piteous*. Perhaps he'd swallowed a thesaurus, to distinguish himself from a "commoner" like her with his SAT-worthy vocabulary. He enunciated every word, like a Shakespearean actor, complete with the accompanying spit. Not once did his eyes stray from her. No doubt, he was used to being the most powerful man in every room, intimidating anyone and everyone with his daunting frame and mirror-like eyes. But Audrey refused to be forced into submission.

"But if those stories *were* true," Robert went on, "tell me ..." His eyes locked onto Audrey, like an owl onto a mouse. "Would I be the sort of man you'd like to cross?"

Every hair on Audrey's neck and arms stood on end. She felt an overwhelming urge to scream, to make a run for it, to pound on every door and let her neighbors know she was in the presence of a mad man. Instead, she ashamedly looked down at her feet, no longer able to meet Robert's piercing gaze.

"What do you want?" she asked, shielding herself with crossed arms.

"Simple. Leave my son, and I'll make sure you have more than enough money to take care of yourself and your ... child. But my son ... he won't be part of that life. And you won't be a Dempsey. Do you understand?"

Her hatred for him gurgled like lava in a volcano, threatening to explode. But Audrey would be damned before she allowed Robert Dempsey to bully her into silence—or force her and Bobby apart. She assumed Robert viewed her as nothing more than a little girl, but he clearly didn't understand how much Audrey's mindset had changed in the past month or so, how much more focused she'd become. Within a few months, she'd be a mother. What kind of mother did she want to be? Did she want to be the kind of mother who would cower from confrontation, or did she want to stand up for what was right, no matter the personal cost?

"I love Bobby," Audrey said, surprised by how steady her voice sounded. "And he loves me. And we're going to have a happy life—one you won't be a part of."

"This ... relationship ... it will never work out the way you want. He isn't ready to be a father—or a husband. And once he's at Columbia, do you really think he'll stay with you? He'll be introduced to so many other women, women far prettier and smarter than you. So, save yourself the embarrassment, and end it now. As I said, I'll make sure you're more than compensated."

"That's all that matters to you, isn't it? Money."

"I think you'll find money is the only thing worth having."

"Bobby means more to me than money, and it's sad you can't see that, that you never appreciated what you had: a son who loved you."

Robert scoffed. "My son ... he's accustomed to a certain standard of living, one he won't be able to sustain without me. The boy you fell in love with ... he had a trust fund, security, prospects. But now ... that's all gone. And I know Loretta ... she's helped with the apartment, but her money ... it doesn't run as deep as mine does. And eventually, she won't be able to support you anymore, and my son will be on his own, trying to make a living off his asinine stories. Is that the life you saw for yourself? Is that what you want for your child?"

"I never cared about any of that."

"So, you're choosing a life of squalor over a life of luxury?"

"Better to live in squalor than end up like you."

Her frankness disarmed him. In a flash, Robert's cockiness was replaced with confusion. It was like he didn't know what to make of her. Undoubtedly, most people he encountered were enchanted by his power and prestige, knowing full well how much money talked—especially in this city. But Audrey wasn't going to live the rest of her life being indebted to Robert Dempsey. She would do every-thing she could to keep Robert away from Bobby—metaphorically, financially, and physically. She would build a wall down the middle of Manhattan, if she had to.

"Audrey." His tone was firmer now, more urgent; his patronizing veneer had finally slipped. "Believe me when I say you *don't* want me to be your enemy."

"And believe *me* when I say I *really* don't give a shit." Audrey stopped dead in her tracks. She was shaking now, but whether from anger or nerves, she couldn't be certain. "All my life, I've heard stories about the 'great' Robert Dempsey, the King of the Upper East Side, a giant among men. But it wasn't until I met you that I realized how very small you are. So, keep your money—and keep your hands off Bobby."

"You little *bitch*." Robert instinctively seized her wrist.

They both stared at Robert's grip, silent. As if burned by fire, Robert yanked his hand away, no doubt noticing the passersby, some of whom were starting to stare.

"What was that you said about Bobby's inane stories?" Audrey asked quietly, rubbing her aching wrist.

With that, Audrey turned and walked away. Once she was safely inside her apartment building, she allowed herself to cry. She'd done it; she'd managed to put on a brave face in front of Robert Dempsey. She wouldn't have to be around him for much longer. Together, she and Bobby would make a clean break from him, and all his threats would be just that—threats.

"What a wonderful man!" Alexander said as Audrey reentered the apartment. "Can you believe it, Audie? Robert Dempsey will be your father-in-law!"

Someday, maybe, Audrey would tell her parents the truth about Robert, but she'd promised Bobby she wouldn't say a word for the time being. It would be difficult, bordering on impossible, but the last thing Audrey wanted to do was betray Bobby's confidence. Besides, she had no business telling anyone—not even her own family—about such personal, sensitive information. Her parents would discover the truth about Robert only if Bobby decided to tell them himself.

"I'm the luckiest girl in the world," Audrey said flatly, her eyes flitting to her wrist, then her engagement ring.

And she was—but because of Bobby, not his father.

CHAPTER 40

Audrey

END OF AN ERA

G RADUATION DAY WAS FINALLY here. All the boys wore gray robes, while the girls donned white robes. Unfortunately, since they were forced to sit in alphabetical order by surname, Audrey wasn't seated by any of her friends, but she somehow managed to make it through the dreadfully boring ceremony.

Principal Waverly talked for far too long about far too many things, none of which Audrey absorbed. She was brought back to her first day at Great Gray, when Principal Waverly had been droning on about school policies. In three years, he hadn't learned how to speak succinctly—or coherently. More than once, Audrey could feel herself dozing off, but she was able to catch herself before she did so.

Chordially Yours was up next. They sang the school song, and Florie was the soloist. Audrey could scarcely believe how far Florie had come. Soon, she would be jumpstarting her music career, letting every music executive in the city know who she was. And Sarah, the salutatorian of their class, was Yale-bound. Truly, Audrey was so proud of her friends; they were well on their way to achieving their dreams, and she couldn't wait to see them succeed.

Bobby, of course, was the valedictorian, and he delivered a powerful, inspiring speech. At the beginning, he thanked his teachers, classmates, and friends. He also made sure to emphasize how much Great Gray had helped him grow as both a student and a person, and he mentioned Mrs. Parker by name, highlighting what a wonderful mentor she had been to him throughout his high school career.

"I'm looking forward to continuing my education at Columbia University this autumn," Bobby concluded, "but I certainly won't forget my time here at Great Gray. It's been the most incredible four years, and I'm not just leaving here with a diploma; I'm lucky enough to have met Audrey, the love of my life. I just know we'll do great things together."

Some of their classmates cheered and wolf whistled, and though Audrey's cheeks were red, she was delighted just the same. Luckily, their class wasn't that big, so it didn't take too long for everyone to receive their diplomas. Then, as the band played the school song, the students dispersed on the field, running off to see their families and friends.

"Let's get a picture of all of you together!" Sophia said to Audrey, Bobby, Florie, and Sarah. "Big smiles, everyone!"

As they posed for an incessant number of photographs—Sophia loved her Polaroid—Audrey studied her friends, one by one, wondering vaguely when they'd all be together like this again. Sarah and her parents were heading off to San Francisco for the summer to see her extended family, and she didn't think she'd be able to attend Bobby's and Audrey's wedding. They'd told her not to worry about it, that they wanted her to spend as much time with her California-based family as possible, but Sarah was still bothered by it. Florie, thankfully, would be staying in New York for the foreseeable future. And Bobby and Audrey, of course, would be busy preparing for their wedding—and their child.

Alexander stood behind Sophia. "All right, one more photo! No, no, Audie. No squirming! Now, everyone, say, 'To the future'!"

"To the future!"

CHAPTER 41

Audrey

A SUMMER WEDDING

O N JULY 11, 1981, Bobby and Audrey were married in a small ceremony attended only by family and close friends. Audrey had always dreamed of getting married in the summer, but she never imagined she'd tie the knot just a few hundred yards away from the Atlantic Ocean. To her delight—and Bobby's chagrin—it was a hot, sunny day. She knew how much he detested the heat, but that, thankfully, didn't dampen his mood. During the lead-up to the wedding, he'd been in high spirits, remarking just how excited he was for Audrey to move in with him so they could officially start their lives together.

So much had changed for them in such a short amount of time, but Bobby's unshakable confidence in their future had rubbed off on Audrey. Even though they were young—far too young to be getting married and starting a family—Audrey knew they'd be okay. At the end of the day, they had each other, and that was all that mattered.

The wedding day was a blur. In keeping with tradition, Audrey wanted to make sure she had something old, something new, something borrowed, and something blue. Her something old, a vintage brooch, came from Aunt Trina. According to Aunt Trina, the brooch had belonged to her and Sophia's mother.

By fastening the brooch to her wedding bouquet, Audrey ensured her maternal grandmother would be with her in spirit on this monumental day. Claire purchased a pair of rose-gold earrings for Audrey, which served as her something new. Sophia, meanwhile, gifted Audrey her old wedding veil, saying it could count as her something borrowed. And for her something blue, Loretta bought Audrey a pair of blue heels.

Audrey remembered putting on her dress—a romantic, lacy number—and walking down the aisle with her father. She remembered seeing Bobby, tears in his eyes, grinning as she made her way toward him. They exchanged their vows, but Audrey had no memory of what she'd said; it was like she'd blacked out. She knew she'd written some heartfelt sentiments about how safe and secure she felt with him, how much she loved his creativity and ambition, but she couldn't be sure if she actually uttered any of those words aloud. Later, when she asked Bobby, he assured her she'd said some lovely things about him and her hopes for their future, which made her feel better. Audrey did, however, remember Bobby's vows; he promised he'd always stand by her side, and there was nothing they couldn't face together.

"We have so much to look forward to," Bobby said, "and I can't wait to spend the rest of my life with you."

They spent most of the evening dancing and conversing with their friends and family. Robert, thankfully, kept his distance, but Audrey could sense his resentment. Though she knew Robert didn't hold any power over Bobby anymore, she was also acutely aware that he wasn't the sort of person to give up without a fight. Someday, she knew, she would be forced to confront him once again, but she couldn't concern herself with that at the moment. This was her and Bobby's day, and they were going to enjoy it.

Sarah had been able to make it to their wedding after all, and she congratulated Bobby and Audrey on their nuptials, telling them how excited she was to meet their baby.

"You're going to be amazing parents," she said, tears in her eyes. "And just so you know, I'll come back to New York for breaks, so it's not like ... it's not like I'll never see you again."

Alexander and Sophia were just as emotional. They told Bobby and Audrey how proud they were of them, and Sophia, dabbing at her eyes, said she couldn't wait to meet her first grandchild.

"It's just so surreal," Sophia blubbered. "I mean, Dad and I ... we're so happy for you. We know this isn't ... this wasn't what you planned, but you have so many people in your life who love and support you, and we'll always be there with you, no matter what."

"Thanks, Mom!" Audrey embraced her. "And you too, Dad! Get in here!"

Alexander pulled his girls into a bear hug. "Come on, Bobby! You're part of this family now too!"

Laughing, Bobby joined in the hug. As they parted, Bobby, his eyes on Audrey, said, "Don't worry, Mom and Dad. Your little girl will be safe with me."

"We know she will," Alexander said, bobbing his head, his arm around Sophia. "We know she will."

For the first time, Bobby and Audrey went their separate ways, as Bobby wanted to catch up with Sebastian, and Audrey was eager to spend some quality time with Florie.

Florie leaned back in her chair, surveying the crowd. "I told you you'd be getting married earlier, didn't I? That you wouldn't be able to wait until Bobby graduated from Columbia."

Audrey laughed good-naturedly. "I think circumstances forced us to move up our timetable, but I'm not complaining." She scooted her chair closer to Florie. "But how are you? Are you excited? Nervous?"

Next week, Florie would start shopping her music around. She'd been finalizing her demo for the past few months, but now everything was coming to a head. There was so much uncertainty, but Audrey knew it would all work out the way it was supposed to.

"All the above! I really ... I have my fingers crossed, but ... I know it'll be a long, tough road."

"You just have to promise me one thing."

"Name it."

"When you become all rich and famous, promise me you won't forget about us little people."

Florie cocked her head to the side. "I'm sorry, and you are ...?"

Audrey laughed, playfully smacking her arm. "But seriously, Florie, I'm so happy for you. I know you'll make it big."

"You've always been my biggest supporter—well, behind my parents, of course." Florie took her hands in hers. "And don't worry. I'll swing by to see you, Bobby, and the baby all the time. What are you thinking? Boy or girl?"

"I haven't really thought about it," Audrey admitted.

"Well, if it's a girl, name her Florence. It's a great name."

"And if it's a boy?"

"Then name him ... Florenzo."

"Florenzo? That sounds like a toothpaste brand!"

"It's a name!"

"Not one I'll be using for my baby! No offense."

"Eh, none taken. But Florence." Florie tapped her nose. "Remember Florence."

Once the reception winded down, Bobby and Audrey retreated upstairs, to Bobby's bedroom, where they spent the night. Felix drove them back to the city the next morning. Audrey couldn't believe she was officially a wife—and Bobby was her husband.

"Someday," Bobby told her as they walked down the hallway toward their new apartment, "I'll be able to take you on a real honeymoon. Where would you like to go?"

"Somewhere warm and sunny."

Bobby laughed. "I should've guessed." He stopped in front of their door and kissed her forehead. "But I hope it's not too much of a letdown, going from the wedding to this."

"Are you kidding? I've been looking forward to moving in with you ever since I found this apartment."

"So, no regrets?"

Audrey pulled him in for a kiss. "No regrets," she said. "I love you, you know."

Bobby smiled. "I love you too." He opened the door. "After you."

CHAPTER 42

Audrey

A NEW BEGINNING

THROUGHOUT THE SUMMER, AUDREY worked as a nanny for one of Loretta's friends, while Bobby worked at a bookstore on the Upper West Side. It was a good routine, and an easy one, and Audrey enjoyed feeling as though she were contributing something to the family. As the summer faded into autumn, Bobby began his first semester at Columbia, and Audrey continued nannying—and growing more confident in her parenting abilities.

Eventually, at the tail end of her pregnancy, Audrey had to stop nannying, and she stayed home, preparing for their baby's arrival. Then, twenty-two minutes after nine o'clock in the morning on January 12, 1982, Emily Sophia Dempsey was born. They hadn't known their baby's sex beforehand, and they hadn't really talked about names all that much, but as soon as Audrey mentioned the name Emily, all other options were pushed aside. Emily heavily favored her father; in fact, the only characteristic of hers that was purely Nielsen was her wispy, blonde hair. But Audrey didn't mind. She knew, of course, that hair and eye colors changed as babies aged, but for now, she was happy their child had Bobby's beautiful blue eyes.

At first, Bobby was nervous about touching Emily, fearing, perhaps, he was more similar to his father than he cared to see, but Audrey reminded him that he was nothing like Robert, that he'd be a loving, warm father—a father who would adore his daughter.

When they were at last able to bring Emily home, Bobby could hardly get enough of her. He'd stand by her crib, looking down at her, unwilling to let her out of his sight. On more than a couple of occasions, Audrey had to pull him away, telling him they needed their sleep as well.

"But she looks so peaceful," Bobby would lament. "And ... I want to know she's safe."

Over the next few weeks, Bobby and Audrey settled into their new lives as parents. There were learning curves, obviously, and they found themselves bickering more than usual, but overall, Audrey was pleased with how well they had adjusted to everything. In particular, fatherhood had imbued Bobby with a new light and energy. Somehow, to Audrey's endless astonishment, Bobby balanced school and parenthood with nary a complaint. In fact, he took great joy in reading his books aloud to Emily.

"Isn't she a little young to understand *Pale Fire*?" joked Audrey, her hands on her hips.

"I think she's a lot smarter than you're giving her credit for," Bobby brightly countered. "See, look!" he added, pointing at the giggling Emily. "She loves it!"

Bobby was one of those enviable people who needed only a couple of hours of sleep at night to function. Audrey, on the other hand, needed at least eight, which she hadn't gotten since maybe October. She was starting to wonder whether she would ever sleep again.

"It'll get better," Sophia assured her one day, after she came over for lunch. "In the early months, you're more frazzled, but before you know it, it'll all settle down. And once Emily is able to sleep through the night, things will be a lot easier for you—and Bobby."

Audrey knew her mother was right, and really, she had nothing to quibble about. Emily was a strikingly well-behaved baby. Sure, she had her moments and tantrums, but on the whole, she was an absolute delight. She didn't cry as much as Audrey had thought she would, and she usually slept during her naps. Though some days were more difficult than others, whenever Audrey looked at Emily, she was reminded of just how lucky she was. She not only had a beautiful, healthy baby girl but also a wonderful, loving husband. She couldn't imagine being any happier than she was right now.

"We're going to be just fine," Bobby said to her one night, his arms wrapped around her waist, his chin resting on her shoulder. "It's all going to be okay."

They were both looking at Emily, who was fast asleep in her crib. They stood there for a few moments, watching as she slept away. She was so unbelievably angelic, so perfect. Audrey still couldn't quite fathom that this little girl was theirs, that they were the ones who had brought her into the world.

"I know," Audrey said, allowing Bobby to pull her closer.

And she believed it—with all her heart.

Resources

The following resources may help readers who are affected by any of the issues raised in this book:

988 Suicide and Crisis Lifeline:

https://988lifeline.org/?utm_source=google&utm_medium=web&utm_campaign=onebox

Call 988, or text 988.

Call, text, or chat with an expert who can help you get the support you need. Available 24/7, 365 days a year. Completely free and confidential.

National Domestic Violence Hotline:

https://www.thehotline.org/?utm_source=youtube&utm_medium=organic&utm_campaign=domestic_violence

Call 1-800-799-7233, or text "START" to 88788.

Call, text, or chat with an expert who can help you get the support you need. Available 24/7, 365 days a year. Completely free and confidential.

About the Author

Brianna MacMahon hails from Corning, NY. A lifelong writer, she began to hone her skills at Hartwick College, where she took many creative writing classes. Even though she was a history and political science major, Brianna wrote as a creative outlet. In the momentous year of 2020, she attained her master's degree in political science from Syracuse University. During the pandemic, she focused more on writing as a legitimate career. She is also the author of the award-winning New Caelus Series, and the first book, *On the Precipice*, is currently available for purchase. When she is not writing, Brianna enjoys reading, hanging out with her family, playing RPGs, and watching her favorite comfort shows on repeat. Follow her on Instagram, @brmacmah, for book updates, and check out her official website, www.authorbriannamacmahon.com, for merchandise, books, and more! If you love the book, please leave a five-star review, as this helps out a ton!

Made in United States
Orlando, FL
28 December 2024

56628626R00193